JORGE AMADO was born in 1912 in Ilhéus, the provincial capital of the state of Bahia whose society he portrays in such acclaimed novels as GABRIELA, CLOVE AND CINNAMON; DONA FLOR AND HER TWO HUSBANDS; and TEREZA BATISTA: HOME FROM THE WARS. His father was a cocoa planter, and his first novel, CACAU, published when he was nineteen, is a plea for social justice for the workers on the cocoa estates south of Bahia. The theme of class struggle continues to dominate in his novels of the Thirties and Forties; but with the Fifties and GABRIELA, CLOVE AND CINNAMON (1958), the political emphasis gives way to a lighter, more novelistic approach. It was in that novel, published in the United States when Amado was fifty and enthusiastically received in some fourteen countries, that he first explored the rich literary vein pursued in DONA FLOR AND HER TWO HUSBANDS. Highly successful film and Broadway musical versions of DONA FLOR have brought to wider attention the colorful and extravagant world of Brazil's foremost living novelist.

Other Avon and Bard Books by
Jorge Amado

DONA FLOR AND HER TWO HUSBANDS
GABRIELLA, GLOVE AND CINNAMON
HOME IS THE SAILOR
TENT OF MIRACLES
TEREZA BATISTO: HOME FROM THE WARS
TIETA
THE TWO DEATHS OF QUINCAS WATERYELL
THE VIOLENT LAND

SHEPHERDS OF
THE NIGHT

JORGE AMADO

*Translated from
the Portuguese by*
HARRIET DE ONÍS

 A BARD BOOK/PUBLISHED BY AVON BOOKS

Originally published in Portuguese as *Os Pastôres Da Noite* by
Livraria Martins Editôra, Sao Paulo. Copyright © 1964 by
Jorge Amado.

AVON BOOKS
A division of
The Hearst Corporation
959 Eighth Avenue
New York, New York 10019

Published by arrangement with Alfred A. Knopf, Inc.
Library of Congress Catalog Card Number: 66-19366
ISBN: 0-380-39990-3
Copyright © 1966 by Alfred A. Knopf, Inc.

First Bard Printing, September, 1978

BARD TRADEMARK REG. U.S. PAT. OFF. AND IN
OTHER COUNTRIES, MARCA REGISTRADA, HECHO
EN U.S.A.

Printed in the U.S.A.

AKP 10 9 8 7 6 5 4 3 2

For Zélia, fanned by the gentle breeze of Rio Vermelho, together with Oxossi and Oxun, on the shore of the sea of Bahia.

For Antonio Celestino, Carybé, Eduardo Portella, Jenner Augusto, Gilbert Chaves, Lênio Braga, Luís Henrique, Mario Cravo, Mirabeau Sampaio, Moysés Alves, Odorico Tavares and Tibúrcio Barreiros, Walter da Silveira, and Willys, Bahians of various origins, but all true blue, who saw Tibéria, Jesuíno and their companions come into being and grow, with the author's friendship.

For the novelist Josué Montello of Maranhão, my cousin.

In the school of life there are
no vacations.

(SIGN ON A TRUCK ON
THE RIO-BAHIA RUN)

A man cannot sleep with all the
women in the world,
but he should try.

(PROVERB OF THE WATERFRONT
OF BAHIA)

Man! That word has a proud sound!
(GORKI *The Lower Depths*)

Preface

WE SHEPHERDED THE NIGHT as though she were a bevy of girls and we guided her to the ports of dawn with our staffs of rum, our unhewn rods of laughter.

And if not for us, punctual with the twilight, lazy wanderers through the fields of moonlight, how would the night, with her lighted stars, her drifting clouds, her mantle of darkness, how would she, lost and alone, find her way through the winding paths of this city of alleys and slopes? On every slope a conjurer's charm, at every corner a mystery, in every nocturnal heart a plea for pity, a pang of love, the bitter taste of hunger in the silent mouths, and Exu at large in the perilous hour of the crossroads. In our boundless pasturing, we went gathering up the thirst and the hunger, the pleas and the sobs, the dung of suffering and the timid shoots of hope, the sighs of love and the lacerated words of pain, and we prepared a bouquet the color of blood to adorn night's mantle.

We traversed the distant roads, the straitest and the most tempting, we reached the frontiers of man's resistance, plumbed his secret, illuminating it with the shades of night, observing its soil and its roots. Night covered all the pettiness and all the grandeur with her mantle, blending them into one single humanity, one single hope.

Leading night as soon as she was born on the wharfs, a trembling bird of fear, her wings still damp from the sea, so menaced in her orphaned cradle, we entered the seven gates of the city with our own private and untransferable keys, and we gave her food and drink, spilled blood and seething life, and under our tutelage she grew, glittering with silver or bedecked with rain.

She sat down with us in the gayest taverns, a maid from the star-studded black. She danced the samba, whirling her golden skirt of stars, voluptuously swinging her black African hips, her breasts like heaving waves. She made merry in the circle of *capoeira* fighters, she knew the master moves and even invented new ones, with the cleverest devising, disregarding the established rules, that madcap of a night! In the circle of the *iawôs*, she was the *orixá* acclaimed of all, the mount of all the saints, of Oxolufã with his staffs of silver, of stooped Oxalá, of Yemanjá spawning forests, of Omolu with his pocked hands; she was Oxumarê of the seven colors of the rainbow, Oxun and the woman warrior Iansã, the rivers and springs of Euá. All the colors and all the beads, the herbs of Ossani and his sorcerers, his spells, his witchcraft of darkness and light.

By now a little drunk and excited, she accompanied us to the poorest brothels where the veterans lived their last span of love and the new arrivals from the country learned the difficult craft of harlotry. She was a debauched night; one man alone did not satisfy her. She had at her fingertips the most refined pleasures and the most boundless violence. The beds collapsed under her milling haunches, her moans of love filled the neighboring streets with music, and the men succeeded one another in her body, where an orgasm took place at every moment in her armpits and thighs, from the soles of her feet to the nape of her perfumed neck. A whoreson night, insatiable and sweet. We slept in the rose of her hair, in her dewy velure.

And the work she gave us when we took her to sea in the swift-running fishing smacks to partake of fish stew, with rum and guitar! She brought, hidden in her robe, the rain and the winds. And when the feast was going along smoothly, the night air serene, the girls enjoying the scent of salt and the sea smell of the tide, she loosed the winds and the tempests. The moonlit fields were no more, the sweet grazing of harmonicas and guitars, warm bodies given over to pleasure; only the depths of the sea when she, the furious and demented mistress of fear and mystery, the sister of death, extinguished the moon, the stars, and the lanterns of the ships. How many times did we not have to take her in our arms so she would not drown in this sea of Bahia and leave the world without night for ever and ever, eternally and for all time broad daylight, sunlight without dawn or dusk, without shade, color, or mystery, a world so bright that one could not bear to look at it?

How many times did we not have to hold her by the legs and hands, tie her to the doorpost of a tavern or to the foot of Tibéria's bed, barring doors and windows, so that she, sullen or sleepy, should not depart too soon, leaving behind an empty stretch of time, neither night nor day, a frozen space of agony and death?

When she arrived in her cradle of dusk, on the ship of an early moon, on the outer fringes of the horizon, she was a poor, meaningless night, lonely, ignorant, illiterate of life or feelings, of emotions, of sorrows and joys, of the struggles of men and the caresses of women. A dull night, nothing but darkness and absence, useless and insipid.

As we grazed her in boundless pastures, shepherding her through desires and ambitions, through suffering and joys, through bitterness and laughter, jealousy, dreams, and the loneliness of the city, we gave her meaning and educated her, making of that small hesitant night, timid and vapid, the night of man. Her shepherds, we impregnated her with life. We built the night out of the materials of despair and of dreams. Tiles of budding loves or of exhausted passions, cement of hunger and of injustice, clay of humiliations and of revolt, lime of dreams and of the inexorable onward drive of man. When, resting on our staffs, we led her to the portals of dawn, she was a maternal night, her breasts turgid with milk, whose womb had yielded its fruit, a warm, sentient night. There we left her, by the edge of the sea, asleep among the flowers of daybreak, wrapped in her mantle of poetry. She had arrived uncouth and poor; now she was the night of man. We would return the next twilight, untiring. The shepherds of night, without course or calendar, without timepiece or fixed occupation.

Open the jug of rum and give me a swallow to clear my

throat. So many things have changed since then, and still more will change. But the night of Bahia was the same, made of silver and gold, of breeze and warmth, redolent of Brazilian cherry and jasmine. We took her by the hand, and we brought her gifts. A comb to dress her hair, a necklace to adorn her throat, bracelets and baubles for her arms, and laughter, moans, sobs, cries, curses, sighs of love.

What I tell I know because I lived it, not because I heard it told. I tell of things that really happened. Whoever does not want to hear can leave; my words are simple and unpretentious.

We shepherded the night as though she were a bevy of restless virgins ripe for a man.

The True Account
of the Marriage
of Corporal Martim,
in all its Details,
with a Wealth of Incidents
and Surprises
-*{ OR }*-
Bullfinch, the Romantic,
and the Pangs
of Faithless Love

1

WHEN THESE EVENTS TOOK PLACE, Jesuíno Crazy Cock was still alive, and Corporal Martim had not yet been promoted, because of his merits and the exigencies of the situation, to Sergeant Porciúncula, something, moreover, which occurred at the end of these labors, as will be seen when the time comes. As for the demise of Crazy Cock, that, too, will be touched upon, if the occasion arises, with the natural reserve and the necessary bearing on the case.

Wing-Foot was coming along the slope, his expression thoughtful, whistling mechanically. His face, grave and bony, with its blue, dull eyes, at times void of all expression, as though he had gone to sea and had left behind him only his feet and hands, his scalp, his teeth, his navel, and his protruding bones. When that look came over him, Jesuíno used to say: "Wing-Foot has taken ship for Santo Amaro." Why Santo Amaro, nobody ever knew; Jesuíno employed certain odd mannerisms in his way of speaking, only he knew why. Wing-Foot was small and skinny, a little stooped, with long arms and bony hands. He made no noise when he walked, as though he were gliding along, and he was lost in meditation. He was whistling an old melody, repeating it, scattering it over the hillside. Only an old man recognized it, startled to hear it, for he had long since forgotten it. He recalled a face lost in the distant past, the sound of a light laugh, and he asked himself when

3

and where Wing-Foot, still under forty, could have learned that old *modinha*.

This was a time when an epoch, a world, was hastening to its close at an ever faster pace. So fast that how was it possible to preserve the memory of events and persons? And nobody else—alas, nobody—will see such things happen and know about people like these. Tomorrow is another day, and in the newly unfolding time, in the flower of man's new dawn, such incidents and persons will have no place. Neither Wing-Foot with his blue eyes nor Negro Massu nor Corporal Martim with his roguery nor the young and impassioned Bullfinch nor Ipicilone nor the tailor Jesus nor the image-maker Alfredo nor our mother Tibéria nor Otália, Teresa, Dalva, Noca, Antonieta, and Raimunda, all the girls, nor other less known folk, for that will be a time to weigh and measure, and they are neither to be weighed nor measured. Perhaps someone will still mention Jesuíno, at least as long as the voodoo rites of Aldeia de Angola exist, on the road to Federacão, where he became a celebrated saint and worthy spiritual guide, the famous Caboclo Crazy Cock. But he is no longer the same Jesuíno; they gave him a cloak of feathers and attributed to him everything that has happened in these parts for the past twenty years.

Wing-Foot, however, was not pondering such philosophies, even though the train of thought that was leading him downhill was no less important. He was thinking about the brown girl Eró, or at any rate, she was the point of departure—as the result of the confusion she had sown —for his cogitations, for a world of mulattas, but the authentic variety, mulattas with all their physical and moral qualities, without omitting a single one. Could Eró be considered a true mulatta, one of the perfect kind? Evidently not, was Wing-Foot's final and irritated conclusion.

In a corner of the pocket of the jacket, many sizes too big for him, which he had inherited from a German client who was almost as tall as Negro Massu, a jacket that covered him to his knees, huddled the little white rat, frightened to death. A little white female rat with a tender snout, blue eyes, a delight, a gift of God, a living plaything.

4

For days and days Wing-Foot had taught her a trick, just one, but that was enough. When he snapped his fingers she would move from side to side and finally lie down on her back, her feet pawing the air, waiting for him to tickle her belly. Who would not have been happy to own an animal like that, so delicate and clean, intelligent and docile?

Mr. and Mrs. Cabral, to whom Wing-Foot sold seashore plants, cactuses, and orchids, were eager to buy her when Wing-Foot proudly showed her off to them. Dona Aurora, the wife, had said: "Anyone would think it came from a circus." She wanted it as a present for her grandchildren, but Wing-Foot stubbornly refused to sell it at any price. He had not trained it as an investment, nor had he spent time domesticating it, teaching it obedience, to make a few milreis. He had spent hours and hours winning its confidence, and he had been able to do this only because it was a very feminine rat. Wing-Foot scratched her belly and she lay motionless on her back, eyes closed. When he stopped, she opened her eyes and waved her legs, asking for more.

He had spent his time and patience to take it as a present to Eró, and by means of this gift to win her smile, her liking, and her favors. The mulatta was a recent and admirable addition to the household of Dr. Aprigio, a customer of Wing-Foot's, and there she exercised with outstanding ability the profession of cook. Wing-Foot, as soon as he saw her, went off the deep end about her and decided to lose no time in bringing her to share his distant abode. The rat seemed to him the most practical and effective means of attaining his coveted objective. Wing-Foot was not a man to waste time and breath on avowals of love, whispered nothings, tender phrases; besides, he saw no percentage in that caterwauling. Now, Bullfinch never did anything else. He was an expert when it came to telling his love; he had even bought a book, *The Lover's Complete Letter-Writer* (with the picture of a couple on the cover, embracing shamelessly) in order to learn honey-coated words and unusual phrases. Yet in spite of all this, nobody ever suffered more deceptions at the hands of sweethearts and fiancées, passing fancies and lovers. For all his literature on love, Bullfinch lived drowning his amorous disillusionments in rum in Alonso's shop or Isidro de Batualê's tavern, the victim of fickle favors.

Night descended gently on the wings of a breeze over the hillsides, the squares, the streets; the air was warm; a languor settled upon the world and its creatures, an almost perfect sensation of peace, as though no danger any longer threatened mankind, as though the eye of evil had been closed for good. It was a moment of perfect harmony, when everyone felt happy with himself.

Everyone except Wing-Foot. Neither happy with himself nor at peace with others, and all because of that incomprehensible Eró. He had spent days thinking only of her, dreaming of those breasts he had glimpsed down the front of her dress when she bent over the stove, setting Wing-Foot's eyes on fire. The mulatta stooped to pick something off the floor, and her burnished thighs gleamed. For the past weeks Wing-Foot had fed his desire, dreaming of Eró, moaning her name in the rainy nights. He had trained the white rat, which was to declare his love. All he had to do was offer it to Eró, make it come and go, scratch its belly, and the mulatta would fall into his arms, overcome and impassioned. He would take her to his distant shanty to celebrate their courtship and marriage, engagement and honeymoon, all at the same time and blended together. In a box, under some dry banana leaves, Wing-Foot had some jugs of rum hidden away. On the way he would buy bread and sausage; they could live there quietly all their life long if they wanted to. All their life or just one night. Wing-Foot did not make detailed plans with a definite time limit or clear-cut perspectives. His objective was single and immediate: to take Eró to his shanty and tumble her in the sand. How things would work out afterwards, that was another problem, to be dealt with when the time came.

And as he proceeded with the white rat's training, he became fond of it; a tender friendship grew up between them to the point where Wing-Foot forgot completely about the mulatta Eró, her very existence, and the tawny color of her thighs. He played with the rat for mere pleasure, without any other intention, just for the fun of it. He spent hours amusing himself with it, laughing, talking to it. Wing-Foot understood the language spoken by all animals.

At any rate, so he stated, and how could one doubt it when rats and frogs, snakes and lizards, obeyed his gestures and his orders?

If he hadn't come to the city to bring some frogs that had been ordered by Eró's employer, a doctor with an experimental laboratory, everything would have been different. But the moment he entered the kitchen Wing-Foot saw her beside the stove, with her profile of a young palm tree, her long legs. "Oh, Lord," he thought, "I forgot to bring the rat." He emptied the frogs into the tank, collected his money, and announced to Eró that he would be back late in the afternoon. The mulatta shrugged her shoulders and flirted her hips as an indication of her complete indifference to that piece of news; he could come back if he wanted to, if he still had some unfinished business. A lot she cared. But Wing-Foot attributed other intentions, sinful ones, to that movement of her body. Never had Eró seemed to him so ardent and inviting.

He returned at the appointed hour, came into the kitchen without asking permission. Eró was sitting at the pantry table, peeling sweet potatoes for dinner. Wing-Foot came over softly and announced himself. Eró raised her eyes in surprise: "You back again? Bringing more animals? What a horror! . . . If it's frogs, put them in the tank. . . . Rats, in the cage. Such filth," she commented, lowering her voice, and went back to the sweet potatoes, paying no further attention to Wing-Foot.

But Wing-Foot did not hear her. He was looking down the front of her dress at the curve of her breasts, and he sighed. Eró spoke up again: "You not feeling good? No wonder; messing around with all those filthy animals you've probably picked up something. . . ."

Wing-Foot put his hand in the pocket of his outsize coat, brought out the white rat, and with tender care set it on the table. The rat sniffed, trying to identify the various and tempting kitchen smells. It stretched its snout toward the sweet potatoes.

Eró leaped to her feet with one bound and a scream: "Get that animal away from there! . . . Haven't I told you not to bring that filth into the kitchen . . ."

She backed away from the table as though the white rat,

7

so pretty and so shy, were a poison snake, like those Wing-Foot managed to catch from time to time and sold to the Institute. She kept up her shrill screaming, ordering the rat and the man out of her kitchen, but Wing-Foot did not hear her, engrossed as he was with the animal.

"Isn't it cute?" He snapped his fingers, and the rat went from side to side and then turned over on its back, belly up, its paws in the air. He tickled its stomach, and once more he forgot about Eró, her breasts and her thighs.

"Out! Get out of here! Take that dirty animal away!" Eró screamed as though she were about to have a fit.

And she screamed so loud that Wing-Foot heard her, rested his eyes on her, recognized her, and remembered why he had come. He took her excitement for natural enthusiasm, smiled, looked at the rat with a touch of sadness, and pointing to it with his finger, said: "It's for you. . . . I am giving it to you. . . ."

And having made the gift, he smiled once more, and stretching out his long arm, caught the girl by the wrist and pulled her to him. He wanted nothing at that moment, moreover, but a kiss of gratitude. The rest would be attended to that night in the shanty.

But Eró, instead of swooning into his arms, struggled to free herself, wrenching herself violently away: "Let go of me! . . . Let go of me! . . ." She managed to disengage herself, retreated to the rear of the kitchen, and shouted: "Get out of here before I call the mistress! And take away that dreadful animal! Don't you ever come back here!"

None of all that was too clear to Wing-Foot. With the still frightened rat in his pocket, he came down the hillside that perfumed afternoon, with a sultry night heavy with clouds closing in, lost in speculation. Why had Eró rejected his gift, fled from his arms, not followed him to the shore, grateful and eager? He could not figure it out.

Many things happen in this world which have no explanation, make no sense, Jesuíno Crazy Cock, a man of vast knowledge, was always saying. It was he who, one night when they were exchanging confidences, defended the thesis according to which mulattas were special beings, miracles of God, and for that very reason complicated and difficult, with unexpected reactions.

8

Wing-Foot agreed; as far as he was concerned, no woman existed who could be compared to a good mulatta. Neither a wheat-colored blonde nor a Negress the color of coal, none. He had discussed the matter not only with Jesuíno; he had even taken it up with Doctor Menandro, an important person whose picture appeared in the newspapers, the director of a center of investigation, but simple and friendly, treating everyone alike, a man without any nonsense about him. He liked to talk with Wing-Foot, to draw him out, to hear him talk about animals, popeyed frogs, lizards as motionless as stones.

Once, on his return from a long trip abroad, Doctor Menandro had lavished praises on French women, clicking his tongue and moving his ponderous, wise head. "There are no women like the French."

Wing-Foot, who up to that point had been respectfully silent, was unable to restrain himself: "Doctor, you will be good enough to excuse me, you are a learned man who invents cures for ailments, teaches in the Medical School, and all that. But you must excuse my speaking out this way: I never slept with any French women, but I can guarantee you that no mulatta has to take a back seat for them. Doctor, sir, they just don't have a mulatta's nature for such things. I don't know if you ever had a fling with a mulatta, one of those the color of elderberry tea, with a backside like an umbrella ant, like a fishing smack rocking on the waters. . . . Ah, Doctor, sir, the day you lay one of them, you'll never went to hear about a French woman again, not even to scratch an itch. . . ."

It had been a long time since Wing-Foot had made such a long speech—proof of his excitement. He spoke out of the fullness of his heart, then respectfully removed his torn hat and grew silent.

Dr. Menandro's reply was unexpected: "I agree with you, my dear fellow. I have always had a high opinion of mulatto women. Especially when I was a student. I was even known as the 'Baron of House Maids.' But who told you that there are no mulattas in France? Do you know what a jewel a French mulatta fresh from Senegal is? Shiploads of mulattas come into Marseilles from Dakar, my dear fellow."

Of course, and why not? Wing-Foot asked himself, finding that the doctor, for whom he had the highest regard, was right. Possibly only Jesuíno Crazy Cock and Tibéria stood higher in the scale of Wing-Foot's admiration and esteem. When he picked up the thread of the conversation again, Dr. Menandro was holding forth on the subject of armpits.

Wing-Foot, as is clear, had not only long experience but also certain theoretical knowledge concerning mulatto women—experience and theory that proved useless when applied to the incomprehensible Eró. Wing-Foot felt defeated and disillusioned. She was more like a lily white, afraid of a poor little rat. Who ever heard of such a thing? A real mulatta? Never.

Wing-Foot was making for Alonso's store. The slope of Pelourinho, which lay ahead of him, was full of mulatto women, real ones. A sea of breasts and thighs, swaying haunches, perfumed napes. They had disembarked by the dozen from the clouds of heaven, which were now black, filling the streets, a sea of mulattas, and on this heaving sea, Wing-Foot set sail. Mulattas were running up the hillside; others came flying; one was standing above Wing-Foot's head; a breast grew until it touched the sky; the path was full of rumps, large and small, all well fleshed; you had only to choose.

Night was approaching, the mysterious nightfall of the city of Bahia, when anything may happen without causing surprise. The first hour of Exu, the hour of twilight shadow when Exu sets out on his travels. The women would have completed their round of visits to all the places of worship, carried out the indispensable ceremony in honor of Exu, or had one perhaps forgotten her obligation? Who but Exu could fill the slope of Pelourinho and the blue eyes of Wing-Foot with beautiful and lascivious mulattas?

On the sea below, the full-bellied sails of the fishing smacks were billowing forward to make port before it rained. Clouds were piling up beyond the bar, driven by the wind, blocking the path of the full moon. A mulatta the color of gold passed, carrying off the melody Wing-Foot was whistling, leaving him only his cogitations. His objective was Alonso's store. His friends would be there, and he could discuss that complicated matter with them. Jesuíno Crazy Cock had the capacity to get to the bottom of it and explain it. He was smart, was old Jesuíno. And if his friends should not happen to be there, Wing-Foot would go to the tavern of Isidro de Batualê, at the Seven Gates; he would go to the waterfront, to the bar of Ciríliaco, skirting the edge of the law with his smugglers and his reefer sellers; he would go to the *afoxé* rehearsal, to Tibéria's brothel; he would go everywhere until he found them, even if he got soaked in the rain that was beginning to come down in torrents. He had to discuss and clear up that confusion with his friends. Mulattas were flying about him, each more authentic than the other.

---※{ **2** }※---

WHILE THE INTRODUCTIONS WERE BEING MADE, Otália now smiled, now turned serious, fingering the sash of her yellow dress, ill at ease, as though asking forgiveness. Timidly she ran her eyes over the group gathered there, let them linger on Bullfinch, her body gently swaying. In spite of her heavily made-up mouth, cheeks, and eyes and her intricate hair-do, it was apparent that she was young, a new arrival, not over seventeen. The errand boy delivered his message quickly, in a hurry to get back: "Godmother Tibéria sent for this girl and says her name is Otália; she has just arrived from Bonfim on the afternoon train, but at the Calçada Station she lost her luggage, everything she had; it seems that it was stolen, but she will tell you everything, and my godmother says it's so you will think up some way to find the lady's luggage and the thief, give him a beating, and I am to come right back, for there's nobody in the house and there's a lot to do, otherwise the one who will get the beating is me."

He caught his breath, showed his white teeth in a smile, brought his hand slowly forward, snatched a tart from the tray, and ran off, followed by Alonso's curses.

Otália stood with fidgeting hands, her eyes on the ground, and said: "I would at least like to find the package. There's something in it I value."

A voice as languid as the approaching night. She raised

her pleading eyes to the two friends, Bullfinch and Negro Massu, each of whom had his glass of rum, and she was taken over and introduced to them, not to the others. Bullfinch, who was wearing a threadbare cutaway, a stovepipe hat, his cheeks painted red, looked like a circus performer. Otália would have liked to ask if he was, but she was afraid of being rude. Negro Massu invited her: "Have a seat, girl, and make yourself at home."

Otália smiled and thanked him. It was a polite suggestion, revealing Massu's innate delicacy, though somewhat platonic, as Otália could observe as she looked about the room. Over by the counter, Alonso was busy; on this side all the boxes were occupied by the habitués, and even so, part of them were standing, leaning against the wall or door as they imbibed their rum. Naturally Massu's invitation was mere politeness, and Otália stood, not knowing what to do with her hands. All eyes were fixed on her, everyone eager to hear her story. The boy had aroused their curiosity, and a good yarn about a robbery, before dinner, is first rate to whet the appetite. Otália took a step toward the counter with the idea of leaning against it to lend herself assurance. But she stopped short as Massu roared: "Haven't you guys got any manners?"

When the Negro had invited the girl to sit down, he had not done this as a mere formality, or speaking empty words. It was a definite offer; she could choose the place she liked best. However, none of the customers who were seated seemed to have heard him: seated they were and seated they remained, comfortable and boorish. Massu was even more comfortably accommodated on a keg of dried codfish. Comfortable but not boorish. On the contrary, deeply concerned with the rites of courtesy. His gaze, in which a spark of anger had flared up, encompassed the semicircle of drinkers and came to rest on Jacinto, a young fop from Água dos Meninos, very cocky, always wearing a necktie, and trying to fill the shoes of Corporal Martim. There he was, sprawled on a box, his syrupy eyes on Otália. Massu spat, stretched out his arm, touched the breast of the good-for-nothing with his finger. The Negro's finger was like a dagger and Jacinto felt it between his ribs. It was said in the marketplace and vicinity that Negro Massu did not know his own strength. "Give your seat to the girl, you big wonderful guy. And be quick about it."

Jacinto vacated the box on the double, leaning up against the door. Massu said, turning to Alonso: "A drink for the young lady, Alonso."

When he had provided her with a seat and a drink, Massu felt a little better. That business of the stolen luggage was going to be a headache for him; he felt it in his bones without knowing exactly why. Besides, that night Jesuíno had not yet shown up, and as for Corporal Martim, he had disappeared from Bahia more than two months before, on the run somewhere along the coast. Jesuíno Crazy Cock and the corporal were good at a complicated business of this sort; they could straighten out the most tangled webs to the satisfaction of all concerned. Naturally he, Massu, would do the best he could; the girl had been sent by Tibéria, and how could one refuse her help? Tibéria's word was law. Bullfinch and Ipicilone would cooperate, but Massu foresaw a difficult night. Not even Wing-Foot had arrived; he was late. There are nights like that, off on the wrong foot from the start, muddled, dark, vexing. What the devil was keeping Jesuíno Crazy Cock? It was already time for him to be telling the experiences of his day, drinking his rum. What good would it do the girl to begin unraveling her story before Jesuíno appeared? Neither he nor Bullfinch nor Ipicilone with all his gift of gab, not to mention that bird-brain of a Jacinto, none of those present, was sufficiently endowed to clear up that matter of the lost luggage whose difficulties Massu could foresee just by looking at Otália, for he did not lack experience to draw conclusions. With these thoughts going through his head, Massu tried to pick up the thread of the interrupted conversation, an instructive discussion about films. As though Otália had nothing to say and nobody wanted to hear it.

"Do you mean to say," the Negro weighed his words as he addressed himself to Eduardo, "that what one sees in the movies is all lies? Phony gun shots, phony punches, and the galloping horses phony, too? Everything? I don't believe it."

"Sure it is," reaffirmed Eduardo Ipicilone, "X, Y, Z,"

so-called because of his *ipse dixit* universal knowledge.
No matter what subject came up, Ipicilone immediately
put his oar in on the grounds that he was a specialist in the
field. "It's all a trick to fool boobs like you. I read it in a
magazine"—and with this argument he flattened out his
hearers. "It's all make-believe. You think the horse is galloping, and what he's doing is playing a part, moving his
legs in front of the camera. You see the hero leap into an
abyss more than a thousand feet deep, and there's no abyss
at all, just a two-foot hole."

Negro Massu carefully considered the statement, but it
did not convince him. He sought the support of the others,
but their lack of interest was all too apparent; the topic had
lost its charm and had become a purely academic discussion, boring, preventing the girl from getting on with her
story. They had all turned toward Otália, waiting. Jacinto
took a pair of small scissors out of his pocket and trimmed
his nails, casting melting glances at the traveler from time
to time. But Negro Massu was not giving up so easily. He
asked Otália: "What do you think? Is everything in the
movies fake, or is Ipicilone pulling our leg?"

"To tell you the truth," she answered "I don't care for
the movies. There is a movie house there in Bonfim, but it
is a dump, with the film always breaking. Maybe those
here are good; that's what they told me; but that one is no
good at all. Even so, I used to go once in a while, I mean
after I became a fallen woman; before that I had gone only
twice because my father didn't let me and I didn't have the
money. Teresa, my sister, is the one who goes a lot; she's
crazy about the movies; she knows the names of all the
actors; she's wild about them, cuts their pictures out of
magazines and pins them up in her room. Did you ever
hear of such a silly thing? Maybe they're not even real
men, but fakes, like that young man says who seems to
know. . . . But Teresa is like that, full of notions. And
speaking of movies, the disappearance of my luggage even
seems like something out of a movie or a book. . . ."

Negro Massu gave a resigned sigh. He had tried to stave
off Otália's story, waiting for Jesuíno Crazy Cock to show
up (where could the old rake be?), and for that reason he
had tried to get the girl into a discussion of the movies to

gain time. But she had managed to bring the conversation around to her getting off the train at Calçada Station and her vanished luggage. Bullfinch could no longer restrain his curiosity: "Yes, what happened to the luggage?"

He is sure looking for an itch to scratch, Massu thought to himself as he heard his friend. All the others wanted to know, too; even Ipicilone let the matter of the films roll in the dust of the store floor. Negro Massu shrugged his shoulders; he foresaw an uneasy night ahead, he and his friends running aimlessly about in search of the new arrival's luggage. He clinked his glass on the counter, asking for a refill. God's will be done. Alonso served him and inquired: "Anybody else?"

He didn't want to be interrupted once the girl began her story; he wanted to hear it in peace. Otália sensed her responsibility, all of them intent on what she had to say. She could not let them down; she took a little swallow of rum, pursing up her lips; she smiled at them all and looked at Bullfinch: was he or wasn't he a circus performer? If he wasn't, why was his face painted red and why was he wearing a cutaway and top hat? Bullfinch returned her smile; he was already on the point of falling in love with her, finding her long hair, black and very fine, and her thin lips and pale complexion most attractive. A wham of a *cabocla*, and with a timid air, like a person in need of protection and love.

Encouraged by Bullfinch's smile, Otália began her story: "Well, as I was saying, I came from Bonfim, where I was living in Zizi's place, and everything was going along fine until the police commissioner began to take a dislike to me and pick on me. All on account of a son of the judge, but was I to blame if Bonfim is a narrow-minded place and if the young man wouldn't leave the house, spending the day in my room? I didn't even care much for him; I don't like those wise kids; they don't know how to talk; they're no fun; whatever comes out of their mouth is nonsense; don't ,you agree with me? But the judge said that he was going to have me put in jail, and his wife called me a dirty name every time she mentioned me, making up that I had cast a spell on her son so he would become infatuated with me. Did you ever hear of such a thing? Me cast a spell to get

16

myself in a mess! . . . The annoyance grew worse, and
what was all of that getting me? Sooner or later, I was
going to land in the clink, and maybe with a knife cut, to
boot. And on top of all that, the judge stopped his son's
allowance, and then Zizi really got annoyed. The
poor devil didn't have the money to pay for a beer, let alone my
room, meals, and other expenses. No money, but jealousy,
the most terrible jealousy, making my life a hell. . . . So
then I . . ."

She was interrupted by Wing-Foot's arrival. He came
whistling, stopped for a moment at the door to wish the
group good evening. Then he went over to the counter,
shook Alonso's hand, received his glass of rum, and came
over beside Massu, looking the company over. Jesuíno
Crazy Cock had not yet arrived. Nevertheless, Wing-Foot
announced: "I have ordered a shipload of four hundred
mulatto girls from France. They will be arriving on
Wednesday." And after a brief pause for a swallow of rum,
he repeated: "Four hundred. . . ."

The announcement was badly timed, interrupting
Otália's story. Wing-Foot resumed his whistling and withdrew into his own thoughts as though the news needed no
further elucidation. Otália, after hesitating a little, was on
the point of continuing when Negro Massu asked: "Four
hundred? Don't you think that's too many?"

Wing-Foot answered, somewhat irritated: "Too many?
And why? Too many, he says. Four hundred, not one
less. . . ."

"And what are you going to do with all those gals?"

"You don't know? What do you think? What a question!"

Otália was waiting for the end of the exchange, to go on
with her story. Negro Massu took this in, and excused
himself: "Get back on the track girl. I was just trying to
find out. . . ."

With a gesture of his hand, he gave Otália the green
light, and she proceeded: "Before that happened, it seemed
to me that the best thing to do was to gather up my
belongings and leave. Zizi gave me a letter for Dona
Tibéria—they're old friends—which I slipped down the
front of my dress. If not, with my luck, I'd have lost the
letter, too, and then what would I do? I left the city, sort of

hiding in the train so the boy wouldn't know about it, otherwise there would have been a terrible ruckus. Only Zizi knew, and my sister Teresa. I got off here with my suitcase and parcel. I put the two things down beside me in the station. . . ."

She was reaching the climax of her story. For that reason she paused. And Negro Massu took advantage of the break to further query Wing-Foot: "You really sent for all those mulattas?"

"To France. A shipload of them. They're arriving on Wednesday. The French women are the best."

"Who says so?"

"Doctor Menandro."

"S-s-sh," said Bullfinch, a finger to his lips, when he saw that Otália was waiting to go on.

She resumed the thread of her narration: "So I set the suitcase and the parcel down beside me, the parcel on top so it wouldn't get crushed, for it was something that meant a lot to me, as I have said. . . . Not that it was anything of value. . : . My dresses, shoes, a necklace the boy had given me at the start of his infatuation—all that was in the suitcase. The parcel was just something I prized, you know. . . . I wanted to go to the toilet; nobody could use the one on the train; it was filthy. There was a gentleman standing near me, dressed to kill, who was looking at me. I couldn't wait any longer, and I asked him if he would keep an eye on the suitcase and package. 'Don't worry,' he said, 'I'll watch them.' "

She stopped again, holding out her empty glass to Alonso. Negro Massu bent over toward Wing-Foot: "How are you going to pay for them?" There was a note of doubt in his voice.

Wing-Foot enlightened him: "I bought them on time."

After being handed back her glass and taking a swallow, Otália resumed: "I went in, and a very decent water closet it was, and when I came back I did not find either the man or the suitcase or the parcel. I went all over the station, looking for him. . . ."

But it was in the stars that Otália was not to have the necessary quiet to tell her story without being interrupted every other minute. This time it was Deusdedith, the master of the fishing smack *Flower of the Waves*, who came into the store asking for Jesuíno Crazy Cock. And as he didn't find him, he said that Massu, Bullfinch, or Wing-Foot would do. He had just come from Maragogipe and had a message for them. "I was looking for you, Mr. Massu. The message was for Crazy Cock first, but if I couldn't find him I was to give it to one of you."

"A message?"

"And urgent. . . . From Corporal Martim. . . ."

A ripple ran through the customers and friends, a display of interest which relegated Otália's luggage, Wing-Foot and his shipload of mulattas, to a secondary plane.

"You saw Martim?" There was a tremor in the Negro's voice.

"I ran into him no later than yesterday in Maragogipe. I was there loading the smack when he showed up, and we had a beer together. He wanted me to tell you that he was coming back and would be arriving in a few days. I even offered to bring him with me, but he still had some business to attend to."

"And is he in good health?" Bullfinch asked.

"Couldn't be better. And besides, married to a woman who is a knockout. What a beauty!"

"A new heartthrob? A mulatta?" Wing-Foot inquired.

"That may delay him," observed Ipicilone, in whose opinion it was sheer madness to speed up a trip when one had found a new girl firend.

"You haven't understood me. I said married."

"Married? You mean bed and board?"

"That was what he told me. These were his very words: 'Deusdedith, my brother, this is my wife; I am married, and have become a family man. A man without a family is nothing. I advise you to do the same.' "

"I can't believe my ears. . . . ."

"Just the way I am telling you. . . . And he asked me to look you up and tell you the news. And to advise you that he would be arriving with his wife this coming week. What a woman, my friend! One like that even I would marry. . . ." And he silently recalled the mole on the left shoulder of the corporal's wife.

The silence, moreover, became general, a worried silence. Nobody, none of the three friends nor any of the other customers, felt up to a word, an immediate comment. That piece of news was hard to digest. Finally Wing-Foot spoke up: "You say that Martim is married? I don't believe it. I am going to give him sixteen mulattas. . . ."

Deusdedith gave a start: "Sixteen mulattas? And where are you going to get hold of them?"

" 'Where?' he asks. From the four hundred I ordered."

The others were gradually coming out of the shock the alarming news had produced.

"Of all the crazy things. . . ." Massu said.

Otália grasped the gravity of what had happened, but nevertheless she tried to get on with her story. However, as the confusion into which the gathering had been thrown was apparent, she first consulted Negro Massu, in whom she discerned a kind of leader, due perhaps to his size: "Can I go on?"

"Be patient, lady, wait just a little while. . . ."

She understood that something serious had happened, something of more weight and importance than the disappearance of her luggage. Even Alonso was astounded: "*Caramba!* Martim has sure put his head in a noose."

Wing-Foot noticed Otália's sadness, lost like her luggage and her story in these new surroundings. He reached into his pocket and brought out the white rat. He put it on the floor, snapped his fingers, and it moved around and then lay down on its back for him to scratch its belly.

"What a darling," Otália sighed, her eyes shining.

Wing-Foot was happy. There was a person who understood him. What a pity she wasn't a real mulatta: "It's so smart it can do everything but talk. I once had a cat that talked. I talked with it all the time. It even spoke a little English."

Otália lowered her voice so as not to be overheard by the others:

"Are you and the other two," pointing to Bullfinch and Massus, "with a circus?"

"Us? I never heard about it; no. . . ."

The rat had gotten up, his nose in the air, sniffing the perfume of the codfish and dried beef, the cheese and the sausage. Otália went on with her questions: "And is it true that you have sent for all those mulattas?"

"To France. A shipload of them. They're arriving on Wednesday. The French women are the best; Doctor Menandro made it clear to me." And in a whisper he passed on to her the great secret he had been keeping to himself. He had not told it even to Massu or to Bullfinch: "Mulattas even to their armpits."

He snapped his fingers; the rat came and went, attracting a number of the group—Bullfinch, Ipicilone, Jacinto, and others. Deusdedith even laughed out loud, he found the trained rat so amusing. Negro Massu was turning the situation over in his mind. He wanted to do something, decided on a course of action. So many things happening at the start of the evening: Otália's vanished luggage, Wing-Foot's four hundred mulattas, and now that incredible news of Corporal Martim's marriage. It was too much for him; only Jesuíno Crazy Cock could assume the burden of so many incidents, straighten out all those tangled threads. Where could the old scamp be?

There he was standing in the door, smiling, greeting his friends, his worn felt hat in his hand, his hair tousled, his big toe showing through the hole of his shoe. Now Negro Massu could breathe easily and give thanks to Ogun, his deity: "Ogun, Ogun, my father!" Crazy Cock had arrived: it was his duty to face the problems, unravel the threads.

He came in and asked, his kindly eyes on Otália: "And where did so much beauty come from?"

Bullfinch gave him a quick rundown. Jesuíno moved forward, took Otália's hand, and kissed it. She, in turn, kissed him, asking for his blessing. One had only to look at him to understand that he was a person whom you ask for a blessing instead of just saying "Good evening," a *babalão* perhaps, perhaps a *babalorixá*, who knows if not an *obá* of Xangó, certainly an old *ogan*, one of those greeted by the drums as he led the voodoo ceremonies, commanding all respect.

"A double rum, Alonso, for it is a rainy night and one to celebrate. Let's celebrate the arrival of this young lady here."

Alonso served the rum and turned on the light. Jesuíno's eyes smiled; his whole being seemed content with life. Drops of water glistened on his coat with its frayed cuffs and collar, on his bushy white mustache. He quaffed his rum in a long noisy swallow, that of a connoisseur.

Negro Massu lowered his big head like that of an ox and moaned: "Father, there are so many things to tell you that I don't even know where to start, whether with the girl's luggage, lost or stolen, or with the mulattas, I don't remember how many, or . . . And do you know, Crazy Cock, the calamity that has happened? Martim has got married!"

"The most stupid thing he could do," Wing-Foot cut in, putting the rat away in his coat pocket. "I was going to give him sixteen mulattas, hand-picked," and to Jesuíno, confidentially, "I sent for a boatload of four hundred. . . . If you like, I can lend you one."

--◦❈{ 3 }❈◦--

CORPORAL MARTIM'S MARRIAGE, which took place during the rains of June, created a sensation. The unexpected and unbelievable news, brought by the skipper Deusdedith, spread like wild fire and superseded all other topics of gossip and comment. The newspapers were full of important happenings, but wherever the corporal was known, the news of his marriage dominated all the conversations.

The weather was tiresome and unpleasant, with heavy rains alternating with a fine, persistent drizzle of the kind that seeps into the bones. Flooded rivers, landslides tearing houses from their foundations on the hillsides, leaving people homeless, the streets asplash with mud, and the consumption of rum on the increase, for against rain and cold, and to avoid grippe, pneumonia, and other afflictions of the lungs, there is no better remedy, as has been abundantly proved. With so much water falling from the sky, the taverns, Alonso's store, and the hospitable whorehouses were crowded. And in all of them the corporal's marriage was the favorite topic of conversation.

Even the recently arrived Otália, who had never before heard the name of Martim, almost forgot her lost luggage, trying to find out the reason for so much hullabaloo and discussion about the corporal's marriage. If he had been a lieutenant or a captain, it would have been more understandable. . . . In Bonfim, a captain of the Military Police had got involved with a rancher's daughter, ran off with her, and it had been one unholy mess. The rancher set his henchmen on him; the captain made himself scarce, leaving behind not only the girl but also his wife and children, for he was married and had four kids. A devil of a ruckus.

Deusdedith went into details: the corporal and his missus were on their honeymoon, so lovey-dovey, so smitten with each other, that you'd have to see it to believe it. Whispering secrets to one another, exchanging kisses in public, calling each other pet names, and a whole series of equally degrading details. Matters for lengthy cogitation and much talk.

A flood of rumors spread from Alonso's store like a crop of weeds, all over the city. On the street corners, in the market places, and in the lowlier brothels the tittle-tattle had no end. In the taverns the conjectures, stimulated by rum, took on an excited tone. Questions and answers succeeded one another, as well as partial and unsatisfactory explanations, a wealth of surmises, and—why not admit it?—bitter words, gloomy predictions.

The mystery of the conjure thrown in front of the corporal's former abode has not yet been satisfactorily cleared up. A terrific hex, the work of a highly competent witch doctor, one of those capable of dispatching to the other world, not merely two impassioned lovers, but a whole family, from grandparents to grandchildren. If Martim's patron saints, especially Oxalá, ancient of days, and Omolu, the divinity of plagues and their cure (Hail, my father!) had not been so strong, if the corporal had not had such firm allegiances in certain holy places, someone who watched over him and rendered conjures harmless by means of even stronger witchcraft, he would have gone straight to the graveyard. He and his wife, the two in one coffin, for if in life they could not bear to be out of each other's sight, they would surely want to remain united in the grave.

The news brought by Deusdedith was soon confirmed and enlarged upon. Riverside dwellers returning from shopping trips to Santo Amaro, traveling salesmen from Cachoeira, sailors from Madre Deus—from every nook of the Paraguassú came dismaying news. The corporal's idyll spread a sheet of tenderness over Bahia de Todos os Santos and the cities and towns through which the newlyweds passed and were seen, hand in hand, eye to eye, their lips parted in a white, happy smile, indifferent to the landscape, the weather, and the inhabitants. In addition to this public display, this lovers' orgy, what aroused wonder and serious concern was the unanimity with which all who had seen him bore witness to the change that had taken place in Corporal Martim's conduct and principles. He seemed a different man: there were even those who had heard him talk about working, looking for a job. Something so preposterous that it would have to be seen to be believed.

Who hasn't heard of the transformations wrought in men's nature by love? The sad become gay; the extroverted, melancholy; the optimistic, pessimistic, and vice versa; the coward acquires courage and the shilly-shallyer, firmness. Nevertheless, no one ever thought the day would come when Corporal Martim, whose integrity of character was so often cited and whose loyalty to his convictions was so deep-rooted, would be talking about a job. Forsaking principles and convictions, sowing alarm among his friends, disillusioning his many admirers, setting a dangerous precedent for the young preparing to face life in the Rampa do Mercado, Água dos Meninos, Sete Portas. How temper the character of these adolescents when the corporal, the figure they most admired, broke with his past in this manner, sank so low? How accept such slander—the corporal looking for work—unless, as Massu suggested, being so in love had addled his brain and he was no longer the master of his deed and words.

Besides, wasn't the marriage itself already proof of madness? Nobody would have been surprised at the marriage of anyone else, Bullfinch, for example. The comments would not have gone beyond a few words concerning the bride's looks and Bullfinch's incurable romanticism. But the corporal had seemed of a different clay.

The most responsible men, the elder citizens, the respectable *ogans*, shook their heads, in alleys and side streets, in dance halls and *afoxés*, at card games, at voodoo ceremonies. As for the women, in the four quarters of the city some wept disconsolately, others ground their teeth, swearing vengeance.

So profuse and varied was the gossip, with the most minute and circumstantiated details, to the point where it was said that the marriage ceremony had been both religious and civil, in the church and before a notary, all entered in the registers with witnesses and acknowledged signatures. It was no good putting forward the argument of Marialva's first marriage, that one really with all the formalities, and she a virgin in flower.

The gossip went on unabated. There were even descriptions of the bride's dress, with veil, wreath, and orange blossoms. Orange blossoms, God save the mark, what blasphemy!

The truth must be told, and in its entirety. Not because she was the wife of a friend should the facts be concealed, especially those generally known and easily substantiated. When Marialva met up with Corporal Martim she had already warmed the bedclothes of three paramours after having left her husband, one Duce, formerly a skilled cabinetmaker and today vegetating, half-sotted, in Feira de Sant'Ana. He can be seen hanging around the market place, offering to carry packages and baskets, the only work he is fit for. What became of his craftsmanship, his liveliness, his ambition? Marialva carried them all off with her when she left, and had there been more, she would have taken more.

Four bedmates, without mentioning her stay in Leonor Coconut Candy's crib, fancy-free and busy. All this lurid past, and people still palming off that story about her marrying the corporal in veil and wreath of orange blossoms, symbols of virginity locked behind seven keys! Virgin she no longer was, Mrs. Corporal Martim, not even as regards the mole on her left shoulder, a family trait her sisters shared, too, very exciting. She knew this, and wore low-necked dresses the better to show off this temptation. The unwary customer who turned his eye on the black beauty spot went off his rocker, lost his head. That must have been what happened to the corporal, in exile and alone, far from his friends, defenseless. In the month of

June, when in Bahia the festivities were at their liveliest. And she, with that mole showing on her left shoulder and those timid, pleading eyes! Eyes imploring immediate protection.

His friends shook their heads, bewildered. They could not think of any way to protect the corporal against so much whispering, so much gossip. It was plain that he was no longer the same man, that he now lived huddled under a woman's skirts like a lap dog. Jacinto and some of the others laughed uproariously as they repeated these stories. Only Jesuíno Crazy Cock, with his invariable sense of justice, did not open his mouth to condemn the corporal. Tibéria, too, maintained her confidence in Martim, like a banner unfurled amid that storm of gossip, fluttering in the wind of all the discussions. She did not believe a word of it. And when Otália asked her who this Martim was that everyone was talking and arguing about, Tibéria stroked her silky hair and explained: "There's not another like him, my child. Without him there is no real fun. Just wait till he comes and you'll see."

{ 4 }

SOME TIME WAS TO ELAPSE before Otália came to know Corporal Martim at first hand and verify the truth of Tibéria's words. For on his return to Bahia, the corporal's behavior seemed to bear out the most dismaying rumors.

That night, however, in spite of the excitement provoked by Deusdedith's news, nobody really believed in the sweeping changes in the corporal's character. And each person there recalled, for Otália's benefit, some incident, some peculiarity, some roguery of Martim's. Thus it was that Otália knew of him before she saw him, and this perhaps explains certain subsequent events or at least aids in their understanding. Matters that will be clarified in due time, for at the moment Otália did not even know exactly who Martim was. She had merely gathered from what the others said that he was a man who shunned shackles of any sort and was zealous of his freedom like no other. This being the case, how was he going to assume the bonds of matrimony, establish a home so firmly founded, become a model husband?

It is worth going into the antecedents of the case the better to understand and discuss it. How could Otália get a clear idea of what had happened if they didn't start from the beginning? If a story is to be understood, one must carefully analyze its beginnings, the roots from which it springs, grows, and spreads, yielding shade and fruits and lessons. Otália, moreover, listened attentively, hanging on the words and incidents as though she had forgotten all about her luggage lost or stolen at the Calçada Station. It was a pleasure to tell things to a person who showed such interest, listened so wholeheartedly. A nice girl, that Otália.

They then explained to her that Martim had been in exile in the Recôncavo for over two months, plying his skills in the somnolent cities along the Paraguassú, with their quiet, uneventful life. Martim had brought to them a sudden vision of progress, a taste of the active and dangerous life of the capital.

He could not complain of his reception. On the contrary, he had found a propitious climate for his novelties, an avid interest, and at no time had he lacked for money. What he did miss, very much, was all that he had left behind in Bahia: the nights of stars and songs, the easy laughter, the drinks and the endless talk, the carefree life, the heartwarming friendships. He had missed the festivals of June: that of Oxossi, which coincided that year with the end of the thirteen-day celebration of St. Anthony, on the 13th; the bonfires of St. John; the abundance of corn pudding and genipap liquor. He had fallen short in his duties toward Xangô, he had not carried out his *bori*. All these shortcomings were excused by his friends and the *orixás*, for they all were aware of the compelling reasons for that voluntary emigration. He had not proceeded in this matter out of choice, but from stern necessity. They missed him, they remembered him every day, and Tibéria threatened not to celebrate her anniversary if he were not back when it came around. "Without Martim there is no real fun," she said.

One thing seemed sure and indisputable: if the corporal had remained among his friends, in his own circle, esteemed by all, respected in the *capoeira* fighting groups, the fair-haired boy of the brothels, he would not have gotten married and given rise to all this talk. But off by himself in Cachoeira, thinking about the festivities of Bahia, he had run across Marialva, with the black beauty spot on her left shoulder peeping out of her low-necked dress. And he had struck his colors. The backlanders had had their revenge.

It was on account of some ungrateful backlanders that he had had to take off precipitately for the Recôncavo. The police were looking for him, and the flatfoots, whose deep-seated antipathy for Martim grew in proportion to the generous palm-greasing of the backlanders, were doing their best to lay him by the heels and put him out of circulation for a while. The only way out was to beat it, without luggage, and foregoing the sighs of Dalva, his heartthrob of the moment.

All this because Martim was not in the habit of attaching importance to or worrying about the sporadic complaints of some of his fellow cardplayers. Complaints, moreover, nearly always muttered, for the one bold enough to speak up was rare. When, by chance, this happened, it was a source of amusement to the group.

The corporal's point of view, repeatedly stated, can be summed up in two clear concepts whose truth is inescapable: "He who lacks ability never gets ahead" and "When you bet, it is either to lose or win." In his calm, gentle voice he would expound his philosophy when doubts or arguments arose. He was not a man given to raising his voice, being a person of breeding, at times so polite that he even annoyed and disarmed fellow players less given to so much etiquette. He was a person who liked a quiet life; to make him fight, one had to offend him in his honor as a soldier. Having been at one time a corporal in the Army, he had acquired obligations toward the "glorious"—the "glorious" being the uniform—and he was very touchy on the subject. Thus he could not tolerate certain offenses, for in his opinion, doubts and insults affected not only him personally, but touched upon the honor of the whole body military, from lowliest private to general. To offend him was to offend the Army. A point of view, moreover, shared, it would seem, by generals and colonels, which puts Corporal Martim in distinguished company.

Thus it was a great source of amusement when some blowhard showed up—generally a newcomer in the area—who, ignorant of Martim's military antecedents, did not know whom he was dealing with. The corporal did not lose his aplomb, did not overstep the limits of the decorum imposed by breeding. The foolhardy bungler, taken in by the corporal's quiet voice, by his politeness, mistaking courtesy for fear, raised his voice in insult: "This is what comes of having to do with a thief. . . ."

The corporal did not turn a hair: "You know something, brother? Go tell the whore who bore you. . . ."

He did not give the complainant time to swallow the remark, for he suited the deed to the word, and the joker fell sprawling on the ground. Martim was a master at *capoeira* fighting, the equal of past and present champions: Querido de Deus, Juvenal, Traíra, Master Pastinha. Of a Sunday afternoon, when acceding to the requests of his admirers or to delight the eyes of some brown girl, he displayed his art in Pelourinho or Liberdade, it was a pleasure to watch him. After seeing one of these exhibitions, a society dame from São Paulo, who was visiting Bahia, lost her head over the corporal and made a show of herself. The sport of Angola held no secrets for Martim.

Breathless and speechless, his eyes popping out of his head, flat on his back, the complainant saw glitter in the sun the famous razor known as "Raimunda," so called in honor of a jealous woman, its former owner, who had tried to establish her claim to being a tough baby at Martim's expense. This Negress Raimunda, whose name the razor commemorated, went on the warpath when she came by irrefutable proofs of certain bedplay between the corporal and the servant girl Cotinha. She stated publicly at a dance in Gafieira do Barão that she was allergic to horns, and that a woman of her standing did not tolerate them; they made her head ache; and besides, her patron saint would not stand for it. She mixed a few glasses of beer with some swallows of rum and took her position at the entrance, waiting for the corporal to show up. If he had not been as agile as he was, she would have scarred his face. The one who did not escape her wrath was poor Cotinha, but the scar, once it had healed, was even attractive, leaving her with one side of her lip raised, as though she were always smiling. While Cotinha was being taken to a first-aid station, the corporal gave Raimunda a few sound slaps, a good cure for unruly nerves, and took the razor away from her. As he led her to a nearby house, he had to subdue her by main force, and as the result of holding her tightly in his arms, Martim got hotted up and forgot all about poor Cotinha, who was waiting for him at the first-aid station with three stitches in her lip. That Negress Raimunda, an *iawô* of Iansã, was quite a woman, more like a mare running about the streets looking for a stallion.

The story of the razor, however, has no direct bearing on the corporal's marriage. It had happened a short time before, and there was no need to tell it to Otália. But that is the way things happen; people begin to tell something, and if they don't watch out, they mix in a lot of other things, going off at a tangent, and before they realize it, they are talking about what they didn't start out to, way off course, lost, without head or tail.

Now the story of the three backlanders, that does have to do with the corporal, with his precipitate trip, and with his much-commented-upon marriage. Martim, as has been made clear, did not take an insult lying down, and for that very reason the number of his cardplaying companions increased. The insinuations regarding the decks (suspected of being marked) which he used and his quick-fingered tricks increased rather than diminished his clientele and consolidated his prestige. The corporal was earning an honest living when he got into the mess with those backland characters.

It would seem that they chanced to turn up in Água dos Meninos. They were visiting the capital, strolling the streets, entering the churches—that of Bonfim to fulfill a vow, that of São Francisco to see the gold ornamentation of its walls—visiting the famous landmarks, and in this way they came to the market of Água dos Meninos. They were smoking cigars and wearing broad-brimmed hats like those used in the movies.

The corporal was minding his own affairs, dealing the cards, acting as banker for some of the stallkeepers, his customary partners. A low-stake game, just a few nickels to lend it interest, a pastime among old friends, with the corporal winning a few cruzeiros here, a few there, the necessary funds for the evening rum. It was more a demonstration of his skill in a cordial, friendly atmosphere than a real game. Tricks were pulled off, laughter exploded, all on a note of good fellowship, one big happy

32

family. From their seat on trucks parked close by, the drivers and their helpers watched, and some of the young fry, standing around, absorbed learning. They had great respect and a high regard for the corporal; from him they learned decorum and manners, drank at the fountain of his many-sided wisdom, with their eyes on his agile hands. That was the university they attended, the school of life in which there are no holidays, and from his chair Corporal Martim freely and generously transmitted his learning, professor emeritus. More emeritus and respectable only Jesuíno Crazy Cock himself, by reason of his age, his boundless wisdom, and all the rest that will be explained in due time. There is nothing worse than telling a story hurry-scurry, slipshod, without carefully analyzing everything.

The three backlanders were strolling about Água dos Meninos, their mouths open, for they had never seen a market like that nor could they even imagine one that size, when they came upon the corporal established in the shade of a tree, with the players seated on boxes and stools, surrounded by the street urchins and the chauffeurs on the bleachers—their trucks. The backlanders stopped to observe Martim's virtuosity. Finally one of them made up his mind, took off his hat, scratched his head, put his hand in his pants pocket, and from its depths pulled out a roll of money. A wad to choke an ox, all bills of one hundred, two hundred, five hundred milreis, so many that the corporal's eyes gleamed, and one of the urchins, nearly full grown and with two entries on the police blotter, sighed. The backlander riffled the bills and chose one of a hundred milreis which he tossed on the queen.

Martim cast up a mental account of his cash on hand. The till was empty but his credit was high. He fell back on some of his capitalist friends, the very ones with whom he had been playing before, the market-stall keepers. With the bank bolstered, the corporal smiled at the backlanders. A cordial smile, as though saying to them that they would not regret the confidence they had bestowed on him; if they wanted to learn how to play, they would never find a better occasion or a more kindly disposed teacher.

The backlanders won the first rounds, naturally. The corporal's good breeding forbade his winning from the

33

start. "The first corn is for the young chicks," was a saying of his. Before you could say scat, Martim was a conto eight hundred milreis in the hole, and the stallkeepers began to get nervous, worried about their money. By this time all three of the backlanders had taken a hand, and the bank began to pick up: a hundred from one, fifty from another, twenty from the third, and a boy was sent off for some cold beers to temper the blazing sun. Some stools had appeared, nobody quite knew how, and the backlanders were comfortably seated, prepared to spend the afternoon there.

And they kept putting their money on the queen, as though they did not know that a woman is a treacherous creature, unworthy of trust. The noble ladies began to fail just as the first of the three backlanders to sit in on the game put up a five hundred milreis bill. Then things followed their natural course.

That night Martim took Dalva a string of beads, the golden beads of Oxum, the patron saint of that skittish mulatta, full of whims, given to swoons, one of the inmates of Tibéria's house. And to Tibéria, for whom he felt the tenderest friendship, the corporal took a gold charm, 18 karat, which Chalub had sold him in the market at cost, without making a penny. The tab for the impromptu celebration was picked up by the corporal, or to be more exact, by the backlanders.

They had arranged to come back the next day, and so Martim counted on a pleasant life with easy pickings for some time, as long as the suckers stayed in Bahia. They wanted to learn to play *ronda?* The corporal would undertake to teach them, to complete their education. Money and amusement would not be lacking in the forthcoming days, not to mention the beers because of the heat. The prospects looked rosy that night of the celebration, nobody had the slightest presentiment, not even Antônio Garcia, with all his spiritism, a medium and everything. Neither he nor anybody, all merrily talking about the return of the backlanders the next day and figuring out how long it would take to relieve them of all their money.

They returned before the appointed time and brought the police. If Martim had not been born with a caul—and

anyone so born is assured the lifelong protection of Oxalá
—he would have landed in the hoosegow. The cops did not
disguise their intentions, they made loud threats, they
talked of giving a lesson they would not forget to those
cardsharpers with their marked decks, who infested the
city, robbing the hard-working people of the market and
the honest rustics visiting the city. They mentioned the
corporal by name, the worst of the lot, in their opinion, the
most despicable and scoundrelly of all, and made no bones
about their intention of giving him free lodging in jail for a
time, with plentiful beatings as rations. Among the most
excited of the flatfoots was a certain Miguel Charuto, especially loudmouthed and insulting, thirsting for the corporal's blood, and everybody knew the reason why. He was
head over heels in love with one Clarinda, a notorious half-
breed Indian with the face of a Chinese, as brazen as they
come. The policeman paid for her flat, her beans, and her
luxuries with the money he squeezed out of the people.
One day he discovered that there was a partner in the firm,
Corporal Martim, a partner who brought no capital, only
the labor of his body. Miguel Charuto did not have the
guts to stand up to Corporal Martim, man to man. He now
took occasion to collect his debt with interest.

At this point in the narration, Otália wanted to know if
the corporal in question was some movie star, since everything that wore a skirt seemed to want to throw herself in
his arms. Weren't his friends exaggerating? They assured
her that there was not the slightest exaggeration. Why the
women fell for him, a long, thin guy, that they couldn't
say; who can understand a woman? The one who looked
like a movie star was not Martim but Miguel Charuto, with
his brilliantined hair, his sideburns, and his cane.

The luck of the corporal was due in large measure to the
blustering of the two-timed Miguel. He boasted about his
bravery and what he was going to do, the news got around,
and security measures were taken. Besides, Martim was
late after the celebration of the previous night and the
morning spent in Dalva's arms.

Street Arabs, stallkeepers, chauffeurs, women vendors,
were on the lookout, stationing themselves at strategic
spots, pinpointing all the routes by which Corporal Martim

might arrive, innocent and smiling, with a clear conscience.

He got word, and beat it. The cops prowled about for several hours, trying to earn the backlanders' tip, but finally had to give up. Not, however, without swearing that they would catch up with Martim; they knew where to find him; he wouldn't get away. Miguel Charuto still lingered on, poking his horns into warehouses and fishing boats, investigating.

When later in the day Martim received a complete report of what had happened, and went about analyzing it in the company of his friends over glasses of wild-cherry brandy, he did not concede major importance to the exciting police story. In his opinion, all that was nothing but a tempest in a teapot: the anger of the hicks and the demagoguery of the cops. The backlanders had probably been listening to talk, perhaps right there in the market, reservations about the decks the corporal used and his way of shuffling and dealing. Backlanders are by nature suspicious, believe everything they hear. They took stock in that tittle-tattle, shot off their mouths, greased the coppers' palms, and stirred up all that hullabaloo. But it wouldn't go any farther; they would go back to their fields, to their hoes and shovels, to their barnyards and pastures, cured for good of the vice of gambling. The day would come, once their anger had cooled off, when they would thank Martim as they looked back serenely on what had happened. Martim's only doubt was whether the backlanders were completely cured, or if there was danger of their forgetting the lesson and relapsing into vice. The ideal would have been at least one more session, one more afternoon of play. The corporal sincerely regretted the breaking-off of those pleasant relations so cordially established the afternoon before and destined, as he thought and hoped, to turn into a solid friendship.

Jesuíno Crazy Cock disagreed with Martim; the affair did not seem to him so inconsequential. Contrary to the corporal, Jesuíno did not believe it would all have blown over the next day, after twenty-four hours of spiritual retreat in Tibéria's house, in the warm embrace of Dalva's arms.

Backlanders are stubborn, proud, vengeful people. Unswerving and obstinate, they do not give up easily. Jesuíno extracted from the knapsack of his varied experience two or three cases, convincing and illustrative, to make his point, one of which was positively hair-raising. It had to do with a backlander who for a year and a half had followed the trail of an insolent rogue who had stolen his daughter's cherry, already—it should be added—somewhat bruised from previous forays, and then taken to his heels. Not even this detail, which considerably reduced the culprit's responsibility, could cool the dishonored father's thirst for vengeance. He set out after the offender, the one fleeing, the other pursuing in an infuriated chase, to the boundaries of Mato Grosso, where the seducer paused briefly, just long enough to deflower another maiden, and at that climactic moment, while hitting on all six cylinders, he was gelded by the outraged backlander, who carried his balls back home with him and thereby ransomed his honor from the byword it had become. He then became reconciled to his daughter, who, moreover, was already installed in the house of the priest as maid of all work, enjoying the vicar's complete confidence and being treated with the greatest respect, as befitted a man of honor and the cloth.

Not even this story shook the corporal's quiet self-assurance; it was impossible—he said—to compare the maidenhead of a virgin, a matter of grave responsibility, with a few contos lost in a poker game on an unlucky day. Neither the honor of a woman nor the death of a man had been involved in his brief dealings with the backlanders. One day—or two, at most—and it would all be an amusing memory. Even more amusing when he, Corporal Martim, discovered the identity of the troublemaker, of the lowlife, who to get even with him had filled the backlanders' ears with lies, and taught him the virtue of keeping his mouth shut.

Jesuíno skeptically shook his silvery head, with the hair growing over his ears, tumbling about his head—rebellious curly locks through which fat Magda liked to run her fingers in moments of tenderness. Jesuíno considered Martim's attitude frankly frivolous. In his opinion, the situation was serious; the backlanders were prepared to spend money; the cops were stirred up; and Miguel Charuto was thirsting for revenge. The corporal should take precautions.

Martim shrugged his shoulders without heeding Crazy Cock's words of warning, as though Jesuíno's opinion were something to be disregarded. And the very next day in the morning he set out for the Model Market, where he wanted to discuss a question of the *afoxé* of carnival with Camafeu, the owner of St. George's Warehouse and an important figure of the aforesaid *afoxé*. The carnival was still a long way off, and naturally the *afoxé* was just an excuse. The corporal never lost an opportunity to go chew the fat at the market, admire the *peji* of Oxossi and Yemanjá, one of the prettiest in the city, play the Jew's harp with Camafeu and Didi, exchange wisecracks with Carybé, talk over the day's happenings.

They almost caught him, for the market was swarming with flatfoots, and the same thing was true of Água dos Meninos, Pelourinho, Sete Portas, and the other places where the corporal was in the habit of making his daily rounds. As though the police had nothing better to do, no other duties, crimes to investigate, businesses to watch over, impudent politicians to protect, upright numbers operators to pursue! As though the taxpayers' money should be used exclusively to run down Corporal Martim! A ridiculous state of affairs which, as is clear, more than justified the indignant imprecations of Jesuíno, whose horror of the police and policemen was well known.

Martim could not even return to Tibéria's establishment, for Miguel Charuto and another disgusting policeman were there, annoying the girls, threatening Tibéria, questioning Dalva. As for the three backlanders, really stubborn customers, they went from one side to the other, egging on the investigators, promising them the world with a fence around it if they recovered the money and put the corporal in the hoosegow. Fortunately it was a question of a card game, and the backlanders would have been satisfied to see Martim behind bars. If a girl's honor had been involved, given their stubbornness, Martim would have run the risk of being castrated.

A hypothesis, moreover, that was aired when some of his close friends, including Tibéria and Dalva, met in the shop of Alfredo, an image maker who had been in business for many years in Cabeça, to lay the plans for his escape and to drink a stirrup cup. Wing-Foot had brought one jug, Camafeu contributed another, and the master of the house the first and the last, as was his duty and his privilege. The conversation touched on this and that and someone recalled the story told by Jesuíno. Bullfinch, who, being young, did not observe the proprieties as he should, laughingly remarked: "Can you imagine Martim gelded?..."

A remote and improbable hypothesis, yet sufficient to wrench from the depths of Dalva's being a howl like that of a wounded animal, the lamentation of one suddenly threatened by the loss of her greatest treasure, the very reason for her existence. The beauty hurled herself on Bullfinch, her nails like claws, and it took all Tibéria's authority to quiet her down.

Not that the girl was not justified, and although the others had trouble putting her in her place, it was easy to understand and excuse her. What good would Corporal Martim be, from her point of view, if the backlanders subjected him to that delicate operation? Who ever heard of a gelded corporal?

Poor Dalva, she could not guess at that hour of leave-taking, her arms about Martim's neck, exchanging vows of eternal love, brimming over with tears and yearning, that the consequences of the corporal's trip would be tantamount, after a fashion, to the conjecture put forward by Bullfinch. And how could she foresee, how could the friends gathered there and the restorer of images of saints even suspect, that the corporal who set out in the dawn hours hidden in Master Manuel's fishing smack would return during the rainy season with that much-discussed Marialva clinging to his arm, with her honey-colored eyes and the black beauty spot on her left shoulder showing at the neck of her dress. From Dalva's point of view, the corporal returned morally gelded.

In Alonso's store, as they told Otália the antecedents of the event, none of those present as yet took in the full extent of the disaster. Only after the arrival of the corporal could they gauge all the consequences. For Martim, given over body and soul to his marriage, did not put in an appearance even at Tibéria's establishment.

That night as they set out to look for Otália's luggage, they were still laughing and joking, dividing up among themselves the four hundred mulattas Wing-Foot had ordered.

⋙{ 5 }⋘

IT WAS WELL INTO THE NIGHT when, ebullient and triumphant, they reached Tibéria's house. The intake of rum had been great during that busy night, first at Alonso's store, where the rain overtook them, then in the peregrination to Caminho de Areia, and, finally, during the moving scenes attendant on the recovery of Otália's belongings. It was still drizzling when they set out for Tibéria's, with the wind carrying sudden squalls of water, drenching the streets and the belated passersby.

They had set out in search of the luggage, taking advantage of a lull in the rain, after threshing out the antecedents of the corporal's marriage, with all and sundry well informed on the matter. At this point the sensational news began to circulate through the city, with Alonso's store as the point of origin, arousing conjectures, curses, reports, and rumors. In the store, sheltered from the heavy rain, from the wind whistling through the old houses, the friends had listened to a repetition of Otália's story. Jesuíno Crazy Cock had insisted on hearing from the lips of the girl the detailed account of the loss of her luggage, beginning with the infatuation of the judge's son in Bonfim and on through her getting off at the Calçada Station with her suitcase and brown-paper parcel. He evinced great interest in the parcel, trying to find out what was in it, but Otália sidestepped the question: "Just a trifle. . . . Of no value."

41

"Just a trifle? But you said that you would prefer to lose the suitcase rather than the package."

"That is . . . just silly. . . . I want to find the parcel because it contains something that means a lot to me. That's all. . . ."

And her smile was so embarrassed that Jesuíno refrained from further questioning in spite of his growing curiosity about the mysterious package.

During the course of the narrative, Wing-Foot, after feeding the white rat a cracker, put the animal in his pocket and dozed off. Negro Massu and Eduardo Ipicilone were sound asleep by this time, the Negro's snores rattling the cans and bottles on the shelves. The rest had left, defying the rain, in their eagerness to spread the news of the corporal's marriage. Only Bullfinch stayed awake, sitting across from Otália, looking at her, feeling a tickling in his breast, shivers of tenderness, the unmistakable signs of a new passion coming over him.

Giving up his efforts to extract details about the parcel from Otália, Jesuíno asked for a description of the gentleman who had offered to look after the luggage while she went off to "attend to urgent needs which nobody else could take care of for her," as he put it.

No sooner had Otália begun her account of him—"A distinguished-looking gentleman, wearing a white suit, well starched, a Panama hat, a bow tie, very spruce"—than a spark lighted up Crazy Cock's eyes. He looked toward Bullfinch as though seeing confirmation of his suspicions, but the lad was not there; he was hanging on Otália's words, listening without understanding, incapable of hearing, much less suspecting, capable only of falling head over heels in love. That was the way Bullfinch was, a heart ever open to love, always responsive to the beauty and charm of women.

"Very spruce . . . and what else?"

"And what else?" Otália searched her memory. "His eyes glued on me just like those of that fellow over there . . ." and she laughed in Bullfinch's face, not scoffing at him, just laughing because he struck her as funny and because of the rum she had drunk.

Bullfinch sat there crestfallen, looking away, self-

conscious. He was shy and easily embarrassed. Otália went
on, laughing: ". . . with his face painted, so funny, and his
eyes on me. The gentleman at the station was the same
way, eating me up with his eyes. Ah!" she recalled, "and he
had a flower in his buttonhole, a red flower."

Jesuíno laughed aloud, pleased with himself. He had not
been mistaken. He winked at Bullfinch, who nodded his
head in agreement with Crazy Cock's confirmed suspicions.
It couldn't be anyone else.

"Let's go," said Jesuíno.

"Where?" asked Otália.

"To find your things . . . the suitcase, the parcel."

"Do you know where they are?"

"Of course. The minute you started telling about it I
knew," he boasted.

"And you know who stole them, too?"

"It wasn't stealing, child, it was just a joke. . . ."

Bullfinch went about waking up the others to take ad-
vantage of the lull in the rain. Massu, Wing-Foot, and
Ipicilone, given the detailed description of the gentleman to
whose care Otália had entrusted her luggage, agreed with
Jesuíno; it could be none other than Zico Carnation-in-his-
Buttonhole.

"He is a good friend of mine . . . a great one for playing
jokes. . . ."

One of his favorite jokes was exactly that: making off
with friends' things, giving them a good scare. A prankster.
Otália timidly put forth an objection: she was not a friend
of the playful Zico, she had known him only by sight when
he gave her the eye in the station, and she had taken
advantage of this state of affairs to ask a favor of him.
Jesuíno ran his hand through his tousled hair and answered
with an argument that seemed to him clinching: "He's
not a friend of yours, but he is of ours, and of Tibéria, and
we are even *compadres*, for I was godfather to one of his
children, one that died, poor thing. That's why he played
the joke."

Otália opened her mouth to say something. She was a
little bewildered, and did not know whether Jesuíno was
right or not. While she hesitated, Jesuíno took the floor
again, prepared to allay any suspicion, any distrust that

might still be troubling her. As they descended Pelourinho slope he held forth at length not only on the subject of Zico's playful nature, but also on the relentless bad luck that pursued him. They were on their way to Caminho de Areia, where Carnation-in-his-Buttonhole lived with his numerous progeny.

They went down the Tabuão, crossed the streets of the poorest red-light district, where they were enthusiastically greeted, especially Jesuíno Crazy Cock, evidently well known and liked in that neighborhood. They stopped to rest in the taverns that were still open, and Crazy Cock's voice took on color and emotion with each drink, his praise of Zico grew more sincere, as did the account of his difficulties, his ill luck, and the iniquitous harassment that "excellent family man" suffered at the hands of the police.

An excellent, a model family man, heavily burdened with sons and daughters, and a person of delicate health. Look how thin he was. Unfit not only for military service, but also for heavy work that called for physical strength. Could Otália imagine the tragedy of Carnation-in-his-Buttonhole's life? A sensitive man, who, like Corporal Martim, could write lyrics to be sung to the guitar, devoted to his wife and children, running about all day long looking for work at which he could make the money needed to support his family, pay the rent, the electricity, the water, the beans, the manioc meal. He went from place to place, and all they offered him were impossible jobs working eight or ten hours on his feet all day, loading bundles and boxes in a warehouse, or waiting on customers in third-rate stores. It was difficulties of this sort that had turned an upright, hard-working man into an idler, unemployed, as though he were a malefactor. For more than four years, ever since the unjustified closing of the gambling houses, poor Zico had been roaming the streets. When the gambling houses were in operation, he had never lacked for work; there was no better "steerer" than he, none more capable, more resourceful. Now that was work suitable for one with his delicate health for it allowed him to sleep all day, quietly. And, as everyone knows, night work is easier; it is not so hot and there are not such large crowds. But the gambling houses were closed down, and at most, Carnation-in-his-

Buttonhole could pick up a little change at certain places still operating outside the law, transitory and dangerous jobs for a man like him, whom the police had their eye on. The police had given abundant proof of the ill will they bore him, they had put up his picture in a gallery of pickpockets and confidence men, and picked him up at the drop of a hat for no good reason, just on suspicion.

Zico suffered greatly with all this. Zealous for his reputation, he saw his name besmirched, the prey of bad luck and the police. However, he did not let himself be discouraged; he maintained his moral fiber, his smile, his unfailing good humor. A delightful companion; nobody could tell a story the way he could, and he had an inexhaustible repertory. To think that a man like that, gay and innocent, should be so miserably hounded.

Jesuíno Crazy Cock did not like the police. He, too, was the victim of cops, detectives, chiefs of police. He had made a careful study of the psychology of policemen and he was against them. With all the professions in the world to choose from, he was in the habit of observing—some laborious, others easy, some calling only for knowledge, cunning, intelligence, while others demanded brute force and the willingness to put your shoulder to the wheel— when a person chose to become a policeman, pursuing his fellow man, arresting him, torturing him, it was because he was good for nothing, not even for collecting garbage. He lacked dignity and human solidarity.

Nevertheless, he asked Otália excitedly, after another drink at a stall still open in Água dos Meninos, who was in command of the world today, who were the lords and masters, above governments and rulers, regimes, ideologies, economic and political systems? In all countries, in all regimes, in all types of government, who was really in command, who ruled, who kept the people in a state of fear? The police, the policemen!—and Crazy Cock spat out his contempt along with the dregs of the rum. The most insignificant chief of police wielded more authority than the president of the Republic. The mighty of the earth, to keep the people in a state of fear and subjection, had been increasing the power of the police to the point where they themselves had been caught in the net of their own weaving. Every day the police commit violence, injustices, the cruelest crimes, against the poor and the free. Who ever saw a policeman punished for a crime that he had committed?

For Jesuíno, refractory to all authority, a free soul and ardent of heart, the world would be a fit place to live in only when the day came that there were no more soldiers or police of any sort. At present, all men, including kings and dictators, not to mention the defenseless poor, were subservient to the police, whose power outranked that of all others. Let her then imagine this immense power turned against a simple family man like Zico Carnation-in-his-Buttonhole, with a smooth tongue, to be sure, knowing how to lead a fool by the nose, but totally incapable of resisting violence. All he wanted was to live in peace, but they did not let him, the cops had singled him out, and bad luck, too. Therefore Otália should not pass hasty judgment on, or form an adverse opinion of a man who was the plaything of fate.

Spelling out the situation, quaffing a glass of rum here and there when the light of a tavern threw its beam across their path, they finally came to a poorly lighted alley where the unfortunate Carnation-in-his-Buttonhole lived. They had left the asphalt and the paved streets and were on a dirt path. Zico's house stood a little apart from the others at the end of the alley, with a small side yard filled with carnations. Drops of water from the recent rain dripped from leaves and flowers.

"He is crazy about flowers, carnations. He puts one in his buttonhole every day," Bullfinch explained, and it was as though with this he gave the final touch to the portrait of Zico, the real one and not the one that had appeared so many times in the newspapers with a number across the chest.

After that panegyric of Carnation-in-his-Buttonhole, confronted by the closed, sleeping house, the silence of that remote alley, broken only by the chirp of a cricket hidden among the carnations, Otália, her legs aching, her head swimming with so much talk and rum, suggested that they give up the search and return to Tibéria's house. But Jesuíno was not willing to tolerate any doubt as to Zico's probity; neither did he want his friend's jest with Otália's luggage to go any farther.

"Every joke has its limits. . . ."

While Ipicilone was clapping his hands at the front door, Jesuíno crossed the bed of carnations toward the rear of the house. Nobody answered the hand clapping, even with Bullfinch and Wing-Foot assisting Ipicilone. The silence continued unbroken, as though nobody were home or they were all dead. Whereupon Negro Massu pounded his fist against the door, making the roof and the walls shake. While this was going on, Crazy Cock had reached the rear of the house in time to see Carnation-in-his-Buttonhole slip through the kitchen door and disappear into the underbrush.

"Hold it, pal. . . . Where are you going? It's just us."

At the sound of a familiar voice the fugitive asked, from a distance: "Is that you, *compadre* Jesuíno?"

"Me and Massu, Wing-Foot and Ipicilone. Come back and open the door."

"And what in the devil are you doing here at this time of night, scaring folks?"

He reappeared, leaping agilely over the puddles of water, attired in a perfectly laundered white suit, with Panama hat, bow tie, and a faded carnation in his buttonhole.

"I came to bring a girl."

"A girl?" There was a note of suspicion in Zico's voice.

By this time a light had come on in the house, and a child's head appeared in the kitchen door. Soon there were three heads, their bright eyes searching the darkness. The remaining friends and Otália had come to the back of the house, crossing through the carnations.

"Yes, a girl. And why were you lighting out in such a hurry?"

"I thought . . . I mean, I was going to the drugstore to buy some cereal for the baby. . . ."

The family had been awakened and got up. Otália had never seen so many boys and girls pushing and succeeding one another in the doorway.

"Come in," said Carnation-in-his-Buttonhole.

From the kitchen they could see the other two rooms of the house, the bedroom and the living room. In the bed-

47

room, seven of the eight children had been piled on a mattress and several straw mats spread on the floor. The oldest must have been about twelve, a pretty young girl on the verge of womanhood. The youngest, about six months old, was whimpering in the arms of its mother, whose prematurely aged profile showed at the open door of the living room, where the married couple slept. The woman looked the visitors over with a weary air.

"Good evening, *comadre*," Crazy Cock greeted her, as did the others, including Otália.

"Good evening, *compadre*. Did you come to look for . . ."

Jesuíno answered: "You see, the girl is one of Tibéria's. That is why I came with her." And turning to Zico: "Where is the suitcase, *compadre*?"

"Whatever suitcase are you talking about?"

"The one you latched on to in Calçada. . . . The girl knows it was just a joke. . . . I explained it to her. . . ."

Carnation-in-his-Buttonhole ran his eyes over the group. "I didn't do it on purpose. How could I tell that she was going to Tibéria's house? She was just asking for it, she even handed the luggage over to me. 'Would the gentleman keep an eye on it while I go in there?' Wasn't that the way it was, Miss?"

He walked past his wife, went into the living room, and came out with the suitcase. Empty. "Please excuse my mistake. . . ."

"But the suitcase is empty, *compadre*."

"So what? Did you think there was anything in it?"

Otália pointed to the woman standing in the door: "That's my nightgown she's got on."

The woman said nothing, barely looking at Jesuíno, Otália, or the rest. The children were observing the scene with whispers and giggles. The second oldest, a girl, too, around ten, was wearing nothing but a pair of panties far too big for her.

"Those are my panties, too."

"Listen, *compadre*!" Jesuíno exhorted.

The woman in the doorway opened her mouth and began to speak in a dull, monotonous voice, without anger or pity: "Didn't I tell you, Zico, that it wouldn't get you anywhere? You're no good for anything. . . . You don't have the knack." Then raising her voice, she ordered the children: "Hand over the young lady's things!"

She drew back into the room, closed the door, and then opened it to toss the nightgown towards Otália. A few minutes later she reappeared wearing an old, patched robe.

From the bedroom and living room the other things began to emerge: a pair of new slippers, bedroom slippers, two dresses draped over the single chair in the room. Carnation-in-his-Buttonhole explained: "You know, *compadre*, we are so terribly short of clothes here. The girls, poor things, it would break your heart . . ."

His wife set out some glasses on an old tin tray and was getting a jug from the corner of the kitchen. Now Zico urged the children on, eager to get the unpleasant episode of the suitcase over with as soon as possible. They were among friends and the occasion called for a celebration. The woman, old before her time, poured out the rum in silence, without laughing but without crying either, just living.

The contents of the suitcase seemed complete, and Negro Massu was about to close it. But Otália spoke up: "My best dress is missing, my prettiest one."

The woman looked at her oldest daughter. The girl lowered her head, went into the bedroom, and came back with a ruffled print dress. It had been a present to Otália from the son of the judge at the beginning of their affair, before his father cut off his allowance. The girl walked slowly, her eyes on the dress, and the grief in her expression was touching.

Otália said to her: "Do you like it?"

In utter confusion the girl nodded her head, and bit her lip to keep from crying.

"Then you keep it."

The girl looked toward her father: "May I keep it, Father?"

Zico swelled with dignity: "Give the young lady her dress, you wretched creature. What is she going to think of us?"

"It's for you," Otália repeated. "Otherwise I'll get mad."

The girl tried to smile, but her eyes were swimming in tears, and she turned, the dress clasped to her breast, and ran into the living room. Carnation-in-his-Buttonhole raised his arms, fervidly: "Thank you, thank you. Since you insist, I will let her keep it so as not to offend you. Thank the young lady, Dorinha—never saw such a mannerless girl. . . ."

At this juncture rum was called for. Otália took the baby in her arms to relieve the mother: "How old is it?"

"Six months, and there's already another on the way."

Ipicilone laughed. "That Zico doesn't let the grass grow under his feet."

They all laughed. Carnation-in-his-Buttonhole decided to go with them. He had to buy some cereal for the baby at the drugstore, and he wanted to make his apologies to Tibéria. They were on the point of leaving when Otália asked: "I had a parcel. Don't you remember?"

"A parcel? Ah, a paper package? It didn't have anything of value in it. I don't know what the kid did with it. Where did you put it?" he called into the living room.

The ten-year-old girl went to look for the package, which was hidden in a corner. The paper came off and a doll emerged, old and raggedy. Otália rushed over, took the doll, and pressed it to her breast. She asked for the brown paper to wrap it up again. The others watched without understanding. Only Wing-Foot remarked: "A doll . . ." And, turning to Otália: "Why all that fuss about a doll? Now, if it had been a live animal . . ."

The children did not take their eyes off the girl. She got up, walked over to her suitcase, put away the package, and Massu helped her close it. They finally left, with Massu carrying the suitcase, and the woman stood watching them from the kitchen door with the baby in her arms. She enjoined once more: "Don't forget the cereal for the little one."

"The kid's got diarrhea. He can't eat anything but canned cereal, and I'm flat broke," explained Carnation-in-his-Buttonhole.

Between them they made up the amount, each contributing something. Zico held out his hand to collect the sum, but Jesuíno put it in his own pocket: "I'll buy it, *compadre*. . . . It's better that way."

"All right. Anything you say."

"No offense intended. You just might forget."

Jesuíno recalled other of Carnation-in-his-Buttonhole's children who had died in infancy for lack of money for cereal. He knew, too, that his friend was forgetful, and above all, could not resist the temptation of trying his luck at the gambling table. He might come upon one on his way home in the dawn hours before the drugstores opened, and with his kind of luck he could lose those few milreis they had deducted from their quota for rum.

When they reached Tibéria's house, all activity had ceased. The girls had gone to bed to rest, alone or with their men. In the parlor the lights were out; the Victrola was silent. In the dining room Tibéria was seated in her rocking chair, her voluminous body filling it to overflowing. She was a stout mulatta, round sixty, with immense breasts, a placid countenance, and eyes revealing firmness and kindness. At that late hour her face, normally cordial and good-humored, was somber, as though something serious had happened. She greeted the crowd with a faint "Good evening." The one who smiled pleasantly was Jesus, her husband, seated at the head of the table, entering the day's take in a ledger.

Jesus Bento de Sousa, clerical tailor, a half-Indian mulatto, with the straight hair and the bronzed color of an Indian, had his glasses balanced on the end of his nose. Some ten years younger than Tibéria, he had been a fine figure of a young fellow when they met almost thirty years earlier, she in the opulence of maturity, with firm dark flesh, queen of the carnival, standard-bearer of her carnival club, a denizen of Aninha's sporting house. He was an apprentice in the Model Tailoring Establishment, who liked his fun, a strummer of the guitar. They had met at an Easter Sunday celebration; that same night they had slept together, mad about each other, and the love had endured, steady and sweet, undiminished by the passing of the years.

When they had been living together for ten years, Tibéria set up in business for herself, and he, too, with his "God's Scissors," a small but well-patronized tailor shop specializing in cassocks and clerical vestments. He was made secretary of the Carmo Sodality, a position he still held, having been elected time after time because of his proved competence, and they had been married by judge and priest. They managed to keep the date of the civil ceremony a secret, divulged only to a few close friends. But on the occasion of the religious ceremony, which took place one Sunday at the church of Our Lady of Carmo at the place called Portas do Carmo, near Pelourinho, the news got around. The church was crowded with women and friends, the girls in their best dresses, the brothers of the Carmo Sodality in their red capes. There was such a hubbub of whores in the church, such an authentic festival air, with perfumes, laces, laughter, and flowers, that Father Melo, with his forty years in the priesthood, said that he had never celebrated a wedding so colorful and so well attended. Tibéria looked like a queen in her dress with a train, a diadem on her head. With the years, Jesus had grown thin and a little stooped. He wore an impeccable white suit. Possibly Father Melo had officiated at richer weddings; but none destined to greater understanding or quieter happiness than this which joined the clerical tailor and the bawd in the bonds of holy wedlock.

Bawd? An ugly word to use in connection with Tibéria. "Mother" was what the girls of the establishment called her. Successive generations of girls came and went, gay or sad, loving or hating their exacting profession, but all knowing that they could depend on Tibéria, rest their head on her ample bosom, pour out to her their sadness, passions, and disappointment, certain that she would stand by them in moments of trial. Tibéria always with the right word, the appropriate gesture, the consolation, and the cure. "Mother" was what her friends of all walks of life and circumstances called her, and there were those who were prepared to kill and die for Tibéria. Her influence was widespread, and few persons were more respected and loved.

Corporal Martim was one of those bosom friends. He would have done anything for Tibéria. He came to see her at her house, regardless of whether or not he was having an affair with one of the girls. He would come to talk with her, to help her whenever she needed him, drink a beer, and then leave. This when he did not come with a group of friends to take the girls off to some party.

It was because of Martim that she had that grumpy look and barely greeted Jesuíno and the others. She was trying to digest the news of the corporal's marriage, which had reached her ears quickly, though distorted. But it stuck in her throat, would not go down. She could not believe it.

She gave the new arrivals a flinty stare: "What kind of hours are these?"

"We were looking for the girl's luggage." Crazy Cock explained, sitting down at the table.

"Did you find it?"

Massu put the suitcase down on the floor: "Zico had taken it to his house so it wouldn't be stolen. . . ."

Tibéria let her gaze linger on Carnation-in-his-Button-hole: "You're never going to learn to behave yourself? And how's your wife? You should get in touch with Lourival, he's got work for you. He's going to start up in business."

"I'll go to see him tomorrow."

Jesus looked up from the ledger: "Is it true that Martim has got married?"

But before anyone could answer, Tibéria burst out: "I don't believe it. I don't believe it, and that's the end of it. And here in my house nobody is going to slander Martim, for I won't have it. Anyone who wants to discuss this matter can get the hell out of here."

With this she got up indignantly. She indicated by a gesture that Otália was to come with her: "Pick up your suitcase and come. Your room is ready."

She was grumbling as she left: "Martim married! Who ever heard of such nonsense?"

The men stayed on in the parlor, around the table. Jesuíno ran his hand through his hair and observed: "This business of the corporal's getting married is more like a revolution."

Jesus nodded his head in agreement: "God help us! When the news first came in, I thought the girls were going on strike. The way they carried on!"

And he got up to serve them a drink.

⊸⊰{ 6 }⊱⊸

IN THE TWO WEEKS' INTERVAL between that rainy night when they recovered Otália's luggage and the luminous morning of the corporal's disembarking with his wife, Marialva, on the Rampa do Mercado, talk reached the boiling point, gossip ran rife, the news spread to the most outlying neighborhoods, suburbs, even other cities. In Aracajú, in the neighboring state of Sergipe, the admired eyes of Maria da Graça, a domestic of vaunted accomplishments, swam in tears. In spite of time and distance, she could not forget that madness of the past year when, after seeing Martim put on an exhibition at the Gafieira do Barão dance-hall, she had left her job and sweetheart to follow him in his devil-may-care life, without home or prospects.

Tibéria alone maintained absolute faith in Martim, unchanged and unchanging. Jesuíno Crazy Cock did not blame the corporal, it is true, nor did Jesus Bento de Sousa, who even went so far as to defend him, trying to explain, find reasons for the much-criticized marriage. They did not, however, turn a deaf ear to the gossip. Only Tibéria would have no part in that character assassination; in her opinion it was all nothing but a malicious lie, the perverse invention of ill-wishers and envious who transmogrified one of those habitual fleeting infatuations of the corporal into a marriage. Tibéria had been witness, and even sponsor, of so many, with girls of her own house. The corporal would turn up madly in love, stating that he could not bear to be separated for a single minute from his heart's desire, saying that he was roped for good. This lasted only until he met another, when off he went, and if a third showed up, he flung himself at her as though he could and should love all the women in the world. How many incidents, squabbles, even physical set-tos had Tibéria not witnessed on the part of Martim's girl friends!

She recalled the case of Maria da Graça, so pretty and innocent, wildly in love, on the eve of her marriage to an excellent young fellow, a Spaniard, with a good job in the grocery store of a fellow countryman and the promise of a share in the business very soon, a fine chap. She had tossed everything over the windmill—her job as nursemaid in the home of Dr. Celestino, where she was treated as one of the family, her sweetheart, her future—to follow Martim. The corporal had rolled her for her two cents, and then he, too, seemed caught up in the maddest passion. There was much talk of marriage, or at least of prolonged togetherness. Corporal Martim was moved; that girl, seemingly so shy, had given up everything for him, without asking anything in return. So charming, moreover, so tender and gentle. Martim had hidden her away in the vicinity of Cabula, and for the first time Tibéria had thought that he was really hooked.

And then, suddenly, when everybody believed him completely immersed in that deep, recent love—not a month had yet elapsed since their first meeting in Gafiera— Martim found himself the center of a scandal: he was attacked by a shoemaker in the neighborhood of Terreiro de Jesus and received a knife wound in the shoulder. The shoemaker, tipped off by a busybody of a neighbor—an old maid, naturally—found his wife in bed with Martim, neglecting all her household duties, in the middle of a weekday afternoon. The shoemaker had been busily at work when the mischief-maker whispered the shocking tidings into his ear. He leaped up, in his hand the knife with which he had been cutting leather, rushed home, and threw himself on Martim, slashing him in the shoulder. The neighbors prevented the row from going farther: the shoemaker wanting to kill his wife, to commit suicide, bent on washing his outraged honor in blood. As a result of the uproar, they all wound up in the police station and the news appeared in the papers, which referred to Corporal Martim as a "seducer." Martim was flattered by this description and carried the clipping in his pocket.

Maria de Graça, however, when she learned of the incident, gathered up her things and left as quietly as she had come. She did not complain, she did not utter one word of recrimination, but neither did she accept excuses or pleas for forgiveness. Martim went on a monumental binge, pickling himself in one of the back rooms in Tibéria's house.

If he had been inconstant even on that occasion, if not even the sweetness and devotion of Maria da Graça had been able to hold his volatile heart, if no woman had ever been able to dominate him, how could this sudden sea change in him have taken place to the point where he was talking about working? Tibéria, mature, experienced, for whom life held no secrets, mistress of a sporting house for over twenty years, was not a woman to be taken in by such chaff.

Jesus Bento de Sousa shrugged his shoulders. Stranger things had happened. There was no man, however much of a chaser he might be, who did not one day get caught, feel the need to settle on one woman, to set up his home, to put down roots in soil that would bring forth trees and fruits. Why was Martim to be the exception? He had married, he was going to work, children would be born, and there would be an end to the old Martim, lawless and masterless, the wastrel par excellence, the buffoon emeritus, the guitar-, Jew's-harp-, and drumplayer, the master of *capoeira* fighting, Martim of the marked decks and the nimble fingers, the swain of all the dark girls, the "seducer." The time for children and work had arrived, it was impossible to escape it. Hadn't he, Jesus Bento de Sousa, been an inveterate reveler, a man with many affairs, the most sought-after half-breed? the tailor asked Tibéria with a smile. The papers of his day had not dubbed him a seducer only because the occasion had not arisen, not because of his lack of merits. Nevertheless, when he met Tibéria, he had changed completely, had given himself over body and soul to work, had become filled with ambition—in a word, another man.

Instead of being moved by his tribute, Tibéria answered harshly: "Are you trying to compare me with that slut?"

"Why do you talk like that when you don't even know the girl, Mother?"

"I don't know her and nobody knows her, but all I hear is that she is a beauty, nobody as pretty as she, wonderful, and I don't know what all. I don't know her, but I can guarantee you that she's not what she's cracked up to be."

Jesus held his peace, understandingly. Ordinarily so pleasant and gay, Tibéria got all riled up at the mere mention of the case when somebody came along with a fresh detail to bear out the veracity of the news. To her, Martim was like a son, naughty, impulsive, and for that very reason dearer to her. And mothers do not like to see their sons married, bound to another woman. During those trying days, her sole distraction was looking after the recently arrived Otália, so countrified, so inexperienced, and still such a child—imagine!—that she played with dolls. In that mysterious parcel, mixed with newspaper clippings, there was an old doll with the sawdust coming out. Tibéria took Otália out for walks, showing her the city, the gardens, the plazas, all the sights.

Only these excursions with Otália took her mind off her growing irritation, which reached its climax when she learned that Maria Clara, the wife of Master Manuel, had rented a house for the corporal and his wife in Vila América, in the vicinity of the voodoo center of Engenho Velho. Martim had given her instructions to that effect and the money when Manuel's smack was taking on a load of bricks in Maragogipe. He had asked her to rent a house and buy furniture: table and chairs; a wide, sturdy bed; a big mirror. He had especially stressed the mirror, at Marialva's request, and Maria Clara had searched half the stores of Bahia before finding it, and it had cost a fortune. Martim, however, had become a spendthrift; nothing was too good for his wife. When Tibéria learned of these activities of the wife of the master of the smack, she became furious with her. Why the devil was she running around renting a house and buying furniture? When she saw her, she would give her a piece of her mind.

However, she reconsidered her aggressive attitude when she learned, in great confidence, Maria Clara's opinion about the much-touted Marialva. The wife of the ship captain confided to her, as well as to other close friends, that she had not had too favorable an impression of the corporal's wife. She was pretentious and haughty. Pretty, that she was—who could deny it? But self-important, full of whims, touchy—in a word, sickening. The worst of it was that Martim seemed to love all that—the whining voice, the affectations, the airs she put on. Tied to her apron strings, he had eyes for no other woman. All the mulattas of the Recôncavo could swing their hips right under his nose, smile their most inciting smiles, the corporal did not notice them. Cooed to rest by his Marialva, he was the perfect husband, a new man. Tibéria would see for herself when he arrived in a few days.

Tibéria's hackles rose as she listened to these remarks. She railed against the newsbearers as though they were in some degree to blame for what had happened. She refused to believe it; they could lay before her the most conclusive proofs; she refused to yield. She would believe it when she saw it—not before.

"Next week they'll be here, and you will see," Maria Clara said as she lighted the brazier to make coffee. Master Manuel listened in silence to the conversation of the two women. He did not want to get mixed up in the affair; he did not butt in. He sat smoking his clay pipe in the prow of the smack.

Of all those reports, of all that gossip, the only thing that interested Tibéria was the news of the imminent arrival of the corporal. She was expecting him without fail at her anniversary celebration. Tibéria's anniversary was an outstanding celebration, an important event in the world of the Mercado, the Rampa, Pelourinho, Feira de Água dos Meninos, Sete Portas, and the Fifteen Mysteries. Each year the solemnity took on greater increment, outdoing the celebration of the previous year. It began with a mass in the church of Bonfim and continued with a monumental *feijoada* for lunch; and the real celebration took place at night, winding up in the dawn hours.

Tibéria saw the date approaching while Martim, an indispensable, an obligatory, figure in the festivity, still was traveling about the Recôncavo, thinking of nothing but that woman. Tibéria could not remotely accept the idea of Martim's absence from the celebration.

Moreover, interest in the arrival of the corporal was not limited to Tibéria. Every day the number of the curious strollers grew, pretending they were not at all interested when their one idea was to find out whether there were any signs of life in the little house Maria Clara had rented for the newlyweds. They felt cheated as they gazed on the closed windows, the locked door. Even Jesuíno Crazy Cock, apparently above such nonsense, could not hide his nervousness. One day, when the subject was under discussion, he lost his self-control: "When all is said and done, what is Martim thinking? That folks have nothing better to do than to be worrying about him, waiting for him to make up his mind to show up with that so-and-so? What he's doing is making fools of us."

The outburst took place at that indefinite hour when it is no longer night and not yet morning. They had attended a festivity of Ogun, Massu's patron deity, and had continued the celebration throughout the night with great enthusiasm. From the voodoo temple they had gone to the saloon of Isidro de Batualê. As always, the conversation, after touching on different subjects, wound up with Martim and his marriage.

At that very hour of still indeterminate light, Martim and Marialva were approaching Bahia on Master Manuel's fishing smack. The boat was moving along lightly, fanned by a brisk breeze. Marialva was asleep with her head resting on her arm, Maria Clara was heating water for coffee; Master Manuel was at the helm, puffing on his pipe. Alone in the prow of the smack, Corporal Martim was trying to make out in the distance the lights of Bahia, faint in the wan dawn of the breaking day. His face was impassive, but his heart was thudding.

He turned his gaze on the sleeping beauty, her breast

rising and falling to the rhythm of her sleep, her sensual mouth, skilled at kissing and biting, half open, her hair loose, fluttering, her low-necked dress, and that black mole on her shoulder. He looked back again into the distance: there was the city, a black mass against the green mountain above the sea, the city and his friends, happiness, life. The lights were dying away in the dawn; the city would soon be awake.

⌐•❈{ 7 }❈•⌐

IT FELL TO THE LOT of Negro Massu to know her before the others, and he would never forget that morning when he saw her for the first time, framed in the doorway. Marialva seemed to him a vision from another world, the world of books, of stories, of films, a princess out of a fairy tale— and Massu adored stories having to do with fairies, giants, princes, and elves—a movie star, one of those seen in films and met anew in dreams, or one of those remote and inaccessible inmates of some distinguished brothel hidden on the beach of Pituba among coconut trees, frequented by select millionaires and ranking politicians, women imported from Rio and São Paulo, even from Europe, the last word, the *ne plus ultra*. On occasion, Massu had caught a glimpse of such women, with their blonde hair, their delicate complexions, their faint perfume, wrapped in fur coats or floating dresses, with their long legs, their heavenly faces, always a fleeting vision getting in or out of an expensive automobile. Ah, to tumble one of them on the sand of the beach! . . . Negro Massu ran his hand over his belly, the color of coal, and a chill ran through his bowels at the mere thought. Now, Marialva might have been one of those, with that infinite charm and the mole on her shoulder, such an impression did she make on him when for the first time he gazed on her face, discovered her eyes, became the slave of her smile, desired her with that desire which is boundless because it is hopeless. He would be satisfied merely to touch that mole on her left shoulder and stand before her, a slave, a dog, a worm of the earth. He lowered his great head like that of an ox and awaited her orders. She merely smiled, the sweetest of smiles, and looked at him with those timid eyes, imploring protection. The Negro's breast swelled like that of a boxer, his muscles stiffened beneath his tattered undershirt. Marialva's smile broadened as she took in the strength of the Negro, and her eyes half closed.

After the introduction, she opened her lips in words of apology, to explain why she did not invite him in: the house was not yet in order and she, at that early hour, was not properly dressed to receive visitors. Corporal Martim stood by, watching proudly as though asking Massu if there were any other man in Bahia who had such a beautiful wife and such a perfect housewife. A lady was Marialva. And at her feet, crawling in the dust, Negro Massu.

Martim had come ashore at half past three in the morning at the Rampa do Mercado; the keys of the house rented by Maria Clara rattled in his pants pocket. For the first time on arriving in Salvador da Bahia after being away from the city, he did not head straight for Tibéria's establishment. Whenever he returned from a brief trip to Porto Seguro or Valença, Cachoeira or Santo Amaro, at the invitation of the masters of fishing smacks or barges, his first visit was to Tibéria. He brought her some souvenir, told her about his trip. They toasted his return, they ate, if it was dinner time, and if he arrived in the middle of the night or toward morning, there was always some girl to take him into her bed, share her pillow with him, protect him from the cold with the warmth of her breast. There were few things in the world Martim enjoyed as much as returning to Bahia after a week or ten days of sailing, and finding himself in the cordial, affectionate atmosphere of Tibéria's whorehouse, seeing her in her rocking chair—which she filled to overflowing—motherly, talkative, surrounded by the girls, Jesus at the end of the table with his ledgers, a family, so to speak, and moreover the only one Martim had ever known and which he had adopted. This time, however, the corporal did not head in the direction of Pelourinho, where Tibéria lived. He had his house, his hearth. His destination was the cottage in Vila América, where he and Marialva arrived accompanied by a cart carrying the suitcases and some household utensils brought from the Recôncavo. The early-rising neighbors saw the couple ascend the hill, the corporal curved under the weight of a big leather trunk, the girl twirling a parasol and casting curious glances around her. The carter was carrying the rest of the luggage, panting up the sheer hillside. The cottage, painted blue, with a window coming off its hinges, overlooked from the hilltop the green landscape of the valley stretching below with groves of banana trees and dotted by tall mangoes and jackfruits.

Martim set the heavy trunk down on the ground, unlocked the door, and he and the carter entered with the luggage. Marialva stood in front of the door and the landscape, examining the surroundings, letting herself be admired by the neighbors, who, so unseasonably awakened, were appearing at doors and windows.

It was one of these neighbors who communicated the news to Massu. At around eight o'clock the Negro was making his daily stop at a numbers game agency when an acquaintance of his, Robelino by name, advised him: "If you want to hit today, play the bear . . . ninety, straight."

"Why? Hunch or dream?" inquired Massu, whose inclinations that morning, for a series of complicated reasons, leaned toward the goat.

"It's the number of Martim's house, there on the hill. It was the first thing that caught my eye this morning. I had just reached the door of my chalet. I was rinsing my teeth when Martim opened the door of the chateau next door, and in the middle of the door was the number 90 in red paint. The funny thing is that my shack, right alongside his, is 126. It should be 92, don't you think?"

Massu caught his breath: "You mean to say that Martim has arrived?"

"Sure, like I was saying . . . he came up the hill carrying a trunk the size of a house, stumbling under the weight. If what's inside it is that lady's dresses, not even the wife of the Governor has as many . . . not to mention the other suitcase the carter was carrying and a big box."

"What woman?"

"The one who was with him. Haven't you heard the word going around that he has got married? You mean to say you didn't know, you who are such a close friend of his? He arrived with her, put down the trunk, opened the door—it was then that I saw the number; I had never noticed it before. The number 90 exploding right there in my face, I played all my savings on it, Mr. Massu."

His voice trailed away as though his mind were on something else, and then grew more confidential: "What a hunk of woman, brother, an image in a procession. What did Martim ever do to deserve such a favor from God? The cream of the crop . . ."

Massu, just in case, played two nickels on the bear, and set out for Vila América. He wanted to be the first to embrace Martim, to bring him up to date on the news, to find out how things had been going with him and meet the lady who had aroused so much comment.

En route he took mental note of the fact that there was a bar at the foot of the hill. He would bring this to Martim's attention; they could begin their celebrations there. That was a day that called for a lot of drinking, from morning until night in the company of all their friends, winding up on the wharf where the smacks put in at sunrise.

He found the corporal, hammer in hand, taking down the front window to fix it. Equipped with nails, pliers, pieces of board, working hard. He threw everything aside to embrace the Negro, inquire about Crazy Cock, Wing-Foot, Bullfinch, Ipicilone, Alonso, all the rest, and above all, about Tibéria and her husband, Jesus. He wiped the sweat from his forehead with the back of his hand, then picked up the hammer again. Massu was looking at the house, at the landscape unfolding downhill, at his friend working. He was thinking of the bar at the foot of the hill: he ought to stand Martim a drink. But the corporal was so absorbed in his work, so determined to fix the window, that Massu decided to wait. "When he gets done, I'll mention the bar, and we'll go and wake ourselves up with a swig of rum." He sat down on a stone, pulled a toothpick out of his woolly hair, and began to pick his white, perfect teeth.

Martim, all the while he was hammering nails, fixing the window, was talking about this and that, the people of Cachoeira and São Felix, of Maragogipe and Muritiba, of Cruz das Almas, for he had been to all those places. Massu, for his part, supplied him with news of what had been going on during his absence, details of the festival of Ogun the night before, the fever that had laid Ipicilone up for ten days, refusing to yield to any of the drugstore medicines and disappearing as by a miracle as soon as they sent for Mocinha, the prayer woman. Ipicilone began praying around eleven in the morning, and by four in the afternoon he was up and asking for something to eat. There was no prayer woman in all Bahia to be compared with Mocinha. Martim agreed and, for a moment, stopped working on the window to praise Mocinha and her powers. How old would she be? She must be over eighty, if not already ninety. Nevertheless, she still danced in the circle of the daughters of the saint in the voodoo rites, and could walk for miles, carrying the sacred leaves she had collected from the *peji* of Ossani. A tough old bird, Aunt Mocinha!

Massu told him, too, about the disappearance of Otália's luggage, one of Carnation-in-his-Buttonhole's little jokes, making them all go out to Caminho de Areia. Martim then wanted to know about Zico, his family, and their cardplaying friends, about Lourival and the folks from Água dos Meninos. Massu gave him the news and then came back to the subject of Otália: a pretty chick, Bullfinch was crazy about her, but that Otália was a little crazy; she made no objection to going to bed with him or any of the others, but she didn't want to listen to any talk of a love affair, she didn't become attached to him or to anyone. When she went out with them to a dance hall or a good fish stew on one of the launches, she took the arm of the first to present himself and stayed with him until the end of the party, giving herself to him with an eagerness nearly always mistaken for love by her partner. But when the night was over, she cared no more for him than if there had been nothing between them. She especially teased Bullfinch, making fun of his sheep's eyes, laughing at his sighs, at his old, mended frock coat and his painted face. It got him nowhere to wash his face, change the frock coat for a ragged jacket, soak his nappy hair with bottles of brilliantine. Nothing moved her. Not even buying a new coat, or a poem he composed in honor of her, a painstaking labor, rhyming Otália with dahlia, morrow with sorrow. She was not attracted by any of this; she did her job at the house afternoon, and evening, and then went out to walk along the wharfs, for she loved to watch the ships. Slightly touched in the head, that Otália. She had sent Jacinto about his business—did Martim remember him?—a strapping young stud, a small-time gambler, who never appeared in public without a necktie. He went and proposed to Otália nothing less than that they shack up together. She answered that she would not even accept him as a client for any amount of money, not even if Tibéria ordered her to; she would rather go back to Bonfim. Just like that, straight from the shoulder, without mincing words. Pretty, yes, not one of those beauties that knock your eye out, but nicely put together. Otália had now become a kind of center of interest for all. Tibéria had taken a liking to her, Jesuíno too, and Jesus had even bought her a new doll, a big one of celluloid, in place of the old, sawdust-spilling wreck she had brought from Bonfim in that brown paper parcel. Yes, she played with dolls like a child. A child, and such a little girl that at times it made one feel sad to see her in the parlor of the whorehouse waiting for a man. When she arrived she had lied about her age, saying that she was eighteen; but Tibéria had made her confess the truth, that she was not yet sixteen.

It was not Massu's intention to stir up his friend by talking about such matters as he sketched the contradictory portrait of Otália that sunny morning. The Negro was not given to such subtleties; he talked about the girl because he liked her, and it made him mad to see her a whore at that tender age. But Massu was not so devoid of the gift of observation that the corporal's indifferent silence did not surprise him, that pounding away at the nails as he repaired the window frame, following the Negro's talk with a smile, but, it was clearly apparent, just out of politeness—and the Corporal's politeness has already been remarked on—and nothing more. Truly, thought Massu to himself, the corporal is a different man, the talebearers were right.

In other days his eyes would have sparkled, he would have put Massu through a cross-examination, he would not have wasted his time fixing windows, but would have set out after Otália. Instead of that, he was listening with only one ear to what the Negro was saying, while the other was cocked toward the inside of the house, awaiting any sound that might come from there.

Up to that moment no reference had been made to Marialva. Not for lack of inclination on the part of Massu, who was crazy to hear something about the wife of the corporal, whom everybody was talking about, because of whom his life had taken a new turn. But he did not feel that it would be right for him to touch on such a delicate subject. It was Martim's place to bring it up, to make the official announcement of his marriage, to talk about his wife, or at least, to give him a lead, some kind of hint that the Negro could pick up and follow. As long as Martim remained silent, speaking of this or that, of everything except what was of real interest, Negro Massu could not touch upon the matter without violating the most basic rules of good breeding.

Who knows, perhaps, when the corporal finished fixing the window and the two of them went down to the tavern, he would lay aside his reserve and take him into his confidence. Massu was turning all these things over in his mind when he saw a change come over Martim's face. The Negro was sitting on a stone with his back to the house, and he turned around. Marialva was standing, as though framed, in the doorway, observing him with a critical eye. But as soon as the Negro turned around, all the hardness, all the distrust vanished from her eyes, and she was transformed into a shy, delicate maiden in peril, instantly recognizing the hero capable of defending her. The change was so swift that Massu immediately forgot that first moment of those cold, suspicious eyes. Her voice, melodious and timid, completed the spell: "Martim, aren't you going to introduce me?"

"Had you already heard that I got married? Well, this is the Missus," and turning to Marialva: "And this tough guy is Massu, my best friend, my brother."

Marialva's small hand was swallowed up in the pile-

driver fist of the Negro, who beamed a smile at her, showing his white, recently picked teeth.

"Pleased to meet you, ma'am. I had already heard about
you. Your fame preceded you. Everybody has been talking about Martim's marriage."

"And there's been a lot of talk about that here?"

"Too much. Nobody talked about anything else."

"And why all this talk?"

"Martim, you know, ma'am, nobody ever thought they
would see him married. He didn't seem the sort of person
to let himself be roped . . ."

"Well, he's married, and well married, in case you want
to know. And if anyone doubts it, let them come and
see."

"Marialva!" Martim cut her short, with a frown.

For barely a second the girl's voice had been as sharp as
a knife, her eyes clouded with anger, but as soon as Martim interrupted her, she resumed the modest air of a timid
gazelle buffeted by the storms of life, her voice lilting, her
gaze timid, imploring love and protection. The change was
so swift that Negro Massu forgot all about it, just as he
had forgotten the first glance that measured him when he
had his back turned and had not seen her. The one who
was right, the Negro thought, was Robelino when he compared Marialva to an image of a saint in a procession,
before whom Massu felt like kneeling in adoration.

Having resumed the modest pose of a gracious housewife, she apologized. "It's such a pity the house is all at
sixes and sevens, or I'd ask you to come in. But Martim
told me that he was going to invite his friends in tonight to
have a cup of coffee with us. I hope you will come. I shall
be expecting you."

"You can be sure I'll be here."

Martim was smiling again. His brow had furrowed at
Marialva's outburst, and with a word he had imposed his
will, had brusquely shown who was boss. Perhaps for that
very reason, he now repeated Marialva's invitation, asking
Massu to transmit it to the friends. And, his smile broaden-
ing, he added, poking the Negro in the belly with the
hammer: "What you need is to get married, Massu, to find
out what is good."

Modestly Marialva lowered her eyes. She took a step toward Martim, the corporal came over, put his arms around her, clasped her to his breast, kissed her on the mouth. She closed her eyes. Massu stood watching them, somewhat embarrassed.

At that moment a package, hurled from the top of a ravine beyond the built-up streets, sailed over their heads and landed a little in front of the house. As it hit the ground, the paper tore and the string came loose. A black hen, dead, with its neck cut off; without doubt the head was lying at the feet of Exu. Yellow manioc-meal mush, prepared with *dende* oil. A piece of cloth, the remains of one of Martim's old shirts. A few coins. Martim set out at a run toward the cliff just in time to see a figure disappearing around the other side of the hill.

Marialva looked at the conjure scattered there near the house. Massu scratched his woolly head and bent over, touching the ground with his hand and carrying it to his head, murmuring: "Ogun be with us, Ogun be with us," imploring the protection of his patron deity, and then said: "God protect us from all spells, God and Xangô."

Once more there became visible in Marialva's eyes that light of cold rage, that sign of careful calculation. She walked over toward the conjure to get a closer look at it, and said: "Let them cast all the spells they like, Martim is now mine, I can do what I like with him."

Martim returned in time to keep her from committing the folly of throwing away, with her own hands, the remains of the conjure. "Are you crazy? Do you want us to die? Leave it there, I am going to send for Mother Doninha, she will make it harmless and purify our bodies. Would you call her for me, Massu?"

"You can forget about it. I'll go and get her."

But before he left, he remembered the bar down below. It was hot and a drink would set very well. He suggested: "Wouldn't you like a swallow first, there's a bar right down there . . ."

Martim smiled: "Let's go, brother . . ."

He took Massu by the arm, which was the size of a tree trunk, and started off with him. From the door Marialva spoke up: "Wait. I'm coming too."

Martim stopped in his tracks, annoyed. He looked at the woman; she was coming. He wanted to say something, stole a glance at Massu; the Negro was waiting. Martim hesitated, but Marialva's victorious air made up his mind for him: "You're not going anywhere. The place of a married woman is in her house, putting things in order. We'll soon be back."

And off they went down the hillside. Marialva could hear Martim's laugh as he chatted with the Negro. "One day he'll pay me out for everything," she thought to herself, her eyes once more clouded over by that cold light of calculated forethought.

❊{ 8 }❊

THE SAINT HAD DESCENDED FROM HER PEDESTAL, but fortunately Negro Massu, her new devotee, did not see her, nor Robelino, the coiner of the metaphor. A frown came over Marialva's face. She could clearly foresee difficulties in Bahia; it was not going to be as easy as the trip through the Recôncavo. They had no more than arrived and he was already giving her orders, telling her what to do, leaving her at home while he went off to swill rum at the tavern. Martim's laughter died away down the hill, answered by the noisy chortle of Massu. Marialva sensed the danger in those peals of laughter, in the air of the city, in the solid, easy-going calm of Massu, in the green landscape of banana trees where the houses flowered in patches of blue, yellow, red, pink. She was going to have to bring them to heel, those famous friends of Martim, put her foot on their necks. Twice that very morning the corporal had raised his voice to her, giving her orders. The first day, when they had only just arrived and entered their house. Where was that impassioned lover, unable to tear himself from her for a single second, crawling in the dust left by her slippers?

The time had come to put the bit on him and, if necessary, give him a taste of the spur of jealousy, make his heart bleed. Marialva was experienced at this game. Getting the upper hand of men gave her pleasure, subduing them, seeing them surrender to her charms and grovel before her. And the greater the number, the keener her pleasure, her sense of power, the voluptuousness of doing what she would with them. She went all out to win them to her, she was meek and timid, in need of them, tender, making herself indispensable. Afterwards she sucked them dry, leaving them without will or purpose, tossing them aside like dry husks when they had lost all their vital impulses, when they had handed everything over to her, even their manhood. Utterly worthless, capable only of desiring her, longing to possess her once more, cursing her, hating her, and dreaming of her. She had been born to dominate men, like a queen trampling slaves under foot, like a saint on a pedestal, perhaps, with the procession of her worshippers kneeling as she passed by. A man-eater, was Marialva.

Up to this point her plans had worked out perfectly. For a long time she had been thinking of leaving the small cities of the Recôncavo for the greener pastures of the capital. But in her wildest dreams she had not envisaged such great good fortune as disembarking there, triumphantly, on the arm of Corporal Martim, with him completely under her thumb. Thus it had happened, and Marialva had every intention of keeping him that way and more and more so. She had come ashore in Bahia, leading by the leash that most admired and freest of men, for whom the women all sighed, the one who until then had remained fancy-free. Wasn't this the subject of all conversations? Now what she had to do was exhibit Corporal Martim bowed to her will. For this she had to ride him on a tight rein. And if he should think he could evade this, she knew another way of making him knuckle under: all she would have to do would be to smile at another, show interest in another man. She would be able to dominate him, keep him impassioned and suppliant, hanging on her movements and words, on her will. For that, God had given her beauty and cunning, and the love of power.

Martim's reputation as a gambler, cardsharper, wolf without peer, chaser, had preceded his arrival in the cities of the Recôncavo. His name came up in the conversations at cathouses, low taverns, fairs, before he landed in Cachoeira. From the cities through which he passed came reports sketching his portrait, setting hearts aflutter.

Marialva, who had spent several seasons in Leonor Coconut Candy's crib, had heard tell of him: the tears shed because of him, the innumerable women pursuing him, begging for a word, a gesture of affection. He slept with this one and that one without becoming attached to any of them; his interest was short-spanned. Marialva swore that she would get him to have and to hold if he showed up. Turn Martim into the docile instrument of her will, and then toss him aside as she had Duca, her husband; Artur, Tonho da Capela, and Juca Mineiro, her lights-of-love; and so many other transients. She would do even more to that conceited popinjay with all that jive about his being irresistible. She would tie him to her chariot wheels, behind her float, exhibit him to the other women, prove her superiority.

It wasn't even too difficult: just a question of the corporal's appearing and laying eyes on her—perhaps thinking only of a night together—but Marialva had laid her plans. She immediately took in the fact that Martim was gnawed by loneliness, far from his city, his milieu, his friends; and all this in the month of festivities—June. He tried to drown in rum and the bodies of women his incurable loneliness. He found those yokels easy pickings and spent his winnings in cabarets and taverns, trying to forget the city of Bahia, where he had acquired his reputation as a rogue.

Marialva immediately took note of the corporal's loneliness, perhaps because she feared and hated loneliness. She lapped him about in affection; she played the role of mother, offering her body and heart in which all the sorrows of the world could be contained and find comfort and cure. Wasn't she herself in need of love and protection? she asked him with those eyes of a timid damsel, victim of misunderstanding and fate. Martim felt himself enveloped in tenderness, warmth to dissipate his homesickness, an arm on which to rest his sadness. Comforted, he plunged into the mysteries of that body whose soul spread protectingly over him.

Ah, there were few women who were Marialva's equal in bed. Fortunate or unfortunate those who slept with her even one night; they became beings apart, different from the others, souls elect. Those who had had this luck or this misfortune ought to get together and form a brotherhood or sodality, a Worthy and Worshipful Order, to meet at a set date and place, at least once a month, and recall her amid tears and gnashing of teeth. Few women like her in bed: a whirlwind unleashed, a bitch, a mare in heat, and then a pool of still water, the sweetness of head rubbing, a soothing breast on which to rest, and then again a tempest-tossed sea and the cooing of doves. Whoever slept with Marialva once would have no rest or happiness until he lay down beside her anew, slaked his hunger, his thirst in hers. A sailor had slept with her, and the next day had left for Salvador to rejoin his ship. He voyaged with the memory of Marialva, and at the first port of call he jumped ship and returned to Bahia to seek her out supplicatingly. A priest slept with her one night and was lost for good.

Martim, too, felt the power of that body. Of that body compounded of mysteries and a heart of maternal kindness to help him bear his loneliness, to restore his joy in living. Thus it seemed to him, when he met Marialva, that he had found the other half of himself, the woman he had sought in all her forerunners, his, his alone and for all time.

Marialva, devoted, flattering, impassioned. Martim wallowed, buried himself in that devotion, that flattery, that passion which knew no bounds. So ardent, so sensual, so timid and reserved at the same time, Marialva confided to him that she had not lived before she met him; only now, with him, had she learned the meaning of life and of love. All that had gone before had been empty and meaningless. The same was true of Martim, and the infatuation grew until it led them away from the Recôncavo as a most perfect married pair on their honeymoon. Martim felt like a knight errant, saving from the degradation of prostitution that poor victim of an unjust fate, born to love and devote herself to one man alone, to be his slave, faithful and exemplary, until death did them part, and even after.

Not to mention the hallucinated nights of bites and sighs; there was no such golden flesh and perfumed nape. A thousand times he died on her breast, a thousand times he came back to life, glorious in her grateful gaze. Marialva devoured the corporal slowly; he was her greatest glory; with him she would arrive in Bahia as his wife, the mistress of his every movement, of his every moment. The girl of Feira de Sant'Ana, daughter of a cook of the Falcão family, had achieved her highest ambition, for wealth did not tempt her, nor did she seek fame. She desired only to dominate men, see them at her feet, hanging on a word or gesture of hers. She was the wife of Corporal Martim, king of the vagabonds of Bahia; he was one of her devotees.

They had no more than disembarked on the Rampa do Mercado, however, than she sensed a subtle change in him. As though, when his feet touched the stones of the city, something began to grow in Martim. Marialva put herself on guard. And afterwards, that same morning, he had spoken sharply to her twice, raising his voice, ordering her to be still once, and later forbidding her to follow him. He would have to be put in his place again, at her feet. Standing in the door of the cottage, hearing the two friends laugh as they went down the hill, she prepared and strengthened herself for any situation that might confront her. She looked at the landscape about her, at the expanse of the city ascending the hill, stretching toward the shore: there was where she would drag Martim at her feet.

Walking down the hillside with Massu on their way to the tavern, Martim sang the praises of married life. He would never have believed he would find marriage so delightful and pleasant. Nevertheless, even though he was head over heels in love with Marialva, happy to possess her and her love, he realized that it was his duty gradually and gently to put her in her place. She had picked up bad habits during their idyll in the Recôncavo, going everywhere with him, continually in his company. Had Massu noticed how he had pulled her up short as they were leaving? Every so often a rap over the knuckles is a good thing in marriage—it makes a wife even more devoted to her husband. And above all, it shows her where she belongs, teaches her just what her rights are. It was a good thing for Massu to take note of all these points, for without doubt, sooner or later he would wind up getting married, establishing a family, giving himself over to the delights of a home.

—◆❧{ 9 }❧◆—

INDEED, THE CORPORAL WAS GIVEN OVER, and with absolute conviction, to the delights of home, as his friends could observe that night; and they envied him. This was the predominant reaction: envy. There were others, too; we are not going to hide them; we shall speak of them, even of those which are hardly to be confessed. For example: the eyes of Carnation-in-his-Buttonhole glittered with rapturous enthusiasm as they viewed the table cutlery. And unconfessable—because indecent—were the feelings of the entire gathering, with the exception of Maria Clara, naturally, toward Martim's wife. Marialva outdid herself in attentions, going from one to the other. From the point of view of affirming their matrimonial happiness, that first gathering was a complete success for the master and mistress of the house. And for Marialva a twofold success; for, which of the guests did not succumb to her beauty, take his place in the cortege of devotees around her float, which consisted of a bed and a mirror?

Nevertheless, when they took their leave past midnight, Jesuíno Crazy Cock, whose experience of life and powers of judgement nobody doubted, shook his head, wrinkled his nose, and prophesied pessimistically: "Too good to last."

This time his friends did not believe him. On the contrary, they considered the transformation of the corporal permanent, and at heart they all envied him. That night every one of them was willing to get married, even Carnation-in-his-Buttonhole, despite the fact that he was already married and the father of so many children. Ah, but if he came upon another Marialva, then even with his poor economic standing, he would have no objections to becoming a bigamist. He would set up a new home, beget more children. To tell the truth, they all envied the corporal, even Jesuíno. How well groomed Martim looked, stretched out in a rocking chair, wearing white pants and a striped pajama coat, carefully knocking off his cigar ash in the ash tray! They observed the corporal, so serene and satisfied, and all of them caressed the idea of marriage, vague, differing in its details, but always to the same wife: Marialva.

All except Jesuíno. Covet her, he did; desire Marialva, he did; but not with a view to matrimony. Even though he avoided any reference to his past, never mentioned the matter, Crazy Cock had once been married, many years back. It was known that his married life had not been happy; there were stories whispered about it, dark secrets. The only thing that was certain was that Jesuíno no longer had a wife and home when he appeared in the streets of Bahia. Of that marriage, according to malicious tongues, the only thing left to him was a dead man on his back, the corpse of a young blade who had been his wife's lover. Whether this was true or made up, nobody ever knew. If it was true, Crazy Cock never felt the need to lay his victim down, not even for a moment, in order to draw a deep breath. No, he never wanted to share his burden with his friends if he was bearing such a burden. And nevertheless, a dead man is a dead weight, a well-established fact that everyone knows. Even if he died a natural death and was at rest in his coffin, but especially if he was stabbed over and over with a dagger dripping hate, as was told of the one Crazy Cock had sent to the other world. Each dagger thrust weighs more than a hundred kilos. Seven times a hundred makes seven hundred, and it must be a chore to carry a dead man like that on your back all your life long. Did you ever think about that? All day long the arms of the dead man around the neck of the living, his hands on his breast, pressing, bowing his back, turning his hair white, constricting his heart. One day the poor devil can stand it no longer, lets the dead man slip to the ground at the most unexpected moment, at the table of a bar, in the bed of a strange woman, at the market full of people, in the middle of the street. Even running the danger of prison or losing his life at the hands of vengeful relatives.

If Crazy Cock carried a stabbed man on his back, he would seem to have found the burden light, for he never shared it with anyone, not even when he slid under the table at Isidro de Batualê's tavern or beside the window in Alonso's store. So many, many years; not even Jesuíno Crazy Cock would have been able to bear such a weight for so long a time, feel the dead man on his back every day, dream of him every night. Probably that whole story of the fourteen dagger thrusts, seven to the man, seven to the woman, he kicking the bucket on the spot, she managing to escape, but a hideous wreck with her face slashed from forehead to chin, was waterfront scuttlebutt. What probably happened was that the fellow did not die at all; as soon as he knew he was in for it, he took to his heels and disappeared.

Be that as it may, as the result of his ill-starred marriage, Jesuíno, though he shared the envy, did not share the general enthusiasm. And, naturally, not Tibéria.

Moreover, Tibéria refused, abruptly and insolently, Martim's invitation, which had been delivered to her by Massu. The Negro had to hear out a diatribe, insults beyond belief, when he showed up at her establishment with the corporal's message.

He found Tibéria seated in her chair during the afternoon lull, with Otália kneeling at her feet. Tibéria was combing the girl's fine hair. She plaited it into braids, tying a blue ribbon at the ends. More than ever, Otália looked like a young girl; who would have dreamed she was a whore? The Negro walked in, said good afternoon, and stood looking at the two women: the fat mistress of the brothel and the young inmate. Anyone would have thought them mother and daughter, Massu mused, and it seemed to him unfair that the two of them should be there in the parlor of a crib. Why unfair, he would not have been able to say; it was just a vague feeling but, nevertheless, strong enough for Massu, who was little given to applying his mental faculties to such matters, to realize that the world was in a sorry state and that change was called for. He would even have been willing to do his share toward this urgent adjustment if he had known how. Mother and daughter, they seemed, with Otália leaning her head against Tibéria's fat knees, her eyes half closed under the caress of the comb and the search for nonexistent lice.

Tibéria smiled at Massu. She was fond of the Negro and invited him to have a seat.

He carried out his job on foot: "I can't stay long, I just stopped by to bring a message. Do you know who has arrived and has sent me here, Mother? Martim and his wife!"

Tibéria let go of Otália's hair, brusquely pushed the girl's head off her knees, and walked over to face Massu: "He's arrived? When?"

"This morning. I heard about it early and went up there. Martim was fixing a window. They sent you a message, Mother. . . ."

"They? Who?"

"Martim and his wife, whose name is Marialva. She looks like a saint in a procession, an absolute knockout. They want you to go there tonight. To pay them a visit . . ."

Tibéria in a fury was as yet a new sight for Otália. As famous as her kindness, her generous heart, were her rages, her tirades. When she got into a temper, she lost her head and was capable of the greatest violence, of assault and battery. This happened rarely, and with the passing of time it was most unusual to see her angry, as though there were no longer room in her heart for fury and umbrage. She was aging sweetly, with charity toward all, compassionate understanding.

When she heard the message, however, her whole bulk, free at that hour of the day of corset and restraint, began to heave; her flesh, her monumental breasts the size of pillows, began to shake; her face turned red; she expelled air from mouth and nose and started to speak in a normal voice, which gradually rose to a scream: "You mean to tell me that he arrived with that cow, and it's me who is supposed to go to visit him? And this is the message you have the impudence to bring me, Mr. Trash who have lost all shame?"

"But I . . ."

"And even to compare that brazen whore with a saint! . . ."

"It was Robelino who said that. . . ."

Tibéria refused to accept excuses. She was beside herself. Otália trembled. Massu wrung his hands, for what had happened was none of his doing. Was this, howled Tibéria, the consideration Martim showed his friends, old and tried friends like herself and Jesus? Always boasting about his fine manners, putting on airs, talking about his strict code of politeness. How, then, did he dare send her a message to come and visit him? It was his duty to come, as he always had, to greet her, to inquire about what had been going on, about her health, to embrace Jesus. She, Tibéria, would never set foot in that house where he had brought that hussy he had fished out of the garbage can, that syphilitic turd, that clap trap. If they wanted to see her, let them come to her house, and the lousy trollop had better take a bath before she crossed her threshhold. Or it would be even better not to bring the slut: Tibéria could get along without her. But if he wanted to, he could bring her, inasmuch as he had already said good-bye to shame and good taste when he tied himself up to that trash; she, Tibéria, was in her house, and there she would receive them if they appeared. Like the well-bred person she was, she would not tell that hustler what she thought of her, she would treat her politely, as was incumbent on a person like herself. But she would not go out, climb the hill to Vila América to visit Martim and that leper pretending to be a married woman. What was Martim thinking about? She, Tibéria, was old enough to be his mother, she deserved more respect. . . .

She finally stopped to catch her breath, panting, her heart racing. Otália ran to get her a glass of water. Tibéria sat down again, her hand on her heart, pushed away the glass, and ordered in a faint voice: "Open a bottle of beer, and bring two glasses, one for me and the other for this shameless black messenger."

Her anger was abating; now she was downcast and sad.

"Do you think, Massu," she asked, "that Martim has the right to do this to me? To me and Jesus? Isn't it his place to call on me first?" And almost whimpering: "You know that next Saturday is my anniversary. . . . If Martim doesn't come, I swear he will never again set foot in my house. I never want to see his face again. My anniversary celebration, that I won't forgive."

Massu agreed. Otália filled the glasses with beer. In the afternoon quiet, the little birds warbled in their cages at the rear of the house.

That night, at Martim's house, Negro Massu recalled the warbling and the beer. There, too, a finch, awakened by the light and the noise, twittered its exasperation while Marialva served first coffee, then rum.

There were memorable moments during the evening. The first was when Marialva took the coffeepot off the top of a kind of small china closet on whose shelves stood cups, glasses, wine glasses. Wine glasses in which rum was served several times after the coffee. The guests opened their mouths in amazement: so much order, such neatness, such comfort. It did not matter that the china closet was wobbly, the left side sagging, that several saucers were missing, that some of the coffee cups lacked a handle, and that no two of the glasses were alike. Glasses and cups, luxuries, the pleasures of a home. And the coffeepot? When they arrived, it was on top of the china closet, like an ornament. Tall, of china, with the chipped side turned to the wall, a thing of beauty. On the stove the water was boiling in a can. Marialva prepared the coffee.

"A little coffee before your drink, to warm the mouth," Marialva announced and they all agreed, even Massu, whose preference would have been for rum right away.

The aroma of coffee filled the room, and they watched her pouring the water through the flannel strainer bulging like a woman's breast. Close at hand, the coffeepot, which had been taken down from the top of the china closet. Ipicilone's eyes beamed: the corporal was a real swell, the owner of a coffeepot. Wing-Foot gave exclamations of admiration. Martim smiled. Marialva lowered her eyes modestly.

Handling the pot with perfect self-possession, Marialva

poured into its rotund belly the freshly brewed coffee, black and fragrant. Then she went around with the coffeepot in one hand and in the other, a tray holding the cups and a saucer of sugar, serving them one by one. One or two sugars, she asked, and then served each according to his taste, accompanying the operation with a smile, a glance, a flirt of her body. Intertwined roses stood out in high relief on the coffeepot. Such a pretty thing!

Sipping his coffee, from the rocking chair where he was sitting, Martim followed Marialva's movements with a tender gaze. He saw the envy mounting in the eyes of his friends, spreading through the room, dominating them all. The corporal wrapped himself about in this envy as in a sheet, completely sold on the delights of a home. Marialva went around again with the tray, collecting the cups. Untiring, she came back with a jug of rum, 100-proof Santo Amaro, and the glasses. She stopped in front of Bullfinch, selecting the glass for him, a dark blue, the prettiest of all. The corporal's enthralled eyes turned from her to his friends as though asking if they had ever met a prettier or better housekeeper. He looked like a gentleman, stretched out in the rocking chair in his white pants, slippers, and striped pajama jacket, taking his ease, master of all he surveyed.

There were his friends, the guests and two or three gate-crashers: Jesuíno Crazy Cock, Wing-Foot, Bullfinch, Massu, Ipicilone, Carnation-in-his-Buttonhole, Nelson Dentadura, a stallowner in Água dos Meninos, besides Master Manuel and Maria Clara. All of them drooling with admiration, even Jesuíno, though it was not as manifest in him as in the others. They watched her, taking in all the details of the house and of Marialva's movements, so absorbed that conversation languished. Following her with their eyes, observing her every gesture, reflecting her every smile.

The second high spot—really sensational—came when she, after having served them rum, and leaving the jug on the table where they could reach it, sat down on a stool and crossed her legs. Her tight dress rode up above her knees, revealing a stretch of thigh. Martim became aware of the breathless silence and the glittering eyes, unwinking, moist with desire. The corporal coughed; Marialva changed position, pulling down her dress and straightening up in her seat. The eyes turned away, too; Bullfinch even got up from the bench and walked over to the window, embarrassed. Only Wing-Foot went on looking and smiling: "You ought to take some sea baths. . . ."

Marialva laughed, agreed, "if he will let me," pointing to Martim. The conversation took on a certain animation, the empty jug of rum was replaced by another, and finally Corporal Martim could not resist the temptation and invited them to see the bedroom. "Our nest," he called it, to Ipicilone's admiration and Jesuíno's disgust. Who ever heard of calling a bedroom a nest? No question about it, Martim had lost his head, had become unbearable. The others, however, found the expression felicitous and apt. It was a small room, barely large enough for the bed with its hair mattress and patchwork quilt, but on the wall hung the enormous mirror above a small table which held Marialva's brushes, combs, brilliantine, perfumes. Martim smiled, pointing to table and mirror: "This is where the missus combs her hair, cleans up her mug, and gets ready for bed at night."

Marialva had remained behind in the parlor, preparing to serve the cornmeal cake, but they all saw her there in the bedroom. Nobody said a word after Martim's remarks; the silence was broken only by Negro Massu's laugh. At the evocation of Marialva's preparing herself for bed, the Negro could not control himself: it was a laugh of uncontainable joy, the thought of Marialva in her nightgown, her hair loose about her shoulders, her lips parted. The others saw her, too, reflected in the mirror. But they did not laugh; they curbed both voice and breath, trying to hide their thoughts. Bullfinch closed his eyes, for he was seeing her naked in the mirror, the black beauty spot reflected a little above her navel, her breasts high and pointed, a bluish rose. The color of the wine glass, a deep blue, a chalice of golden honey. He shut his eyes, but he kept on seeing her. He left the bedroom hurriedly, in need of air.

But she was in the sitting room as though waiting for him, standing tall and serene. She smiled at him, her eyes on his, questioning him, as though trying to divine all that had gone on in his heart. And they turned supplicating, those eyes, imploring protection and friendship, and it was evident that Marialva was the purest of women, the most lonely and forsaken, misunderstood. A victim, beyond a doubt. Hadn't Massu told Bullfinch how that very morning, more than once, and roughly, Martim had shouted at the poor thing? Was it for this that he had gone to the Recôncavo to find her and marry her? Sad eyes gazed on Bullfinch as though begging for a little understanding and tenderness. Nothing more than the tender affection of a brother, platonic, the sympathy of a friend. But Marialva's lips parted, showing her white teeth, the red tip of her tongue, her full lips made for kissing and biting. . . .

Bullfinch put his hand over his mouth as though to cover up the evil thought, but he could not hold back the sigh that escaped him. Marialva sighed too, and the two sighs met in the air, mingled, died together. The others returned from the bedroom. Ah, if Bullfinch could, he would have thrown himself on the floor, like an *iawô* before the *iyalorixá*, and kissed the sole of Marialva's feet.

They all sat down except Bullfinch, Martim in his rocking chair, as Wing-Foot asked: "Did you know that at the bottom of the sea there is a sky just like the other one? With stars and everything? Well, there is—a sky even fuller of stars, with sun and moon. Only, in the bottom of the sea there is a full moon every night."

Marialva stepped forward to serve the cake; Bullfinch filled the dark blue glass with rum and drank it off at one swallow.

--⟨ 10 ⟩--

"MARTIM IS MY BROTHER, alas, my brother! Not only my brother-in-devotion, both of us sons of Oxalá (*Exê ê ê Babá*), but my best friend, sharing all my hours, all my joys and sorrow. For him I would knock myself out, run any risk. So how can I look at his wife, his real wife, the mistress of his house, with eyes other than those of a friend, how can I cherish for her any feeling other than pure brotherly affection? Alas, Martim, my brother, your brother is a scoundrel." These were the thoughts that were running through Bullfinch's head during the time between his visit to Martim's house and the great celebration of Tibéria's anniversary.

They were bitter days for the spieler, filled with dark thoughts, mixed emotions. The last time he had seen her, one Sunday morning, she had stood waving good-bye to him from the window of the house and then, for no good reason, had stuck the tip of her tongue out at him. A chill ran through Bullfinch's body, a shudder. "Alas, my brother, I don't have the strength! Oxalá, my father, save me, I will have prayers said over my body so I can resist the spells of this woman, the witchery of her eyes." At the door of the "World's Bargain Center," distracted from his duties, Bullfinch realized that the suggestive gesture of Marialva and his feverish response lacked all fraternal character, that aura of purity called for in exchanges be-

85

tween brother and sister. On the contrary, they were indicative of highly dubious feelings, sinful intentions. "Oh, my brother, when did one ever see—*Exê ê ê Babá*—a brother shiver with cold and feel the fever burn his face at the sight of the full lips of a sister, her tongue moving like a snake's?" If Bullfinch and Marialva were, so to speak, brother and sister, such feelings could only be classified as incestuous. Bullfinch clasped his head between his clenched fists. What to do?

Mention has already been made of Bullfinch's highly romantic nature, of his wild infatuations, of his love letters, hundreds and hundreds of them, of his repeated engagements—always at some woman's feet, almost always rejected and left to suffer. That he should have fallen in love with Marialva was no surprise. All of them were more or less in love with the corporal's wife, even Wing-Foot. When it came to women, Wing-Foot was a purist, hard to please. Too light, lacking that caramel color, Marialva fell outside the narrow circle of true mulattas described by Wing-Foot. Nevertheless, he made an exception for her, offering her the white rat and promising her a green bullfrog.

In love they were, true, but platonically, without even thinking of the possibility of any evil intent. Wasn't Marialva the wife of Martim? Silent adorers, her devoted slaves ready to obey her orders, but nothing more. They came to visit her, drink her rum, listen to her talk, look at the black beauty spot on her shoulder, the swaying of her body, and that was all.

But in the case of Bullfinch it was different; passion went beyond the limits of the loyalty due a friend. Bullfinch felt himself dangerously close to that line beyond which lay ingratitude, disloyalty, hypocrisy. He lived dramatic days, his head aching with warring emotions, his breast heavy, his heart sore. He saw himself as a drowning man, with open eyes taking in all that was going on around him, conscious but incapable of staying afloat, of swimming, irresistibly sucked into the depths of the sea. Where was his sense of honor? He swore he would resist—all the women there were in the world!—swore he would be worthy of Martim's friendship, and yet one look from

Marialva was enough to completely shatter his purpose. He was turning into a weathervane.

He was so distraught that he began to neglect his work, and Mamede began to demand a little more enthusiasm in his spieling: "Hey, Bullfinch, do you expect Chalub to pay you for lying down on the job? What goes on here? Where are the customers?"

Ah, Mamede, what do you know about a man's moral sufferings? Bullfinch felt like resting his heavy head on the Arab's shoulder and telling him all, giving vent to his heart ache.

A professional spieler, or "head of commerical propaganda," as he was called, Bullfinch was hired, from time to time, by the Arab Mamede to attract customers. He stationed himself in front of the doors of the "World's Bargain Center," which opened on to Baixa do Sapateiro, to proclaim the excellence of the pants of tweedy cotton mixture of third-rate quality, and of the cheap gewgaws that Mamede sold at high prices. Dressed in his threadbare cutaway, wearing a top hat, and with his face painted like a circus clown, Bullfinch bellowed to the four winds the innumerable advantages of the Arab's store, especially on the occasion of the sweeping sale advertised on a poster with huge red letters covering the front of the establishment:

"The Sale of the Century! Everything given away!"

Twice a year, at least, on the most varied pretexts, Mamede "gave away" the merchandise on hand, renewing his stock. Bullfinch played an important part in this commerical maneuver. It was his duty to bring in customers to acquaint themselves with the generosity of the Arab, a generosity that verged upon madness, and to purchase those articles sold at unbelievably low prices, practically given away. The public at large, walking indifferently along the Baixa do Sapateiro, did not seem aware or appreciative of Mamede's generosity. For that reason, Bullfinch was supposed to carry on a noisy propaganda designed to halt the hurrying passersby. At times he went so far as to take one of them by the arm and drag him into the shop. He was not only competent, he was also conscientious, and he worked for his money.

That was why Mamede was surprised to see him dejected, without his usual wit, his abundant repertory of jokes and wisecracks, tricks, all that made people stop, gather about him, with some of them finally deciding to go into the store. Once they were in, they bought, for Mamede took it upon himself to convince the unwary customer. But that morning Bullfinch lacked vivacity, *élan*; he was listless, sad. Maybe he was sick, the Arab thought: "Are you sick or hung over?"

Bullfinch did not answer, shouting at the top of his lungs: "Come in, come in, everybody! The Arab Mamede has gone crazy and is selling off everything for less than cost! He's selling the store, he's going back to Syria, he's closing out. Come in everybody! Take advantage of the opportunity! Hurry in before everything is gone!"

How could he answer without telling all? The passion that was devouring him, how he couldn't get her out of his mind for one second, seeing her there in front of him, her eyes pleading, that poor victim of life and Martim? Victim of Martim? Bullfinch tried as hard as he could to discover signs of ill-treatment and abuse on the part of the corporal, but could not find them. Could he have done so, it would have helped to quiet his remorse.

The message of Marialva's suffering eyes seemed clear to him: she was a victim; she was there against her will. God only knew the schemes that Martim, with his fast tongue and wiles, had used to make her his! Not that she had told him anything—it was just the way she looked at him. Bullfinch, up to that point, had avoided a frank talk, mutual confession, even though Marialva more than once had tried to see him alone. Bullfinch was afraid.

But against whom could Marialva's eyes beg for protection and help if not Martim? Even though Bullfinch had not heard a single harsh word from the corporal to his wife, even though he saw him most affectionate and impassioned, ready to satisfy Marialva's every whim, he could not imagine any other source of oppression or violence.

But none of all this justified Bullfinch's passion. Even if the corporal had kicked her around, dragged her by the hair, flailed her bottom and ribs, she was his wife; he had a right to treat her any way he liked. And if she did not agree, she could go, leave her husband and home. When time had elapsed after this, perhaps Bullfinch could then come forward and present his candidacy. But with her in Martim's house, all lovey-dovey with him, sitting on his lap, and he, with the greatest tenderness, doing everything she wanted—you would have said there was no better husband—how explain the long looks, the shivers, the half-open lips, the tip of the tongue? Bullfinch did not even have the right to think of her lustfully. Nor Marialva of him.

Bullfinch threw himself despairingly into advertising the sale at the "World's Bargain Center." His voice rang through Baixa do Sapateiro, bellowing the usual wise-cracks, the jokes that never failed. But under the white lead and the red paint that covered his face, there was a blush of shame, of shame that he should be harboring treachery toward a friend. Ah, Martim, my brother, your brother is a low scoundrel! His voice lacked its usual drollery, his gestures were mechanical, there was no joy in his heart. Love always made him excited and happy. But now, when he felt that he had found the love of his life, incommensurable, total and eternal, his heart was full of sadness and remorse. Oh, if he could forget her, if he could wrench her saintly image from his breast, and be able to look Martim in the face once more, be worthy of his friendship!

Yes, he must wrench her from his heart, drive her out of his thoughts forever. Even if this meant that he was never to see her again, never to go back to the corporal's house or even attend Tibéria's anniversary celebration, where he would be sure to meet the couple. Of course, not to go to the celebration would be terrible. Tibéria would never forgive him. But he ought to do it; he must do it. Martim would not do otherwise if he, Bullfinch, were the husband in danger. Bullfinch even recalled an instance that put him under still deeper obligations to the corporal in affairs of the heart. He had been making up to a high yellow at the Gafieira do Barão dance-hall. They had covered a lot of ground, were almost sweethearts, when Martim, without knowing a thing, ignorant of all these details, had asked the girl for a dance and had propositioned her. She had melted in his arms, the slut. She was prepared to take him up, and all the while she was putting on a big act with Bullfinch, pretending to be a virgin, a respectable girl. When, however, they made their plans to meet after the dance, she warned Martim that they would have to give Bullfinch the slip because she was practically engaged to him, and if he should become suspicious . . . Martim would understand . . .

What the two-timer did not expect was Martim's reaction. He let go of her right there on the dance floor, with a face like a thundercloud. So she was bespoken to Bullfinch, practically engaged to him, and was accepting an invitation to lay the first fellow who showed up? How cynical and indecent could you get? Didn't she perhaps know that he and Bullfinch were practically brothers, bosom friends? Less than two weeks before, the two of them had carried out their vows together, washed their heads, slept side by side in the chamber of the saint, like blood brothers in the same bed. If they hadn't been in public, he would have given her a few slaps to teach her to respect her man.

And when Bullfinch arrived, all starched, in a new suit, Martim told him about the indecency of the high yellow, who was watching them from a distance, with misgivings. Bullfinch wanted to raise hell and send her packing with the greatest contempt; but Martim, who was experienced in such matters, dissuaded him. First pretend to be very angry, he advised him, then generously forgive her, but demand in return that she go to bed with him that very night. And only after they had slept together was he to tell her what he thought of her and throw her out. And so Bullfinch did, although it was hard for him to put on the act and then throw the tramp out of bed. Never would he be able to master women the way Martim did; he was incurably sentimental.

Yes, there was nothing for him to do, if he did not want to behave like the most unworthy of friends, but to wrench that love out of his heart, never more let his eyes rest on Marialva or say a word to her. He knew, with that knowledge that leaves no room for doubt, that if he met her, if he let his eyes meet her imploring eyes, he could not hold out, he would confess his passion, betraying his friend, his brother-in-devotion. Bullfinch stopped shouting his spiel.

He had made up his mind: he would never see her again, would suffer for the rest of his life the sorrow of having lost her; he would never again be able to love another woman, wretched forever but worthy of Martim's friendship, loyal to his brother. Ah, Martim, my brother, I am going to be miserable for your sake, but that is the way friends should behave! Bullfinch felt heroic and was moved. He looked around the street and saw her. There she was, standing at the door of the movie house, which was still closed at that hour of the morning, and she smiled at him. She raised her arm and beckoned to him with her hand. Bullfinch thought he was seeing a mirage; he closed his eyes and opened them again. Marialva's smile broadened, and her gesture grew more urgent. Bullfinch saw nothing more; all his good intentions, his heroic decisions melted away. There in the back of his mind the figure of Martim arose, but Bullfinch dispelled it. After all, what was there wrong in saying "good morning" to the wife of a friend, chatting a little, talking about this and that? It would even look odd if he refused to see her and talk to her. All this ran through his head in less than a second, in less time than it takes to wink an eye. He jammed his hat on his head and leaped across the street in a spectacular bound without heeding the streetcar coming in one direction and the truck in another. He avoided them both by a miracle. Mamede let out a yell, thinking that he had been crushed under the wheels. What the devil had got into Bullfinch that day? A sudden attack of madness preceded by a fit of melancholy? His curiosity aroused, the Arab went into the street just in time to see Bullfinch turning the corner in animated conversation with a woman who would stop the traffic. He shook his head; there was no doing anything with that Bullfinch. And as though he did not expect to see him back that morning, Mamede raised his voice with his special Levantine accent and began to proclaim the marvels of the "World's Bargain Center," the sensational sale, the goods being given away free.

⋯⊰ 11 ⊱⋯

THERE WAS NO WAY OF GETTING USED to the radical
change in the corporal's life. To see him now one had to
seek him out in his house; no longer did he show up as
before; he had become difficult. To be sure, he went back
to his old stamping grounds in the Market and Água dos
Meninos for a few games of cards, he resumed his sleight
of hand performances with the deck for the delight and
edification of the rising generations. But a bare minimum,
just enough to earn the necessary chicken feed for beans
and dried beef, manioc meal and *dendê* oil. Aside from
this, the pleasures of home took care of all his needs.

There were those who looked upon him as irretrievably
lost, without hope of salvation. That woman had him completely under her thumb; he was putty in her hands; she
was the boss; she rode him on a tight rein. It had taken the
corporal a long time to fall in love, to surrender, but when
he did, it was unconditional. Friends and acquaintances
recalled the old Martim, free as the wind, elbow bender,
capoeira fighter, past master of the dance, the life of every
party. That one was now gone for good, transformed into a
henpecked husband who had to account for every minute
of his time.

All this, assuming that nothing worse happened, for
there were those who began to comment on the frequency
of Marialva's and Bullfinch's meetings, their long conversa-

tions interspersed with giggles and ogling. True, Martim and Bullfinch were intimate friends, like brothers, devotees of the same saint, making their annual *bori* together, and perhaps that intimacy with Marialva was nothing more than politeness. Even so, one couldn't help wondering. Martim alone seemed oblivious of this, given over to his infatuation, to the delights of his new existence.

For it must be stated for the record that the criticism of the corporal's behavior and the chorus of lamentations that rose about him did not exclude that initial envy already mentioned.

It did not remain at the white heat of the first days when all his friends dreamed of marriage. The enthusiasm cooled off somewhat, in view of the limitations imposed on and accepted by Martim, but even so, the vision of the order, the comfort, the warmth of a home now and then disturbed Ipicilone and Negro Massu, not to mention Bullfinch, for he dreamed of nothing else: getting married, assuming that sweet ball and chain, but, of course, to Marialva.

And there was the catch. The idyll that had begun that morning of their meeting on Baixa do Sapateiro in front of the "World's Bargain Center," when they went off together, shy and a little abashed, grew. They were silent for a while, not knowing how to begin.

They walked side by side, their eyes on the ground, now smiling, now serious and lost in thought, grave thoughts. Finally Marialva took the initiative, in a voice that was barely a whisper: "I had been wanting to talk to you . . ."

Bullfinch raised his eyes to the innocent, sad face of Martim's wife: "You wanted to talk to me? What about?"

"To ask something of you . . . I hardly know . . ."

"Well, go ahead. . . . I am here to do whatever you want."

"You promise?"

"It's a promise."

"Well, what I wanted . . ." and she turned even more timid and sad.

"What? Go on. . . . Tell me."

"What I wanted to ask you was not to come to the house anymore."

It was as though she had dealt Bullfinch a blow in the breast. He had expected anything but that, that brusque cutting off of his hopes. In spite of the fact that he had decided of his own accord not to return to the corporal's house, that request of Marialva's wounded him deeply. An expression of utter dismay came over his face, for a moment he could not answer, and stood there rooted in his tracks. She, too, stopped, looking at him sorrowfully. She put her hand on his arm and said:

"Because if you keep on coming, I don't know what may happen. . . ."

"But why?"

Marialva lowered her eyes:

"Can't you see? Martim is getting suspicious, he's already got a flea in his ear. . . ."

Another blow in the breast for Bullfinch. What was he to do if Martim already had his suspicions? Ah, my brother, what a horror!

"But nothing has happened. . . ."

"That's just it, and it's better for us not to meet again . . . as long as nothing has happened. . . . Afterward it would be worse. . . ."

At this point Bullfinch, mad with love, beside himself, without seeing what was going on in the busy street around him, took Marialva by the hand and asked in a voice husky with emotion: "And do you find that . . ."

Once more she lowered her eyes: "I don't know about you. . . . As for me . . ."

"I can no longer live without you."

She moved ahead, saying: "Let's keep walking; people are looking at us. . . ."

As they walked on she explained that this must not be. She was under obligations to Martim; he had brought her; he gave her everything; there were no limits to his kindness; he was devoted to her heart and soul, mad about her, really mad, even capable of committing a crime. How could she leave him, even if she did not love him, even though her heart yearned for another? Both of them, she and Bullfinch, must sacrifice all not to wound Martim, not to cause him such sorrow. She, at any rate, was prepared never to see Bullfinch again, however much suffering this decision entailed. And he ought to do the same; he was Martim's friend; that love was doomed from the start. She had come looking for him to get him to promise that he would never see her again.

Bullfinch swore, overwhelmed by emotion, that Marialva was a saint and that he was completely unworthy of her love. She had led him back to the path of honor, of loyalty to a friend. True, he would suffer like one condemned to the depths of hell, but he would never seek her out again; he would strangle that guilty love; he would be worthy of his friends. His breast swelled, and Marialva watched him out of the corner of her eye. He swore, kissing the cross of his joined fingers, and rushed away brusquely, to avoid temptation. She watched him leave, and a smile flowered on her lips. She made her way through the crowd that filled Baixa do Sapateiro, taking in with satisfaction the remarks and whistles that greeted her passage. She did not turn to look back, merely emphasized the swinging of her bottom. Bullfinch disappeared down the side streets, looking for a tavern, caught up in a whirlwind of emotion, a foundering ship with tattered sails and broken rudder.

For three days Bullfinch wandered about the city of Bahia, drowning his sorrow, his sacrifice, his heroism, in rum. His friends were unable to discover the reasons for this celebration, whether it was the beginning or the end of an affair, whether he was engaged or had been sent packing by some heartthrob. His conversation was muddled, but a certain pride could be sensed amid that tribulation. Jesuíno, who had gone to see Martim the second day to discuss some bets on a cockfight, told him about Bullfinch's desperation, his drinking until he passed out, with the air of a martyr, and his talking about killing himself. Martim stated categorically: "What Bullfinch needs is to get married."

Marialva was standing in the door of the sitting room, listening to the conversation, and she smiled. Martim went on: "What a woman was born for is to look after a man in his home," and addressing himself to Marialva: "Come on, beautiful, how about a drink for Crazy Cock and your hubby here? Something select in the way of rum."

Marialva crossed the room to fill their glasses.

The next day, when Bullfinch, unshaven and dirty, was ordering his first drink of the day in Isidro de Batualê's tavern, a street urchin approached him and whispered in his ear: "Young man, there's a lady outside wants to talk to you. She sent me to call you. . . ."

"I don't want to talk to anybody. Scram!"

But his curiosity got the better of him, and he peeped out of the door. A few houses farther down, there she was, and he rushed toward her: "Marialva!"

"Dear God, look at the state he's in! I never thought . . ."

According to her subsequent confession, it was at that moment, when she saw him filthy and reeking of rum, that Marialva succumbed to that guilty love. She began to cry, and her tears laved Bullfinch's soul, leaving him, a few hours later, clean and unburdened.

This was their first meeting, but several others followed in the space of a few days: Marialva, swept off her feet by passion; Bullfinch—it goes without saying. They met briefly, in church naves, on the wharfs, they talked hurriedly, in fear of Martim. They had agreed not to see one another at Marialva's house. When she could, she would go where he was working, and they would walk along the street, down steep Tabuão, losing themselves among the crowds, two fellow souls, two lovers mad about each other, yet two noble souls.

Yes, for they had decided not to betray Martim. That vast and boundless love, roweled by white-hot desire—they would subdue it, keeping it on a purely spiritual level. They loved one another, true, and they could do nothing about this, for it was stronger than they. But they would never let this love become sinful; they would resist all desire; he would never touch her, never betray Martim. Bullfinch lived days of almost frenzied excitement; his friends did not know what to make of it.

Marialva poured out the bitterness of her soul to him. It had always been like that with her. Nothing good ever came her way; she was the victim of fate, pursued by bad luck. What better example of this could there be than what was happening between the two of them? When she found love, when finally, after so many cruel years of suffering, life offered her a recompense, she was bound by ties of gratitude to a man whom she did not love but to whom she owed respect and friendship. And as Bullfinch was his best friend, fate seemed determined to rob her of all opportunity to be happy.

She told him, after her own fashion, the story of her life. It was worth listening to her to hear her version of the facts. According to her, the cabinetmaker Duca—a meek soul who wouldn't say boo at a goose—was a wild beast brimming over with hate, making a martyr of a poor little girl of fifteen. Marialva had practically been sold to that bandit by her wicked stepmother. Duca was transformed into a bandit, and kindhearted Ermelinda, her father's mistress, who had patiently put up with the misbehavior of her stepdaughter, became the stepmother of cheap melodramas, persecuting and finally selling the unhappy orphan, and so on and so forth. Naturally, in this version, there had been no other man in the limpid, suffering life of Marialva in the time between Duca and Martim. Fat Artur, Tonho da Capela (a sexton by calling), Juca Mineiro (a storekeeper), disappeared as though wiped off the face of the earth. The days in the whorehouse and the one-night standers, the chance passersby, were summarily eliminated. On the contrary, when Duca had left her penniless after a life of sacrifice, cooking and washing for him, when he had become a habitual drunkard, she went to work as a laundress in the home of a wealthy family, washing and ironing so as not to fall into a life of degradation. It was while thus employed that she had met Martim under circumstances designed to win her affection and gratitude. Sick from so much work, with a chest cold that was threatening to turn into consumption. It was thus that he had made her acquaintance, and he had been kind to her, bringing a doctor, buying her medicines, without asking anything in return. When she got better and was able to be up and around, planning to go back to work, he had suggested that she come to Bahia to live with him. She had accepted, even though she did not love him. But she liked him; she respected him; and besides, she could not bear the thought of going back to the washboard and the iron. Had she done so, before long she would have been in the charity ward of a hospital with a lung eaten away. There was the story of her life, a rosary of sadness, a sea of tears.

Bullfinch suffered as he listened to her, tenderness welling up in him. Hand in hand (they had decided not to regard this as improper behavior, merely a form of solidarity, proof of spiritual alliance between two noble souls), they walked along the waterfront and dreamed how good it would be if they could join their loneliness, their previous disappointments, their tattered pasts, and begin a new life together—leaning on one another, supporting one another. But this they could not do; Martim stood between them, good Martim, friend Martim, who had once given proof of his loyal friendship, Martim, his brother through devotion to the same saint, a tie as sacred as that of blood brother, Martim, ah Martim, that son of a bitch of a Martim, why in the hell had he had to get mixed up with Marialva?

·{ 12 }·

DURING THOSE DAYS immediately preceding the celebration
of Tibéria's anniversary the latest bulletins from Corporal
Martim's matrimonial front reported the following de-
ployment of forces: the corporal, taking his ease in his
rocking chair, gave the impression of being the happiest of
husbands; Marialva, looking after her house and her man,
hovering about him, aroused the envy of the mulattas of
the neighborhood; Bullfinch, tried and loyal friend, was
sighing with passion and sacrificing himself for his brother-
in-devotion; the rest of Martim's friends deplored the loss
of him, the great enlivener of the night, but all were agreed
on the matter of his tranquil happiness, and all envied him
a little. Martim had become a gentleman, and although he
had not gone so far as to get a job and go to work, a
complete change had come over his life. Jesuíno alone held
out: that farce would be short-lived.

Did this information, however, tell the whole truth?
When the corporal sat sipping his rum in silent reflection
after his return from quick forays in search of money, was
this to be taken as a reaffirmation of the wisdom of his
marriage? Happy, beyond a doubt. Too happy. . . . That
was exactly it: too happy; and this he found cloying.

Out of the corner of his eye he watched Marialva moving about the house, coming and going, dusting, scouring
the knives and forks, the coffeepot, washing the cups, look-

99

ing after everything not so much to have the house in order and shining clean as to display her own perfection. Too perfect; it positively turned his stomach.

At times a strange thought came into Martim's mind: how had he got mixed up with Marialva? One of those unforseen things that can happen to anyone. A situation develops; an obligation is impulsively assumed, giving rise to comments; interests become involved; and before the person realizes what has happened, he is ensnared and has to go through with it and play his role. Not that he disliked that of happy husband: he had a pretty woman with a black beauty mark on her left shoulder, the hottest number he had ever shared a bed with, a first-class housekeeper, everything clean and in order, everything on time and as it should be, so what more could he ask? Why did he find the pose of married man, of perfect spouse, of happy husband, so burdensome? He even had to admit that he had thoroughly enjoyed it for a while. But now he was beginning to weary of so much comfort, of such a well-run house, of such a model wife.

When he had met her in Cachoeira in the whorehouse, when he had been so much in need of someone to comfort with the warmth of tenderness his loneliness in exile, he had vaguely thought, as he looked into her eyes, of shacking up with her, and had suggested it in passing. She had taken him up on it, had collected her belongings, and had mounted on the saddle behind him. He was so avid for company and affection that he had decided to take her with him for a few days and then turn her loose a few cities farther on, before he returned to the capital. But he had reckoned without Marialva's experience, her capacity for making herself indispensable. Martim found himself enveloped in that love, grateful to that woman for whom he was everything, who was groveling at his feet. He got in deeper and deeper, and before he knew it, it was he, Martim, who was tied to *her*, with fetters on his wrists and a chain around his ankle. Who had decided the return to Bahia? he asked himself, seated in the rocking chair, casting up accounts of what had happened. Who had decided to rent a house, buy furniture? Who had broadcast the news of their marriage, even inventing details? Who had charted the course of a new life for Corporal Martim? Marialva, she and nobody but she, leading him, and he letting himself be led, agreeing with everything, backing up all her decisions and ratifying her statements. That was how it had happened, and when the corporal came to his senses, he was married and set up in a house, enjoying innumerable advantages.

He had had his fun, too: the surprise of his friends, their envy, Tibéria's anger, Jesuíno's doubts and Jesus's justification, the atmosphere that had sprung up around the affair, the gossip and tittle-tattle, the bets, the jujus thrown in front of his door, all that had led him to enlarge his real well-being into a show of absolute happiness. Little by little it began to pall on him. So many interesting things happening outside, and Martim having no part in them. He was no longer the leader, the standard-bearer, the man who made the decisions. Nobody came any more to invite him to the celebrations. They had even forgotten to send for him on the occasion of the elections in the *afoxé*. Moreover, for this reason Camafeu was not elected to the presidency and they all realized the consequences of this grave error: the *afoxé* did not win first place that year, thus losing the triple championship. Before leaving for the Recôncavo, Martim had launched the candidacy of Camafeu, and with the corporal's prestige, skill, connections, and friendships, victory was assured. Camafeu had accomplished many things on behalf of the club; he was active and well liked. Valdemar da Sogra, who had been the almost lifetime president, could no longer promote the *afoxé;* it had grown greatly in numbers and importance, and Valdemar's hands had become too weak for the job. They were going to keep him on, however, in order not to hurt his feelings and because there was no other likely candidate. That was when the corporal took matters into his own hands, thinking of the triple championship, and put forward the name of Camafeu. It was received with sympathy and support, and everything was going fine, when Martim had to light out and disappear in the Recôncavo. He had returned shortly before the elections. Camafeu's candidacy, without the corporal's direction, had declined, withered; he was unable to prevent the re-election of Valdemar da Sogra. So married and withdrawn was Martim that nobody gave him a thought, not even Camafeu himself called on him, sent for him. He did not even go to vote, and he only learned the results days later.

He was getting fed up, too, with Marialva's perfection. And he began to give her a slap once in a while just so she would not think she was mistress of all she surveyed. Naturally, not before his friends, in public. He went on playing the part of the most impassioned lover, the most devoted spouse, the model husband. He enjoyed seeing and feeling the envy in the eyes of the others, envy of his complete happiness. At such moments, Bullfinch died of envy; he was capable of picking up the first brown girl he came upon in the street and marrying her, just to imitate Martim.

Amusing, without a doubt, but it was beginning to get tiresome. His departures "to get some dough for expenses" grew more frequent; and his sojourns in the street, longer. If anyone had mentioned this beginning of boredom, if anyone had suggested the possibility of that famous union's coming to a speedy end, Martim would have protested, denied it with emphasis and violence. Because he was not thinking, even to himself, of leaving Marialva, of breaking up his home. Nothing of the sort. It was just that everything was so good and so perfect that he was getting tired of it. How is it possible for a thing to be too good?

Marialva was aware of all this; she did not miss even the most carefully stifled yawn. It was as though she could guess his thoughts, as though she could read his heart: the corporal was no longer the same as when she had met him in the Recôncavo. She had begun to feel it the very day they arrived in Bahia, during that morning visit of Negro Massu, and had seen the slow growth of that sensation of satiety. Martim was beginning to get fed up with that life and with her, Marialva. She could feel it in the air, in a certain haste in his kisses, in a certain reluctance to come to bed, but she gave no sign of her awareness. It was not that she cared so much about losing Martim or the breaking up of that home. She had broken up others before, and a lover more or less didn't make much of a dent on her. What she would not accept was that he should take the initiative, give the first yawn; that it should be he who turned her out on the streets of Bahia as though she were a nobody like her predecessors. If anyone was to do this, it would be she, Marialva, and she'd do it when and how she wanted to.

She felt him withdrawing from her little by little, so slowly, so gently, that another woman, less discerning, would not have noticed it. Marialva, however, had no intention of letting Martim make himself important at her expense. She was not going to allow his boredom, his surfeit, to grow. She would not allow him to take off suddenly one day, leaving her with the house and the furniture, the glasses and the coffeepot. She would work out a plan of attack: she would wound him so deeply in his vanity that he would drag himself on the ground, weeping at her feet, begging her pardon. Not for nothing did she know how to deal with men. A better weapon than jealousy did not exist. Marialva would demonstrate her power, and for this, she counted on Bullfinch. And who better? Bullfinch, Martim's best friend, his brother-in-devotion, both of them sons of Oxalá. Martim would pay for his daring to tire of her body and her smile, of getting bored with her. Nothing of the sort had ever happened to her before; it was always she who sent the man off, impassioned, supplicating. But before Martim was fed up and had made up his mind to leave, she would trample him underfoot on the arm of her new lover and would order him to get out, to go back into the street where he had come from. The man she chose would sleep in her house, in her bed, and for him Marialva would primp in front of the great mirror of her room.

Bullfinch, innocent of all these subtle machinations, of the beginning of the tedium of the corporal (whom he believed to be more and more deeply in love, in which idea he was confirmed by Marialva in their surreptitious exchanges along the water front), of Marialva's plans of revenge, suffered the pains of the damned and enjoyed the delights of paradise, the pains and delights of one who is experiencing a great love. At their meetings, Marialva, dramatic and hapless, not knowing what to do, left him in panic and delirium. She became fearful, risking her reputation and her life, to meet him, a platonic meeting, nothing more than breathless conversations, handclasps, eyes looking into eyes, mounting desire, and Bullfinch on the point of losing his mind.

She told him of Martim's love, how he could not be without her for a moment, that when he went out to get some money (she took advantage of such occasions to meet Bullfinch), it was always in a hurry, returning on the double, as fast as he could. At night when their bodies were tearing one another apart in bed—Bullfinch ground his teeth with hatred—he threatened to kill her if she ever even thought of betraying him, of leaving him, of going off with another man. He swore he would stab her to death (which is the worst death there is), strangle her partner, and then commit suicide to complete the tragedy. There you see how much she risked to talk to Bullfinch just for a moment, press his hand, look into his eyes! Did he really deserve so much, did he really love her, was he not taking advantage of her, of her candor, of her innocence? She came like a fallen woman or a madwoman just to see him, drawn by that love without prospects, without hope. Nor could they think of going farther with it, for it would be the death and dishonor of them all. Ah, if Martim even suspected . . .

This was how she talked, in a kind of frenzy. And at the same time, as though she could not restrain herself, she indulged in the most hallucinating dreams: could Bullfinch just imagine how sweet and wonderful it would be if the two of them could live together always, free, loving each other without threats or perils, Marialva's house even better ordered than now, with curtains at the windows and a rug at the door? And she to look after him, at last free to live with the man she loved, he rising in his profession, giving up his jobs at Syrians' stores, and striking out on his own, selling wonder-working cures or modern inventions for housewives, traveling through the country with her and his merchandise. This was what she dreamed of, a dream never to come true, the dream of a madwoman, but she could not accept the terrible reality, the impossibility that one day, cost what it might, she would be his, wholly his, and his alone.

She left quickly, fearful that Martim might return before

she did and not find her home. He would demand to know where she had been, whom she had seen, what they had talked about. She might lose her head and tell him everything, everything, which was really nothing, but enough to make Martim think that he had been deceived, cuckolded, and right there on the spot he would finish her off with a kitchen knife. She left Bullfinch in a state of despair, at war with himself, torn between loyalty to his friend and a love that brooked no restraint, with desire raging in him, and his romanticism, his fondness for noble and tragic gestures. To him, Marialva was the purest, most put-upon and long-suffering of women. What could he do to free her, liberate her from the prison where Martim kept her, and bring her into his arms, his bed?

Yes, to tumble her in bed; for however romantic Bullfinch was, he did not exclude from his remote and impossible dreams laying Marialva in the bed that at the moment belonged to Martim, clasping her in his arms, diving into her breasts, wrapped in her hair, buried in her rose.

Even without knowing all these details, Jesuíno Crazy Cock did not take much stock in the bulletins from the front. With that kind of sixth sense he possessed, he had misgivings about the outcome of the corporal's marriage. And he confided his doubts to Jesus over the stein of cold beer whose foam covered his mustache: "It's not going to last, Jesus, it's not going to last. There's no need for Tibéria to get herself so worked up. This will be short-lived. A day sooner, a day later, and Martim will be here, tossing off a beer with us."

It was just an intuition, but Jesuíno was rarely mistaken in his diagnosis when the ailment was infatuation, passion, or love. In his opinion, love is eternal only because it springs anew in the hearts of men and women, not because there was any love that lasted a lifetime, always waxing. He smacked his tongue, savoring the beer, and shook his head with its thatch of white hair: "I know that type of woman, Mr. Jesus. She is one of those who drive men crazy. They have no peace until they have slept with her. But after that, they want to leave. For what she wants is to boss, to get her foot on their neck. Do you think Martim is going to take that?"

Jesus did not want to pass opinion. For him the human heart was a mystery that had no explanation, full of surprises. Take that girl Otália, for example. She seemed just a silly young thing with nothing special to her, pretty and that was all. But under closer scrutiny she was a pool of complications, full of inlets and outlets, of mysteries to be deciphered.

{13}

JESUS WAS RIGHT ABOUT OTÁLIA BEING COMPLICATED and
surprising. Little more than a child, and yet capable of
facing up to the most complicated situations, as she proved
at Tibéria's party.

The echoes of that celebration still resound today along
the shore of the sea of Bahia, on the waterfront, in the
markets and environs, not only because of the joy that
reigned supreme, the quantity of rum and beer that was
consumed, but also because of the moral fiber Otália revealed when circumstances demanded it. It is at times like
that, of weighty decision, that one can accurately measure
a man or a woman, can see a person's true face. One often
thinks one knows a person in all his intimacy, and suddenly, when the occasion arises, he turns out to be completely different—the timid, daring; the coward, foolhardy.

Perhaps it was because Tibéria had been vexed by so
many annoyances since the corporal's disembarkation,
fretted by worries, that she decided to make that celebration of her birthday an outstanding event. An apparent
impasse had developed in her relations with Martim after
the invitation transmitted by Negro Massu and so
brusquely turned down by her. So she wouldn't come to his
house, Martim fumed. All right, then he wouldn't go to her
place either. The corporal, who was versed in matters of
protocol and etiquette, argued that it was Tibéria's place to

visit him first, for he had returned from a trip, and married, to boot, and it behooved his friends of such long standing to come to meet and greet and welcome Marialva. Trifles, tommy rot, nonsense coming between friends tried and true, and then all the tittle-tattle of the talebearers, ruining a valued attachment. And it was a sad thing to see an old friendship like that of Tibéria and Martim destroyed. Tibéria, when she learned of the corporal's interpretation of the proper procedure in the matter of visits, stated to anyone who cared to hear her that Marialva had better sit down while she waited for Tibéria to call on her, for she would have to wait a lifetime. It was not the place of Tibéria, an honorable and respectable woman, to leave her house to go to welcome a trashy backlands whore.

Tibéria did not mention the corporal's name, she avoided all reference to him and Marialva. She feigned her usual good humor, but those closest to her knew that she was wounded and hurt, and for that very reason they gave her every proof of affection on the day of her celebration. From early in the morning, at five o'clock mass in the church of Bonfim. Many had been invited to the *feijoada* at noon, many would come at night, there would be drinking and dancing. But only the closest of friends attended the mass: the inmates of her sporting house (they all chipped in to pay the priest and the sacristan and to buy the candles and flower for the altar of the miracle-working saint) and close friends. It was to avoid the attendance of the curious, of strangers, that Tibéria had the church service at this early hour.

She arrived on Jesus's arm making the trip in the taxi of Hilário, her *compadre*. Her friends were waiting on the church steps, Crazy Cock in front. The girls formed a sprightly group to escort her in.

For Tibéria this was the moment of deepest emotion. With a black mantilla on her head, partly covering her face, a prayer book, bound in mother-of-pearl, bearing witness to her devotion, wearing a black, high-necked dress, she knelt in the front row with Jesus beside her. The girls took their places in the other pews, the friends in the back, beside the font of holy water.

She knelt, folded her hands, lowered her head, her lips

moving. She did not open her prayer book, as though she did not need it to remember the prayers she had learned in childhood. Jesus, practically a man of the cloth, for from his hands, his scissors, and his needles had emerged the cassocks and sacerdotal vestments used there, completely at home among those sacred objects, stood waiting impassively for the tears to start. For the tears burst forth infallibly every year during mass, and the barely repressed sobs that made Tibéria's breast, as broad as a sofa, rise and fall. What were the emotions that agitated her at this solemn hour of the mass of her anniversary? What the memories, the incidents, the faces, the places, the dead, that filled her for the half hour she was alone with herself, her lips ruminating prayers, her thoughts lost perhaps in the days of her childhood and adolescence? When the tears began flowing and her breast heaving, Jesus stretched out his hand and rested it on his wife's shoulder, at one with her. Tibéria reached for this comforting hand, and pressed it to her lips in gratitude. She raised her eyes, smiled at Jesus, and the moment of tears was over.

That year, as she got out of Hilário's taxi and went up the steps of the church, Tibéria took in at a glance the people who were there. The girls were laughing loudly, excited by this morning festival, overcoming their sleepiness with the fresh vision of the day. Accustomed to sleeping until late, they knew nothing of the life of the city in that dawn hour. When, by chance, they happened to be up at daybreak, it was because they had not yet gone to bed, and even so, they did not see the dawn, for they were still at work, enveloped in smoke and the fumes of liquor, wearied with the prolonged night and the obligation of being merry. It was different the morning of Tibéria's feast. They scrambled out of bed at break of day, put on their most circumspect clothes, almost no make-up, and gathered about Tibéria. They seemed like members of the family, daughters and nieces, who had assembled to participate in the celebration of a beloved relative.

They surrounded her on the stairs, their laughter breaking out at the least pretext. But Tibéria, after receiving the embraces of her friends, moved quickly into the church, trying to discern in the muted light of the atrium the figure of Martim. He had never failed to be present in previous years. He was the first to embrace her, kissing her fat cheek like a son. He would come dressed to the nines, his white shirt shining with starch, his pointed shoes gleaming. When she saw that he was not there, Tibéria lowered her head; her feast was off to a sad start.

She knelt as she did every year, in the same spot, clasped her hands together, and her lips began to murmur the old prayers. But her thoughts did not follow their usual course, did not make their way through memory to the far-off nooks of her girlhood, bringing to the surface that fat, lively young girl of the little provincial city at the time of her first flirtations. She could not even recall the figures of Father and Mother, lost so early and forever. Martim had not come; there had never been such ingratitude, so false a friend of such fickle affection. It was enough for some trashy slut to cross his path, and he cast off his old and tried friendships. Tibéria lowered her head over her folded hands, and that year the tears threatened to arrive before their usual hour.

She felt the pressure of Jesus's fingers on her shoulder. Jesus understood: he knew how devoted she was to Martim, how she loved him like a son, the son she had always longed for, the great void in her life. She had so wanted a son, she had undergone long medical treatments, to no avail. Martim had fallen heir to all this tenderness which had accumulated over the years.

Jesus squeezed her shoulder; she was about to take his hand and kiss it when he whispered: "Look! . . ."

She turned her head. There stood Martim in the door of the church, the light falling on him, his white suit resplendent, his black pointed shoes gleaming. He smiled in her direction, Tibéria wanted not to smile, to turn a stern face toward him, show all the anger that had built up during those weeks, but how could she resist him? Martim smiled at her, winked his eye, and she smiled back. She bent her head once more, and this time she found all the old images, her girlhood and Father and Mother. The warm comforting tears ran down her face, her breast began to heave, and Jesus laid his hand on her shoulder.

To tell the whole truth, it must be stated that Martim's

action had not been quite as spontaneous as was to be desired. Late the preceding evening, Jesuíno Crazy Cock had showed up at the corporal's house and had stayed for a while talking. Marialva had served them rum and had hung around listening to what they had to say. Jesuíno touched on this, that, and the other, and Marialva realized that all that talk was merely by way of an opening gambit. Crazy Cock had not yet showed his hand. But after savoring the rum, he said: "Do you remember, Martim, that tomorrow is Tibéria's anniversary?"

The corporal nodded his head, his eyes veiled. Jesuíno went on: "The mass is at five in the morning at the church of Bonfim, you know. . . ."

Marialva's eyes went from one to the other: this was a matter in which she had a special interest. There was a brief silence. Martim looked through the window into the street, but—Jesuíno could have sworn—without seeing anything, not even the street urchins playing soccer with a cloth ball or the streetcar creaking along the rails.

"You know, Crazy Cock, that I am not going."

"And why not?"

"Tibéria has not behaved right toward me or Marialva. She has offended me."

Jesuíno picked up his empty glass and looked into it. Marialva got up to refill it.

"Thank you," he said. "Of course, if you don't want to go, don't; that's your business. But there's just one thing I want to say: when one has a difference with one's mother, it's she who is right, and no one else."

"With one's mother? . . ."

"That's what I said."

He drank his rum. Marialva came over to him: "As far as I am concerned, I think Martim should go. Dona Tibéria doesn't like me; I don't know why; probably someone stirring up trouble. But that is no reason for Martim to quarrel with her. I already told him . . ."

"If it was me," Jesuíno wound up the matter, "I would go by myself to the mass, which is for her closest friends, and then afterwards the two of you should go to the *feijoada*. There would be no better present for Tibéria."

Martim did not answer. Jesuíno changed the subject,

took another swallow of rum, and left. As he was starting down the hillside, he heard a voice calling to him out of the dark. It was Marialva, who had come around the back way to say to him: "Leave it to me. I'll see that he goes. He doesn't want to because of me, but I'll bring him around. . . . He does what I want him to," she laughed.

Martim went alone to the mass, and arrived at the lunch with Marialva. The Homeric *feijoada* was cooking in two kerosene cans, pounds and pounds of beans, sausage, sun-dried meat, smoked meat, fresh beef and pork, pigtails, pigs' feet, spareribs, bacon. Not to mention the rice, the hams, the tenderloins, the chicken in brown gravy, the fried manioc meal, food enough for an army.

The number of guests was not quite that of an army, but they ate for a battalion, trenchermen worthy of all respect. Rum, vermouth, and beer to float a battleship. Some of the guests certainly would not make it to the evening celebration; they would pass out there at the lunch. Bullfinch, for example, who did not eat a mouthful, but tossed off one glass of rum after another without pause.

Seated in her rocking chair, her poise regained after the contradictory emotions of the mass, Tibéria received congratulations and gifts, embraces and kisses, serene, happy, and in full command of the feast. From time to time she called to one of the girls, ordering her to serve so-and-so, on the alert to see that her guests lacked for nothing. Jesus moved about the room without going too far from Tibéria's side, preparing her plate himself, serving her vermouth, which was her favorite drink, stroking her hair. His gift to her had been a pair of long earrings which she was wearing, and she looked like a monumental oriental statue.

When they arrived, Marialva went straight over to Tibéria, outdoing herself in bows and flattering phrases. She wanted to get into the good graces of the mistress of the establishment, a person of importance in her milieu, whom she might someday need. Nothing like being on the safe side. Tibéria accepted her attentions unperturbed, nodding her head as though in approval of the fawning words, interrupting the speaker to give orders to the boy who was helping, then, with a condescending gesture, inviting her to continue. When Marialva had finished, Tibéria smiled at her, treating her politely but distantly, without expressing pleasure at her coming to the party or congratulating her on her marriage, as though she did not know she was the corporal's wife, without even praising her beauty. Although she could not deny Marialva's beauty, she avoided admitting it. She treated her cordially, invited her to be seated, ordered one of the girls to serve her. As though this were a formal visit, without making any reference to her connection with Martim, the much bruited wedding, the home set up in Vila América. Neither to Marialva nor to Martim, whom she treated with the same friendship as before, as though nothing had happened, as though he had not even gone to the Recôncavo.

Martim tried to force the situation, break the equivocal barrier Tibéria had set up. He asked her point-blank: "What do you think of my wife, Mother? Isn't she something?"

Tibéria pretended that she had not heard him, addressing herself to one of the guests. Martim repeated his question, touching her arm.

"Each to his taste," she answered.

The reply was so deliberately maladroit that Martim tried to discover its malice, irony, meaning. He finally shrugged his shoulders and went over beside Marialva, who was seated close by. It was plain that Tibéria was not yet ready to make a gesture evincing sympathy; she was still hurt; she refused to include Marialva in her tenderness. How long would she hold out? Martim knew her well; it was impossible for her to harbor hate, dislike, grudges. For the moment she was observing the code of strict good breeding, even stressing a certain solicitude, the attention due a guest, overwhelming Marialva with food and drink, ordering her served more every minute. This was less with the intention of making herself agreeable than to show the affluence of her house, to throw the lavishness of her party, the prodigality of food and drink, in her face.

The other women, the inmates of the house and the guests, did not hide their curiosity; they elbowed one another to see Marialva, size up her dress, her slippers, her hair-do, commenting on everything with giggles. This was really Marialva's first public appearance, her presentation to local society. And if there had been a society reporter on that night-life beat, in that atmosphere of cheap happiness, he would surely have recorded the fact, embellishing it with adjectives and exclamations. Marialva felt herself the cynosure all eyes, and the superior, aloof air she assumed toward that gaggle of indiscreet women was in marked contrast to her meekness and humility before Tibéria. Clasping Martim's arm, very much his beloved, showing her owner's rights over the corporal, she looked down at the others from her superior vantage point. She whispered to Martim, nipped his ear, exchanged kisses with him, her voice dripping affection. The women criticized her, but it was pure envy.

And also because the men had eyes for no other, even those who had already met her and hobnobbed with her at Martim's house, during the conversations when she served them coffee and rum. Marialva had made ready for the party; she was wearing a new dress with a tight skirt, revealing every curve, upper and lower, and when she sat down, showing her legs and knees. A good seamstress, she cut and made her own clothes. The only one who avoided her, who kept his distance, was Bullfinch. He had barely tasted the food and had flooded himself with rum.

The incident with Otália took place at night when the celebration was at its height. Many of the guests had not even gone home; they had telescoped lunch and the evening dance. Marialva, however, had gone to change her dress, and she now appeared in a blue one, cut very low, with her hair loose. When she entered with Martim there were already couples dancing in the front parlor, where on work days the girls waited for their customers. As she came in, the music almost foundered, for André, the flute player, missed a note, and Tibúrcio's eyes popped out of his head and he dropped his ukulele. This Tibúrcio was a law student, a notorious reveler, a great friend of Tibéria's and an excellent ukulele player. He had joined the combo of two guitars, harmonica, and flute, the players all friends of the house. Marialva, hanging on Martim's arm, crossed the length of the room to the rocking chair like a throne, where the celebrant sat, surrounded by the girls of the establishment, receiving more greetings. They brought her as a gift material for a dress, presented it to her, and then started dancing.

Now, everyone knew about the corporal's accomplishments as a dancer. He was in the habit of putting on an exhibition at the dance hall of Gafieira do Barão; he loved to dance, and he was a wonder at it—it was like a show. For a long time he had not done his stuff in Bahia, and that day he put his heart and soul into it. Marialva was not in his class, but she made up for her shortcomings with the movements of her body, yielding, retiring, giving herself over, asking for a bed and a man. It was not the pure dance of Martim, that lightness of a bird, almost ethereal in its agility and grace. But who would not enjoy the sight of those flanks of hers moving to the rhythm of the music?

When the dance was ended, the corporal left Marialva in the parlor while he went to have a drink with his friends at the rear of the house. There they all were, with the exception of Bullfinch, who had passed out after lunch and had had to be carried away: Jesuíno, Negro Massu, Wing-Foot, Ipicilone, Carnation-in-his-Buttonhole, Isidro, Alonso, and many others. They were doing little dancing, but by way of compensation they were drinking deep. The corporal joined them; he was happy, the tiff with Tibéria the only thorn in his flesh. For the first time since his return he had been drinking with his old friends ever since morning, and he found everything amusing.

In the parlor, seated proudly in an arm chair, Marialva allowed herself to be admired. She glanced about looking for Bullfinch. When she had gone home after lunch, the poor spieler had been on his last legs, babbling things that made no sense. They must have taken him away by now. It was a pity; Marialva liked to see him in that state of complete abandon because of her, drunk for love of her, from so desiring her. A rag, a husk of a person. That was the way she liked to see men, at her feet, dragging themselves along. She could feel their eyes on her, lingering over her legs, the low neckline of her dress. She crossed her knees, cunningly revealing and hiding expanses of thigh.

The music struck up a samba, one of the irresistible kind. Marialva would have liked to dance it. Why hadn't Martim come back? He was guzzling rum; Marialva had never seen him knock back so much. The room quickly filled up with lively couples. The samba is made for milling the haunches, lighting desire in men's eyes, a dull, yellow glow. Why didn't Martim come to dance with her? The others did not venture to: she was the wife of the corporal; it wouldn't look right. Besides none of them danced like him, with his grace and roguishness, and he was hers alone, exclusively hers.

No, he was not exclusively hers, as Marialva could verify when she saw him appear suddenly in the parlor, with Otália in his arms. She had not seen them come in; she had not witnessed the beginning of that shameless performance. Where had he dug up that tramp, skinny, not a pick on her, with braids and a dress with a sash? Otália was wearing the same dress she had worn to mass that morning, and she really looked like a little country girl, a mere chit, with those braids sticking out at her neck.

She went whirling around the room, smiling in Martim's arms. The corporal, too, was smiling, brimming over with satisfaction. Anyone who did not know him well would not have realized that he was drunk, for aside from the well-being that shone in his eyes and his unrestrained laughter, he gave no other sign of the load he had taken aboard. Nevertheless, he had been drinking ever since the conclusion of the mass. Right there, in the vicinity of the church, he, Jesuíno, and Massu had taken several eye-openers to mark the beginning of the celebration. Now he was smiling at Otália, encouraging her. She danced without any of the bodily voluptuousness of Marialva; she was a leaf floating on the breeze; her feet did not seem to touch the floor—a sweet child brought to life, born of the music, a dancer who was the corporal's peer.

It was such pure dancing, so pure and beautiful, that the other couples left the floor, one by one, preferring to watch, giving over the stage to the real dancers. Whereupon Martim released Otália and began to dance before her, with a speed and a variety of steps that left the spectators agape, while the girl circled, completing the man's dance. After this exhibition, they moved through the room again, birds on the wing, the bearers of grace and joy. Before, the men had watched Marialva dance, their eyes inflamed with desire. Now men and women were looking at Otália, filled with tenderness. Martim laughed, his feet moving ever more swiftly through the steps of the dance.

Never in all her life had Marialva felt so insulted and affronted. She closed her eyes in order not to see; she gritted her teeth in order not to scream. She went pale, and a cold sweat broke out on her forehead and hands.

She saw them go whirling about before her, a smile on Otália's lips, a gleam in Martim's eyes. A cloud passed over her, dimming her sight and understanding. When she came to herself, she was in the middle of the parlor, making for Otália and screaming: "Get out, you poor excuse for a person. Let go of my man!"

It all happened so quickly and unexpectedly that there were those who did not arrive in time to see it, like the drinkers in the back room, who missed the best of the celebration. Marialva advanced toward Otália, and with a shove, tried to separate her from Martim.

But Otália did not give ground. She went on dancing. Martim, laughing, flaunted himself between the two women, opening his arms first to one, then to the other, proud to be the apple of discord. Otália smiled and danced as though nothing were happening. A general enthusiasm reigned in the room. Is there anything more exciting than a fight between women?

Marialva stood stock-still, her mouth half open, hardly breathing. When she recovered, she advanced once more on Otália, insulting her: "Whore! Consumptive snot!"

But Otália was on the alert, and without interrupting the rhythm of the dance, she gave Marialva a kick on the shin as she reached out to grab her by the braids. The corporal's wife fell back, holding her leg and howling. In view of her screams, several women went over to the dance floor to restrain Otália, but the girl fended them all off without breaking step, and even managed to give Marialva two slaps. Only then did Tibéria assert herself, calling for the respect due her house and the occasion. In the opinion of Jesuíno, she might have done so sooner. She had even, according to Crazy Cock's version, prevented Jesus's earlier attempt at intervention when Otália raised her hand to Marialva's face. Finally, majestically, she descended from her throne and went over to Otália, who was out of control: "Come, my child, don't lower yourself. . . ."

Marialva was led away screaming. Martim laughed, harder and harder, as with the help of Negro Massu and Wing-Foot they led her off in tears.

The corporal could not decide whether, when they got home, he should give his wife a beating or tell her she was right and comfort her. He had not managed to get mad at anyone that night. Not even at Tibéria, in spite of her needling him as he went by: "Take your bundle of rags away from here, son. The next time you get married, consult me first. . . ."

He was not even mad at Otália because of the slaps she had given Marialva. A spirited girl who knew her own mind. Nor was he cross with Marialva; it was jealousy that made her behave like that. He wasn't mad at anybody. On the contrary, he went along the street happy, the falling-out between him and Tibéria over, good old Mother Tibéria, there was not another friend like her. As he pushed Marialva onto the street car, Corporal Martim was discovering his city all over again, as though he had just come ashore that day, as though the weeks before had been a dream.

Negro Massu and Wing-Foot had to help him, for Marialva did not want to go. She struggled. She bit Wing-Foot's hand. She tried to scratch the corporal's face, screaming to the amusement of a few passengers on the street car: "You dog! Fooling around with that broomstick! Trash! Fairy!"

Martim was laughing his head off; Negro Massu laughed too. Wing-Foot spread his arms, maintaining an uneasy equilibrium, and explained to the passengers, to the conductor, to the motorman: "There's no celebration like Tibéria's. . . . Not even in Germany, in the days of the Emperor of the World, not there or anywhere. Is that so or isn't it?"

The street car moved ahead, scattering Marialva's howls and the corporal's laughter through the streets in the new dawn.

⋯⊰{ **14** }⊱⋯

FROM THE DAY OF TIBÉRIA'S PARTY, events took on an accelerated rhythm.

There is always a moment in any story when "events take on an accelerated rhythm," and it is, as a rule, a moment charged with emotion. For some time now it would have been desirable for this to happen in this account of the corporal's marriage, in which, if the truth be told, little took place and that at a slow pace. Even now, the announcement of the acceleration of events does not mean that they advanced at break-neck speed, but just that things began to boil. Paving the way for the dénouement of Bullfinch's and Marialva's tragic love.

When the crisis quieted down and Marialva's nerves allowed her to reason, she began to live for her revenge. The scandal which had upset Tibéria's party had given visible shape to her worst fears, to that feeling of danger surrounding her ever since her arrival in Bahia. Either she took steps or the corporal would wind up being the boss, bridling her and giving her a taste of the spur. And one day, calmly and when least expected, he might take off, throwing her aside like a dirty clout. This, however, she would not permit. She would take advantage of his still being in love with her; she would show him the stuff Marialva was made of and would bring him to his knees. For this she counted on Bullfinch and his wild passion. For it is curious to note that in spite of all the commotion that had taken place on the day of Tibéria's anniversary, Marialva bore no grudge against Tibéria or Otália. Naturally, she wanted to show them, as well as the other women of the brothel and vicinity, her power over Martim, how she could make him cry and could laugh at him. The rage she felt was toward Martim, toward his laughter, to be more precise, at the way he had amused himself at her expense. Instead of immediately dropping that broomstick and coming back to her side, humble and contrite, explaining the unimportance of his having danced with another, he had stayed with the two of them, practically egging them on to fight, flattered in his vanity at being fought over with slaps and kicks on the shin. Ah, no, things would not remain like that. She would have her revenge. And quickly, the quicker the better, before the echoes of the set-to and celebration died away. They would all see Martim's humiliation, and her laughing in his face, making him the object of the jibes and derision of all. They would point him out, his airs and pretensions blasted for good.

Her plans, however, were seriously hampered because of an initial lack of collaboration on Bullfinch's part. Marialva had intended to throw her affair with the spieler in the corporal's face, to display Martim's horns in the market place. But to do this, it was necessary first of all to put the horns on his head, to become Bullfinch's mistress. This did not seem difficult to her. On the contrary, wasn't it his longing to sleep with her that was consuming Bullfinch? One word or gesture of hers would be enough to send him head over heels.

But things did not work out as she had thought. Although more impassioned and beside himself with every passing moment, Bullfinch possessed reserves of moral fortitude that were practically inexhaustible. To betray his friend was out of the question; he would die of love and desire, but he would not go to bed with the wife of his brother (in devotion).

It was two days after the events, when comments were still running high, that Martim, who apparently had resumed his quiet life of a home-loving husband, had to go out to get funds for them to live on. He had spent a lot on

Tibéria's celebration, a present for her anniversay, material for Marialva's dresses, slippers, stockings, bracelets, and earrings. The cashbox was empty; Martim put the deck of cards in his pocket and set out to look for players. Marialva quickly sent word to Bullfinch by the street Arab and got herself dolled up, with a fancy hair-do, perfumed, and wearing a dress that showed off her figure to best advantage. She went down along Unhão, to the deserted bridge, where she waited for him.

Bullfinch wasn't even working those days. He was so out of hand that he did not even look for work; he owed money in every tavern, and if he still got credit, it was only because they were sorry for him. They had never seen him so desperate before, poor Bullfinch, always in love and always thwarted. This time, however, the business seemed serious, for it was lasting longer than usual. Two, three days of rum guzzling had been enough to cure his previous passions. This one, however, outstripped all forecasts; he was even talking of committing suicide. The kid found him in the saloon, in the vicinity of the Market, sitting alone with a glass of rum.

When he reached Unhão, she was already there waiting for him, as melancholy as she was beautiful, sitting on the bridge, looking out at the sea, her eyes lost in space. Bullfinch sighed. No more unhappy man ever lived; no matter what happened to him during the rest of his life, no matter what misfortune, he would never be so marked down and pursued by bad luck as now. He loved and was loved—he could hardly believe he deserved so much—by that beauty of beauties, but, dear God, as faithful as she was beautiful, as decent as she was gentle. Linked, as she was, by bonds of gratitude to a man she did not love, she was nevertheless faithful to him, restraining her desire and passion, limiting it to a longing without hope, an unfulfilled desire, a platonic love. How could one be more unhappy? Impossible.

But he was to come away from their meeting even more unhappy and wretched. Pleased with himself, nevertheless, proud of having found the strength to resist when she, routed in battle, gave herself up, and Martim's head came within an ace of sprouting antlers. Bullfinch proved himself a worthy and upright friend.

For no sooner had he arrived and they exchanged their first emotion-filled words than she took his hands in hers and declared: "Beloved, I can bear no more. . . . No matter what happens, come what may, I want to be yours. . . . I know this is wrong, but what can I do?"

Bullfinch's eyes opened wide, he was not sure that he had heard right; he asked her to repeat what she had said, and she did so in a voice even more agitated, consumed as by an inner flame, on the point of throwing her arms around Bullfinch's neck there and then, and kissing him, that first kiss previously denied him.

Bullfinch hesitated. He so desired her, he dreamed of having her during those nights tormented by sleeplessness, at the tables in the tavern he saw her leaning on his arm, her head on his shoulder, and through the haze of rum she undressed herself for him, not one time but many, her alluring body covered with black beauty spots, her dewy belly and the rose with velvet petals. He loved her deeply, true, and had been suffering because of his love of her, but on the other hand, he was at peace despite his drama, for from the start Marialva had put up the barrier of the impossibility of that love's reaching fruition. In fact, at no moment was he obliged to choose between the love of Marialva and loyalty to Martim, a friend like a brother. And now here she was, without any forewarning, offering herself, prepared to do whatever he wanted and desired— go away with him for good or just sleep in his bed and then go back home.

Bullfinch was engulfed by his tragedy; he was a willow in the wind, a sail buffeted by the gale. Before him, Marialva, all that he aspired to in the world. But between them stood the figure of Martim. What was he to do? No, no, he could not raise the dagger of betrayal against his brother, and least of all, stab him in the back. He couldn't.

"No, no, we can't," he sobbed in despair. "No, it's impossible."

It was a heart-rending cry, a suicidal but irrevocable decision. He covered his face with his hands. He had just liquidated his life, wiped out every and all hope of happiness, but he had proved himself a true and loyal friend.

Marialva had not expected this; she had not come prepared for a refusal. She thought she would see him beside himself with joy, in a hurry to get her to his room in Pelourinho, in the attic of an old run-down mansion. She had even thought of ways to restrain his enthusiasm, yielding to him little by little on that first day of kisses, of embraces, inflaming his desire, arranging for another meeting when she would make him her lover and have her revenge on Martim. And what she had run into were Bullfinch's moral reserves, insurmountable.

No, Bullfinch explained to her, taking her hands in his, it could not be. There could be nothing between them; their love was one of sacrifice and renunciation. If they were to belong to one another someday, there would have to be no bond between her and Martim, no commitment of any sort. As she herself had said repeatedly, she was under obligations to Martim, she owed him gratitude. She had no right to lose her head as she was now doing. Neither she nor, much less, he. His friendship for Martim was of long standing, since when he, just a kid at the time, was begging alms in the streets, one of many street Arabs. Martim held an outstanding position in the group and extended his protecting hand over the newcomer, saving him from torment or abuse at the hands of the older boys. Later on came girls when they were initiated into the rites of manhood, and in the *candomblé* they discovered that they were both devotees of Oxalá, Martim of Oxalufa, old Oxalá, Bullfinch, of Oxuguian, young Oxalá. Together they carried out their *bori* on more than one occasion, the priestess pouring the blood of the sacrificial animals over their heads, the same blood purifying them both. On a certain occasion they had offered up a goat to the divinity, sharing expenses. Then how could he go to bed with Martim's wife, even though he was madly in love with her? No, Martim was a hallowed being as far as he was concerned, and he preferred to kill himself and kill Marialva.

This was in no wise part of Marialva's plan, to let herself be killed or commit suicide. She was smarting under the snubs she had received at Tibéria's party, but the idea of death was far from her mind. What she did want was to avenge herself on the corporal, to see him at her feet, humiliated, his reputation destroyed.

In the midst of that display of despair and tears, of vows of love and threats of death, in which Bullfinch intermingled passages he had learned by heart from *The Lover's Complete Handbook* with words of absolute sincerity, one phrase caught Marialva's attention and gave her the clue to the best solution from her point of view.

It was when she, attempting to raise his spirits and also because she was disgusted, wounded in her vanity, rejected for the first time by a man—a man to whom she had offered herself, she who was continually pursued by them —spat out her contempt: "You are a coward, you are afraid of Martim."

Bullfinch trembled. Fear? He was not afraid of anybody in the world, not even of Martim. He respected him, that he did, he was a friend of his, devoted to him. How could he then betray him, stab him in the back, deceive him on the sly? If at least he knew about it . . . frankly, straightforwardly . . .

If at least he knew about it . . . Marialva's voice once more became honeyed, she was again the impassioned, kind, and loyal Marialva of before: "And what if we told him about it? Suppose you went and said to him that we were in love and wanted to live together?"

That was a new idea. One could not say that it exactly swept him off his feet at first, but how could he refuse to do it? As for Marialva, she was wildly enthusiastic. It was exactly what she most wanted: Bullfinch telling Martim of their love and she witnessing the scene, Martim casting himself at her feet, perhaps throwing himself in a rage on Bullfinch, the two men fighting over her, capable of killing and dying for her. She would have had her revenge on Martim, and she could decide with which of the two she would live, and with which she would just sleep. Perhaps she would stay with Martim—she had already set up housekeeping with him—but she would two-time him with Bullfinch. Or she could stay with Bullfinch, inheriting the furniture and the house, and going to bed now and then with Corporal Martim. When all was said and done, he was a pleasant bedfellow and she didn't want to lose him either. That would be her day of glory, when Bullfinch crossed the threshold to deliver his official communiqué.

Bullfinch shook his head. No, it would not look well to go and tell Martim everything. What for? Had Marialva thought of what might happen? How much Martim would suffer? What folly he might commit? Marialva smiled, basking in the thought; it was her revenge, her day of glory, her triumph. She would not yield; Bullfinch had no way out. He would have to come before Martim and tell him everything, vie with him for his wife.

She ran her hands over Bullfinch's hair: "You did not understand anything of what I said when I came. You thought that what I wanted was to go to bed with you—to deceive Martim behind his back?"

"And wasn't that it?"

"Who do you think I am? Do you think me capable of such a thing? What I wanted was for you to go and talk with Martim. I am sure that he will understand. He will suffer a little, for he is crazy about me, but he may understand. And even if he doesn't like it, our obligation toward him will have been fulfilled, and we can go. Don't you think so?"

"What you mean is that if we tell him about it, even if he does not agree, we can go?"

"Naturally."

"He's never going to agree."

"Of course not. But we will have fulfilled our obligation toward him. If you are in doubt, ask Jesuíno. What you cannot do is betray him behind his back, nor I, either. So we'll go there and tell him. And then we can do as we like."

It all seemed clear to Bullfinch.

"I think you are right."

"Of course I am."

And for the first time she kissed him, a long kiss, one of the sort that only she knew how to give, with lips and tongue; he had to struggle to free himself.

"Not yet, only after we have talked with him."

"And when are you going to do it?"

But Bullfinch asked for time; he wanted to accustom himself to the idea. It was not as easy as it looked.

⊰ 15 ⊱

ON THE CONTRARY, IT WAS DAMNED DIFFICULT. The problem was hedged around with all sorts of complications. Bullfinch could not carry the weight of such worry alone, and decided to share it with his friends. In a voice tremulous with shame, with wild gestures, phrases memorized from books, he vomited the whole tale into the fraternal and curious ears of Jesuíno Crazy Cock. He also vomited up the rum and remnants of sausage that was all he had eaten that day. He was gaunt and pale, with circles under his eyes, his hair a disheveled mop. Later on, Negro Massu and Ipicilone were informed of the matter, and Wing-Foot, more or less. He could not understand all that confusion—was Bullfinch going to take Martim's girl away from him or wasn't he?—but he could not withhold his silent solidarity in such dire and dramatic moments.

There followed disturbing days of confabulations, prolonged examinations of the various angles of the situation, warnings, advice, plans, and the corresponding consumption of rum. It seemed like the meeting of an international assembly: they argued and argued in a debate that at times became heated, only to realize at the end of the night that the negotiations had made little progress. According to Jesuíno, the business called for tact and care, the counsel of men with long experience of life, and careful study, in view of its delicacy. What was at stake was the long-standing friendship of two comrades, two brothers-in-devotion, not to mention such lesser matters as honor, morality, and peril of life. And so the advice of certain venerable old men and of specialized technicians on certain points was sought. And the news was broadcast, as Marialva, laughing in her house, had wanted. She woke up in the night to laugh to herself.

Opinion was divided. Negro Massu found it all a mistake, one of those crazy projects of Bullfinch, whose head was always full of notions and got completely out of hand when it came to a woman. In his considered judgment, Bullfinch had only two paths open to him, and neither of them led past the corporal's house.

What were these two paths? they all wanted to know. Massu began with the most practical and prudent: for Bullfinch to clear out and disappear for a while in Alagoinhas or Sergipe. Sergipe was a land of good rum, where there was a future for an able spieler. Moreover, he, Massu, knew a fellow who was looking for a spieler to travel through the backlands advertising and selling a miracle-working cure he had invented. He was one of those persons who knew a lot about herbs, who had lived for a time with the Indians, had learned from them about native cures, and had discovered a sure-fire remedy for blennorrhagia made of the bark of a tree and the root of a wild plant. There wasn't a case of clap that could hold out against it.

He needed someone to sell the product in the backlands, at fairs and public gatherings. Bullfinch turned down the offer; in his long experience as a spieler he had always avoided selling those infallible cures. You invariably wound up in the cooler, with druggists and doctors sicking the police on you. But, answered Massu, that was in the capital, where the police received a pay-off from the druggists. For that reason his friend wanted to corner the market in the backlands. He could not expand his business in the capital, where he had even been threatened with jail. Just because he did not have an M.D. degree they would not approve his formula, and the doctors, envious of his knowledge and fearing his competition, had unanimously declared, after examining a bottle of Arise, Club (what a wham of a name!) that it was a case of criminal quackery.

What the medicine did, according to them, was to collect the gonoccoci and spread them through the blood stream, with unforeseeable future consequences. As for the author of the formula, he was a charlatan who was looking for a long jail term.

All calumny, envy, fear, for the remedy was really good; after three or four doses, there was not a case of gonorrhea that did not yield to it; the discharge and pain disappeared; and all for a ridiculously low price and without that torture of irrigations of permanganate. The worthy inventor of the formula, the sometime guest of the Indians, had tried out his remedy on more than one sufferer, with positive results in every case. True, the doctors attributed the fact that Arlindo Pretty Boy was bedridden at the age of twenty-eight to these experiments. He had caught a terrible case of clap; he had been treated by various doctors without getting better. He went through hell when he had to pass water, not to mention the foul smell. Finally, on the advice of his friends, he tried Arise, Club and it did the trick: before finishing the second bottle, he was a new man. True, a few months later he was in bed, paralyzed as though all his nerves and muscles were tied up in knots. But why connect this severe rheumatism of Arlindo Pretty Boy (so called because of his former good looks, which were no longer what they had been) with Mr. Osório Redondo's remedy? It was nothing but the ill will of the doctors. However, because of this infamous persecution, Osório could not sell his beneficent formula in the capital, and he had to make do with the backlands, where he traveled from fair to fair bringing health to the yokels. But as the backlands were vast, he was looking for someone who, in return for a good commission, was willing to help him in his crusade against venereal diseases. If Bullfinch so desired, Massu would take him to meet Mr. Osório, who lived over Corta Braço way and had in his house some special kinds of rum treated with herbs that only the Indians knew, and which left a man more spirited than a stallion or an alley cat when the moon is full. He had a large clientele of old men.

Bullfinch refused the tempting offer; he did not want to earn his living in the backlands or break off with Marialva.

Jesuíno Crazy Cock, however, became keenly interested in such a worthy citizen as Mr. Osório, and held a visit to his house to be in order; they should show their solidarity with this persecuted philanthropist. Jesuíno himself knew something about herbs and many of the secrets of plants, being a devotee of Ossani.

Bullfinch inquired about the second path: perhaps that would be more advisable. Negro Massu did not need to be coaxed. Now, if Bullfinch did not feel up to breaking off with the dame and going out into the world curing the unfortunate sufferers from one of life's plagues, then there was only one thing left for him to do. What was that? Grab the trollop some moonless night, disappear with her, hide away where Martim could not find him, and never come back. Go way off into the backlands, get lost somewhere in the Northeast, disappear on the roads of Piauí or Maranhão, places Massu had heard of, faraway countries at the end of the world. Because, let Bullfinch never doubt it for a minute, Martim would turn into a raging beast when he came home and did not find the beauty with the black mole on her shoulder, his honorable spouse. And if he ever got hold of Bullfinch, her seducer, not all the Arise, Club in the world would do any good.

These were the two suggestions of Negro Massu. He saw no other course, for that idea of Marialva and Bullfinch's going before Martim to tell him their shameless plan, to laugh in his face, give him a certificate of cuckoldry, as for that . . .

Bullfinch got mad and yelled excitedly that there was no shamelessness of any sort nor any certificate of cuckoldry. Massu was insulting a pure platonic love and offending Bullfinch's dignity. They had behaved, he and Marialva, with the greatest loyalty toward the corporal. For the moment, the whole thing had not gone beyond lyrical conversations, plans and dreams, without a single caress that was out of bounds. And why did they want to go to Martim if it was not to continue along these lines of absolute loyalty? That was why they did not sneak off in the dead of night like fugitives, so as not to stab a friend in the back. They wanted to go to him, tell him how they had been overwhelmed by love, by an uncontrollable passion. Uncontrollable, and yet they had controlled it because of their loyalty to friendship and gratitude, because of their loyalty to Martim, and had kept it on a plane of pure platonism. And there they were to tell him, loyally and honorably, that they could not live without one another, and for that reason they were asking him to scram, to leave Marialva's house and Marialva herself.

Marialva's house? Ipicilone was taken aback at this rapid and definitive occupation of the house with the corresponding furnishings of sitting room and bedroom, from bed to coffeepot, from long mirror to cups. Wouldn't that all be Martim's, bought with his money earned by the sweat of his brow and at the risk of losing his freedom because of crooked card games? Not satisfied with the suffering he would cause his friend by robbing him of his wife, did Bullfinch also want to latch on to his furniture and his house? Who ever heard of such a thing?

Bullfinch defended himself: as far as he was concerned, he did not want anything. Having Marialva, he had all the riches of the world; he asked nothing more. As for the house and the furnishings, however, if they thought the matter over carefully, they would see that the question of ownership was not quite so clear. When in his whole life had Martim had a house, a known address? At times, true, he rented a room in which to hang his clothes and lay chicks. But could these temporary quarters properly be called a home, when he left them as soon as he became infatuated with some girl in a brothel and took to sleeping in her room, to whose closet he transferred his white suits? How many times had Martim brought his traps to Bullfinch's room in Pelourinho, or to Jesuíno's, in Tabuão, or to the remote shack where Massu lived with his grandmother, or even to the shanty Wing-Foot had put up on the beach, because he had no place to put them when he broke off with his passing fancy? He did not take them to Ipicilone's house because that one never had even a rented room, much less a shack or shanty. He lived any old way, sleeping in the taverns or in Alonso's store, on the counter or turning a sack of dried beef into an odoriferous mattress.

If at the moment Martim enjoyed the luxury of a house and furniture, it was thanks to Marialva. She had demanded a house, decent furniture, and the corporal, to win her (for she had done everything not to go with him, had resisted as long as she could, and had acquiesced only out of gratitude, as they all should know in order to judge her fairly) had given her everything and would have given her more if she had been a gold digger, a self-seeker. For her and not for himself Martim had rented the house in Vila América, so it was morally hers. Could they imagine Martim living alone in a house? As for the furniture, the matter was even more crystal clear. He had bought it for Marialva, to make her comfortable, to insure her affection. They were Marialva's belongings, in addition to being the only thing the poor creature owned aside from her clothes and some necklaces and earrings which were worth very little. Who had given her those necklaces and earrings, clothes and shoes, if not Martim? Moreover, was Martim perchance going to take her shoes and dresses, leaving her naked in the street because she did not want to live with him any longer? Of course not. Why, then, would he want to hang onto the furniture when the same thing held true of it as of the clothes? And the house, too. Bullfinch trusted Martim: he would not stoop to such petty vengeance; he was generous of heart; Bullfinch knew of nobody so open-handed and disinterested as the corporal.

Ipicilone was not convinced by this subtle argument, and as in the meanwhile the learned gathering had been joined by gay Carnation-in-his-Buttonhole, who was a recognized authority in matter of other people's property and rentals, his opinion was requested, and he found against Bullfinch. The master of a house, its true proprietor, was the person who had rented it, the one who was responsible for the rent even if he did not pay it on time. Wasn't it Martim who had taken the house, signed the paper, or at least given his word to pay the rent? In that case, the house was his; Marialva was there as a boarder, a guest, to enhance the atmosphere. So true was this that he, Carnation-in-his-Buttonhole, had not paid the rent of the house where he lived for more than six months, and even so, the Spaniard who owned the dump could not evict him, even though he had hired a lawyer. What better proof could there be? As for the furniture and other things, it was even clearer that they belonged to Martim, who had bought and paid for them. Bullfinch, not content with wrecking his friend's life, wanted to rob him of his house and furniture in the bargain. Carnation-in-his-Buttonhole was amazed. It was a wonder Bullfinch didn't demand the corporal's fine clothing, his tight-fitting white pants and long coats, the striped shirts with attached collar, the pointed shoes. . . .

Bullfinch snorted. They did not understand. If Martim wanted to, he could keep the house and the furniture, even the girl's clothes and trinkets. The only thing he wanted and laid claim to was Marialva herself. They loved one another; they could not live apart or go on as they had up to now, stifling in their suffering breasts their wild desire, bereft of affection, of the simplest caress, keeping away from one another so as not to fall into temptation when they strolled along the waterfront discussing their problem, the width of the sidewalk between them.

"Don't give me that stuff! You were walking hand in hand with her; people saw you." Jesuíno, who had taken no part in the discussion up to then, cut him short.

But before he could continue, he had to listen to Bullfinch's explanations. They might have held hands once in a blue moon, when the outlook seemed grimmest, when they found themselves hemmed in by impossibility, covered by the "black clouds of the gale of their existence" (a phrase from *The Lover's Complete Handbook* which Bullfinch aptly inserted in his defense speech). With their heads burning with fever, their hearts thudding, it was possible that they had joined hands the better to bear their suffering, their star-crossed love, "this cursed love that battens in my tempest-torn breast. . . ." Incidentally, did any of them know what in the devil "tempest" meant? It was a tricky word used frequently in *The Lover's Complete Handbook;* perhaps Jesuíno or Ipicilone knew what it meant.

"It means 'storm,' you dope," Jesuíno explained, demanding at the same time further details: "Now you tell me in all sincerity if you didn't go on from holding hands, if you didn't go farther. . . ."

Bullfinch would have liked to deny the kisses, that first one on the ruins of Unhão bridge when they had decided to talk to Martim. And the others which followed, that same day and the next week while they were discussing the details of the visit to the corporal. Marialva put forward two considerations with regard to the kisses. First, weren't they going to live together after they told Martim everything? Then what difference did a kiss make? It was nothing serious; it was not like going to bed together: an explanation which absolved them from sin and remorse. On the other hand—and there was a certain contradiction in this—she fretted after the kisses, using them as an argument for hastening the decisive step, the interview with the corporal. Before the kiss, she had adduced its lack of importance. Afterwards, she had found it to be the very road to perdition. In this backing and filling, the kisses grew in number and ardor, some leaving them breathless, others practically tearing away pieces of lip, as prolonged as life and death, sucking, biting kisses which descended dangerously down Marialva's shoulder, and rose along the curve of her breast.

They could not delay the interview, otherwise they would be stabbing Martim in the back. Marialva trembled in his arms; if Bullfinch was truly a friend of his friend, he ought to arrange for the visit to the corporal as soon as he could. Clinging to Bullfinch, kissing him, biting him, she sighed with remorse, she owed Martim gratitude, how could she be doing that? It was a wild love that was dragging her down the path of dishonor. . . . Bullfinch must make haste before the irremediable happened.

Bullfinch would have preferred not to talk about the kisses, or at least to omit certain details, but he knew it would do no good to lie to Jesuíno. Crazy Cock had the reputation of being clairvoyant, one who could read people's eyes and thoughts, practically a *babalaô*. It was useless to try to hide the truth from him. He would find it out.

"Well . . . a kiss or two is nothing serious."

"A kiss? Where? On the forehead, the hand, the face, the mouth?"

To the vast entertainment of the others, Jesuíno made a detailed interrogatory, cross-questioning Bullfinch, making him regurgitate every kiss, as well as the suckings and bitings, and the path along the shoulder with the pretext of the beauty spot, skirting the mounds of the breast.

"It is really best for you to go and talk with Martim quickly before this winds up badly. If you went and talked with him, you would be acting as you should, like a decent person. Then if he gets mad, he'll be the one who's in the wrong."

Ipicilone found the undertaking dangerous, for it seemed to him that nobody could tell what the corporal's reaction might be. Suppose he lost his head and killed Marialva and Bullfinch? The latter shrugged his shoulders, heroic and resigned; life without Marialva meant nothing to him. If the corporal killed him, he was within his rights; he had raised his eyes to the wife of a friend; he loyally acknowledged this.

"Only the eyes? And what about the kissing and the biting?"

It was this, the kisses, that Bullfinch had in mind when he spoke of raising his eyes to the forbidden fruit of a friend's wife. He did not accuse himself of other things, for other things he was not to blame. If he deserved to die, it was because of those few kisses, but the taste of Marialva's mouth made death worthwhile.

It was only at this point that Wing-Foot really became interested in that whole business. Taste? What taste? What was the taste of that woman's mouth? He, Wing-Foot, had once known a woman, a long time ago, whose kisses tasted like shrimp stew, really wonderful. He had made a big play for her, but she had disappeared and he had never again found the same taste in another's mouth. What was the taste of Marialva's kisses?

Bullfinch did not answer him, for he was interested in hearing Jesuíno's opinion. Crazy Cock paused to think; the light fell upon his hair; they were all hanging on his words. He did not believe that Martim would start shooting, and attack Bullfinch. Why should he do this when his friend had behaved decently, loyal to the sacred bonds of friendship? The interview might be painful, true. If the corporal was so much in love with that woman, devoted to the point of not being able to live without her, the news was going to be a shock to him, a terrible shock; it might even unhinge his mind. And if that happened, then nobody could rightly say what he might do.

Massu, thinking of the corporal's suffering and rum, suggested that they all go with Bullfinch when the time came, and in that way they could witness the scene and prevent any desperate act on Martim's part—a proposal which aroused great enthusiasm among all present, with the exception of Jesuíno, who opposed it firmly and for good reasons. That was a delicate matter involving the honor of the actors, and nobody should mix in it except those having leading roles. They should not go with Bullfinch. At most, they might accompany him to the foot of the hill and stay in the tavern there at the bottom, having a beer. In that way, when Martim left his house, bowed down and grief-stricken, they could lend him their moral support, sharing his suffering. Or they could run toward the house if they heard any noise indicating violence or despair.

All agreed, and Bullfinch set the date for the next morning, before lunch, when Martim was sure to be home. Jesuíno pointed out the need for haste, that any delay might be fatal. How long would Bullfinch be able to hold out against Marialva's kisses? He was on the brink of the abyss, and at any moment he could slip over into the depths.

That was the same thing Marialva had said over and over again when they embraced and kissed on the deserted bridge, she and Bullfinch. That afternoon she did not have to. Bullfinch arrived all excited, informing her of the decision he had taken and agreeing with her on the hour: ten in the morning. As a rule, at that time Martim devoted himself to his guitar after taking care of the birds.

Bullfinch's face had a dramatic air: the next day he was going to drive a dagger into the bosom of his best friend. If Martim killed him, he could not complain. Perhaps it would even be better. If Martim killed him and her, the two lovers (platonic), they would lie together in the morgue, and they would be carried together by their friends to the grave. He saw himself dead, a flower on his breast, and Marialva beside him, her hair loose, her throat cut.

-->{ 16 }<--

OR HIMSELF STRETCHED COLD AND BLOOD-STAINED, and Marialva with a knife in her breast, or alive and having to witness Martim's despair. There were moments when he even preferred the first hypothesis because of the horror the second aroused in him, the sight of a man as virile as Martim humbled, destroyed for good. Because without Marialva life would be sad and meaningless.

Bullfinch imagined the scene. He would arrive, look at his friend, tell him all. No, not all. He would not mention the kisses, the bites, the hand working down from the neck to the delights of the breasts. What he would do would be to tell him of that mad, doomed love, instantaneous, love at first sight, and the terrible suffering, the relentless fight to suppress it and tear it from their hearts. They had kept it on a plane of pure friendship, like brother and sister. But who is there that can gainsay love "when two hearts intone in unison the song of sacred nuptials" and "neither the tempest gales nor threats of death can separate them," as *The Lovers' Complete Handbook* so rightly put it? They had not been able to quell their increasingly violent emotions, yet by sheer strength of will they had managed during all this time to respect Martim's honor, keeping it immaculate and intact, despite the tremendous effort it cost the two lovers. Marialva did it out of gratitude, not to hurt Martim, who was so crazy about her and devoted to her;

136

Bullfinch, out of friendship, loyalty to a brother-in-devotion, a tie as sacred as though he were a blood brother. Intact, immaculate, unpolluted, was Martim's honor, not the smallest blot (oh, those kisses, he must not make any mention of them, nor of holding hands), yet love went on devouring them like the flames of hell. They would not be able to endure that equivocal, terrible situation much longer, he and Marialva. And that was why he was there before Martim, solemn and grave, to leave the decision in his hands, the fate of the three of them. Without Marialva he could not live, he preferred death. He knew how painful this would be for Martim, however . . .

He saw his friend suffering before his eyes. Humiliated in his masculine vanity, his fame of lady-killer—hadn't a newspaper once referred to him as a "seducer" and the police been after him? Supplanted by Bullfinch, the luckless Bullfinch, so often abandoned, flouted by sweethearts, fiancées, mistresses. Wounded in his vanity . . . But that was as nothing compared with the deeper sorrow, that of losing Marialva. Because of her the corporal had changed his way of life. The inveterate Bohemian, the unregenerate night-owl, the loafer without fixed abode or schedule, had become transformed into a law-abiding, orderly citizen, a model husband, home-loving, attentive, thoughtful, tender. Metamorphosed from a tramp into a gentleman, almost a swell. His home was the envy of all his friends. And there was Bullfinch, his brother-in-devotion, his intimate friend, prepared to destroy all that happiness, rob him of his wife, take over his brother's home like an enemy force occupying the lands and cities of an invaded country, ravishing wives, sweethearts, and sisters, stealing the most valued possessions, destroying lives. A sinister task, a tragic love!

Bullfinch walked aimlessly through the streets, chewing the bitter cud of these horrors, touched and somewhat heroic. Heroic because the affair was not devoid of danger. There was the possibility of death, with him stretched out at Marialva's side. And then Martim bowed down under this weight for the rest of his life. Bullfinch felt like crying at the thought of his own fate and that of Martim. At times he even forgot Marialva. That night he was seen in a saloon memorizing phrases and paragraphs from *The Lov-*

er's Complete Handbook, the strongest, the most moving.

The friends, too, were getting ready for the events of the following day, which called for strength of soul. Nothing better to temper one's mettle and establish one's emotional equilibrium than a few well-measured and -weighed glasses of rum imbibed the night before. This they did in Isidro de Batualê's saloon, where Bullfinch was pointed out by the curious. For, nobody knew how, the news had trickled through the closed circle of friends and was circulating in various sectors. Certain things do not need to be told or revealed; they are guessed at, picked up by people's sixth sense, suddenly and without explanation. This was what happened with Bullfinch's planned visit to Martim. Bets were even laid on how the corporal would react. Most of the wagers backed the corporal to give Bullfinch a beating, with a few whacks left over for the quasi-unfaithful spouse.

When he heard how the smart money was going, Bullfinch shivered; the prospect of a beating was neither pleasant nor elevating. It lacked the heroism of death, it was low and indecent. But his mind was made up. He would not turn back.

Marialva, bathed in a glow of happiness, sang as she tidied the house, smiling, cheerful, the disagreeable incident at Tibéria's house a few days before completely forgotten—so it seemed. Martim, lolling in the rocking chair, was drawing up a complicated list of the numbers he planned to play, interrupting this delicate intellectual operation to watch her come and go with girlish verve, laughing to herself in the corners.

Laughing to herself, savoring beforehand the morning's emotions, when Bullfinch would come into the room and she would see the two men face to face, standing up to each other, armed with hate, capable of everything from aggression to assassination, and all because of her. The two friends whose intimacy went back to their vagabond boyhood as street urchins, the two brothers-in-devotion to their patron Oxalá, who had carried out their *bori* together, who had poured the blood of cocks and goats upon their heads, swearing loyalty to one another, and now, for love of her, were facing one another like walls of hatred, their eyes calling for death and blood. Perhaps it wouldn't go that far, maybe they would just roll to the floor in a fight, in which case the corporal would have the advantage, for he was a famous *capoeira* fighter. Bullfinch was no match for him. Martim would have the physical advantage, but he would be left with a thorn piercing his heart because Marialva had turned her eyes on the spieler, had exchanged words of love with him, had addled his brain to the point where he was willing to confront Martim.

She saw the corporal humiliated before her, begging her to stay, dragging himself at her feet. The victor in the fight, but wounded for life, never to be the same Martim again.

Marialva could then decide as seemed best to her. She could stay with Martim, a Martim bowed once and for all to her will, the while she met Bullfinch from time to time to cure his wounds with the balm of her promises and her kisses and—who knows? Or she could share bed and board with Bullfinch, ideal as a husband, so docile, so romantic, yet sleeping with Martim now and then. He was nice to sleep with, she could not deny that. Anyway, the decision would be hers and she would make it within the hour, on the inspiration of the moment, depending on how the interview went. Marialva laughed as she moved about the house, laughed so much and with such satisfaction, that Martim wanted to know the reason for it: "What's got into you?"

She came over and sat down at his feet, taking his hands in hers, and turning on him those familiar eyes of entreaty and fear, the eyes of a victim. Begging, pleading for affection. Mechanically Martim ran his hand over Marialva's hair. What was she up to? When that expression came into her eyes, when she garbed herself in humility and sweetness, she had something up her sleeve, some plan she was concocting. Martim pondered that woman he had met in Cachoeira on a day of desperate loneliness, when a man is fearful of dying alone like a dog. Since then he had followed her uphill and down dale, and his whole life had changed. If anyone had told him this would happen, he would not have believed it.

"You love your sweetie pie, black man?"

Martim caressed her hair still more, as though in answer to her question. But his thoughts were far away and he was

seeing the youthful face of Otália. She was cute, that girl.
. . . He shook his head, withdrew his hand from Marialva's
hair, longing to free himself from all of them, from all
women. It was not possible for one man alone to sleep with
all the women in the world, but he should try, according to
the lore of the old sailors on the waterfront. Martim did his
best, but it was impossible, there were too many of them,
no man had the time and strength for an enterprise of such
dimensions. He wanted to go back to the list of numbers he
planned to play that morning, a task that called for
thought and deliberation, difficult calculations and specialized knowledge, the ability to interpret dreams. But Marialva was distracting his attention, demanding affection,
proofs of love. Martim yawned; this was not the time; he
was torn between the peacock and the elephant; he had
dreamed of Wing-Foot riding on a cloud of peacock feathers. "Not now."

Marialva got up quickly and went off with a swish of
skirt and petticoat. Tomorrow he would see, tomorrow he
would pay dearly for the lack of attention bestowed on her
today, tomorrow morning, around ten o'clock.

And what if Bullfinch didn't come? Wouldn't it be a
good idea to send the street urchin with a message? But
why would he fail to come? He was crazy about her,
crawled at her feet. Just as Martim would when Bullfinch
showed up and told him everything. Marialva could see
them, the two facing one another like mortal enemies, the
two bosom friends, the brothers-in-devotion. Clutching the
daggers of desire, of jealousy, of hatred, prepared to do
battle for love of Marialva, without whom they could not
live, without whom, apart from whom, they did not want
to live.

17

THE FRIENDS STAYED BELOW, at the foot of the hill, in the tavern. The group had grown with the presence of certain gate-crashers, people who had put money in the kitty of the bets, which had run amazingly high on the preceding night. From there, from the tavern, in spite of the hill which separated them from Martim's house, they could, after a fashion, follow what was taking place. They would hear any outcry, their ears alert to the sound of fighting or the report of a revolver, alterations in the tranquil rhythm of the corporal's conjugal life. They were excited, and some of them patted Bullfinch's back and shoulders to give him courage. Especially those who had laid money on the violent reaction of the corporal and foresaw at the very least a beating, perhaps a few stabs in the spieler's belly. In the tavern they ordered a first round to buck them up. They offered Bullfinch a drink before he started up the slope, but he refused. He had drunk too much the night before, he had a bad taste in his mouth, his tongue was furry, and his head was heavy, just when he most needed a cool head and a nimble tongue. Whereupon they raised their glasses and drank to him in a silent but meaningful toast. He took a long look at his friends, one by one, touched and grave. He pressed Jesuíno's hand and started up the hillside. All those present stood solemn and moved, too, clearly aware of the fact that they were living a historic moment. Bullfinch disappeared around the curve of the muddy slope. The acacias were being whipped by the wind, carpeting the path with their yellow corollas.

Bullfinch was dressed as befitted the occasion. He had laid aside his work clothes, the frayed cutaway and striped pants, the old starched bosom shirt, the chalk and grease paint. He had put on his good clothes, necktie and jacket, had shaved, and he looked gaunt, his face pale and with deep circles under the eyes. He ascended the hill with measured tread, his gaze melancholy, his face solemn. Moreover, a certain solemnity encompassed his whole being, a solemnity that verged on the lugubrious, gave a funereal air to that ascent of the hillside. Bullfinch had prepared himself in this fashion, dressing as he did only on rare and solemn occasions, so that from the minute he came in, Martim would realize that there was something exceptional about the visit, how serious it was. That was why, at the point where the path made a right-angled turn and Martim's shack came into view, Bullfinch stopped to arrange his clothes and give even greater solemnity to his gait. At the door, Marialva was waiting for him impatiently; the clocks had just struck ten. She beckoned to Bullfinch to urge him on, but he continued at the same slow pace. It was not the moment for haste, for flippant eagerness. He was about to shatter the life of a friend, and the spieler's heart was bleeding. Might it not have been better to accept and follow the advice of Negro Massu, pick up the flasks of the wonder-working cure for blennorraghia, and set out for Sergipe to mourn the absence of his beloved? The minute he came in through the door, Martim would realize the dire nature of the visit as soon as he took one look at Bullfinch's dramatic air.

But when he reached the threshold of his friend's house, which he was about to cross, sly and dissolute, worse than a thief or a murderer, leaving in his wake inconsolable sadness and desolation, he heard Marialva hissing recriminations between her teeth: "I thought you were never coming, that you had got cold feet...."

This was a flagrant injustice for he was there right on the dot, at ten o'clock, as they had agreed. Never in his whole life of obligations assumed and carried out had he been so punctual. His friends, supporting him in that tragic moment of decision (and also interested in the outcome of their bets), had taken it upon themselves to see that he got up and had awakened him way ahead of time.

Marialva's face was flushed, her eyes glittered restlessly, giving off a strange light, and everything about her was different, as though she were hovering in the air, as beautiful as a fairy, but with a certain stamp of cruelty about her beauty, a Satanic expression due perhaps to her fancy hair-do, with two rolls that looked like devil's horns. Bullfinch had never seen her like that, she seemed another woman, he did not recognize her as that sweet Marialva of his, swooning with love.

"Come on, he's in the living room." And she walked quickly ahead of him, announcing: "Darling, here is Bullfinch who wants to talk to you."

"Why the devil doesn't he come in?" Martim's voice answered, a little blurred as though he were talking with his mouth full.

It was necessary, Bullfinch reassured himself, to reveal to Martim by his first words and gestures the gravity of the visit, the fact that it was something out of the ordinary. In view of this he asked before entering the room: "By your leave ..."

No friend had ever asked leave to enter the corporal's house. Martim therefore must surely realize the tragic nature of the business in hand as soon as Bullfinch came in stiff-gaited and then stopped even stiffer, pale, almost as though the blood had drained out of him. But to the disappointment and despair of the impassioned spieler, the corporal noticed nothing, remarked nothing, completely absorbed in the contemplation of a honeyed, yellow ripe jackfruit on the table. He had just cut it and the pulp exhaled an aroma, the juice running out on a piece of newspaper spread over the table, and the sight of the fruit aroused greediness and desire. Martim did not even look around. All Bullfinch's effort to maintain his difficult pose was lost. Moreover, the perfume of the jackfruit penetrated his nostrils, reaching his stomach. Bullfinch had not tasted a morsel of food that morning of betrayal and death.

Martim's fraternal voice enveloped his friend: "Sit down, brother, and have some jackfruit. It's delicious."

Bullfinch came over at the same measured gait, his face funereal, his bearing emphatic, almost majestic. Marialva leaned against the door of the room, at a vantage point from which she could follow every detail of the scene about to unfold. Martim munched a bit of the jackfruit, the scent filled the room, who could resist that odor? Bullfinch resisted it intrepidly. Martim turned toward him, surprised by his gravity: "Has anything happened?"

"No, nothing, I just wanted to talk to you. To clear up a matter . . ."

"Well, sit down and talk, and if it is in my power, it will be done."

"It's a serious business, so it's better to wait until you get through."

Martim gave his friend an appraising look: "You look as though you had swallowed a broomstick. But you're right, it's better for us to finish up the jackfruit and then talk. Sit down and pitch in."

The juice of the fruit dripped between the corporal's fingers, the fragrant pulp the color of gold. Bullfinch had eaten nothing that morning; it was no time to be eating, but to cry and to screw up his courage. He had not been hungry; there was a lump in his throat. But now it was past ten, his friends had awakened him very early, way ahead of time. His stomach felt empty, and a sudden hunger came over him, asking, demanding, that he accept the repeated invitation.

"Come on, fellow, what are you waiting for?"

The jackfruit became irresistible; it was Bullfinch's favorite fruit, and the sight of the juice running down Martim's fingers and lips, and the air heavy with that intoxicating perfume . . . what difference did a few minutes sooner or later make? Bullfinch took off his coat, loosened his tie, for it is impossible to eat jackfruit all dressed up. He sat down, put in his fingers, drew out a section, put it in his mouth, and spat out the seed: "Swell!"

"First-class," Martim agreed. "It's from a jack tree nearby that's absolutely loaded."

The dialogue was interrupted by the violent slamming of the door to the room. This was Marialva's way of attracting the attention of the two friends. Her eyes were blazing and the rolls of her hair looked more than ever like the horns of the devil.

"Didn't you tell me you had something important to talk over with Martim?" she asked Bullfinch in a harsh voice. She was furious; she could not wait for their conversation to begin. Was this, then, that love of Bullfinch's, so vaunted, so mad, so boundless? Unable to resist the temptation of a ripe jackfruit!

"When I finish, I'll talk. In a little while."

"There's a time and a place for everything," Martim opined.

With a brusque gesture, Marialva angrily entered the room. "I can't stand jackfruit. I like only apples or pears."

"You don't say so!"

Bullfinch licked his fingers. Jackfruit is a good fruit, especially in the morning on an empty stomach. How was it possible not to like jackfruit and be crazy about pears and apples, insipid fruits? What taste was there to an apple? Even a sweet potato has a better flavor, not so flat. Having thus voiced his opinion, Martim felt satisfied and wiped his fingers on the pieces of newspaper. Bullfinch helped himself to a couple more sections and laughed with satisfaction. A swell fruit, the jack, and this one was out of this world. Martim picked his teeth with a matchstick, and said: "Now what's this business of yours?"

Bullfinch had almost forgotten the reason and the solemnity of his visit; the jackfruit had left him at peace with life, ready for a good chat, a detailed discussion of the most varied topics, as always happened when those two friends got together. Martim was pushing him once more toward that tunnel without light or air, and he had to traverse it. He got up.

Marialva had appeared again in the door of the room, her eyes shining, her nostrils dilated, a race horse ready to take off, just waiting for the signal. Bullfinch knotted his tie, put on his coat and his solemn expression, that funereal air it was now harder for him to assume. His stomach was no longer empty; instead of that bitter taste in his mouth it was now perfumed with jackfruit, and the ideas of suicide and death were far removed. Nevertheless, he achieved a fairly good result, so much so that Martim, as he turned

his rocking chair the better to hear him, was surprised by
his expression and behavior: "You look like you was at a
wake."

Bullfinch stretched out his arm in an oratorical gesture
and spoke in a choked voice. Standing there in that pose,
he looked exactly like one of those statues of important
personages set up in public squares for the admiration of
their fellow countrymen. Martim was so intrigued by Bullfinch's gestures and attitude that he hardly took in the first
words of his rhetorical discourse.

Martim must try to understand—Bullfinch orated—it
was difficult, without doubt, but there was no choice. He
unwound the speech he had worked out beforehand with
the help of *The Lover's Complete Handbook* and Jesuíno
Crazy Cock. There might exist a friend as loyal as he, but
none more so. Loyal, dying all the while for love of Marialva, that pure, saintly woman, that "chaste and immaculate matron," a more loyal spouse did not exist. Theirs
were two lives caught up in the juggernaut of destiny,
marked down by adverse fate, ill fortune not to be con-
jured away, hopelessly jinxed. Playthings of destiny, toys
of fate.

Standing in the doorway, Marialva could not control
herself. It was hard in that glorious moment to play the
part of the poor victim, the persecuted damsel. An aura of
triumph haloed her face. Her eyes went from Bullfinch to
Martim, she was getting ready to trample the two of them
under foot, waiting to be contended for by steel and fire.

Martim did his best to understand the complicated explanation of his friend, bristling with long words, the result
of Bullfinch's mania for buying and reading pamphlets and
books. He frowned with the effort. Desperation, Marialva
imagined. Horror at the betrayal of a friend, thought Bullfinch. But the truth was that it was nothing but the effort
to follow that farrago of words, embellished with terms
from a sermon or a dictionary. There was the real reason
for Bullfinch's lack of luck where women were concerned;
it was all that book talk; there wasn't a chick who could
take it. However, thanks to this supreme effort, Martim
began to get the drift of it, catching a word here, another
there, at times a whole phrase, and all the while taking in

out of the corner of his eye the act Marialva was putting
on in the doorway, with that sublime air reflected in her
face. He realized the why and wherefore of Bullfinch's
attire and melancholy: apparently the poor dope was infatuated with Marialva, crazy about her. Could it be possible, my Lord of Bonfim, Oxalá, my father (*Exê ê ê
Babá*)? Could it be possible? And she, too . . . Would it be
to this that Bullfinch was referring with those high-flown
allusions to twin souls, platonic relationship, sundered
lives? He began to understand: Bullfinch was crazy about
Marialva, but restraining himself because of his friend, not
to put horns on him, respecting the honorable head of his
friend. Top notch, that Bullfinch.

The best thing, however, was to clear it up at once. He
interrupted the speech at a particularly moving passage,
and asked, raising a suspicious hand to his smooth head:
"Have you been two-timing me with her?"

Bullfinch shuddered. All in vain had he poured out his
talent and his erudition. He had not been understood;
Martim had not recognized the purity of his intentions. He
answered in a way that left no room for doubt: "No! What
have I been telling you from the start?" Then he added, to
keep the record straight: "I didn't, but I longed for her."

"So you longed for her? And she for you, too?"

Bullfinch picked up his cue and resumed his speech; he
was not going to give it up for that unseemly and unforeseen dialogue. Yes, he was reciprocated, but she, an illustrious matron, was the first to raise the barrier of impossibility. . . .

Corporal Martim smiled, but he was touched. Such loyalty on the part of Bullfinch made his eyes smart, his heart
melt. He knew how much Bullfinch suffered when he fell
in love, and now, when it involved Martim, he must be
suffering like a mangy dog just to be loyal to his brother-in-
devotion. Such dedication called for payment in the same
coin, and he, Corporal Martim, a man of breeding and
honor, could not fall short in devotion, in proofs of friendship. They were brothers-in-devotion, as Bullfinch had
pointed out, they had made their *bori* more than once
together; for that reason he was loyal to him; he suffered
rather than betray him, suffered like a mad dog, suffered

the pangs of hell. He deserved a reward, Martim would not be outstripped in this contest of friendship, menaced but victorious. "You really like her? Honestly?"

In the solemn and sonorous silence, as Marialva held her breath, for the hour of victory had arrived for her, Bullfinch lowered his head, and after a long moment of hesitation, reaffirmed his love.

Martim looked toward the door. Marialva seemed to grow in stature, radiant, a princess at whose feet men crawled, offering up their maddened hearts, a beauty without peer, laying the strongest males in the dust, a fatal woman never to be forgotten. Ready to answer, cruel and cunning, Martim's inevitable questions.

The corporal, however, asked her nothing. He merely looked her over with a cold eye. A fatal and definitive woman, definitively fatal, born to trample men down, drag them in her train, that was Marialva, beautiful with that black beauty mark on her shoulder. Fatal, who could resist her fascination? At times, a little tiresome. Even very tiresome. Bullfinch was welcome to her; Martim felt as generous and noble as a knight of old. The kindliest feelings swelled his breast, somewhat oppressed by all the jackfruit he had consumed.

His voice echoed amid the solemn silence and the wafted breeze: "Well, my brother, I understand everything. Your longing and suffering. It is a fine thing to see; you are truly a brother. And I say to you, the one who deserves her is you, and you may take her. She is yours." And turning toward the door of the room: "Marialva, gather up your belongings, for you are going with Bullfinch." And smiling at his friend: "You are going to take her with you right away; it wouldn't look good for you to leave your woman here in my house with the reputation I've got. . . ."

Bullfinch's jaw dropped, and he stood there slackmouthed, totally bewildered. He had expected anything: screams, curses, despair, knife poised, revolver—who knows?—physical redress, tears, horror, suicide, murder, a tragedy with headlines in the newspapers, anything but that, that wholly unexpected solution. When he finally managed to speak, he sounded as though he were drunk: "Take her? Right away? And what for?"

Marialva was pale, motionless in the doorway.

"Right away, for as of now, she is yours. And it doesn't look good . . ."

But Bullfinch still tried to bring him to his senses: "You're going to suffer a lot, too much, all alone. . . . I prefer . . ."

Marialva, teeth clenched, eyes popping out of her head. Martim, generous and logical: "You have already suffered because of me. . . . To play square with me. Now it is my turn. I, too, have the right to suffer for a friend; you're not the only one."

Such capacity for renunciation raised that friendship to the pinnacle of universal glory. The two men were deeply moved. In the door of the room, Marialva began to fade out.

"But the fact is . . . You are her husband, perhaps the best thing would be for me to go on suffering, set out for Sergipe to sell a cure, great stuff; I have had an offer; you won't see me any more. So you won't suffer. You keep her; I'm going away right now. Good-bye forever. . . ."

He was turning around when Martim's harsh voice riveted him to the spot. The corporal was mad: "Take it easy, brother, where are you going? Be patient; you are going, but it's with her; you have a yen for her; she has a yen for you; and what am I doing interfering with the two of you? Eat food another is longing for? You take her, and right now. As for me, everything is over; I don't want her any more."

Bullfinch raised his arms; he was in a blind alley. "I have no place to take her."

Martim settled the problem, more and more generous and firm: "Don't let that stand in your way, brother, you stay here with her; I'm leaving. I will go to Tibéria's place to forget. Who knows? She may have some pretty new girl. . . . I'll tell her that she is not to expect you soon because you have got married, and a married man is not supposed to go sniffing around a whorehouse. You keep everything; I'm just taking my clothes."

"Everything? I . . ."

"Everything. Table and chair, mirror, I'm even giving you the coffeepot, which is valuable."

"And what am I to do with all this? No, I can't accept. It is very kind of you, but . . . ."

Marialva had lost the desire to scream, to scratch their faces; she no longer looked feverish, her eyes darting daggers. She had endured it all; she was now shrinking in the doorway, her hair falling down around her head, all awry. Martim smiled at her. She was very tiresome, that was a fact; Bullfinch would not take long to rue his bargain.

He was already ruing it.

"You want to know something, brother?"

Martim got up with the somewhat ceremonious air reserved for visitors: "Yes?"

"Let's leave what was said unsaid, and everything as it was before, for to tell you the truth I don't feel a yen for her any more. . . ."

"Ah, no, brother, that can't be. You came for her; you keep her. As for me, I don't want her any more, neither as wife nor servant. You can't imagine, brother, how tiresome she is. A real puke."

"But I don't want her, either. I was beginning to have my suspicions. All that love had to have a reason. And I'll tell you something else: she's not a decent woman. If it depended on her, you would have more horns than a barnyard ox."

Martim laughed, pointing to Marialva in the doorway, all her airs laid in the dust: "And that tramp thought she was going to stir up trouble between the two of us, who are closer than brothers. It makes me laugh." And he laughed heartily, that old, untrammeled guffaw of his, recovered and for good. Bullfinch laughed, too, and the gay laughter of the two friends rolled down the hillside to the tavern, where the bettors tried to identify and catalogue that strange sound coming from the house above.

Martim went to get the bottle: "How about a drink to celebrate?"

Bullfinch was agreeable, but he remembered: "It's not good to drink so soon after eating jackfruit."

"Right you are. Rum on top of jackfruit can give you a stroke."

"Too bad," Bullfinch mourned.

The friends' eyes met over the remains of the ripe jack-fruit. The pulp the color of gold gleaming invitingly.

"The thing to do is to finish up the jackfruit. Tonight we'll celebrate."

Bullfinch took off coat and necktie, and his funereal air disappeared. They waded into the jackfruit again.

In the bedroom Marialva was collecting her belongings. The two friends seemed to have forgotten all about her, laughing and eating. She crossed the living room and they did not even look up.

"I would say that nobody had won his bet," Bullfinch observed thoughtfully. "Let them save their money for tonight. We could have a fish stew on Master Manuel's smack."

"And take some girls from Tibéria's house. Tell me something, Bullfinch: that little country girl with the straight hair who danced with me at Tibéria's party, is she still there?"

"Otália? Yes, she's still there."

Marialva descended the hillside, and the gang waiting in the tavern looked at one another as they watched her go by. From the house on the hilltop came the sound of laughter. No doubt about it, Martim and Bullfinch were laughing together. They all decided to go up and find out why Corporal Martim's marriage had wound up in those unexpected guffaws.

In the street, resting her bundle on the ground, Marialva, a poor, lonely girl, almost shy and frightened, was waiting for the streetcar that would carry her to Tibéria's whorehouse.

Interlude
of the Christening
of Felício,
Son of Massu
and Benedita

OR

Ogun's *Compadre*

1

THE CHILD WAS FAIR, with straight hair and bluish eyes. Well, not exactly blue. "He has eyes the color of the sky," malicious tongues wagged, but that was not true. Blue or not blue, the insinuations regarding the Gringo's being his father were nothing but the vulgar surmises of low-minded people, quick to misconstrue everything or nothing.

Besides, it was easy to unmask the allegations, show up their falsity. The Gringo had been completely unknown along the waterfront; he had not yet come ashore, nobody knew from where, with his steady, silent rum-bibbing and his sky-blue eyes, when Benedita gave birth to the child and went about showing it off to the neighbors. Furthermore, even afterwards, the Gringo and Benedita were never seen to be on an intimate footing, and probably didn't even know one another, for that liar, after her unforgettable appearance and disturbing stay of several months, had suddenly left for good, and reappeared only when she came to leave the child. Even so, her stay was brief, just long enough to give up the poor little thing, state that he had not yet been baptized because neither had she the money nor was she in shape to do this, and then disappear once more, without leaving any address or clue as to where she was going. Some said she had returned for good to the state of Alagoas, where she came from, and that she had died there, but such suppositions lacked proof. They were based on the deplorable state of Benedita's health when she came back. Nothing but a rag, gaunt, her cheeks sunken, her bones showing through her skin, and with a cough that never let up. Why in the world would she have brought the child and left it in Negro Massu's hands, if she had not known her days were numbered? Because, according to the reports of neighbors, you could say whatever you wanted to about Benedita: flighty, fickle, cynical, a liar, a lush, but there was one thing you couldn't accuse her of, and that was of being an unnatural mother, heartless enough to abandon her child not even a year old. Ah, if there were a good and devoted mother, she would be like Benedita, but not better. Solicitous, even exaggeratedly fond of the baby, utterly devoted. Once when the poor little fellow had a severe stomach upset, Benedita spent night after night without sleeping, weeping and watching over the sick infant, in a state of alarm which was repeated every time it caught a cold or had a pain in its stomach.

When the baby was born, she had even thought of giving up her profession and finding a job as waitress or laundress. She went hungry so the child would lack for nothing. She bought it expensive embroidered and lace-trimmed dresses; it looked like the child of rich parents, capitalists.

If she had come to hand over her son, separate herself from him, it was because, the general opinion went, she felt that her end was near, with a fever that never let up, and spitting blood all the time. And as in the bustle of that quick visit she had told an acquaintance that she did not want to die without seeing once more the region where she had been born, they concluded that she had died in Alagoas, in the vicinity of a village called Pilar.

Who knows, though? She might even have died there in Bahia, in a charity hospital, which was the word spread by one Ernestina, an old friend of hers, whose mother, too, was dying there. On a visit to her mother, she had come across Benedita in the incurable ward, so thin that Ernestina had not recognized her, racked with a cough as she lay stretched out on the bed, if hospital cots can be called beds. She had asked for news of the baby and begged Ernestina to keep her whereabouts a secret. She did not want anyone to see her in that state, and she made her friend swear she would not say a word to anyone.

Ernestina brooded over her promise for three nights, but the evening before visiting day she broke her oath and told the secret to Tibéria and Negro Massu.

The next day the three of them set out for the hospital, taking fruit, bread, cakes, and medicines recommended by Dr. Filinto, a friend of Tibéria's, and house physician of the brothel. They had talked about whether to take the child or not and had concluded that it was better to wait until later, as it might be too much of a shock for her. In her state of weakness and debility, it might kill her.

But when they got there, they did not find Benedita, and nobody was able to tell them what had become of her. The nurses were in a hurry; the orderlies, in a bad humor; none of them could give them any definite information. That was a charity hospital; they couldn't expect it to have the order and organization of a private institution. And so they could not find out whether she had been discharged (and a discharge there did not mean a cure, but rather the impossibility of a cure) or was on the list of the three paupers who had died in the last few days.

And that was the last they heard of gay Benedita, so pleasant and so harum-scarum, nobody knew whether she was alive or dead. No friend was present at her burial. Who knew? She might turn up, when least expected, to claim the child, though in all probability, as Tibéria explained, she was dead and buried, and the child was motherless. With Jesus's approval, she herself, when she came back from the hospital, had wanted to take Massu's son to raise. But the Negro would not even discuss the matter; he flew into a rage. He and his grandmother, Vevéva, who was getting on for a hundred, but who still took part in the dances of the *iawôs* in the *candomblé*, could certainly look after the child. She, too, was outraged. Give up the child, Massu's son? Never!

Now, if Benedita could only have conceived by the Gringo on the occasion of her return, when she was already sick, to bring the child and leave it with Massu, how in the world could that impossible paternity be laid at the door of the blond seaman? Nothing but malicious prying into other people's lives, the inventing of slander. Any child can have bluish eyes, even if the father is a Negro, for it is impossible to sort out and classify the different bloods of a child born in Bahia. All of a sudden a blond crops up among mulattoes, and a pickaninny among whites. That's the way we are, praise be to God!

Benedita said the baby was white like that because it took after her grandfather, a big blond foreigner, a great beer drinker, a weight lifter and tightrope walker who left the yokels at fairs agape with amazement. A perfectly credible explanation except that viperous tongues refused to accept it and went on attributing fathers to the boy, as though Massu weren't enough, a father and a half, an upright and respected citizen with whom people minded what they said, and crazy about his son. Not to mention the grandmother, old Vevéva, with the babe in her arms. Tibéria, herself a woman of stern and inflexible opinions, had pronounced judgment when she gave up the idea of adopting the child. It was in good hands, she said; it couldn't be better cared for or have a more devoted father, a sweeter grandmother.

As for its paternity, no one was in a better position to decide this matter than Benedita and Massu. When the girl had had to give up the baby so that she could die at peace, she had sought no other father, and she must have known what she was doing. And Massu had never evinced the slightest doubt, the least misgiving, not even the shadow of a doubt, regarding Benedita's behavior in the whole matter. When she disappeared from their midst, she had already told her friends that she was pregnant. Why wouldn't he be responsible for her condition, when the two of them had taken a tumble in the sand by the waterfront warehouse one night when they were drunk?

Benedita was the group's constant companion, they had only to call her and she came; she drank, sang, danced in the dance halls, and at times, slept with one of them. There was talk of somebody she was in love with, a certain Otoniel, a clerk in a store, whitish, dopey-looking. However, there was nothing preemptive about this. She was free to do as she liked, and Otoniel had nothing to say about it.

That was how it happened one night when they had really been knocking it back and were all three sheets to the wind, even Jesuíno Crazy Cock, who was so rarely seen blotto. The only one still on his feet was Negro Massu, who never lost his strength or his senses. He took Benedita to the sand, and she let him have his way with her, never suspecting, poor lass, the old stifled passion of Massu, dying for love of her. They had a ball, the Negro bellowing like a pricked bull. Benedita received him joyfully; she was always gay and pleased with life.

Others had passed over her, her body and her joyousness, without leaving a trace. But not Negro Massu. Not only had he marked her whole body with his fists and teeth, leaving her as red as though she had been beaten; he wanted to keep her within certain bounds dictated by his desire and his jealousy.

The next day he went looking for her, to take her back to the sand with him, and as he could not find her, he flew into a rage, threatening to wreck Isidro de Batualê's tavern, and it was a hard job to restrain him. When he found out afterwards that she had had a date with that Otoniel who clerked in a store in São Pedro, he set off for there like a madman. He picked the clerk up from behind the counter, threw him against the kitchen equipment—it was a place that sold pots, refrigerators, kettles—beat up two clerks and the manager, and started chasing the owner. It took four soldiers to quiet him down, dragging him through the streets, beating him with their leather knife sheaths.

Benedita took advantage of Massu's term in the jug, halcyon days after the tumultuous events, and after announcing her pregnancy, disappeared. Otoniel disappeared, too, but not with the girl. He was not crazy enough to risk his life, for Massu had threatened to kill him if he ever went near her again. He asked his boss for a letter of recommendation and went off to try his fortunes in Rio de Janeiro. When Massu was finally set free, thanks to the intervention of Major Cosme de Faria, he could not find even a trace of Benedita. He went around for a while scowling, grumbling about everything, until in the end he recovered and forgot the girl's face and the night on the sands. He became once more the kind, friendly Massu from Sete Portas; he did not even remember Benedita any more.

When, lo and behold, one night she appeared at his house with the child and left him there to stumble through his first steps, falling and getting up, clinging to Vevéva's legs, laughing with that droll little face. He was the son Massu had sowed in Benedita's womb when they had been lovers some months back, perhaps Grandmother Vevéva had heard talk about it. Massu had knocked her up and then had cast her aside. She had had the baby, that beauty of a boy, and she would never have parted with it if she hadn't been sick and had to go into a hospital for treatment. Under those circumstances, where should she leave the child except with its father? One thing she knew for sure: Massu was good; he wasn't going to let the child suffer neglect.

It was at that very moment, as Benedita was saying all this, that Massu happened to arrive. He had come to bring some money for his grandmother's marketing needs. He heard Benedita's talk, saw the baby crawling around the house, getting to its feet and falling. In one of these tumbles the scamp looked at Massu and laughed. The Negro shivered. What had Benedita been doing to become so skinny and ugly, so aged, her arms like those of a skeleton? But the child was strong and healthy—what legs and arms! —his son. If only he had not been quite so white and his hair had been kinkier, it would have been better. But after all, what difference did it make?

"He takes after my mother's father, who was white with blue eyes and talked some crazy language you couldn't understand. He could just as well have turned out black, but it was my blood that came out on top. But his build is yours, exactly. And his way of laughing."

His way of laughing: there was nothing more captivating. The Negro squatted on the floor, and the child came and pulled himself up between his legs. And said "Papa" over and over again. Massu's peals of laughter rang out, rocking the house. Then Benedita smiled and left, satisfied. Her tears came only from having to leave the child, not because of fear and despair.

No one had ever seen a father and son so fond of each other, such friends. The child rode around the room on the

Negro's back. The two of them laughing together, and the grandmother with them.

The only thing left to do was to baptize him. Who ever heard, asked Grandmother Vevéva, of a child eleven months old and still a heathen?

⁌❦ 2 ❧⁍

BAPTIZING A CHILD seems a very simple matter, but when you get down to it, it involves a whole series of complications. It's not just a question of picking up the baby, getting a few friends together, setting out for the nearest church, speaking with the priest, and finished. If that were all there were to it, there would be no problem. But first you have to select the priest and the church—taking into account the devotions and duties of the parents and of the child itself, the *orixás* and charms by which they are bound —prepare clothes for the occasion, choose the godparents, give a party for the friends, get hold of money for the expenses, no small consideration. It is a laborious task, a heavy responsibility.

Old Vevéva turned a deaf ear to all excuses: the child was not going to round out a year of his life as a heathen, like an animal. Vevéva was scandalized at Benedita's neglect. She was really a flibbertigibbet, a bird-brain. She was satisfied with giving the child a name, calling it Felício, nobody knew why. Not that it was ugly, but if she had had the choosing, Vevéva would have preferred Hasdrubal or Alcebíades. But Felício would do; any name was all right as long as the child was christened, not in danger of dying without having received the sacrament, condemned never to enjoy the delights of paradise, to spend an eternity in limbo, a damp, rainy place, in Vevéva's opinion.

Massu promised her he would take all the necessary measures. But he would not do things in a rush. The child was in no danger of dying, and a baptism arranged helter-skelter might complicate its whole life. He was going to discuss the matter with friends, begin the preparations. Vevéva set him a strict time limit: fifteen days.

Fifteen days seemed too short a span to Massu, but when he consulted Jesuíno Crazy Cock, the latter found it reasonable, taking into account the fact that the child's birthday, which should not be celebrated without his being baptized, was at hand. That was the first decision they arrived at: baptism and birthday should be jointly celebrated, and in this way they would have twice the fun for half the expense. The wise solution Crazy Cock had hit upon absolutely bowled Negro Massu over. What a guy that Jesuíno was; he had an answer for everything! Whereupon conferences were begun, and prolonged by multiple rounds of rum, to settle the sundry problems to which Felício's christening gave rise.

At first there was no major difficulty. Jesuíno found a way of handling each situation, always with sensible arguments, and if everything was not settled in one night, it was because this would have been too much work, too exhausting a task for those of them who were getting on in years, as was the case with Jesuíno himself and Carnation-in-his-Buttonhole. They and Eduardo Ipicilone had proved very helpful in the discussion, in which Wing-Foot, Corporal Martim, and Bullfinch also participated.

Wing-Foot had contributed one bright suggestion, and then had said no more: "If the kid was yours truly's," he said, "I would baptize him in every kind of religion: with the priest, the Baptists, Jehovah's Witnesses, all the Protestant sects, and spiritists, too. That way he would be absolutely guaranteed and couldn't miss out on heaven."

But this strange proposition did not arouse much enthusiasm, nor did Wing-Foot insist further. He did not bring ideas and suggestions to the conference table to see them debated, praised, or attacked, or to show off. His sole motive was to be helpful, and his contribution was gratis. Moreover, that first night he was the one who was paying for the rum; the others were broke; even Corporal Martim didn't have a dime. As a rule the corporal always had some change, his gambling take. But that afternoon he had gone out with Otália and had bought her a bunch of magazines, besides taking her to see a wedding. Otália adored weddings.

The first night they threshed out most of the matters. The christening outfit would be contributed by Tibéria, Massu would raise the money for the party with the help of his friends. The church would be that of the Rosary of the Negroes in Pelourinho, not only because Massu had been baptized there some thirty years before but also because they knew the sacristan, Mr. Innocence of the Holy Ghost, a sharp mulatto who in his off hours was a policy runner. He wore dark glasses and always carried an old breviary that a priest of Conceição da Praia had given him, between the pages of which he hid his list of bets. He was a very dependable runner, for he managed to slip through every police net. Not to mention his being a first-class sacristan, with more than twenty years of experience. From time to time he would let fall in the conversation a *Deo gratias* or a *per omnia secula seculorum*, church Latin he had picked up which added to his prestige among his listeners. He was frequently consulted, was even said to be clairvoyant, but there was no proof of this. With his sanctimonious air, his dark glasses, and his prayer book, he was a welcome guest at any birthday, baptism, or marriage, a good trencherman, and with an eye to a pretty dark wench, provided it didn't attract too much attention, for he had to protect his reputation from malicious gossip. And there was one detail on which he and Martim were in complete agreement. Just as the corporal linked his honor to that of the whole glorious national army, so Innocence considered his reputation part and parcel of that of the ecumenical church itself. Any stain that besmirched the sacristan sullied all Christendom. Hence he was very cautious and did not get himself involved with just anybody.

In view of the foregoing, it was natural that the Church of the Rosary of the Negroes should have been their choice. But in addition, Mr. Innocence owed Bullfinch a great favor, and Negro Massu, too, for they had both helped save his reputation.

Massu had introduced Bullfinch to a friend of his, Osorio Redondo, a self-styled druggist with a knowledge of herbs, who manufactured a miraculous medicine for the cure of blennorraghia. Bullfinch had taken a few bottles to sell in the suburbs and had given one to Mr. Innocence.

The sacristan had been taken in by one of those hussies who pretend to be strait-laced and even very devout. The slut began showing up in the sacristy every morning, her mouth brimming over with prayers and her eyes fixed on Innocence with a candor that was touching. The sacristan took a chance on running his hand up her fanny; she let him, and he glimpsed greener pastures. She put up a show of modesty, just for the record, and Innocence struck while the iron was hot, taking the citadel. He was enchanted with the affair; true, the mettlesome miss was not sweet sixteen, but on the other hand, she was refined, of good family, and Innocence was so flattered in his vanity that the next day he did not pay his usual visit to the mulatta Cremildes, to whom for a long time he had rendered virile homage every Tuesday. The result? Three days later he suffered the painful consequences in his own flesh: the pious hypocrite had given him a nasty disease. That was a serious dilemma for the sacristan: either he risked general censure if he were seen going to one of the many doctors who have their offices in Terreiro or on the Square, specialists in such diseases, or he rotted in silence. Just let one of the old hens see him going up the steps of one of those specialists, and the news would be spread over seven states. He might even lose his job.

It was then that he heard someone in Alonso's store telling of the miraculous properties of the medicine peddled by Bullfinch. He knew the spieler. They were on friendly terms, they often ran into one another in Pelourinho. Light flooded Innocence's troubled soul; at last he glimpsed a way out of his misfortune.

He looked Bullfinch up and told him an involved story: a friend of his, a connection of his family, had picked up a V.D. and couldn't get rid of it. He was ashamed to come to Bullfinch in person to get the medicine and had asked him to do it. Even so, he, Innocence, wanted his charitable intervention kept a complete secret, otherwise gossiping tongues were capable of inventing all sorts of scurrilous things, like spreading it around that it was Innocence himself who needed the medicine. Bullfinch not only promised absolute secrecy but even gave him the wholesale price on a bottle of Arise, Club. And a week later, Innocence could return, humble and repentant, to the clean sheets of misprized Cremildes.

Linked by such close ties to the group, naturally Innocence would spare no effort to give all possible luster to the christening of Massu's son. He could personally supervise the necessary measures for the ceremony. And he would speak to Father Gomes, recommending the child, his father, and his father's friends. Felício would receive the baptismal waters with style and perfection.

The church, the sacristan, and the priest were now chosen; but the thorniest problem still remained, that of the godparents. They would leave that for another night, as it was an extremely delicate matter.

Moreover, Jesuíno washed his hands and bowed out of the discussion when it came to the godparents. It was clear from his attitude that he felt sure this honor would fall on him. After all was said and done, he was an intimate friend of Massu's, had known him for years and years, had helped him out of many a tight spot, not to mention his contribution to this matter of the baptism.

He said he did not want to influence or exert pressure on Massu, and for that reason he would not take part in the debate. The choice of godfather and godmother depended exclusively on the preference of the parents, and nobody should stick his nose into the business. They should be sought and chosen among the closest friends, those for whom they had the highest regard, to whom they owed the most courtesies and favors. Godparents were like close relatives, brother and sister, so to speak. Nobody should meddle in the matter or, once the choice had been made, either criticize or oppose it. That was why, once again setting a good example, Crazy Cock withdrew from the discussion and advised the others to behave as he did, with the same loftiness of spirit. This was the only attitude that behooved each and every one of them: to leave the father and mother free to assume the responsibility of such a

weighty decision, which in this case, moreover, fell solely
upon the father, for unfortunately the mother, the late
lamented Benedita, was no longer with them. If she were
alive, he, Crazy Cock, knew full well on whom the choice
would fall. But now . . .

Really retire, completely withdraw from the discussion,
none of them did, not even Jesuíno, in spite of his eloquent
speech. They lost themselves in veiled suggestions, half-
voiced phrases, Ipicilone even going so far as to mutter
something to the effect that he was in the habit of making
lavish and frequent gifts to his godchildren. An affirmation
received with general and hilarious skepticism, for Ipicilone
did not have a penny to bless himself with or any godchild
on whom to bestow gifts. In any case, Jesuíno considered
this insinuation in deplorable taste and highly improper,
and his opinion had the full backing of the others.

It was thus that Negro Massu came to realize that they
were all, without exception—Jesuíno, Martim, Wing-Foot,
Bullfinch, Ipicilone, Carnation-in-his-Buttonhole, even the
Spaniard Alonso—each and every one of them, waiting to
be asked to act as the child's godfather. At the moment,
they were seven; the next day there might be ten or fifteen
candidates. Massu's first reaction was one of satisfied
vanity—all of them vying for the honor of calling him
compadre, as though he were a politico or a businessman
of the City! If it depended on him, he would ask them all,
the seven who were present and many others, all his friends,
those of the waterfront, the fishing smacks, the markets,
of Sete Portas and Água dos Meninos, of the houses of
worship, the *capoeira* circles, and in that way the child
would have innumerable godfathers. But though the candidates were many, only one could be chosen; only one
godfather could be selected from the lot of them, and
suddenly Massu realized the nature of the problem that
confronted him, and could see no way out. The only thing
to do was to put the matter off, leave the decision till the
next day. Otherwise, how could he go on drinking in peace
and good fellowship? Furtive glances, words with double
meaning, vinegary phrases were being exchanged.

So the night might end on a note of perfect friendship,
they reached agreement as to the godmother: Tibéria. She

had missed out on being Felício's mother; she had wanted to adopt him; she was going to give him his christening outfit. The choice was self-evident, admitted of no argument. Martim went so far as to suggest the name of Otália, and Ipicilone that of the Negress Sebastiana, his current flame, but as soon as Tibéria was proposed, the other candidates were withdrawn. It was now their duty to go to the bordello and bear her the good tidings. Who knew but what, high-flown with the emotion and joy of the news, she might open a jug of rum or bring out some cold beers to toast her *compadre?*

They left Alonso's store, once more brothers all. But between them, like an invisible sword blade separating them, like sand in the gearbox, went the problem of the choice of godfather. Massu swung his big head back and forth as though trying to shake off a worry; he'd decide in the course of the week; after all there was not such a great hurry. Vevéva had given him a limit of fifteen days, and here on the first night most of the problems had been settled.

— ❧{ 3 }❧ —

MOST OF THEM, YES, BUT NOT THE HARDEST ONE. It certainly was difficult to choose a godfather, Massu became convinced, when three days after that night of the first, felicitous conversations, the situation remained unchanged, the child continued godfatherless.

To say it remained unchanged is a manner of speaking. The fact of the matter is that it had gotten worse. They had not advanced one step in the direction of solving the problem, and instead there hung over the group the threat of serious dissension. Outwardly that long and devoted friendship continued perfect, without having suffered the slightest scratch. But a careful observer would have sensed, with the passing of nights and drinks, a growing tension marking words and gestures, casting long silences in the midst of the conversation. As though afraid of offending one another, they were overly polite and ceremonious, without that carefree intimacy of so many years' and drinks' standing.

All of them, however, very attentive to Massu, treating him with the greatest deference. The Negro could not complain, and if it had not been for that time limit set by old Vevéva, he would not have asked for a better life, a father surrounded by generous aspirants to godfathership.

Carnation-in-his-Buttonhole offered him cigars, strong, black ones from Cruz das Almas, superfine quality. Bullfinch brought an amulet to protect the child against fevers, bad luck, and snake bite, in addition to some ribbons from Bonfim. Ipicilone invited Massu to a stew of lights and liver at the house of the Negress Sebastiana, washed down with rum from Santo Amaro, and tried to get him tipsy, possibly in the hope that he would decide in his favor. Massu ate and drank till he was as full as a tick, but the one who rolled under the table, out like a light, was Ipicilone. Massu, moreover, took advantage of the situation to give Sebastiana a few squeezes, and if he didn't go any farther, it was out of consideration for Ipicilone, who though drunk, was nevertheless present. It wouldn't have looked right, with his friend in the other room.

Corporal Martim was the one who displayed exemplary solicitude. Meeting the Negro on the road to Barra, sweating under the enormous basket of groceries he was carrying on his head and with an earthen jug, heavy and awkward, under his arm, the noonday sun beating down on him, he came over and offered to help him. Another person would have ducked around the corner to avoid meeting him. Martim took over the jug, thus relieving the Negro of part of his load, and set out with him for Barra to keep him company and shorten the trip with his ever-pleasant and instructive conversation. Massu was grateful to Martim, not only for lightening his load—one of those big jugs is a mean thing to carry; it doesn't fit well under the arm; and he had the basket on his head—but also for his conversation, which kept him in a good humor, for before meeting him the Negro had been vexed by life, cursing the devil. He had taken that job of carrying the purchases made by an elegant lady of Barra at the market of Sete Portas, groceries for a whole week, because he was flat broke and Vevéva was asking for money for the child's cereal. The little rascal loved bananas with manioc meal, ate like a horse, and he, Massu, was having the worst kind of a run of luck: not once did he hit.

Martim, trying to fit the jug comfortably under his arm —he refused to carry it on his head—was telling him the news. He hadn't shown up the night before because he had gone to the great celebration of Oxumarê at the *candomblé* of Arminda de Euá. What a show, brother! It couldn't have been better! In his whole life as a participant in *macumba* rites he had never seen so many deities descend at the same time; of Oguns alone, there were seven, each better than the other.

Negro Massu stopped to listen. He was a son of Ogun and also his *ogã*. Martim told him about the celebration, the dance, and the singing. In spite of the basket on his head, precariously balanced, full of breakables, Massu went through a few dance steps. Martim, too, gave a twist, and struck up a chant to the god of metals.

"*Ogun ê ê!*" shouted Massu.

And he had an illumination, as though the sun, that cruel, punishing sun, had exploded in yellow; he almost lost his senses; it was like a blow across the eyes, a vision: in the nearby woods he saw Ogun laughing at him, all appareled in his implements, telling him to relax because he, Ogun, his father, would settle that problem of the child's godfather. Massu was to come to see him. And with that, he disappeared, and all that remained was a dot of light on the Negro's retina, indubitable proof of what had happened.

Massu turned to the corporal and asked him: "Did you see?"

Martim had resumed his walk: "A hunk of perdition, isn't she? What a backside! . . ." and he smiled, his eyes following the majestic mulatta disappearing around the corner.

Massu, however, was remote from such distractions, still in the grip of his vision. "I'm talking about another matter. Something serious."

"What, brother? Is there anything more serious than a dame's tail?"

Negro Massu told him of his vision, of Ogun's promise to solve his problem, and his order to go to see him. Martim was impressed: "You really saw him? You're not just pulling my leg?"

"I swear it. There's still a red spot dancing in front of my eyes."

Martim turned the matter over in his mind and felt encouraged. In the last analysis, he was the one who had brought the conversation around to the subject; he was the one who had talked about the various Oguns dancing at

Arminda's clearing. If Ogun was to indicate a name, why couldn't it be his, Martim's? "Ah, my brother, what you must do is go right away. Who is it you are going to consult?"

"What a question! Mother Doninha, of course."

"Then go right away."

"I'm going today."

But that day the priestess Doninha, *iyalorixá* of the famous Temple of Media Porta where Massu was a trained and ordained *ogã* and where Jesuíno held an eminent post, a distinction of the highest order, that day she was unable to take care of the Negro's problem or even to see and have a word with him. She was in the chamber of the *iawôs* on a difficult assignment, something she was doing for one of her daughters-in-devotion who had come from out of town. She sent him a message to come back the next day, any time in the afternoon.

That night, gathered at Isidro de Batualê's tavern, the friends heard from Massu's lips the exact version of what had happened. Martim had already regaled them with part of the story, but they wanted to hear it from Massu himself, in all its details.

He was going with Martim, the Negro told them, along the road to Barra, carrying a basket and jug, when he began to hear the beating of drums and certain of the god's songs. At first very low, muted, then growing louder, like a celebration. There was Martim to bear him out; he would not let him lie.

Martim not only confirmed what he had said, but added a detail: just before it happened, they had been talking about the feast of Oxumarê in the *candomblé* of Arminda de Euá, and when the name of Ogun was mentioned, both Massu and he had felt the thud of the deity on the nape of their necks, and their bodies had jerked as though Ogun had mounted them and they were in the circle at the voodoo clearing. As though they were going into a trance. He, Martim, even felt a quiver in his legs.

Then the music grew louder, and that was when Ogun appeared out of the thickets beside the road. An enormous Ogun, more than three yards high, bedecked with all his insignia, and his voice dominating everything. He came over and embraced Massu, his *ogã*, and told him not to worry his head any more about the business of the god-father of his child, for it was up to him, Ogun, to decide the matter, thus freeing Negro Massu from that aggravation, that vexatious difficulty of not knowing whom to choose among friends he valued equally. Wasn't that the way it was, Martim?

Once more Martim backed him up, but was unable to confirm the exact height of Ogun, it could just as well have been three yards as a little more or a little less. More, he would think, closer to three yards and a half. And what about the voice? A voice like a gale, drowning out every other sound. The others looked at the corporal out of the corner of their eye. It was plain that he was flattering Ogun, trying to curry favor with the deity.

Massu wound up his story with satisfaction. Ogun would decide who should be the godfather of the child, and any-body who wanted to argue about the choice would have to be crazy, for Ogun was not a divinity to suffer an affront.

There was a silence fraught with agreement and respect, but also with silent interrogations. Might that not all be a scheme of Corporal Martim's? Might he not have convinced good old Massu of that strange vision at midday with *macumba* music and the deity dancing on the public highway? Martim was a sly, tricky customer. That could all be a carefully thought-out plan: in the first vision Ogun had promised to settle the problem, and in a second, again unseen by the others, Ogun—an Ogun who existed only in Massu's imagination, with an assist from the corporal—would state that he had chosen Martim to be godfather. Eyes darted from Massu to Martim, uneasy, without concealing their suspicion. Finally Jesuíno took the floor: "So what you mean is that Ogun is going to choose? Wonderful. But how is it to be done? He said you were to go to see him. Where? How are you going about it?"

"Consult someone who can clear it up for me. I already went, today."

"You already went?" There was a note of alarm in Crazy Cock's voice. "Who was it you consulted?"

Would it be Martim himself or someone primed by the corporal?

"I went to see Mother Doninha, but she was busy and couldn't take care of me until tomorrow."

Jesuíno gave a sigh of relief, as did the others. Mother Doninha was above suspicion, deserving of absolute confidence. Who would dare to raise the slightest doubt as to her trustworthiness, not to mention her powers, her intimacy with the deities?

"Mother Doninha? You did right; for such a serious matter there is nobody like her. When are you going back?"

"Tomorrow, without fail."

Only Wing-Foot persisted in his earlier advice: "If it was me, I would baptize the little devil with the priest, the spiritists, in the churches of every faith—there are a lot of them, more than twenty, all having different ceremonies. For each christening, you could choose a different godfather."

A practical and original solution, perhaps, but unacceptable. What in the devil would the child do all his life long with so many religions? He would have time for nothing but to run around from church to church. He had enough with Catholicism and Voodoo which, as everybody knows, blend with and understand one another. He would baptize him with the priest, and pledge him to the deity at the voodoo center. What need for more?

The next afternoon, Massu set out for Retiro Hill, where Doninha's place of worship was. It was one of the biggest temples in the city, a huge clearing with several buildings, houses for the initiates, votaries and guests and a big shed for the celebrations, the house of the *eguns* and the little house of Exu close by the entrance.

Doninha was in the house of Xangô, the presiding deity of the *axé*, and there she received Massu. She gave him her hand to kiss, invited him to be seated, and before getting down to business, they talked of various things, as well-bred people should. Finally Doninha made a pause in the conversation, asked one of the initiates to bring them coffee. Then she folded her hands, canted her head in Massu's direction as though to indicate that she was ready to listen to him, that the hour for consultation had arrived.

Massu then unfolded his tale of woe, telling about Benedita's showing up with the baby, well cared for, fat, but unbaptized. Benedita had never been very religious; she was flighty, had never taken anything seriously in her life. Poor thing, she had kicked the bucket in the hospital, at least that was what they said, though as for seeing her, nobody saw her or went to the funeral.

The priestess listened in silence, nodding her head, muttering words in Nago from time to time. She was a Negress about sixty years old, stout and deliberate, with huge breasts and keen eyes. She wore a full skirt and a loose white blouse, leather sandals, and a string of beads knotted around her waist; her throat and wrists were loaded with necklaces and bracelets, and she had the majestic air of a person conscious of her power and knowledge.

Massu spoke without fear or hesitations, confidently, for there existed between him and the priestess, as between her and the other persons of the *axé*, a close connection, almost a relationship. He told how distressed Vevéva was about the child's not being baptized, a concern Doninha found fully justified. Vevéva was her sister-in-devotion, one of the oldest of the house. When Doninha entered the temple, Vevéva had already completed her seven years as a novice. And Vevéva had set him a limit of fifteen days to have the child baptized; she did not want to see him round out his first year still a heathen. Everything had gone well with their preparations, including the choice of the godmother, who everybody agreed should be Tibéria. But the insurmountable stumbling block had been the godfather. Massu was friendly by nature and had so many close friends, not to mention his profusion of acquaintances, that how was he to choose among them? Above all, when it was a question of the five or six who met every night, brothers were never more inseparable. Massu could not sleep; he spent his nights comparing the qualities of his friends and could not make up his mind. Never in his whole life had he known what it was to have a headache, and now he had such a throbbing in his temples, such a buzzing in his ears, that his head felt as though it were splitting. He could already see himself on bad terms with his friends, deprived of their company, and how could he live without the warmth of human companionship, an outcast in his own country?

Doninha understood the problem and nodded her head in agreement. Then Massu came to Ogun's intervention: "I was going along the road, loaded down like a pack mule, and Martim alongside, chatting with me, when without warning or anything, my Father Ogun appeared at my side, a giant more than five yards high, bigger than a telephone pole. I knew him right off because he was wearing all his insignia and because of his laugh. He came over and told me that I was to see you, Mother, that he would tell what he had decided in regard to the child's godfather. To leave the matter to him, that he would solve it. That's why I came yesterday and am here today, to find out the answer. When he had finished speaking, he laughed again and flew through the air toward the sun, entered it, and there was an explosion—everything turned yellow as though it was gold."

When Massu had finished his story, Doninha informed him that she was more or less acquainted with the situation, that it was no surprise to her, for the evening before, when he had been there and she had not been able to see him because she was engaged in a difficult and delicate operation, something very strange had happened. At the very moment that Massu arrived, she had begun casting the shells to ask Xangô for answers to the distressed questions of the woman she was helping—a votary of his who had been away from Bahia for many years, living in São Paulo, and who was involved in a mess such as Massu couldn't imagine. Suffice it to say she had come from the South posthaste to carry out her duties to Xangô and put herself under his protection. Well, as she was saying, she had cast the shells and called upon Xangô, but instead of Xangô, the one who appeared and talked a lot of nonsense (or so she thought at the time) was Ogun. She cast the shells, called upon Xangô; Ogun took the lead and came out with all that rigmarole. And Doninha, without knowing anything, ignorant of what was happening to Massu, trying to get rid of Ogun and calling upon Xangô. She had even thought that this was the doing of Exu, who was capable of pretending to be Ogun just for a lark. Doninha was beginning to get mad, the votary's hair was standing on end, for with the shape her affairs were in, that additional confusion left her crushed. How could she bear another cause for worry, when she already had enough and to spare?

At this point, Doninha, suspecting some disturbing influence, had sent one of the initiates to find out who was in the vicinity of the temple at that hour. And she had come back with Massu's message. At the time, Doninha had not connected the visit of Massu with the appearance of Ogun; she had simply sent word to him to come the next day. How could she receive him with all that hubbub going on?

But the minute Massu had gone through the gate of the clearing, Ogun had left, too, and everything had returned to normal. Xangô had been able to appear in all his majesty and answer the girl's consultation, settling her problems most satisfactorily, and the poor thing was so happy it was a pleasure to see.

Afterwards, turning over in her mind what had happened, Doninha had begun to put two and two together and had reached this conclusion: Ogun had come because he had some business afoot with Massu. So she waited for the visit of the *ogã*. Even now, as they were talking, she had felt something in the air, she would swear Ogun was close by, listening to their whole conversation.

She got up cumbersomely from the armchair, resting her hands on her thighs, which were as broad as the waves of a storm-tossed sea, and told Massu to wait. She was going to clear everything up immediately; she was going over to Ogun's house, which was on a little slope beyond the ravine. A votary appeared, carrying a tray holding cups and a coffeepot, kissed Massu's hand before offering him the hot, fragrant coffee. The Negro felt comforted and almost calm for the first time in several days.

Doninha did not take long to come back, walking with her short, quick steps. She sat down and explained to Massu Ogun's instructions. The Negro was to bring two cocks and five doves, in addition to a platter of fried bean cakes and bean tamales to nourish the *orixá's* head. After that he would attend to the problem of the godfather. On Thursday, day after tomorrow, at sundown.

Doninha would take care of the preparation of the bean

cakes and tamales; Massu gave her the money she would need. He would bring the cocks and the doves the next day. On Thursday he would come with his friends; they would eat the deity's meal with Doninha and such of the votaries as might be present. There would be pineapple cider.

They all lived in a state of suspense those two days, asking themselves on whom Ogun's choice would fall as the most worthy to be the child's godfather. The problem took on a new dimension. One thing was the choice made by Negro Massu, who might easily go astray, commit an injustice. But Ogun was not to be fooled, would not commit any injustice. Whoever he chose would be recognized as the best, the most worthy, the exemplary friend. They all felt their hearts shrink, now that uncontrollable forces had entered into play, above and beyond any deal, scheme, or manipulation. Not even Jesuíno, occupying such a high post in the hierarchy of the *candomblés*, could have any influence. Ogun is the deity of metals, his decisions are inflexible, his sword is of fire.

⟿❦{ 4 }❦⟾

IN THE DISTANCE THE LIGHTS OF THE CITY sprang up, darkness thickened between the bushes on the road to the *axé*. They walked silent and thoughtful. Tibéria had come with them, she insisted on being present, considering herself directly involved in the matter as godmother. Goats and kids skipped along the slopes, homeward bound. Shadows dropped over trees and passersby, and farther ahead the darkness was rising like a wall.

In the *axé* there was a silence of dim lights and quiet footsteps in the houses where the votaries lived. The yellow pallor of kerosene lamps filtered through the cracks of doors and windows. In the house of Ogun, lighted candles illuminated the shrine. As they entered the gate and greeted Exu, a daughter of Oxalá, dressed in ritual white, emerged from the darkness and murmured: "Mother Doninha is waiting for you. In Ogun's house. . . ."

A chintz curtain covered the door, hiding the entrance. They went in one by one, bowing before the altar of the deity, then lining up against the wall. The priestess was seated on a stool, with a plate of cola nuts before her, and she gave them her hand to kiss. Darkness was slowly descending over the fields. As the room was small, it could not hold all of them; only Massu, Tibéria, and Jesuíno stayed inside with Doninha. The other friends and votaries gathered in a group outside, the curtain having been lifted.

One of the votaries approached Mother Doninha and kneeling before her handed her a clay plate with the two big sharpened knives on it. Another brought the two cocks. The priestess began a chant; the votaries answered. The rite had begun.

Doninha put her feet on the first cock and set the clay trough between her feet. Holding the fowl by the head, she took the knife, cut its throat, and the blood flowed out. She then pulled out feathers, adding them to the blood.

The second cock was sacrificed; the chants in honor of Ogun pierced the night and rolled down the hillsides toward the city of Bahia.

An initiate came and brought the frightened white doves. Their blood was collected in another vessel and to it were added selected feathers.

Doninha got to her feet, took up the bell, and with it led the music. The words of the offering were spoken, turning the dead animals over to Ogun. Massu was kneeling to the ground; Jesuíno, too. With her fingers dipped in blood, Doninha touched the head of each, those who were in the chamber and the others. The choice could fall on any of them. The votaries carried away the dead animals to prepare the meal for the gods.

After this they all went outside into the clearing and stayed there talking while activity mounted in the kitchen. The night enveloped everything; the stars were innumerable in that sky without electric lights. Nobody made any reference to the matter that had brought them there. It was like a social gathering, friends having a chat. Doninha narrated incidents of her distant childhood, recalled persons who were no more. Tibéria contributed her share of recollections. And so they sat on until Oxalá's priestess announced that dinner was ready.

The daughters-in-sainthood came in a row, carrying trays of food, the bean cakes, the tamales, the fricassee. The sacrificial animals were now the fragrant, colorful food. Doninha selected the ritual pieces for the deity, adding to them the bean cakes and tamales. The plates were set before the shrine; the votaries sang, with Doninha leading the songs.

She then picked up the shells and cast them. The friends

poked their heads through the doorway so as not to miss a detail. She cast them and called upon Ogun. He was satisfied, it was apparent, for he came laughing and leaping, and greeted them all, and very especially Mother Doninha and his *ogã* Massu.

Doninha thanked him and asked him if it was really true that he was ready to help Massu in that difficult predicament of choosing a godfather for his son from among his friends. It was for this that he had come, he answered, to give thanks for the meal offered by Massu, the blood of the cocks and the doves, and to talk with them, to give them the longed-for solution.

It was then Massu's turn to give thanks and transmit his warmest greetings. For there he was confronted with that confounded problem of the christening of his son, a pretty, bright little fellow, full of life and mischievous, a very devil, he even seemed one of Exu's. And Massu having to select a godfather from among his friends, so many and so good, and being able to choose only one. He wanted to know how to proceed so as not to offend the others. For that reason he had come and brought the cocks and the doves, as Ogun had ordered. Wasn't that the way it was?

That was just the way it was, Ogun agreed, it was all absolutely true. Seeing his son Massu so troubled, he had come to help him. Massu did not want to offend any of his friends and didn't see how to avoid it, wasn't that it?

They all followed the conversation through the casting of the shells. Doninha grew before them, the mistress of unknown powers, of magic and the Yoruba language, of definitive words and mysterious herbs.

And what was the solution? Massu asked the deity, Ogun, his father, and all of them, including the priestess Doninha, awaited the answer in tense silence. What was the solution when they could see none?

Then inside the shrine the clanking of iron was heard, the sound of steel on steel, the clash of sword against sword, for Ogun is the lord of war. A gay merry laugh rang out, and it was Ogun, wearied of the slow dialogue by means of the casting of the shells, who wanted to be in more direct contact with them; it was Ogun mounting one of the votaries, his daughter. She rushed through the door, greeted Doninha, stopped before the shrine, and raised her voice: "I have already made my decision. Nobody is going to be the child's godfather. The godfather will be I, Ogun." And she laughed.

In the frightened silence that followed, Doninha asked for confirmation: "You, my Father? You the godfather?"

"I myself and nobody but me. From now on Massu is my *compadre*. Farewell to all of you. I am leaving now. Prepare the celebration. I will return only for the christening."

And he took his departure instantly, without even waiting for the farewell chant. Mother Doninha said: "I never before saw this; it is the first time. A god the godfather of a child, a deity having a *compadre*, I never even heard tell . . ."

Massu was high-flown with vanity. *Compadre* of Ogun! None had ever existed before, he was the first one!

·◄{ 5 }►·

YES, THE SOLUTION WAS PERFECT, wonderful, left them all satisfied. None had been chosen; none stood higher in the scale of Massu's friendship than the other. Above them, only Ogun, the god of metals, the brother of Oxossi and Xangô. The solution pleased them all. Yet, in spite of this, one could not say that the problem of the christening had been completely settled.

On the contrary, if Ogun's decision had broken the impasse regarding the choice of godfather, it had created a new and unforeseeable one: how to get Ogun to the Church of the Rosary of the Negroes and have him bear witness there to the Catholic rite? The deity was not a human being; he could not give a power of attorney to one of the friends to act for him. Moreover, this dilemma, which Bullfinch had called attention to, brought them right back to the previous problem: who would be chosen to represent Ogun? Whoever it was would, up to a point, be the godfather of the child. No, such an idea had to be completely discarded.

Even Mother Doninha admitted she was perplexed. How was the matter to be dealt with? Ogun had calmly stated that he would be the godfather of the child, Massu's *compadre*, and before long the news would be all over the city, with everybody talking about it. A deity had never been seen acting as a child's godfather; it was the first time anyone was a god's *compadre*, and Negro Massu would take on new importance, with everybody wanting to attend the christening to see how the father and his friends would work it out, how they would manage to have Ogun present at the ceremony. The deity had proclaimed himself the godfather. All good and well, but he had left them—Massu, Doninha, Jesuíno, Tibéria, Martim, and the others—holding that hot potato: how was Ogun to participate in the act?

Mother Doninha wore herself out casting the shells, calling on Ogun, beating the invocation to the deity on the drums, singing his chants, imploring him to come. Had he not promised, with merry laughter, to return only on the day of the christening? He seemed determined to keep his word. Doninha had power with the saints, nobody in the *candomblé* circles of Bahia knew as much as she, her powers were the greatest ever conferred on any priestess. Yet in spite of being so in favor with the deities, even employing every resource, calling upon Ossani and using the most secret herbs, offering, at her own expense, a goat to Ogun —not for all this could she get him to return, exchange a word with him, hear the slightest explanation of how she was to proceed. Ogun had disappeared, and not only from her temple, the Axé da Meia Porta, but from all his sites in Bahia. He did not descend to any of them, creating panic among his votaries and priests, for he did not respond to any call; he did not come in search of the food set out for him or the animals sacrificed in his honor.

The drums were beat; the blood of cocks, doves, ducks, lambs, and kids flowed; the handmaidens danced in a circle; the chants rose on high; the beads and shells were cast by the highest priests and oldest and wisest priestesses. Ogun did not respond. The news spread to the four corners of Bahia, from mouth to mouth, from ear to ear: Ogun had decided to be godfather of the son of Massu and the late Benedita; he had disqualified all the other candidates, and after deciding this, had departed to return only on the day of the christening. This would take place the following week, on the child's first birthday, at the Church of the Rosary of the Negroes in Pelourinho, with Dona Tibéria acting as godmother. She was preparing the infant's outfit, a wealth of linen and cambric, with dark blue, Ogun's color, predominating, and as all the girls of the brothel wanted to collaborate, at least with a gift, the christening was beginning to assume grandiose proportions. Curiosity mounted. Since the news of the marriage of Corporal Martim to the beauteous Marialva, today a star at a night club on Ladeira da Praça, where she displays her black beauty mark and her coyness, calling herself a singer, there had been no news that aroused such wonderment.

It affected even respected and highly regarded intellectuals, all of them distinguished students of the Afro-Brazilian cults, each with his own personal theory regarding the various aspects of *candomblé*. They disagreed on many points, but they were all as one in considering completely absurd this story about a deity acting as godfather at the christening of a child. They quoted English, American, Cuban—even German—authorities to prove that there was no such category as that of *compadre* in the hierarchy of the *candomblé*, neither here nor in Africa. They were all, eminent ethnologists or mere charlatans, determined to learn whether the *compadre* of a god ranked above the *ogãs* or below the *obãs*, to what veneration he was entitled, if he should be greeted before or after the assistant priestess. For even though they took exception to this innovation, which broke the purity of the ritual, they could do nothing about it, for it was the work of the deity himself. What they did want was to be present at the christening; they ingratiated themselves with members of the cult to make sure of an invitation.

With all this, Massu became as vain as a peacock; nobody could stand him those first days, such a conceited ass, so self-important had he become. But he was brought back to the bitter reality by Jesuíno and Martim, by Tibéria and Ipicilone, and above all, by Doninha. How were they to bell the cat?

To act as godfather at a christening, you have to go to the church, be present at the ceremony, hold a candle, recite the Creed. How could Ogun do this? Massu shook his big ox head and ran his eyes over the group, waiting for the lifesaving answer to come from one of his friends, for he, Massu, had none, could see no way out of the complication.

Doninha tried everything until the day finally came when she admitted defeat. She was unable to establish communication with Ogun; all her efforts had been unavailing. Only the god himself could find a way out; Massu would have to excuse her; she could do no more.

Then once again Jesuíno Crazy Cock covered himself with glory. He spoke and gave the solution. Crazy Cock's equal did not exist; we might just as well stop beating about the bush and admit the truth. This is not to belittle or offend anyone, for with the passing of time all came to agree on the proven superiority of Jesuíno. Even though at that moment Crazy Cock had not risen to his full stature, as happened later on, they already paid him homage and did not compare themselves to him. Such a simple solution, that which Jesuíno came up with, and no one else had hit upon it!

Massu had come back from the temple, where he had heard Doninha's disheartening message. The Negro decided to put off the christening until Ogun was ready to cooperate. The delay would be a blow to old Vevéva, so determined to see the child baptized, but Massu could think of nothing else to do. So he stated to his friends in Alonso's store.

"I think maybe I've hit on the nub of the matter," Jesuíno announced. But he refused to reveal his idea without first hearing Doninha's opinion, for the carrying-out and the success of the plan depended on her approval. In a state of great excitement, they decided to go to her place of worship immediately.

In Doninha's presence, Jesuíno set forth his idea. He began by asking whether the manner in which Ogun had behaved on the day they consulted him had not surprised them? He had been answering by way of the shells; suddenly he had come in person, mounted on one of his votaries: wasn't that so? And thus, through the mouth of the handmaiden, he had taken on himself the duty of acting as godfather and had stated that he would return on the day of the christening. Had he or hadn't he? And hadn't they all been surprised at the lack of co-operation on the part of Ogun, at his disappearing and leaving them to suffer when they had to settle a problem of such dimensions? However, when the day came, Ogun would take care of everything, indicate what should be done, supply the solution to the problem.

The friends looked at one another with a dazed air. Wing-Foot voiced what they were all thinking: "As far as I am concerned, you might as well be talking in German. I don't understand a word."

Jesuíno gave a gesture of his hands to show how easy it was. All you had to do was to use your head a little. But they did not find it so easy. Only Mother Doninha, who had closed her eyes and concentrated, guessed the solution. Relaxing her fat body in her rush-bottomed chair, she opened her eyes and smiled at Crazy Cock: "You mean . . ."

"Of course."

". . . that Ogun will descend in one of his daughters the day of the christening, and she will be the one who will act as godfather, only that she will not be she, but he?"

"Don't you see? Isn't it simple?"

So simple that they still could not understand, and Jesuíno was obliged to explain: the one who would go to the church would be a votary of Ogun's but acting for the deity, that is to say, being merely the god's horse. Now did they get it?

Their faces lighted up in smiles of satisfied understanding. Yes, sir, that Jesuíno was a card all right; he had hit the nail on the head; he had found the way out. The votary would arrive at the church, mounted by Ogun, who would be the godfather.

"Except that a woman can't be a godfather," Bullfinch pointed out.

No, not godfather . . . She would have to be godmother.

"I've already got the godmother. Tibéria," Massu reminded them.

"Nor would Ogun want to be a godmother," Doninha added. "He's a man-god, he wouldn't want a woman's job. He can't be the godmother."

They suddenly seemed to be right back where they had started. But Jesuíno was not dismayed.

"It's just a question of getting hold of a son of the god's, a male votary of Ogun's."

But of course, how simple! They were so balled up they

couldn't think straight; everything had seemed lost. Without a doubt the problem was settled.

Only, at the moment, at Doninha's place of worship there was no son of Ogun's, no manservant of the deity's. There were devotees of the deity, initiated like Massu, but these would not do; the god did not enter them. The only two trained by Doninha had moved away from Bahia; one of them was living in Ilhéus and the other in Maceió, where, incidentally, he had opened a house of worship.

"Let's talk with one of another house," Bullfinch suggested.

The proposition seemed reasonable enough, but Doninha raised a number of doubts. Would it work? Would Ogun approve of getting a person from another place? For Massu was an *ogã* there, not in another temple. It was there, through Doninha's lips first and then through a votary of the temple, that Ogun's will had made itself manifest.

As they were in the midst of these considerations, adrift once more, from outside the house of Xangô, where they were talking, they heard a handclap and a voice asking for Mother Doninha.

"I know that voice," the priestess said. "Who's there?"

"A friend, my Mother."

There appeared in the doorway old Artur da Guima, an artisan with a shop on Ladeira do Tabuão, a good friend of them all. It was a pleasure to see him, and if they had not been so downhearted, he would have been greeted with hugs and pats on the back.

"Just imagine," he said, "me climbing these hills to kiss Mother Doninha's hand and ask her if there was any truth in the story that is going the rounds, with people talking about nothing else, of my Father Ogun offering to be godfather at the christening, and I find the whole crowd here! Greetings, my Mother. Greetings, my brothers."

He bent over to kiss the hand of Doninha; she looked at Jesuíno; Martim smiled. Martim was a close friend of the artisan, who was one of his gaming companions. Artur was an inveterate crapshooter. And Martim spoke up in a tremulous voice, so astounding did the arrival of his friend seem: "Artur is a votary of Ogun and one who belongs to this house."

At first they all stood with mouth agape, realizing what had happened. Then came the embraces, the handclasps, the general and bubbling-over happiness.

Because Artur da Guima was a son of Ogun, who had received his preparation there, in that temple, except that it had not been Doninha who had laid her hand on his head and made him a votary. He had been a votary for more than forty years; his group had been initiated before Doninha was a priestess, when the temple was still in the hands of the late Dodó, of unforgotten and revered memory. That was why, in recalling the sons of Ogun in the city of the temple, Doninha had not included Artur da Guima, her brother-in-devotion, and not her son, Artur da Guima, who had certainly been led there at that very hour by Ogun—who could doubt it? Nobody did, not even Artur himself when Jesuíno explained everythng to him down to the last detail.

An elder of the temple, where he held a high post, Artur appeared only on the occasion of the great festivities or during the period of indispensable rites. And never, or hardly ever, was he seen in the circle of dancers. When he put in an appearance, he would sit in a chair behind the priestess, and as a rule she would ask him to lead two or three chants to his patron. He did this modestly; he did not like to show off, to make himself seem important, take advantage of his seniority. Once in a blue moon, Ogun mounted him and he danced in the circle. But his Ogun was little given to taking on human habitation; he was a difficult Ogun who rarely manifested himself, the same as Massu's, moreover, though the Negro was merely an initiate, not a votary of the deity's.

Doninha and Jesuíno eyed one another, the priestess lost in admiration in spite of all the things she had seen in her lifetime; Jesuíno, just a mite vain at being able to say that he had collaborated with Ogun, shared knowledge of his plans, helped carry them out.

"A son of Ogun and from this temple," Doninha repeated.

"And for over forty years," Artur da Guima proudly confirmed. "It will be forty-one years since my initiation. There are few left from those days. . . ."

"I was a girl of thirteen," Doninha mused. "Only two years afterwards, I entered the shrine to serve the deity."

"A tiptop god is Ogun," Massu certified.

Artur da Guima agreed—with some reluctance, for as has already been stated, he was a modest, timid soul, who stayed in his own corner except when he came out to gamble, an incorrigible crapshooter who almost always lost but who could not restrain himself. His Ogun appeared only at rare intervals, months went by without his manifesting himself, merely asking for the observance of a rite from time to time, food for his head. But to make up for this, when he did descend, he was full of life, gay, talkative, very friendly, greeting and embracing his acquaintances, his *ogãs*, and the members of the *candomblé*, all laughter, twisting and turning, dancing a lot, in a word, a first-class Ogun, top-flight, not any old god, a beauty of a god, and when he descended, the whole temple greeted him with enthusiasm. Artur da Guima demanded one thing, and this was that Doninha be present at the ceremony. Only she, with her power, would be able to control this vagabond, noisy Ogun, suddenly loose in the streets of Bahia, treading the flagstones of a church, acting as godfather at a christening. He, Artur da Guima, refused to take the responsibility. He had only to recall that time, some years back, when he was waiting for a bus to Feira de Sant'Ana one Sunday afternoon, on a serious matter that made it necessary for him to go to the nearby city, serious enough to make him miss Ogun's celebration that night. Well, Ogun had descended right there at the bus stop, grabbed hold of him, and before he knew it, he was at Dodó's place of worship, having crossed the whole city with the god mounted on his neck. But to start off, Ogun had given him a thrashing to teach him to respect the days of his celebration, had thrown him on the ground, had beaten his head against the paving stones. Then, shouting and laughing, he had set off for the temple. They had arrived accompanied by a small crowd. Artur da Guima learned about all this afterwards from the others.

So he had experience. That Ogun of his was a roisterer; he had to be controlled; otherwise Artur da Guima would not be responsible for the consequences.

But nobody paid much attention to him, they were all so excited by the solution to the final problem of the christening. The news would warm the heart of old Vevéva; the ceremony would take place on the appointed date.

⊷❧ 6 ❧⊶

FATHER GOMES'S GRANDFATHER HAD BEEN A SLAVE, one of the last to make the trip in a blackbirder. His back was welted by the lash, his name was Ojuaruá, and he was a chief in his own land. He had run away from a sugar plantation in Pernambuco, leaving the overseer in a pool of blood, had taken part in a slave revolt, had wandered about the forest, and in Bahia had taken up with a light free mulatta, ending his days with three children and a grocery store.

After Abolition, his elder daughter, Josefa, had married a young clerk, a good-looking white Portuguese who was crazy about the mulatta with her swaying haunches and shining teeth. Old Ojuaruá had caught the two of them lying along the wall, and as he was still as strong as a bull, he squeezed the lad by the throat and did not let up until they had set the date for the wedding.

That marriage seemed to blast the youth's fondest hopes, for the owner of the store where he worked, his fellow countryman, a widower and childless, had planned to marry him off to a cousin, the only relative he had left, from a village back in Trás-os-Montes. The owner was fond of the clerk, but he also felt himself under obligations to the distant cousin to whom, from time to time, he sent a few *patacos*. The ideal arrangement would have been to marry his faithful employee to his relative, and when he died, leave the flourishing store to them. Josefa came to demolish this plan. In a fury, the Portuguese threatened to send for the cousin, marry her himself, being still sound in wind and limb at sixty-two, and leave everything to her.

Josefa, however, was not prepared to lose the store or the regard of its owner. She knew how to ingratiate herself; she asked the Portuguese to act as best man at the wedding; she danced attendance on him, joked with him, called him father-in-law, scratched his head. The truth was that the storekeeper forgot to write the letter he had threatened to send inviting the cousin, whose picture, when he showed it to Josefa, made her roll on the ground with laughter. The boss deserved something better than that scarecrow: was a man like him, so good-looking and strong, going to gnaw on those bones? The Portuguese let his eyes rest on Josefa, on her solid flesh, her firm breasts, her swinging hips, and agreed.

In this way Josefa helped her husband, a good worker in store and bed, a delight of a man, but shy on brains, become the boss's partner and the sole owner of the store after his death. And when Josefa had her first child, a son, the Portuguese went crazy over it, was as fond of the little mulatto as though he were its father. Moreover, gossiping tongues would admit no argument: if the old Portuguese wasn't the father, he had certainly added the finishing touches to the confection of the child. Hadn't he taken the couple to live in his big widower's house, and hadn't he spent hours there alone with Josefa while her husband sweated in the store? Josefa shrugged her shoulders when anybody came to her with that tittle-tattle. She had developed into a fat, serene mulatta who could look after two Portuguese without any trouble, frolic with both of them, leaving them both happy, the young one, a rearing stallion, the old one a rutting billy goat.

While his wife was alive, the old man had longed for a son, and had longed for him to the point of making a vow: if the newborn child was a boy, he would send him to the seminary and have him ordained a priest. But his wife did not give him this happiness; she could not hold on to the children she conceived; she lost four or five, and in these alternating pregnancies and miscarriages she aged before her time, and authorities carried her off. Now the Portuguese was fulfilling his vow; he intended that the child should go to the seminary. As for Josefa, she was a devotee of Omolu; she had been initiated while still a girl; her father Ojaruá was an *obã* of Xangô, and attended the *candomblé* of Engenho Velho, hidden underground, persecuted in the most difficult days. That was why the future priest in his early infancy was often taken to the festivals and rites of the *orixás*, and if it had not been that he went off to the seminary, he would certainly have become an initiate or votary of one of them—Ogun, undoubtedly, who was Josefa's choice as soon as he was born.

In the seminary the young mulatto forgot the colorful sight of the *macumbas*, the harmonious circles of the votaries, the sound of the drums calling the deities, the presence of the gods in the ritual dances; he forgot the name of his grandfather, Ojaruá. To him his grandfather was the Portuguese store owner, the best man at his parent's wedding, his godfather, the patron of the family.

Josefa, too, stopped frequenting the voodoo ceremonies, and only very much on the sly did she carry out her duties toward Omolu, the elder (*âtoto*, my father, give us health!). It did not look right for the mother of a seminarist to be seen associating with the people of the *candomblé* or, much less, frequenting the site of ceremonies to the *orixás*. Even before the husky young mulatto had become transformed into the frail Father Gomes, ordained and having celebrated his first mass, she had completely given up old Omolu; she no longer gave him food; she carried out none of her obligations, appeared no more at Engenho Velho.

In addition to the seminarist, she had one daughter, Teresa, who had died at the age of eleven of variola, and later Josefa herself died of black smallpox. Whereupon the old crones would have it that she had been punished by Omolu, the god of health and sickness, lord of pox and pestilence, as everybody knows. Hadn't they both, mother and daughter, been devotees of Omolu, and hadn't the old deity come more than once to demand his young horse, insist upon her going to the shrine to anoint her head and receive her deity? But Josefa, out of respect for her son the seminarist studying to become a priest, would not allow her daughter to carry out her devotions, had rebelled against the rules. Nor did she herself, formerly so zealous of her god, pay any attention to him now, foregoing her obligations completely. She had failed to carry out her *bori*; for years she had not danced at her deity's feast. That was what the old crones said, the repository of secrets, the intimates of divinities and priests.

The two Portuguese, partners in business and bed, fathers of the recently ordained priest, died, too. Father Gomes sold the store, bought two houses in Santo Antônio beyond Carmo, one to live in, the other to rent out. As a matter of fact, both of them were rented for years while he was officiating in the interior, in São Gonçalo dos Campos and in Conceição da Feira. After this, he never again left the capital, and he grew old in the Church of the Rosary of the Negroes, held in high esteem by the faithful, and assisted by Mr. Innocence of the Holy Ghost. Saying his masses, performing christenings and marriages, moving placidly amid that motley crowd of artisans, dockworkers, prostitutes, loafers, clerks, and people without gainful occupation or with none they cared to admit to. He got along well with them; he was a cordial Bahian without a trace of bigotry about him.

If anyone had reminded him that his maternal grandfather had been an *obã* of Xangô and his mother a votary of Omolu, an Omolu famous for the bright coloring of his straw vestments and the violence of his dance, he would not even have believed it, so completely had the scenes of his early childhood been obliterated from his memory. He recalled his mother as a fat, pleasant woman, very devout, who never missed mass, an excellent mother. He did not like to remember her last days, in bed all swollen, her face, arms, and legs covered with pustules, smelling badly, devoured by smallpox, muttering unintelligible phrases, strange words. He would have been scandalized if some old woman of those bygone days had turned up and had revealed to him that all that was the doing of an exasperated Omolu riding his horse on its last journey.

Father Gomes was well aware—how could he ignore it?—that the city was full of *candomblés* of many different kinds, Yoruba, Congo, Angola, Caboclo *candomblés* in profusion, temples that functioned the year around, voodoo sites where the drums beat every night, swarming with believers. The same who filled his church at Sunday mass, the same ardent devotees of the Catholic saints.

The great majority of his parishioners who never missed a mass, who carried the floats on their shoulders during the processions, the heads of the sodalities, also belonged to the *candomblé*, merging the Catholic god with the African *orixá*, fusing them into a single deity. In the shrines of the *candomblés*, he had been told, pictures of Catholic saints hung alongside fetishes, Negro sculptures, St. Jerome in the shrine of Xangô, St. George in that of Oxossi, Saint Barbara on the altar of Yansã, St. Anthony on that of Ogun.

For his flock, the church was like a continuation of the place of voodoo worship, and he, Father Gomes, was the priest of the "white gods," as they called the Catholic saints. By this designation they stressed their community with the African *orixás* and at the same time their difference. They were the same, but in the guise in which the white and the rich worshipped them. For this reason Father Gomes also was at a greater distance from them, from their respect and esteem, than the priests and priestesses, the *babalaôs*, the old men and women of the cult. Father Gomes vaguely realized all this, but it did not bother him too much, for he was a tolerant person. When all was said and done, they were good people, those of Pelourinho, Catholics each and every one. Even though they mixed saints and *orixás*.

On one occasion Father Gomes was surprised to find the church full of people dressed in white—men, women, children, all in white. He asked Innocence if there was a reason for this or if it was mere coincidence that they should all be so impeccably turned out in white clothes. The sacristan reminded him that it was the first Sunday of Bonfim, Oxalá's day, when it is the duty of all to dress in white, the color of the greatest of the divinities, the father of the other deities, Lord of Bonfim, to put it more clearly.

Out of the corner of his eye, and with a certain surprise, Father Gomes took in the immaculate whiteness of Innocence's own attire, his gleaming white trousers, his white shirt, his coat shining with starch. Was it possible that even his sacristan . . . ? Father Gomes preferred not to delve into the question.

In spite of this discretion, which characterized him, he could not fail to notice the extraordinary attendance at seven o'clock mass on the day set for the christening of Massu's son. A weekday, not a holiday or a Sunday, and the church was full, or rather, it had begun to fill up at dawn. When Father Gomes arrived, at half past six, a small crowd was already chatting on the steps. After returning their greetings, the priest made his way past Negroes, mulattoes, and whites amid conversation and laughter. It was a festive atmosphere. How odd: most of the women were wearing the typical multicolored costume of Bahia, and some of the men, as he could observe, had bows of dark blue ribbon on their lapel.

Inside, the church was equally crowded, and the full skirts swept the nave, where countless slippered votaries and initiates glided along as though moving through the measures of a dance. Fat and aged *iyalorixás*, gaunt and devout old women with white woolly hair, sat on the benches, their arms adorned with bracelets and beads, heavy necklaces at their throats. The church was more lighted up by the colors of these ornaments and the flowered fabrics than by the wan light of the candles on the altars. Father Gomes wrinkled his brow; something out of the ordinary must have happened.

In answer to his question, Innocence reassured him. Nothing special. Just a christening that had been set for that day and all those people had come to attend it.

A mere christening? Then the parents must be very rich, distinguished people. Was the father a politician? Or a banker? The children of bankers were not as a rule baptized in the Church of the Rosary of the Negroes in Pelourinho, but in that of Grace or Piety or St. Francis, or at the Cathedral. Maybe it was a politican who had brought his son to that humble baptismal font as an act of demagoguery?

Neither a politician nor a banker nor the owner of a store nor even a stevedore. Negro Massu, the father of the child, did odd jobs, mostly carrying bundles and boxes, when he was really hard up. Aside from that, what he liked to do was go fishing with Wing-Foot, kibitz at a good game of cards or dice, engage in a chat over a glass of rum. As for the mother, she had been gay and pretty, a good kid, but a flibbertigibbet, a feather wit, who had died of tuberculosis in a hospital.

And why had so many people come to attend the christening? the priest wondered when he had been informed of these details. What could have attracted them, when Massu was a poor devil who could offer them nothing, neither public office nor literary glory, nor even lend them money?

Ah, Father Gomes could not imagine how well liked Massu was and, in his way, important among those people. Without being a politican or a banker, he had already done many favors. What kind of favors? Well, for example, once a rich young punk, one of those pampered brats of the Corredor da Vitoria, thinking he owned the world because of Papa's money, had tried to pull a fast one with a girl of sixteen, a daughter of Carnation-in-his-Buttonhole. . . .

"Of whom?"

"That's his name. You know him, he's around Pelourinho a lot, he always wears a flower in his buttonhole. . . ."

Well, as he was saying, the fellow ran across the girl alone at night, looking for her father, with a message from her mother, an urgent matter, sickness. The girl was walking fast, her father was working, he was . . . well, a kind of night watchman in a store. The fellow saw that the girl was alone, came up to her, grabbed her, really latched on to her. . . . The only reason he did not take advantage of the poor thing was that she screamed, people came, and he beat it. But he was recognized, for it wasn't the first time he had tried to pull a stunt like that—a scoundrel who, not satisfied with cows of his own class, tried to molest the daughters of the poor. . . . The girl had showed up all scratched and sobbing at the circle of the . . . that is to say, where her father worked, and Negro Massu happened to be there and heard the whole thing.

While Carnation-in-his-Buttonhole went with his daughter to take care of the matter about which his wife had sent for him, Massu set out for Terreiro de Jesus and environs, looking for the young pillar of society and future benefactor of his country. He found him drinking at Tabaris, a cabaret on Praça do Teatro, where they did not want to let the Negro in because he was wearing sandals and no necktie. Massu, however, pushed aside the whole lot of them; the policeman, who was an acquaintance of his, gave ground and disappeared; the Negro made his way in and grabbed hold of the playboy with such fury that one of the musicians choked on a note. What a beating, Father, what a beating! No dude had ever gotten one like it in Bahia, and when the Negro had finished with him, the tarts applauded, for he was not well liked; he was in the habit of using their services and then not paying for them, and the musicians and customers applauded. When the police, who had been called after considerable delay, finally showed up, Massu had already had a beer and had left, and all that the flatfoots could do was to pick up the little angel and take him home. There his parents sent for doctors and raged against this city without police and full of bums, where a lad of good family and good habits like their young son-of-a-bitch (if Your Reverence will excuse the word) could not even go out at night. For that and other reasons, Massu was popular and had many friends. The godmother was popular, too, one of the kindest and most obliging of persons, with a vast circle of friends, including people of quality, doctors, judges, congressmen. She was Dona Tibéria, proprietress, that is to say, married to a clerical tailor by the name of Jesus, owner of "God's Scissors," Father Gomes must know him. Yes, Father Gomes knew who the tailor Jesus was; when young he had spent his savings on a cassock made by him, the first and the last, for his was a high-priced establishment, all right for monsignors and canons, but not for the likes of him, a modest priest of a poor parish. He also knew who Dona Tibéria was, didn't she always contribute generously to church celebrations? Perhaps in that way she hoped to obtain forgiveness for her sins, for her immoral trade. Innocence nodded his head; he never disagreed with the priest.

And to change the subject, he mentioned the old Negress Vevéva, Massu's grandmother, respected for her age and her knowledge.

"And what kind of knowledge can an ignorant Negress have? And who is the godfather? Is he popular too?"

Was he! Innocence choked, for this matter of the god-father was a problem if ever he saw one. Nevertheless, he had to manage it somehow. Father Gomes did not know the godfather, he was a craftsman with a shop on Tabuão, who worked wonders with his hands, carvings in stone, ivory, wood.

"On Tabuão? Maybe I might know him. What's his name?"

"His name is . . . Antônio de Ogun."

"How's that? Ogun? What a strange name, Ogun."

"Clever, Father, you never saw anyone so skillful. Most of the dice used in the city—I mean, he is a fine worker. . . ."

But the priest was pursuing that far-away sound in his memory: "Ogun . . . I've heard that somewhere. . . ."

That's the way with these Negroes, Innocence explained, they sometimes used the most extraordinary monikers, African names. Didn't Father Gomes know Isidro de Batualê, who owned a tavern in Sete Portas?

No, no, he didn't know him. How could he? Honestly, people come up with the craziest names. The godfather, moreover, was not a Negro, probably not even a mulatto, maybe a long way back. He could pass for a well-born white man. And he had that slave name of Antônio de Ogun. Innocence knew a Maria de Oxun, who sold manioc mush on the Ladeira da Praça.

When Father Gomes reached the door that separated the sacristy from the nave of the church, he peeped out. The throng was growing; the ranks of the Bahian women with their full skirts were now swelled by prostitutes with contrite faces. The priest felt his breast oppressed by a suspicion he could not put words to. The name of the godfather nudged a vague memory, but he could not place it. It calmed him, however, to see Innocence so relaxed and free from misgivings. What he did not know was that the sacristan's calm was only surface deep. As a matter of fact, he was dying of fright: what if Father Gomes happened to know Artur da Guima? He'd surely want to know the reason for this change of name, why Artur da Guima had become Antônio de Ogun.

The Christening of Felício

Ipicilone was the first to want to know. He was very touchy; he did not want to be fooled; he insisted on the greatest propriety in every detail of that affair. And when he set forth his doubts, they met with general approval. According to him, if the name given as that of godfather was Artur da Guima, then he would be officially the god-father of the child even though he was not in fact, but was acting in that capacity merely as the deputy of Ogun. However, only a few persons knew this, and with the pass-ing of time, the fact would be forgotten, the child would grow up, and as far as he was concerned, his godfather would be Artur da Guima. Was that so or wasn't it?

Artur da Guima himself agreed. They ought to use the name of Ogun, beyond a doubt. But how to do it? Once more Jesuíno Crazy Cock rose to the occasion. Wasn't Ogun Santo Antônio? Then all you had to do was use his full name, Antônio de Ogun. The only drawback was that Innocence knew Artur da Guima. Bullfinch, to whom the sacristan owed his health and his unsullied reputation, was entrusted with the matter of going to see him and explain-ing the matter to him.

Innocence hesitated, but finally gave in and became an accomplice. How could he refuse them his solidarity when he was in Bullfinch's debt? The only thing that worried him was that the priest might know Artur da Guima. When they asked Artur, he said he couldn't be sure. He did not know if the priest had ever noticed him; he knew His Reverence very well. Just to be on the safe side, Innocence drew up the baptismal certificate at once. And there it stood: Godfather—Antônio de Ogun.

In the doorway connecting the sacristy with the church, Father Gomes watched the crowd grow. People were arriv-ing every minute. Among those present, it seemed to him that he even recognized Dr. Antônio Barreiros Lima of the Institute of History, an illustrious member of the Medical School. Could he, too, have come for the christening of Negro Massu's son?

It was time to put on his vestments for the mass, which was to be followed by the christenings. In the Square, visible through the door of the church, a kind of small

201

procession appeared. Bahians, men and women, and the sound of voices. Probably the christening party. They advanced slowly. The priest hurried, for he was late.

Innocence said to him, as he helped him get ready: "It's going to be a celebration that will make news. . . ."

"Which? What celebration?"

"That of the christening. Dona Tibéria is paying for it. She, Alonso of the store, Isidro, and other friends of Massu. The sky's going to be the limit. I even wanted to talk to you, sir; I won't be able to be here this afternoon, as I've been invited to the lunch."

"Have I any engagements?"

"No, sir."

"Then you can go. I just wish I could remember what the name of that godfather reminds me of. . . ." He stood thinking for a moment before he picked up the chalice and moved toward the altar. He murmured under his breath: "Ogun . . . Ogun . . ."

Ogun came across the square with dancing step, free from all constraint, ready for anything, and let out a yell which shook the windows of the old mansions and made all the Bahian women gathered in the church shudder. The child in Tibéria's arms smiled, old Vevéva came slowly to Ogun's side, Massu, wearing a suit of blue worsted in which he was suffocating, shone with vanity and perspiration. Ogun broke away from Doninha's hands and ran ahead to mount the church steps.

⚜ 7 ⚜

ON THE EVE OF THE CHRISTENING, Tibéria, Massu, and Artur da Guima slept in the *axé*. Mother Doninha had informed them beforehand that the three of them—the godmother, the father, and Ogun's horse—would have to make their *bori*, cleansing their bodies and feeding the head of the god.

They had arrived early in the evening as the shadows were flitting along the path of São Gonçalo, descending over the mysterious hillsides, the hiding places of Exu. Exu let himself be glimpsed among the thick woods, at times as an attractive young Negro, at times as an old beggar leaning on a staff. His foxy, devil-may-care laugh echoed through the lianas and the branches of the bushes in the soft twilight breeze.

The three who had been summoned did not arrive alone. They were accompanied by their friends, for all the gang wanted to be present at the ceremony. Mother Doninha had invited several initiates of the temple, carefully chosen, to help: preparing the herb baths, lighting the big wood-burning stove, sharpening the knives, scattering myrtle leaves over the floor of the freshly swept chambers and parlors. They made everything ready for the solemn ritual of the *bori*.

But in addition to those who had been chosen, a number of others showed up, drawn by curiosity, and a buzz of talk and laughter filled the cermony grounds as though it were the eve of one of the great annual feasts obligatory on the calendar of the *axé*, a basic celebration in honor of Xangô or Oxalá, of Oxossi or Yemanjá.

A little after seven, Mother Doninha, grumbling about having to get up early the next day, rang her bell, and they assembled in the house of Ogun. There were too many for them all to be able to get in; some had to stay outside.

The priestess made her way through the visitors: "Nobody sent for them; they came because they wanted to. Now let them make out as best they can."

Artur da Guima and Massu were already waiting in the shrine itself, the room where the fetishes of the deity were kept, his apparel, his implements, his food, all that belonged to him. The Negro and the craftsman had taken their bath of herbs in a first cleansing of their body against the evil eye, envy, and any other ill. They were dressed in clean white clothes: Artur in pajamas, Massu in shirt and pants, and were seated on mats spread before the shrine.

Tibéria, who had also just emerged from her bath, came led by an *iyalorixá*. Wrapped in a gleaming white robe the size of a circus tent, she smelled of wild herbs and coconut soap. She waited in a little room next to the shrine, where a beautiful old chest held the clothing of the deity. She seated herself on a mat, her flesh free of girdle or stays, and she looked like a monument, placid and good-humored. Jesus, her husband, mingling discreetly with the other spectators, smiled with satisfaction at seeing her in such a state of repose.

The bells sounded. Mother Doninha took up the sheets, one by one. First she covered the two men, the sheets falling from their shoulders to their feet. Afterwards, the woman. The three were seated in ritual posture, the soles of their feet and the palms of their hands turned toward the priestess. Doninha settled herself on a stool and sighed; there was a lot of work ahead of her. She began a chant; the votaries responded in chorus, almost under their breath, the Yoruba song of greeting to Ogun.

She then busied herself with the water—pure water in the small clay water jugs. She poured a little out on the ground, wet her fingers, touched the feet, the hands, and the head, first of the men, then of the woman. She then cut the cola nuts and the *orobos*, one cola nut and two *orobos* for each person, separated certain pieces to be cast, and gave other pieces to the three of them to chew.

Ogun replied to her casting of the nuts and said that he was ready for the next day. Doninha could set her mind at ease; everything would go well. He sensed that she was worried and wanted to reassure her. What he did recommend, and this emphatically and insistently, was that they should not fail to make their promised sacrifice to Exu, his propitiative ceremony, first thing in the morning, at the break of day, so that he would not come and upset the festivity. Exu was roaming the neighborhood that night, scaring people on the roads, and they had to be on guard against him. But cautious and experienced, Mother Doninha had already set aside a guinea hen as a sacrifice to Exu before the ceremony, at the first ray of dawn on the christening day. Exu himself had selected the fowl some days before. Ogun wished everybody success and happiness, especially his *compadre* Massu, and then withdrew, to return when the meal was ready.

The hens were then sacrificed, their blood cleansed the heads of the men and the woman. They were now ready for the next day, eased of all evil.

In the meantime, while the votaries were cooking the deity's food, they talked of a number of things, but avoided the subject of the christening. Finally the meal was served —the chicken fricassee, bean cakes, bean tamales—first the deity his favorite pieces, and then Massu, Artur, and Tibéria, and then, in the dining room the others. There was all the food anybody could want, and Jesus had brought two crates of cold beer and several jugs of sweet wine. They sat around talking for a while, even though Mother Doninha reminded them of all the work she had to do the next day first thing in the morning.

In the shrine and the small parlor, at Ogun's feet, wrapped in sheets, branded with the blood of the sacrificed animals, with chicken feathers stuck to their toes, fingers, and head with blood, and the food of the deity inserted in the hair on the crown of their heads and all tied in place with a white cloth, Massu, Artur, and Tibéria had lain down to sleep. Artur was wheezing; Massu was snoring;

only Tibéria was still awake. Covered with the sheet, that strange hood on her head, the heavy necklace over her immense bosom, and a smile on her lips.

The friends had wanted to sleep in the temple, but Doninha had refused. She wanted no crowd on the way to the church. The fewer people who went with Ogun, the better; in that way they would not attract attention. She made a single exception for Jesuíno; she ordered a mat spread for him in the dining room. A man of wisdom and prudence, he might be useful if something unexpected came up. She took brief leave of Martim and Wing-Foot, Ipicilone, and Bullfinch. Martim had been entrusted with the responsiblity of getting old Vevéva and the child to the church with the help of Otália. They arranged to meet the next day at seven in the morning in Pelourinho Square.

But the orders of the priestess proved of no avail, for the next morning before the sun had risen, the paths to the *axé* were already being tramped by votaries, devotees of St. Cosme and St. Damian, Negroes, mulattoes, and whites, all wanting to be present from the beginning. Not only those of the ceremonial grounds of Meia Porta, who had been initiated or trained there. Not only those of the Yoruba rite, which was that of the temple. They came from all the houses of worship, the Yoruba, the Congo, the ceremonial centers of Angola, and the Caboclo *candomblés*. Members of the cult, without differentiation, not one wanted to miss the unheard-of spectacle of an *orixá* entering a church to christen a child. Nobody had ever heard the like. They hastily ascended the hillsides of mist and shadows among which Exu was roaming, a vagrant, a good-for-nothing, waiting for his sacrifice.

Votaries put down their trays of fried bean cakes and bean tamales, their cans of manioc and tapioca porridge, their pans of fried crabs, deserting the four corners of the city, with no thought for their customers. Others left un-kindled the stoves in the rich homes where they exercised the supreme art of cooking. Or threw to the wind duties and family obligations. Up the hillside they went, wearing their most colorful outfits, the initiates of Ogun especially attired. At times with small children straddling their hips. Important figures also showed up. The *babalaô* Nézinho of Maragogipe, so often consulted by priestesses and priests. He had come especially to witness this unheard-of event. He arrived in a taxi in the company of the no less famous Father Ariano of the Morning Star, whose Caboclo deity was not too happy about the business. Agripina de Oxumaré, who sold porridge on Ladeira da Praça, also came: a large, handsome woman the color of copper, with the body of a goddess. Her deity descended at any center since the disappearance of the Candomblé da Baixada, where her Oxumaré had called out her name twelve years before, when she had still been a child. This beautiful Agripina was a marvel dancing; it was a sight to see her possessed of the deity, dancing with her stomach to the ground, the sacred serpent. A professional dancer of Rio had copied her dances and won success and the praise of the critics with them.

Doninha had got up very early, while it was still dark, and had called Stela, her assistant. They then awakened several of the votaries to take care of Exu's sacrifice. Massu's snoring in the altar chamber was like the whistle of a steam engine. Doninha, accompanied by Stela and the votaries, set out for the house of Exu. One of the women went to get the guinea hen.

She came back frightened: the guinea hen was gone. It had managed, God only knows how, to get loose from the string by which it had been tied to a guava tree and had run off, disappeared in the clearing.

At the very moment that she was telling Doninha what had happened, a mocking laugh, long drawn out and cynical, was heard in the bushes. The priestess and Stela exchanged glances; the votaries shivered. Who could be laughing like that, so insolently, except Exu himself, the most moot of all the *orixás*, rascally, irresponsible, a prankster, a lover of practical jokes? He had played so many that people had come to confuse him with the devil. Whereas each of the *orixás* had its counterpart in a saint of God—Xangô, St. Jerome; Oxossi, St. George; Yansá, St. Barbara; Omolu, St. Lazarus; Oxalá, Our Lord of Bonfim; and so on—Exu had none, and those who were not well versed in the cult accused him of being the devil. Everyone was afraid of him, and the first ceremony at all the festivals was always for him, and the first songs. He had asked for a guinea hen; would he be satisfied with some other animal or would he be annoyed?

Mother Doninha sent for three white doves she had in a cage. She hoped to placate Exu with them. She sacrificed them, asking him to accept them in the place of the guinea hen. Exu seemed to be satisfied, for his laughter was heard no more and the atmosphere remained calm. When the offering had been carried out, Doninha returned to Ogun's house for the last part of the ritual cleansing, to remove the sheets from the heads, the feathers from the feet and hands, the food of the saint from the hair.

When, accompanied by Massu, Tibéria, and Artur da Guima, Doninha came into the big shed, even before the morning mists had lifted, she was confronted by that world of people. It seemed the occasion of some great festivity, one of those marked in red on the calendar of the temple. The priestess frowned; she did not like that. Her intention had been to conduct Ogun accompanied by only four or five votaries in addition to herself. And now she found this noisy, excited crowd there. Not to mention the guinea hen that had run off in the night and the laughter of Exu. She shook her head, worried. She knew the talk that had been going on in *macumba* circles: there were many who criticized her for having assumed the responsibility of such a dubious undertaking. Who knows? they might be right. But now it was too late; she had begun it; she would have to see it through. Besides, she was only obeying the orders of the deity. Ogun would surely help her out.

So she crossed the shed with head high, making straight for the armchair to whose back a bow of red ribbon was tied, Xangô's color, a chair she alone was entitled to occupy, a symbol of her rank and standing. There she received the greetings of Nézinho and of Ariano and invited them to sit down beside her. The votaries came and threw themselves at her feet, kissing her hand.

The drums boomed; the dance circle was formed. And as though by previous decision, general agreement, votaries of other temples took their place in the circle alongside the votaries and initiates of the house. Everything was different on that day, Nézinho observed, deeply impressed, but the changes in the ritual maintained a perfect rhythm, as though obeying an order established beforehand by the priestess. Only Doninha felt uneasy; the changes in question were not in obedience to any orders she had given.

Doninha struck up the first song; the votaries answered. In the middle of the circle, Artur da Guima began his dance. There was a general excitement; the votaries nudged one another, laughed about nothing, and the circle had no more than begun to move and the first songs to ring out when a Iansã descended, bucking and curveting, throwing a votary against the walls, violently. Her war cry awakened the still sleeping birds and scattered what was left of the night. The votaries applauded; the dance grew swifter. There was unusual excitement in the air; the priestess felt it; anything might happen.

Mother Doninha asked Iansã to leave: nobody had summoned her there; it was neither her feast nor her rite; Iansã would please forgive her, but she must go. The deity, however, did not want to obey. She went from side to side, shouting noisily. She was determined to stay and dance, ready to accompany Ogun to the church and even to take Tibéria's place as godmother, if need be. Mother Doninha had to exercise all her persuasion and all her power.

Finally, Iansã took her leave, but she had no more than departed, under protest, when two other votaries fell into a trance: one possessed of Nãnãn Burokô; the second of Xangô. To avoid complications, Doninha allowed them one dance, but only one, and ordered them to withdraw into the shrine. Quickly, for Iansã was threatening to return. It was necessary to send the three votaries away from the shed to the house of the devout women, the *ayabás*.

And the excitement mounted; the votaries danced with growing enthusiasm; the orchestra player ever louder, Agripina circling light and beautiful. Mother Doninha felt somewhat nervous. Everything should be transpiring quietly and almost secretly, not with this frenzied dancing, the house full of people, the very opposite of the arrangement made with Ogun. The saint did not want a fuss or a lot of people or an uproar. And why was he taking so long to descend? If he waited much more, the other deities would begin to arrive, and by the time there were six or eight in the shed, how could she, Doninha, control that many *orixás*, subdue them, send them away? Impossible. Not even with the help of Nézinho and Jesuíno or with the collaboration of Saturnina de Yá, the priestess of Bate Martelo, who at that very moment was entering the door of the shed with three votaries.

In the center of the circle Artur da Guima was dancing. His age did not allow of much dash or imagination, but his dance was full of dignity. Doninha made up her mind: she got up from her armchair and went over to dance beside Artur.

All those present got to their feet and with hands outspread greeted the priestess. All the votaries, including Saturnina de Yá and her three daughters-in-devotion, entered the circle.

Doninha grasped the tools of Ogun and touched Artur lightly on the nape of the neck with them. The artisan's whole body gave a shudder. She then touched him in the middle of the head, and Artur da Guima swayed as though shaken by a high wind.

Always dancing around the son-of-the-saint, Doninha unfastened her bright shawl from her belt, threw it over Artur, and made him dance beside her, fastened to her, in rhythm with her. Artur trembled, jerked as though he were receiving electric shocks. Dancing, the priestess touched him on the head, the neck, and the chest with Ogun's tools. The orchestra plunged furiously into the summons to the saint.

Suddenly Artur da Guima wrenched himself out of Mother Doninha's arms and went stumbling about the shed. The saint had finally arrived; he came wild and fierce, throwing his horse from one side to the other. Artur groaned and guffawed, collided with the walls, rolled on the ground; never had anyone seen Ogun so dreadful, so devastating. Mother Doninha hurried over and helped him to his feet.

In a storm of laughter, the saint threw Artur's shoes far away, then went out to greet the woods, came back, crossing the shed to greet the orchestra at the other side. Like a typhoon.

And he danced. How beautifully he danced! A gay dance with many flourishes, the war dance of Ogun, but modified, full of roguishness and virtuosity. Artur da Guima was free of the weight of age and the sleepless nights at the gaming table. He was a young man in his full vigor, his feet stamping, whirling faster and faster in a dance of challenge and greeting. He came and embraced Mother Doninha, pressing her to his breast. She freed herself, amazed at so much enthusiasm on Ogun's part. He was moved by this business of being godfather of the child; that was evident. He embraced Massu, dancing before him in a marked display of friendship. He embraced Nézinho, Ariano of the Morning Star, Saturnina de Yá, Jesuíno Crazy Cock, Tibéria. He even went to the circle and danced there in front of Agripina, took her in his arms, and nuzzled the nape of her neck. The girl laughed nervously. Doninha was shocked; she had never seen that before, a deity nuzzling a votary.

When the orchestra fell silent, the deity's horse went from side to side and finally stopped in front of the priestess, demanding the festive attire. He wanted his richest and finest clothes and his tools, too.

His festive attire. His tools? Was he, perchance, out of his wits? Mother Doninha asked, her hands on her hips. Didn't he know that it was impossible to go into the church in his holiday attire, brandishing his irons?

The saint stamped his foot on the ground stubbornly, grimaced, and demanded his clothes. Patiently but firmly, the priestess explained things to him. He knew very well the reason why he had descended that morning, on a day not scheduled on the calendar. It was he himself, Ogun, who had decided the matter of the christening of Massu's son, appointing himself godfather. Then why was he bringing up all that nonsense of his holiday attire, his tools? They had to go to church; it was already time, and he must try to behave in such a way that not the priest or the sacristan, none of those present at the mass, would suspect the imposture, would unmask Artur da Guima. He had to go in very circumspectly, as discreetly as possible, without making a noise, without calling attention to himself. Only in that way could they christen the child. Had he thought of the expression on the priest's face if he even remotely suspected the identity of the real godfather? The christening would be off; the child would go on being a heathen with no godfather to stand up for him.

The deity seemed to agree with her. In the church, when they got there—he said—his behavior would be exemplary, nobody would suspect that it was he and not Artur da Guima who was holding the candle and supporting the head of his godchild. But here, in the shed, he wanted to have fun, amuse himself with his sons and daughters, with his friends who were there, with his *compadre* Massu. He wanted to dance. Let Doninha order the songs to begin; let the orchestra strike up.

But Doninha did not grant him even this. They were late; they had to start. Not one more dance, not even a song. There was only a little time, and they had quite a way to go, partly on foot, partly by streetcar. The god's horse, however, stamped his feet, walking from side to side menacingly.

Doninha got mad. Then let him do what he liked, but afterwards he was not to come blaming her for what happened. Let him dance all the dances he felt like, put on his holiday attire, and take all the time he wanted. But he was not to count on her any more. He could go to the church alone and fend for himself.

In the face of such threats, he grudgingly gave in. Even so, they had trouble persuading him to put on his shoes. He flatly refused. Who ever heard on an *orixá* wearing shoes! They finally reached a compromise: he would put on his shoes when they got to the streetcar.

On the way to the car stop, they had to go after him and bring him back from the woods three times, for he jerked away from the group and ran off. More nervous with each passing moment, Mother Doninha prayed to Our Lord of Bonfim that everything should go well. She had never seen Ogun like that, so out-of-hand, like a mischievous urchin. Even taking into account the circumstances, the fact that it was the first time an *orixá* was going to a Catholic church to christen a child, even so.

8

So colorful and gay a streetcar as the one coming from the direction of Cabula around six o'clock in the morning had never run along the rails in the city of Salvador da Bahia de Todos os Santos. It was on its way to Baixa do Sapateiro, brimming over with votaries in their bright full skirts, their starched petticoats, their turbans, necklaces, and bracelets. As if they were going to a *candomblé* festival.

In the midst of them was a turbulent customer who looked as though he were drunk, wanting to dance on top of one of the benches. A fat woman was trying to control the impulsive and amusing roisterer. Passersby recognized her as the priestess Doninha.

The motorman, a strong young Negro, had lost control of the vehicle and did not seem to care. The car moved first at a snail's pace, as though no such thing as a schedule existed, as though it had all the time in the world, and then at full speed, breaking all traffic laws, in haste to arrive. The conductor, a cross-eyed, mulatto with stiff, kinky hair, rang the bell, for no good reason, to the rhythm of *macumba* music. Moving along the running board, he refused to charge for the ride. Nézinho had wanted to pay for everybody, but the conductor returned the money to him. "Everything for free, on the Company," he said laughing, as though they had taken over, assumed control of the streetcar line, the motormen and conductors, the workers in the carbarn. As though that morning a state of general happiness and frank cordiality had been decreed.

The incidents which had begun at the temple were rushing headlong. An unclouded atmosphere filled the city; dawn hung in the air, the people along the sidewalks laughed.

They got off the street car at Baixa do Sapateiro and set out for Pelourinho Square. It was a small conglomeration in bright hues, swelled by the curious and passersby.

The streetcar was left standing there on the rails, empty, for both the conductor and the motorman, as though by common consent, had deserted the vehicle and joined the throng. This gave rise to the traffic tie-up which caused so much confusion in the city, upsetting commerce and industry. Several truck drivers at the same time and without previous agreement left their big trucks in Sete Portas, in front of the Lacerda elevator, on the docks, at the Calçada Station, at the bus stop of Amaralina, at Pitangueiras, and in Broatas, and all set out for the Church of the Rosary of the Negroes. Three buses full of workers decided by a quick vote to call a holiday and went to the festival.

The *orixá* ascended Pelourinho slope amid the greatest turmoil, disobedient, attempting to jerk loose from Doninha's hands, trying out dance steps in the street. From time to time he let out a loud guffaw, which nobody could resist, and they all laughed with him. "Where were his solemn promises?" Doninha asked, but he paid no attention, he was the master of the city.

At the Square, the two corteges met, that of Ogun coming from Baixa do Sapateiro, that of Vevéva from Terreiro de Jesus.

That of the deity, with priestess and votaries, *babalaôs* and *ogãs*, with three *obás* of Xangô, the motorman, the conductor, several chauffeurs, two policemen and a soldier of the army, Jesuíno Crazy Cock, the sculptor Mirabeau Sampaio and his wife Dona Norma, he dressed in white like a good son of Oxalá's, she very gay, embracing acquaintances—and she was acquainted with everybody—wanting to go through a few dance steps in front of the saint. And the populace in general, without counting the kids.

And the cortege of the baby and old Vevéva. In the lead, a cart in which Vevéva, the baby, and Otália were riding. Behind came Martim, Bullfinch, Wing-Foot, Ipicilone, all the neighbors of Negro Massu, the personnel of the *capoeira* ring of Valdemar, people from the Mercado Modelo, Didi and Camafeu, Mario Cravo with Master Traira, skiffmasters and whores, a whole orchestra of ukuleles and harmonicas, Cuíca of Santo Amaro and the celebrated fortuneteller Madame Beatriz, newly arrived in the city and recommended to Bullfinch.

The meeting of the two groups took place just in front of the Capoeira School of Angola, and Master Pastinha and Carybé helped old Vevéva out of the cart. Tibéria, all dressed in silk and lace, kilometers of lace from Sergipe, carried the child in her arms, as she was the godmother. Martim held out his hand to Otália, and the girl gave an agile leap, to the accompaniment of wolf whistles from the teen-age onlookers. The *orixá* laughed a merry chuckle.

He moved ahead; he came dancing, oh, what a wonderful dance of greeting and friendship. He came dancing and stopped almost directly in front of the old Negress Vevéva as though about to embrace her, but she threw herself to the ground right there in the street, pounding her head against the stones in homage to the deity. He stretched out his hand and helped the old woman to her feet, then pressed her to his breast three times. Doninha gave a sigh of relief. It was Ogun, thank God, treating the old Negress with respect and affection. So far, so good. But how would he behave in the church? She had never expected that of Ogun. She had been deceived.

The *orixá* came dancing, circled about Tibéria, came still closer, gave a hoarse cry, and pulled out from under his shirt a hidden iron tool—not one of Ogun's—and touched the child's head with it. The procession advanced to the steps of the church. New doubts assailed Doninha; why had Ogun pinched Tibéria's bottom, why that lack of respect? Pressing through the throng, the priestess came forward, prepared to do whatever was necessary to avoid a scandal. Jesuíno followed close beside her, sharing her misgivings.

At the head of the stairs, as he passed between people

with their hands stretched palm upward to greet him, the *orixá* let out that laugh of his, so jeering and cynical, so lacking in respect and so knavish, that not only Doninha understood, but also Nézinho, Ariano—whose Caboclo deity did not like that whole business and was worried about how it was going to turn out—Vivaldo, Valdeloir Rego, and other important members of the sect. Their breasts were filled with fear. Only the babe in Tibéria's strong arms smiled in rapture at the turbulent deity.

·⊰{ 9 }⊱·

WHEN THE *orixá* ENTERED THE DOOR of the Church of the
Rosary of the Negroes with his cortege, Father Gomes,
who was in the sacristy removing his vestments after saying
mass, asked Innocence if the people of the christening
party were ready. He wanted to get it over with as soon as
possible, as he had an ulcer and could not go too long
without eating.

Innocence, a little frightened by the unusual bustle in
the church and the noisy crowd in the Square, went out to
see. It was at this very moment that the organ let out a
hoarse note, in spite of the fact that it was locked and there
was nobody in the choir loft.

Perplexed, Father Gomes came as far as the door,
looked up into his church, saw the choir loft empty and the
organ locked. Apparently all was calm, except that the
church, even though mass was over, was still full, crowded.
I'm getting old; I must be hearing things, Father Gomes
thought to himself. He shook his head in melancholy confirmation, but his attention was at once attracted by the
congregation. Bahian women in holiday attire whose efful-
gence lighted up the penumbra of the temple; men wearing
blue suits or blue ribbons in their buttonholes, many people. Father Gomes decided that friendship was worth more
than wealth and social standing. Here was the child of a
poor Negro, a vagabond, being christened, and the turnout
was like that for the christening of the child of a banker or

217

a politician in power, even bigger, and certainly more sincere.

Around the font a small group had gathered, made up of the deity's horse and Tibéria, Massu, Vevéva, Doninha, Otália, Jesuíno Crazy Cock, Corporal Martim, Wing-Foot, Bullfinch, and a few others.

Nearby, the spectators were craning their necks to see. In the Square, the many who had not managed to get into the church were elbowing one another, and more and more people kept arriving, coming from all over the city, carrying musical instruments and out for a lark. The *orixá* went through some dance steps, laughed his mocking laugh, made as if to go dancing down the aisle. Doninha shivered with fear, as did all the priests and priestesses present who realized what was happening, they and Crazy Cock. From the moment they had entered the church they had taken in the terrible truth.

Father Gomes came walking toward the font; Innocence handed the godfather the candle with blue decorations. The priest patted the face of the smiling child, who did not take his eyes off the deity's surrogate, and looked over the group before him.

"Who is the father?"

Negro Massu stepped forward, modestly: "Your humble servant, Father."

"And the mother?"

"God took her away."

"Oh, yes. Excuse me. And the godmother?"

He cast a quick glance at Tibéria, he had met her somewhere. But where? With that kindly visage, a face reflecting a pure and generous soul, he could only have known her through the church. He smiled at her approvingly and then suddenly remembered who she was. But he did not retract the smile, so innocent and devout was Tibéria's face.

"And the godfather?"

The godfather was obviously drunk, thought the priest. His eyes glittered, he swayed from side to side, laughed between his teeth, short, nervous laughs. He was the man with that weird name, the artisan of Ladeira do Tabuão. The priest had often seen him at the door of his shop, he would never have imagined he had such a bizarre name. How was it again? The name of a Negro slave. Fixing him with a stern, censorious gaze, he asked: "Exactly what is your name?"

It would seem that the customer had been waiting just for that. The most cynical and unrestrained, the most jeering, laugh resounded through the nave, crossed the church, echoed in the Square, scattered throughout the city of Bahia, breaking windows, raising the wind, stirring up a dust cloud, frightening the animals.

The *orixá* gave three bounds, and shouted: "I am Exu! I am the one who is going to be the godfather! I am Exu!"

Never before was there and never again will there be such a silence. In the church, in the street, in Terreiro de Jesus, Ladeira da Montanha, Rio Vermelho, Itapagipe, Estrada da Liberdade, Farol da Barra, Lapinha, Quinze Misterios, in the whole city.

Everyone stood frozen in his tracks, there and everywhere. The only one who was wandering desperately around the church was Ogun. The rest was silence and stillness.

It was then that the most unexpected and extraordinary thing was seen. Father Gomes shook within his cassock, leaped out of his shoes, swayed on his foundations, twirled a little, and half closed his eyes.

Jesuíno Crazy Cock watched attentively. Could his eyes be deceiving him? Doninha, Saturnina, Nézinho, Ariano, Jesuíno, several others, realized what was happening, but did not become frightened, for they lived on intimate terms with the *orixás*.

The priest murmured something; Mother Doninha respectfully went over beside him and spoke a greeting in Nago.

Ogun had been delayed that morning of the christening; he had had to be present at long-drawn-out rites in Nigeria, and at an important celebration in Santiago de Cuba. When he finally hurried to the shed of the temple of Meia Porta, he found his horse, Artur da Guima, mounted by Exu, his irresponsible brother. Exu laughed at him and imitated him, complaining that they had not given him what they had promised, a guinea hen. For that reason he was getting ready to start a ruckus and put an end to the christening.

Like a madman, Ogun had searched the city of Bahia for a son of his into whom to descend to put things back in their place and chase Exu away and christen the child. First he looked in the temple. None. Daughters, yes, a lot of them, but what he needed was a son. He went to the Opa Afonjá *candomblé* to see if he could find Moacir de Ogun, but the lad was somewhere around Ilhéus. He went to other temples, and found no one. He set out in despair for the city while Exu was carrying on his pranks in the streetcar. The motorman was a devotee of Omolu; the conductor, of Oxossi. The soldier of Oxalá, Mario Cravo, of Omolu, too; none of them of Ogun. There in the Square he was an eyewitness to Exu's jiggery-pokery. He saw how he took them all in, how he allayed Doninha's suspicions when he raised Vevéva from the ground with delicacy and respect.

In the greatest distress, he followed him into the church. He wanted to talk, to unmask Exu, take his place, but how do it when there was not a single male horse of his whom he could mount?

He was skirting the four corners of the church as the priest approached and began his questioning. Then, suddenly, as he looked at the priest, he recognized him: it was his son Antônio, born to Josefa de Omolu, grandson of Ojuaruá, *obã* of Xangô. Into him he could descend; he had been intended to be his horse. True he had not carried out his obligations at the time he was supposed to, but in an emergency like this he would do. A consecrated priest in a cassock, but not on that account less his son. Moreover, there was no choice: Ogun entered the head of Father Gomes.

And with a strong and determined hand, he fetched Exu two good slaps to teach him to behave himself. Artur da Guima's face bore the red marks. Exu realized that his brother had arrived, that the fun and games were over. It had been fun; he had had his revenge for the guinea hen promised him and of which he had been cheated. He quickly left Artur with one last gaffaw and went to hide behind the altar of St. Benedict, a saint of his own color.

As for Ogun, even more quickly than he had entered, he left the priest and occupied his old, familiar horse, on which he would have come to the church if Exu had not balled everything up. It all happened so quickly that only the most knowledgeable took it in. The ethnographer Barreiros, for example, noticed nothing; all he saw was the priest slapping Artur da Guima because he thought he was drunk.

"There's not going to be any baptism. The priest is going to throw the godfather out," he concluded.

But the priest was himself once more. He knew nothing about slaps; he did not recall anything, saying as he opened his eyes: "I had a kind of dizzy spell."

Innocence came over solicitously: "Shall I get you a glass of water?"

"No, thank you, it's over."

And turning to the godfather, he asked: "What did you say your name was?"

Hadn't this man been drunk a little while before? Well, he had gotten over his jag; he was now steady on his feet, head up; he looked like a warrior as he smiled: "My name is Antônio de Ogun."

The priest picked up the salt and the consecrated oils.

In the sacristy afterwards, when the ceremony was ended and he had signed the certificate, the priest shook hands with the father, the godmother, the great-grand-mother, Vevéva, who was almost a hundred years old, as well as the godfather.

When the godfather's turn came, Ogun took three steps backward and three forward and came in a dancing movement to embrace Father Gomes three times. Father Gomes, who was also Antônio de Ogun. It did not matter that the priest did not know it, but he was a son of Ogun, of Ogun of the mines, of iron and steel, of shooting irons. Ogun the warrior. The deity clasped him to his breast and rested his cheek against that of the priest, his beloved son in whom he was well pleased.

–•❧ { **10** } ❧•–

AND THIS WAS HOW MASSU'S SON WAS CHRISTENED. A complicated and difficult affair, bristling with problems, but all of which were solved, thanks first to Jesuíno Crazy Cock, a man of great sagacity, then to Mother Doninha, and finally, to Ogun himself.

The celebration in the house of the Negro was one of the greatest, and everywhere in Bahia, wherever there was a daughter of Ogun, the dancing went on until dawn of the next day. In Pelourinho Square alone, when they came out of the church, Crazy Cock recognized more than fifty Oguns doing a victory dance. Not to mention the other deities. They all descended, without exception, to celebrate the christening of the son of Massu and Benedita.

Hidden behind the altar of St. Benedict, Exu went on laughing for some time, recalling his prank. Then he fell asleep, and while asleep he seemed a child like any other. Nobody who had seen him would have suspected that this was Exu of the crossroads, the *orixá* of motion, so knavish and unbridled that people confuse him with the devil.

And this was how Massu became the *compadre* of Ogun, which gave him great prestige and standing. But he was the same kindly Negro he had always been, now with his hundred-year-old grandmother and his baby.

After this, many people invited different *orixás* to act as godfather or godmother of their children. Oxalá, Xangô,

222

Oxossi, Omolu, are very much in demand as godfathers; Yemanjá, Oxum, Iansã, Euá, as Godmothers; and Oxumarê, who is male and female, in both capacities. But so far, none has accepted, perhaps distrustful of Exu's pranks. Only one *compadre* of a god exists, the Negro Massu, *compadre* of Ogun.

The Invasion
of Cat Wood

-❦{ *OR* }❦-

The Friends
of the People

◦⊰❧{ 1 }❧⊱◦

WE ARE NOT GOING TO DIVIDE THEM UP into villains and
heroes—who are we, disreputable vagabonds of Rampa do
Mercado, to pass judgment on such transcendental matters? The newspapers are full of the controversy, with sup-
porters of the administration and members of the opposition accusing one another, calling one another names,
praising one another, each trying to make all the political
hay he can out of the invasion of the lands of Cat Wood,
beyond Amaralina, behind Pituba. Apparently from the
start, and even before the invasion began, there was a
complete and total solidarity with the invaders, nobody
took a stand against them, and there were some, like Congressman Ramos da Cunha of the opposition and the
journalist Galub, who ran serious risks in defending them.

We are not going to blame anybody; we are not a court
of justice, and nobody tried to find out whether one or
several were guilty of the death of Jesuíno Crazy Cock, for
they were all too busy with the celebrations. But neither
are we going to join the chorus singing the praises of the
governor or the congressmen, of the government or the
opposition, or of the Spaniard who owned the lands, old
Pepe Eight Hundred, as the millionaire, José Perez, owner
of a chain of bakeries, cattle ranches, leagues and leagues
of land, not to mention houses which he rented out, was
nicknamed. Yes, because he too was praised in the verse of

Cuíca, styled a generous man with the heart of a turtle-dove, capable of sacrificing his own interests for the good of the people. Can you imagine! The poet must have got a fat fee; he's a good guy; everybody likes him; but he is always ready to hand out praise or abuse for a consideration. Poor fellow, you can't blame him, with that big family he's got, and having to earn his living—and the cost of living being what it is—exclusively by his intellect. Cuíca wrote his tales in verse, some of them very nice, and he himself set them up and printed them, designed the cover and peddled them at the market and along the waterfront, beside the Lacerda elevator or in Água dos Meninos, calling out the titles and proclaiming their merits.

He praised the Spaniard Pepe Eight Hundred, forgetting to include the reason for the nickname—the eight-hundred-gram kilograms he used in his warehouses and bakeries, which constituted the basis of his fortune; he praised the governor, the lieutenant governor, congressmen and aldermen in general, all the press, and particularly, Jacó Galub, the fearless reporter:

> Hero of Cat Wood Hill
> The journalist Jacó,
> Threatened with assault,
> And having to eat dust,
> Friend of the people, he,
> The dauntless champion
> Of giving them roof and bread,
> Galub the people's friend.

He praised everyone, or nearly everyone, cadging a hundred milreis from one, two hundred from the other, and considerably more from the Spaniard Eight Hundred, I hope, but he was the only one in all that vast news coverage to mention Jesuíno Crazy Cock and recall his figure. The newspapers and radios ignored him. Fulsome praise of the governor or Congressman Ramos da Cunha, of the valiant policemen, of the chief of police, thanks to whose prudence combined with his determination not to give in, et cetera, et cetera . . . But of Jesuíno, not a word. Only Cuíca, in his pamphlet "The Invasion of Cat Wood Where

the People Built a Community in Forty-eight Hours," devoted one verse to his memory. Because Cuíca, even
though he twisted the truth a little, knew how things had
happened, without the drooling or the trimmings that came
later. Poor fellow, he needed the money, and he sold the
truth down the river.

It will not be we who criticize him—why should we? He
was a favorite poet of the market place, with his sprung-
rhythm verses, poor of rhyme, positively destitute at times,
but with touches of genuine poetry now and then by way
of compensation. He altered facts and opinions depending
on which side his money was coming from. But isn't that
what great poets do, here and in foreign parts, with their
names in the papers and statues in the parks? Don't they
adapt themselves to the interests of the wielders of power,
and do they not behave in this fashion or that, according
as they are asked, ordered, or commanded? Depending on
what they are paid, depending on the highest bidder.
There you have the truth, spelled out with all its letters.
Didn't they change school, tendency, label, opinion, or the
same filthy lucre for which Cuíca changed his opinions?
Money or power or luxury or position, awards, their name
in the papers, laudatory speeches, what difference does it
make?

We are not going to blame anybody—that is not what
we are here for—but to narrate the history of the invasion
of Cat Wood Hill, for it has its humorous side and its sad
side, like every story worth telling. We are not going to pull
the chestnuts out of the fire for anybody; it so happens that
we were there and we know all that took place.

That was the time of Corporal Martim's infatuation—
was it really infatuation?—with Otália, and of the
lachrymose passion of Bullfinch for Madame Beatriz, the
celebrated East Indian fakir (born in Niterói), and we
would like to tell of these loves. So we will find some way
of intermingling the facts, the romantic and the heroic,
those having to do with the passions of the corporal and
the spieler, as well as those relative to the invasion of the
lands formerly the property of Commander José Perez,
illustrious bastion of the Spanish colony, distinguished son
of the church, respected in diverse sectors of the life of

Bahia, an outstanding citizen. Forgive us if we present here side by side the governor and Tibéria, madam of a cheap whorehouse, congressmen and loafers, sobersided politicians and gay ragamuffins, the street Arabs, Congressman Ramos da Cunha and Wing-Foot, the reporter Galub and Corporal Martim, on this occasion, moreover, promoted to Sergeant Porciúncula. We cannot handle it differently; intermingled they were, the poor and the rich, the lighthearted and the solemn, the people and those described in the newspapers as the friends of the people. But, and I repeat, we are not blaming anybody.

We don't blame anybody even though nobody was interested in finding out whether someone deserved punishment for the death of Jesuíno Crazy Cock. They were all very busy with the celebrations. They say the governor, a sensitive soul when it came to manifestations, was moved to tears as he embraced Congressman Ramos da Cunha, his political adversary, who drew up the expropriation plan. But he smiled when he appeared in the balcony in answer to the applause of the crowd in the Square.

---◦◦◦{ **2** }◦◦◦---

CUÍCA EXAGGERATED WHEN HE ALLUDED in the long title of his chapbook to a community built by the people in forty-eight hours. It took that invasion, the first carried out in Bahia, exactly a week to achieve the appearance of a neighborhood. Today Cat Wood is a real borough, and already the fancy façade of the Madrid Bakery, one of the chain belonging to Pepe Eight Hundred, has gone up there right across from Negro Massu's house. Other incursions were afterwards successfully carried out, whole developments sprang up beside Liberdade, to the northeast of Amaralina; there was the invasion of Chimbo on Rio Vermelho and the Lacustrians with their city above the waters. The poor have to live; they have to find lodging somewhere; nobody can be in the open all the time; one has to have a roof over his head; and who has the money to pay rent?

Even we incorrigible night owls have to have a place to rest our heads once in a while, a home to go to. To live without a home is impossible, and even Wing-Foot, a man without a schedule or steady work, catching his frogs and rats, his snakes, green lizards, and other animals for research and experimental laboratories, accustomed to the wind and the rain, loving to sleep on the beaches and tumble mulatta wenches there—for he is crazy about them —even Wing-Foot, whose nature can adjust to everything, the same as his animals, felt the need of a hole he could call his own. He was the forerunner of the invasion, so to speak.

On those lands of Cat Wood he built out of coconut-palm fronds that grew there, pieces of lath, boards from boxes, and other materials that cost nothing a kind of hut where he lived and which was his center of operations in his search for animals. There was no lack of frogs and toads in the brook just a few steps away. Rats of every kind and size proliferated in the vicinity, especially in some farms close by on the way to Brotas. In the woods of the surrounding hills there was everything: lizards, snakes, poisonous and non-poisonous, iguanas, tegus, and at times a rabbit or a fox. And fish from the river and the ocean for food. Not to mention land and water crabs.

He built his hut and lived in it for a long time without being disturbed. It was far from the center of the city; almost nobody ever came there to visit him, except when he dragged some friend out for a fish stew or some swinging chick to see the moon rise. Wing-Foot had never bothered his head about whether those vast and deserted tracks of land had an owner, whether he was committing an infraction of the law by building his miserable shack there.

And that was what he said to Massu when the Negro turned up one day at his invitation to share a fish stew. Wing-Foot cooked well; he was a master hand when it came to a bouillabaisse of pike, red snapper, grouper, mojarra, all caught by him. Many a time he had taken as a gift to Tibéria or Master Manuel fish weighing from eight to ten pounds or strings of sardines, octopi, or rays. And he would go to cook the stew on Manuel's skiff, rocked by the waves, smiled upon by Maria Clara or surrounded by the girls in the big kitchen of Tibéria's whorehouse. Fish cooked by Wing-Foot was a real treat.

Only once in a blue moon did he cook in his hut in Cat Wood and invite a friend. His regular diet was a piece of dried beef, a little manioc meal, and brown sugar. Wing-Foot was easily satisfied, and there was a time in his life when he didn't even have dried beef, only brown sugar and meal. Those were the days when he traveled about the interior and carried on the devout profession of helping the dying to die.

You know how it is: those stubborn die-hards who won't die, ready to disencarnate but reluctant to leave, not wanting to hang up, taking days and days to die, bollixing up the life of their relatives and friends. Perhaps it was because they still had unatoned sins to expiate on earth and for that reason needed prayers. Now, Wing-Foot had specialized in helping these fussy customers cross the threshold of the other world, leaving their families free to get on with the tears the situation called for, the preparations for the funeral, the food and drink for the wake. The finest wakes imaginable, with rum flowing freely and food fit for a banquet.

So anyone who had a cranky relative given up by the doctors, with one foot in the grave, but clinging to the flicker of life, without wanting to let go, knew what to do. He sent for Wing-Foot, agreed on the terms of payment— his fee was not excessive—and Wing-Foot took charge of the patient. Sitting beside the bed, he began the prayers, encouraging the relative: "Come, now, God is waiting for you. God and all His angels." And in his deep voice he chanted: *"Ora pro nobis . . ."*

There were other pray-ers, male and female, in the neighborhood, but none so quick and dependable as Wing-Foot. In half an hour, or at most an hour, the dying person snuffed out his candle and went to enjoy the delights of the paradise promised him by Wing-Foot. He made only one demand on the family about to be plunged into mourning: to leave him alone with the patient, not to upset him by their presence. They all went out, and behind the closed door the voice of Wing-Foot could be heard in prayers and advice: "Depart in peace, brother, with Jesus and with Mary. . . ."

On one occasion, a more inquisitive relative suddenly opened the door and could bear witness to the efficacy of Wing-Foot's aid, which went beyond prayers. He helped the dying person with his elbow, too, burying it in the aforesaid customer's belly, cutting off the little breath he still had left.

The relative raised a great howl, and that was the end of Wing-Foot's career as pray-er for the dying. Threats of vengeance brought him to the capital. It was then he built

233

his shack and met Jesuíno Crazy Cock when he offered his service as pray-er to a friend of the old vagabond whose husband did not want to abandon his earthly envelope. At that time Wing-Foot had not yet devoted himself to science as an important collaborator of research laboratories.

But all this curious and rich past of Wing-Foot has little bearing on the invasion of Cat Wood. We mention it merely to testify to the presence of at least one resident in those lands well before the coming of Massu.

Negro Massu, stretched out on the sand, sipping a drink of rum, breathing in the appetizing smell of the fish stew, looked over the landscape, the blue sea, the white beach, the coconut trees swaying in the breeze, and asked himself why he wasn't already living there. It was an ideal place to live; there couldn't be a better.

Negro Massu was suffering a serious crisis at that moment. The owner of the shack where he had been living for years in the company of his aged grandmother and his young son had finally got tired of trying to collect the rent, on which Negro Massu was four years and seven months in arrears, the exact time he had been living there. He had never paid one cent. Not because he was by nature a dead beat. On the contrary, there were few persons as serious and reliable as he. He did not pay for the simple reason that at the end of the month he never had the money. At times Massu made an effort; he saved up the few cents he had earned here and there, running errands or playing the numbers, with the rent in mind, the obligation he had assumed. But something unexpected always came up, an important celebration, a feast he could not miss, and there went his savings, his fragile nest egg.

Once the owner of the shanty, who had a slaughterhouse in the neighborhood, came in person to collect. He found only old Vevéva at home; he did not have the heart to turn her out, and left a message for Massu. The next time he came he found Massu fixing up the roof, which was full of leaks. The Negro was furious: a roof you could see through, a shanty not worth pissing on, sky-high rent, and the butcher yelling for his money, wanting the rent all of a sudden. The Negro snorted, came down from the roof; his muscles gleamed in the sun; he shouted still louder. The owner left without further talk and even promised to have the leaks fixed.

But recently a company had bought the lot and the shanty. The butcher had sold it relatively cheap because he saw no prospect of getting any income out of it or of Massu's moving.

The company planned to build a factory; it had bought up a big tract of land, was tearing down houses and shacks, and gave the occupants a month's notice to get out. And offered work, first in the building and afterwards in the factory. Negro Massu realized that he had no choice but to find new quarters.

And there, stretched out in the sand, eating the excellent fish, he asked Wing-Foot: "Who does this land around here belong to?"

Wing-Foot turned the question over thoughtfully in his mind: "I don't know. . . . It doesn't belong to anybody."

"When did you ever see land that didn't have an owner? Everything in this world belongs to someone."

"I think it belongs to the government. . . ."

"Well, if it belongs to the government, it belongs to the people."

"Does it really?"

"Don't you know that the government is the people?"

"Do you believe that? The government belongs to the police; that's for sure."

"You don't understand. I know; I even heard it said at a meeting. The trouble with you is you don't go to meetings, and that's why you don't know."

"What do I want to know for? What good would that do?"

Negro Massu let the oil trickle down the corner of his mouth. What delicious fish! There was no better place to live.

"You know, Wing-Foot, I'm going to be your neighbor. I am going to build a shack here for me. To put the old lady and the kid in."

Wing-Foot waved his hand generously: "You won't want for room, brother. Or for palm fronds."

Thus it was that several days later Negro Massu returned accompanied by Martim, Ipicilone, Carnation-in-his-

Buttonhole, and Jesuíno Crazy Cock. In a cart they brought some tools, a saw, hammer, and nails. Wing-Foot collaborated by cooking another fish stew. Only Bullfinch did not come, occupied as he was with Madame Beatriz.

Massu built his shanty, and it even turned out pretty. Carnation-in-his-Buttonhole, who had been taught the trade of house painter in his youth, chose the colors for doors and windows, blue and pink, and picked up the brush. But he did this only as an *aficionado*, as a favor to friends. At heart he had a horror of that work.

Ipicilone, sitting down, his belly full of fish, watched Carnation-in-his-Buttonhole painting windows and doors while Massu, Martim, and Jesuíno raised the mud walls. He sighed: "It makes me tired just to watch you work."

Ipicilone was like that, devoted to his friends; wherever they went, he went. Always ready to collaborate with advice and suggestions, expert at many things, an intellectual; he even read magazines. But physically weak, he tired easily.

While they were building, they enjoyed the beauties of the site. That night Jesuíno sang the praises of Cat Wood to Tibéria as he had dinner at her place.

Massu moved, Tibéria came to visit him to see her godson, and she and Jesus fell in love with the countryside. In so many years of hard work, she running the whorehouse, he cutting and sewing cassocks, they had not managed to put by enough to buy a home for their old age. Why not build it there little by little, buying the bricks and mortar, a few yards of gravel, some roof tiles?

With those two houses, that of Massu, of board and mud and wattle, and that of Tibéria and Jesus, of brick, the invasion got under way.

How the news reached so many people, nobody knows. But a week after Jesus had started his house, some thirty shacks had sprung up on Cat Wood in an extraordinary variety of building materials and with a profusion of children of all colors and ages. And every day new carts came bringing people and boards, boxes, laths, old tin cans, anything that was useful for building.

Mention must be made of the fact that Wing-Foot moved. He went far away, leaving his straw hut, which was immediately taken over by Dona Filó, a businesswoman harried by the police, especially by the juvenile court. She trafficked in children, who incidentally were her own. She had seven, the oldest nine years old, the youngest five months, and she rented them out by the day to beggar-women she was acquainted with to help them collect alms. With a small child it was much easier to touch the hearts of passersby. Filó had a child a year; she only had to go to bed with a man once to get up pregnant; there was no way of preventing it. Each child had a different father, but she did not bother any of them. With her own children she earned her living, and the oldest was already being trained by the juvenile delinquents in the way he should go. He had even been arrested for breaking into a candy store.

Thus it was that the invasion of Cat Wood began.

–⚬⦗ **3** ⦘⚬–

THERE WAS SUCH EXCITEMENT, everybody building houses
on the lands of Cat Wood, a pretty hill from which one
had a magnificent view of the sea and a steady breeze so
that one never felt the heat. Only Corporal Martim sat
tight. His friends were all in a flutter, each one selecting
the place to put up walls and roofs, he helping them all he
could, but beyond this he did not go. Ever since his shattered marriage to the beautiful Marialva, he had never
again thought of setting up a house, much less, building
one. He had had his fill of home life, he was satisfied with
a little attic room in a run-down old mansion of
Pelourinho.

Even though he was more wildly in love than ever. A
passion that was devouring him inwardly, leaving him
idiotic, like a teen-ager, like Bullfinch when he fell in love,
that crazy Bullfinch in the case of Marialva, remember?
Well that was the state Corporal Martim was in now with
all his bagful of tricks, his famous savvy. The object of
his passion had been rightly guessed by all: Otália, that girl
who had come from the city of Bonfim to follow her trade
in Bahia.

Martim had not been able to get her out of his head
since the day of Tibéria's party, when she had stood up to
Marialva while dancing with him. He spent long spells
without seeing her, but he kept the memory of her in his

mind, certain that he would meet her one day and fix up things between them. When Marialva finally decided to admit defeat and left the house in Vila América, Martim, after a lapse of a few days, put on his best suit, polished his patent-leather shoes, put brilliantine on his hair, and went out to find Otália.

That Otália was something, a mixed-up kid, full of the weirdest notions. She did her job at Tibéria's place; she had her steady clientele; she made a great hit with older men because she was gentle and sweet, like a pampered little girl, and Tibéria loved her as though she were her daughter. After hours, she did not get intimate with any of the friends of the house, people like Martim who slept around with the girls, became infatuated with them, passions at times terrible and dramatic. Hadn't Terencio once pulled out a knife and finished off Mimi, the one with the face of a kitten, because of stupid jealousy?

Otália did not take up with anyone. If she wasn't too tired, she was glad to sleep with whoever came seeking the favor, and if she went to some party, she left on the arm of the one who pleased her most. She was sweet in her love-making, allowing herself to be enfolded and possessed, a helpless little girl. Not like Marialva, with whom this was nothing but an act. Otália was really a child, perhaps not more than sixteen.

Corporal Martim had no trouble propositioning her. Otália seemed to be waiting for him, and when he arrived, with a melancholy air, in the role of deserted husband, brokenhearted and in need of consolation, she received him without surprise as though his coming and their meeting were inevitable. Martim even found her too easy, and that annoyed him a little.

Naturally, he did not want to spend weeks courting her, wooing her, saying sweet nothings. He did not know how to do this; he was not Bullfinch. But neither did he like to go to bed with her when he had no more than held out his hand and told her he did not mind Marialva's desertion, for ever since that day of the dance he had been thinking of nobody but her, had had no other woman in mind. As a matter of fact, it was he who had got rid of Marialva, had she heard the story? To be free to come looking for Otália.

Otália smiled and said, yes, she had heard all about it. She knew about Bullfinch's passion—who was there in the city that didn't?—his despair, Marialva's plans for revenge, the interview between the two friends, she knew it all, and what she didn't know she guessed. She had seen Marialva come to the crib, her face as long as a horse's in the rain, without talking to anybody. She had shut herself up with Tibéria in the parlor for an interview. She had then taken the room in the back which Mercedes had left vacant when she went to Recife. Then Otália had expected Martim, certain that he would come, for she, too, had been waiting for him for a long time. Even before knowing him, when she had just heard talk about him, the comments on his marriage in the Recôncavo. The very day of her arrival in Bahia, without knowing anything about the capital, fleeing from the persecution of the judge in Bonfim because of his son. The boy had taken a shine to her; the mother had raised the roof, and the father too. And when she had just landed in Bahia, they had stolen her luggage. . . . Well . . . Afterwards it turned out to be a joke of Carnation-in-his-Buttonhole's, as Jesuíno had explained to her. Well, that day all the talk was about Martim, about his marriage to Marialva. That so-and-so, incidentally, could not stand Otália; she had even given her a dirty look when she came into the house. But she, Otália, wasn't mad at her, bore her no grudge. What is to be, will be. She had known beyond the shadow of a doubt that Martim would get tired of that dressmaker's dummy and would come looking for her. Don't ask how she knew; one of those things you can't explain. There are so many in life, aren't there?

She held out her hands and lips, smiling her smile of a child. Too much of a pushover, thought Martim; it was no fun.

But here was where the corporal, so versed in the ways of women, made a mistake. Otália took him by the arm and suggested that they go for a walk. She just adored walks. The corporal preferred it that way, too; bed came afterwards, when she had finished her work. He would come to the house around midnight, have a snack with Jesus, down a beer, talk about this and that. And when Otália had finished with her last customer, had taken a bath, put on a house dress, resumed her face of a young girl, then they would initiate their first night of love. Even so, it was a little too quick; the courtship generally lasted three or four days. But it would have been worse if she had invited him to go to bed that same afternoon, when Martim had just begun to talk to her. Good Lord, he wondered what she would be like, so quick to accept him, putting no obstacles in the way, not playing hard to get, saying right off that she had liked him for a long time and had been waiting for him.

They strolled past Barra, walked along the beach, picking up shells, while the wind played with Otália's fine hair. She ran over the sand; he pursued her, took her in his arms, crushed her lips with kisses.

They came back toward the end of the afternoon. Tibéria was strict about the schedule. Otália had not worked that afternoon, so she had to be on hand that night. Martim agreed to meet her there in the house after midnight.

He went off to round up some partners for a card game. That way the time would pass quickly and he would make a little money for his first expenses with Otália, a present of some kind.

This was the time when a new chief of police, an ill-natured customer who prided himself on being very efficient, decided to put an end to gambling in Bahia. He outlawed the numbers game, put several runners in jail, and had the police raid the places where card or crap games were going on; he raised Cain. But he didn't do anything about rich people's gambling, about those who played roulette and baccarat for high stakes in hotel rooms, in the fine houses of Graça and Barra. He turned a blind eye on those dives; gambling for him was only the gambling of the poor.

Therefore Martim had a little difficulty finding a partner that night. But he finally got up a crap game and won a few dollars. The best loser was Artur da Guima. He had no luck at gambling, and his patron saint had ordered him more than once to give up crap shooting, but to no avail; the habit had too much of a hold on him.

It was already past midnight when Martim returned to the whorehouse. Otália was waiting for him in the parlor with Tibéria and Jesus, all of them sitting around the table. Martim had bought a bag of candy, which he offered them. Jesus poured him a glass of beer, and they drank one another's health. Then Jesus went off to bed; Tibéria, to close up for the night.

"Shall we go too, beautiful?" Martim suggested.

"Oh, yes, let's . . . go for a walk; the moon is just beautiful."

It wasn't a walk Martim had had in mind. For him it was time for them to go to bed, not to go out in the street. But he didn't say anything. All women have a right to their whims, and he was willing to satisfy her. And so they set out through the streets, admiring the moon, exchanging vows of love, declarations of eternal fidelity. Like sweethearts in a tender conversation. A woman like Otália, so sweet and artless, the corporal had never met before. Martim was letting himself become enmeshed in the sweetness of that wandering about without any fixed purpose, under the light of the moon, stopping in doorways, stealing kisses.

Finally they got back to the whorehouse, and at the door Otália held out her hand in farewell: "Good-bye until tomorrow, my black boy."

"What did you say?" Martim asked, not taking in what she had said. And he followed her in. She, however, was inflexible. She was not yet ready to sleep with him. Who knows? someday, later on . . . That night she was tired; she wanted to rest, be alone, recall the hours she had spent with him, a day so brimful of happiness. She raised her lips to kiss him, pressed against him, body to body. Then she ran off to her room, locking the door after her. Martim was left flabbergasted, with the taste of Otália on his lips, the warmth of her body, and her absence.

From inside the house came the authoritative voice of Tibéria: "Who's there?"

He took off in a fury. Determined never to see that crazy thing again, with her little-girl face and her idea of making a fool of him. He left cursing.

All this the very opposite of his earlier reactions, as leaps to the eye. Before, it had annoyed him to think she was too easy to go to bed with, to the point where it lost all its poetry. And now, when he saw that it was not going to be so quick, that it would take time, that the girl wanted to be courted first, he got mad, turned into a fury, kicking the paving stones truculently.

In a foul humor, he went off to look for his friends, but the only one he found was Jesuíno Crazy Cock in a bar on São Miguel, engaged in conversation with a *candomblé* priest. He sat down at the table with them and ordered a drink. But even the rum was flat that night. He had the taste of Otália on the tip of his tongue, on his fingers, her scent in his nostrils. Nothing else had flavor or meaning.

Jesuíno, ignorant of the way things had been shaping up since Marialva departed from the shanty in Vila América, leaving Martim and Bullfinch finishing up a ripe jackfruit, was flabbergasted. Had that business of Marialva affected the corporal to the point of doing away with his good humor and thirst? Martim told him, however, that he was wasting no regrets over Marialva, one of the most tiresome, boring women he had ever met. She could go to hell for all he cared. As for Bullfinch, he was his brother; if they had been born of the same mother, twins, they couldn't have been closer and better friends. It was other things that were getting him down. Jesuíno did not question him further; he never pried; if people confided problems and plans, sorrows and dreams, to him, he listened and tried to help them. But he never forced anybody's confidence, however great his curiosity. Besides, his talk with the priest was very interesting and instructive: mysteries of *eguns*, that old man of Amoreiera knew all there was to know on the subject.

Martim made up his mind not to see any more of Otália, but his determination dissolved with sleep, and at the close of the afternoon there he was back in the brothel. Tibéria laughed when she saw him: "You're infatuated again? With the girl, aren't you?"

Her approval was apparent in her voice. She loved to act as sponsor of Martim's affairs, and she was very fond of Otália; she treated her like a daughter. This was different from Martim's marriage to Marialva, entered into without her knowledge, and the corporal setting up housekeeping, withdrawing from his friends.

Otália received him with the usual tender smile, the same intimacy, rapturously happy to be loved and to love.

"Why didn't you come sooner? Where are we going today?"

He had come in a frame of mind to settle the matter quickly, to take her to bed no matter what. But in her presence, in the face of her candor, her ingenuousness, his courage deserted him; he said nothing, totally disarmed, and went out with her for a walk. That second day they went to a festivity on the Square, with a kermis and a band. When they returned to the the brothel, Otália once more took leave of him with an ardent kiss.

Martim was completely flummoxed. How long was that going to go on? Far longer than he had imagined. The days went by, the walks grew longer, they visited one spot of the city after another, went to parties, *candomblés*, fish stews, dances, holding hands, with eyes only for one another, sweethearts. And at the brothel they said good-bye. She did not sleep with the corporal, but, of course, she would never again sleep with anyone for pleasure; she did her job, and that was the end of it. There was no man in her life except Martim.

If she had been a virgin, the corporal's wooing could not have been more proper. Wasn't it incredible? Falling in love with a girl from a whorehouse, a prostitute, available to anyone who had the money to pay!

And more proper with every passing day. With the others, even those who still had their cherries, the caresses rose in crescendo to their logical conclusion, until he generously serviced them. With Otália it was just the opposite. The longest time he had enjoyed her caresses was the first day, feeling the weight of her breasts, the curve of her buttocks, the warmth of her thighs. She went on giving him her mouth avidly and pressing herself against him when they said good-bye, but that was all.

Moreover, as time went by, she grew more and more withdrawn as regards the matter of bed. A trust was growing up between them, a gentle love, an intimacy, but the advance on Otália's bed, which his body desired, did not progress. At most, during the long walks or amid the gaiety of parties, the dances at Gafieira do Barão, Martim managed to steal a kiss, sniff the nape of her neck, touch her breasts lightly, play with her smooth hair.

And this had been going on for over a month to the amazement of his friends. As for Otália, she confided her happiness to Tibéria, her love for Martim, her infinite tenderness. She said she was his sweetheart.

Sweetheart or no, the corporal was not interested in putting up a house at Cat Wood. He had had his fill of homes. . . . Alone or with Otália, he would turn up there to help his friends. Tibéria was building what was far and away the best house there, of brick, with real roof tiles, and whitewashed. Bullfinch, too, was putting up his shanty, getting ready for the future, not to mention Massu, who had already moved in with his belongings, his grandmother, and his son. At times Martim brought along his guitar and sat around singing.

The houses came into being in response to the direst need. The residents did not have the money to pay the rent of house or room, not even in the most tumble-down quarters, in the stinking tenements of the old city, where family upon family was crowded into small, dark cubbyholes. Here, at least, they had the sea and the sand, the sight of the coconut trees. They were poverty-stricken people, the poorest of the poor, really of the lower depths, living by odd jobs and the most backbreaking toil, but even so, they did not let themselves be crushed by poverty; they rose above it; they did not give way to despair; they were neither sad nor devoid of hope. On the contrary, they triumphed over their wretched state and could laugh and amuse themselves. The walls of the adobe houses went up, those of straw, boards, strips of tin, tiny shacks, the meanest huts. Life took on an intense, impassioned quality. The clapping and stamping of the samba groaned throughout the drum-filled night. The ritual drums called to the festivals of the *orixás*, the *berimbaus*, to the sport of Angola, *capoeira* fighting.

Only at the end of the first week, when some twenty houses had already gone up, did Pepe Eight Hundred, the owner of all that stretch of seafront that abutted on the Navy's property, including Cat Wood Hill, learn one Saturday, through an agent of his, of the invasion of that small parcel of his holdings, of those buildings of tin and boards.

Pepe had bought that land for practically nothing years before. Not only Cat Wood Hill but large tracts, whose existence he did not even recall for months on end, though he had a plan to divide them up into lots and develop a residential district there when the city expanded toward the ocean. A vague long-term plan, not to be carried out in the immediate future. The rich still had enough vacant land in Barra, Morro do Ipiranga, Graça, Barra Avenue, so that they need not move out along the roads leading to the airport. The increase in value of that area would not come so quickly.

But in any event, he was not going to tolerate squatters' shacks on his land or the presence of trespassers, especially that pack of vagrants. He would order the shacks razed, that squalid blot defiling the beauty of the beach.

One day buildings would go up there, true. But not those miserable huts. They would be spacious houses with broad verandas, apartment houses designed by famous architects, with all the refinements of good taste and of the most expensive materials. Homes and apartments for wealthy people who could pay the price of Eight Hundred's lands and build on them with beauty and comfort. As for Cat Wood Hill—he had thought of putting that aside for his grandchildren, the boy and girl, Afonso and Katia, he in his first year at law school, she preparing to enter college. Darling children, with leftish inclinations in keeping with their age and the times, pretending to be independent, too, with their cars and their launches at the Yacht Club.

Gardens would be laid out there, women of perfect beauty would walk among the flowers in their bathing suits, tanning their bodies on the beach and in the water, making them more desirable and more agile for nights of love.

BEAUTIFUL, WITH HER SINUOUS BODY, was Dagmar, a
mulatta whose appearance on Saturdays at the Gafieira do
Barão dance hall always aroused renewed enthusiasm. She
had been living of late with Pretty Hair, a *capoeira* champion and a bricklayer in his spare time. She had held classy
jobs before falling in love and taking up with Pretty Hair:
waitress in a home in Graça, nursemaid of the children of
a rich family. But when Pretty Hair assumed the responsibility for that apotheosis of a woman, he would not consent to her spoiling her poise and elegance by dusting the
furniture in the home of some scoundrel or putting up with
spoiled, whining, unbearable brats. He didn't want his
brown girl to have her nerves shot to pieces.

Out of love for Dagmar, he took up his bricklayer's
trowel and built a daub shack on Cat Wood Hill. And after
he had built his, he helped put up others, earning a modest
sum from those who could pay it, helping others free of
charge; for he was skilled at his trade and liked to give a
helping hand to a friend in need. Even now, on that Sunday morning, while Dagmar, tired of waiting for him, was
making her way to the beach, Pretty Hair was helping with
the swift erection of the shanty of Edgard Chevrolet, a
former taxi driver, retired as the result of an accident in
which he had lost his right arm and left eye.

Dona Filó, too, was making for the beach, with five of

her seven children. On Sundays she refused to hire any of them out, no matter how much money she was offered. Sunday was mother's day for her. She spent it all with the children, bathing them, washing their hair, fine-combing it for lice. It was a pleasure to see them in their clean clothes; she had lunch with them, a Sunday dinner which she cooked herself; she told them stories. She made up for the week she had to spend without them while the children were helping beggars at the doors of churches or in the streets, going into restaurants and bars, dirty and in rags, with a starved air. The two older ones were up on the hill, playing soccer on a field that had been improvised behind the shacks. The second of them had real skill as a goalkeeper; he did not let a ball get by him. With the help of God, he might one day become a professional and earn a fortune.

It was a calm, sunny morning, not too hot, the breeze blowing through the coconuts, the sea smooth, tatters of white clouds in the sky. Automobiles were speeding along the road to the airport as Dona Filó crossed the highway with her five children. Several young men in sport cars turned around to admire Dagmar's dark body. From the direction of Amaralina came the sound of police-car sirens. Nobody on the hill or the beach paid any attention to them. They were undoubtedly heading for Itapoã.

Jesuíno, as well as Martim and Ipicilone, had come early in the morning to spend the day with Massu. The only one absent was Bullfinch, his house was not yet quite ready, for he was busy with the affairs of Madame Beatriz, the fortuneteller, who was preparing to present herself before the public of Bahia buried alive, spending a month in a coffin, without eating, without drinking, something sensational. Martim was tuning his guitar, sitting on a kerosene crate, with Otália's head resting on his knees as she stretched out beside him on the ground. In addition to the house of Edgard Chevrolet, three or four more were in the process of construction, but only Edgard was working that Sunday. The other residents were resting, lying on the ground or inside their shacks.

The three big police vans, carrying more than thirty officers and detectives, did not keep on to Itapoã. In front of Cat Wood, they turned off the highway, on to the dirt road, and stopped at the foot of the hill. Pathways had been opened through the woods by the new residents.

It was all unexpected and quick. The policemen went up armed with picks and axes, some of them carrying cans of gasoline. One of them, the head of the gang, blew a whistle. This one was to achieve notoriety as a result of the invasion of Cat Wood. He was known as Chico Pinóia and he was really a trashy customer, as will be seen.

They advanced on the shanties without asking anyone's permission. Besides, to say without asking permission is meaningless, for a bunch of them, armed with light machine guns, drew up in front of the shanties, and Chico Pinóia called out: "If anyone tries to interfere with the work he'll get a bullet in his belly. . . . Whoever wants to go on living had better behave himself."

Others marched on the shacks and, wielding pick and ax, tore them down, destroying not only the houses, but also the furniture, if those boxes, tables, and broken-legged chairs could be called furniture. But it was all their owners possessed.

A third squad came with cans of gasoline, poured it over the boards, the straw, the clothes, and struck a match. The flames rose in a succession of bonfires. The inhabitants came running out, not understanding what was happening, but prepared to defend their belongings. They stopped short, however, at the sight of the machine guns, forming a group of hatred and protest.

Negro Massu alone was so blinded by rage that he did not take in the machine guns, only Chico Pinóia and his whistle. He threw himself on Chico, while five detectives grabbed hold of him, but even so he gave as good as he got, and he got plenty. "Give that impudent Negro a beating," Chico Pinóia ordered.

From the beach, Dagmar, Dona Filó, and her five children came running. They could do nothing; the police had accomplished their glorious mission. Of the twenty-odd shacks with their motley furnishings, all that remained was a few handfuls of ashes scattered over the hill by the steady breeze. Filó still had time to shout: "Cowards! Dogs of hell!"

Chico Pinóia ordered: "Put her in the wagon too."

Two policemen dragged her to the van in which others were holding Massu down. But when they prepared to take off, they found that every one of the tires had been punctured: the collaboration of the street Arabs, free of charge. From the flaming hill the despoiled residents could see the infuriated police in their useless vans, and Chico Pinóia standing in the middle of the road asking for a lift. Faced with the problem of having to walk to the city, the police finally commandeered an empty truck returning from the airport. With all this confusion, they let Massu and Dona Filó go; there would be no lack of opportunity to arrest them again. They squeezed into the truck, police and detectives, leaving several to look after the vans while they waited for new tires.

From the hilltop the residents of Cat Wood watched them without knowing what to do. The fire, after destroying the shacks, went crackling through the underbrush, burned down some bushes, and then died out. The heavy silence of impotent rage was broken by a woman's sobs. For the first time in her life the poor creature had had a house, and her happiness had lasted only two days.

It was at this point that Jesuíno Crazy Cock came out of his corner, took several steps forward to the middle of the scorched earth, and said: "My people, don't be discouraged. They tore down the houses; we'll build them up again."

The silence grew alert. The woman stopped crying.

"And if they tear them down again, we'll build them up again. We'll see who is the most stubborn."

Negro Massu, still bleeding, roared: "You're right, father, you are always right. I am going to build my house again, and now I'll be on guard; just let me see some coward of a policeman come to tear it down. He'll regret it."

He went over to old Vevéva, who was holding the baby. Though he was only one, the determination written on his face made him seem an army.

A little while later, all were once more putting up their shacks with great animation. Needs must when the Devil drives, for they had nowhere to live. They were all working, including the beautiful Dagmar, Otália, Dona Filó and her children, all the young loafers. Even Ipicilone, who was born tired, worked that Sunday. Martim playing the guitar, the others working and singing. A celebration which at night turned into a dance.

From the foot of the hill, beside the waiting vans, the police who had been left in charge of them watched the work that was going on above. Seen from below, it was a curious sight. It aroused the curiosity of the journalist, Jacó Galub, the leading reporter of the opposition newspaper. He was coming back from the airport, where he had gone to see a friend off, and that cloud of smoke and those people milling around attracted his attention. He stopped his car, went up, inquiring what had happened. In the name of the residents, Jesuíno Crazy Cock spoke with him, telling him what the police had done.

‒‹{ 5 }›‒

ON TUESDAY THE MOST SENSATIONAL NEWS of the year exploded in banner headlines on the front page of the *Gazette of Salvador*, the newspaper of the opposition, at that moment in dire need of funds and readers. It was still feeling the effects of the defeat at the polls. The editor of the paper, Airton Melo, had run for a seat in congress, had spent a lot of money on his campaign, mostly that of his backers, but the paper's reserves, too. He had come in fourth, and out of self-respect he could not as yet support the government. Looking at the pictures taken on Cat Wood Hill (where Jacó had returned with a photographer on Monday), and with a grimace of disgust at the sight of Dona Filó looking into the camera with her toothless mouth open in an immense smile and with children clinging to her arms and flanks, Airton Melo, the upright journalist, "the watchdog of the public funds" (as his newspaper had called him during the campaign) explained to Jacó: "A few cracks at the Spanish colony will do us no harm. Those *gallegos* are getting greedier all the time, not one penny could I get out of them. Put the heat on that thief Perez and spread the story of the eight hundred grams. In that way the paper won't be defaming too many of them. Be sure to mention the honorable exceptions. You'll see how they loosen up, and we really need the money. Things are tough, Jacó."

"And what about the government?"

Airton Melo smiled. He looked upon himself as a politician of high merit, extremely subtle, heir to all the tricks of the old Bahian trimmers; "Give it to the government, my boy. Hard and heavy, no holds barred. "But"—here he lowered his voice confidentially—"go easy on the governor. Appeal to his conscience, to his heart. Undoubtedly he is unaware of what is going on, etc., etc. You know the line. But don't spare the chief of police. He is the leader of the campaign against gambling, saying that he is going to wipe out the numbers racket. Unfortunately the paper can't come out in favor of gambling or the numbers racket. But with this story of the invasion of Cat Wood Hill, we can give Albuquerque (that's his name, Nestor Albuquerque) the treatment, and maybe even get him kicked out. And we'll have financial backing for the campaign—the numbers crowd." He lighted a cigar and blew out the smoke. He looked at Jacó affectionately: "And if it works out, I won't forget you. You know I am not ungrateful."

He felt generous as he glimpsed the possibility of big money. He was under heavy expenses, with two families, a home and a home away from home, and his wife Rita and his mistress Rosa vying with one another to see who could spend the most. The two R's, the Rapacious Rats, as he himself described them cynically and wittily, were gnawing away his bank account.

Jacó Galub looked at his editor tilted back in his easy chair. A great man, in his way. But if he, Galub, were to trust to his promises and wait for his generosity he would die of hunger. And Jacó Galub had no intentions of dying of hunger. He was ambitious, he had plans, side lines he was following up, and if he did not make an issue of the miserable salary Airton Melo paid him, it was because he was using the columns of the newspaper for his own advancement. He was alert and intelligent; a good journalist, he knew all there was to know about the newspaper game; he was one of the best reporters in the city, and he was devoid of any bias, as well as of all sentimentality. Cold, though he gave the impression of being dedicated, his ambition was to make a name for himself, get a job on one of the important newspapers in Rio, with a big salary and nationwide prestige. And he would bring it off; of that he was certain. So he, in turn, smiled at the "upright journalist": "You can rest easy; we will launch a full-scale campaign. The reputation of the paper will go up by leaps and bounds. Not to mention the circulation. I'll lead the attack."

"Put lots of emotion into your coverage, heart; make everybody weep with pity for those poor people, destitute, without a roof to cover them. . . . Heart!"

"Leave it to me."

As soon as Jacó went out, Airton Melo lifted the telephone receiver and waited impatiently for the dial tone. When he finally heard it, he dialed a number, and when it answered, he asked: "Is Otávio there? This is Dr. Airton Melo."

And when Otávio Lima, the head of the numbers racket in the capital and neighboring cities, came to the phone, he said: "Is that you, Otávio? We have to get together, old man. At last I've got the trumps I need to unseat Albuquerque."

A pause while he listened: "This time I've really got them. A sensational campaign. But I can only explain it to you in person."

He smiled at the other's suggestion: "At your office? Are you crazy? If they see me there, in no time the word will be around that you are buying my paper. . . . At my house."

Another pause as the king of the numbers game asked him something.

"In which one?" the journalist repeated thoughtfully. "At Rosa's. We'll be more at ease there."

And so, on that Tuesday, with a story that took up all of page 8, with headlines on the first page—and a picture of the toothless, many-childed Dona Filó, whose statements wrung the reader's heart—under Jacó Galub's by-line, the *Gazette of Salvador* initiated its campaign "in defense of the homeless poor forced to squat on vacant land," a campaign that set a record in Bahian newspaper history.

During the first week, Jacó Galub displayed untiring activity. He spent much of his time at Cat Wood, listening to people, encouraging them, promising them that with the support of the *Gazette of Salvador* they could rest assured and build all the houses they liked. And truly, his stories were a veritable lure. The first invasion of the hill was almost a private operation among friends carried out by Massu, Jesus, Bullfinch, Pretty Hair, all acquainted with one another—*compadres*, relatives, drinking and talking companions. But after the fires set by the police and the beginning of the *Gazette's* stories, people began to turn up from everywhere, transporting boards, boxes, anything that could be used for building. Ten days later there were more than fifty houses, and the building boom gave every sign of growing.

Jacó's stories faithfully reflected Airton Melo's instructions. Give it to the government: a chief of police who was brutal and incompetent, in the pay of the magnates of the Spanish colony. In his first story, Jacó described how it had all begun, basing his account on information given him by Jesuíno and the other squatters: homeless folk who had chosen those neglected lands to put up their houses. Then the complaint to the police of "the millionaire José Perez, who for many years has borne the comic nickname 'Pepe Eight Hundred Grams'" and the ruthless measures taken by Chico Pinóia—the habitual torturer of prisoners—under the orders of Albuquerque, "the saturnine chief of police, the overbearing lawyer with little learning and great conceit." The beating given to Massu was described at length: the Negro defending his dwelling place, the life of his grandmother and his infant son, the police holding him back while they set fire to his house. It had really happened this way, except that Jacó made Massu get the beating ahead of time, and omitted all mention of the Negro's retaliation. Massu did not like that. In the story he seemed like a poor devil who had been beaten up by the police without doing anything about it. Jacó had quite a job to explain it to him and placate his resentment.

In his attack on the goverment and, above all, the chief of police, the journalist made no charges against the governor. He dedicated words of praise to his kind heart and appealed to it. To his patriotism, too. It was time for the government to bear in mind the fact that we were an independent country and not a "Spanish colony." There was a strong Spanish colony in Bahia, made up for the most part of upright, industrious men who had contributed a great deal to the progress of the State, but among them there were also outstanding rogues who had accumulated ill-gotten fortunes, as the *Gazette of Salvador* planned to reveal in another series of articles. But there was a difference between Bahia's having a Spanish colony and being "a colony of the Spanish colony." Meanwhile, the chief of police, Dr. Albuquerque, so relentless in his pursuit of the policy agents (one could not help wondering why), was at the orders of Pepe Eight Hundred Grams when it came to driving off vacant, idle, uncultivated land Brazilian citizens, honest and hard-working, whose only crime was poverty. In the eyes of the chief of police, said Jacó, no worse crime existed; he was a henchman of the wealthy and above all, as was evident, of the Spaniards who grew rich by giving short weight.

It had been a long time since such a sensational and violent news coverage had been seen in the Bahian press, involving such important persons. The first day's edition was completely sold out, and more copies of subsequent issues had to be printed during the days that followed.

Some of the residents whose photographs appeared in the paper, were interviewed by Jacó; Dagmar the beautiful appeared in a bathing suit, looking like a movie star, which earned her several sound slaps from Pretty Hair. A woman of his was not going to be showing off her thighs and breasts in the pages of a newspaper. Chastened, Dagmar accused the photographer of fraud, of taking her picture without her knowing it, a debatable statement, not to say a downright lie. But these are family affairs, and we are not going to get mixed up in them. We will merely state for the record, adding to our experience of women and of life in general, that after the slaps Dagmar not only became more discreet but also much more affectionate.

The one who played a stellar role was Dona Filó. Scrawny and disheveled, her black dress torn, a child on each hip, one at each breast, and the others circled around her, she was the very image of poverty. As events developed, even magazines in Rio bought pictures of her for publication. That is to say, they bought them from the photographer. Filó did not see a penny of the rights. But by way of compensation she was aglow with pride at having her picture in the papers. She began to charge more for the hire of her children; they now had fame and name. Jacó had attributed to her the phrase of Jesuíno: "They tore down the houses; we'll build them up again." But with the passing of time, the phrase came to be the invention of Galub himself, for he repeated it again and again in his articles, as an affirmation and a threat, without recalling its authorship, finally persuaded that the celebrated phrase was really his. A paternity disputed by Congressman Ramos da Cunha, leader of the opposition in the state legislature, a fiery orator. In one of his speeches, the statesman lashed out with a dramatic peroration: "The despotism of the chief of police, the arrogance of the millionaire Perez, the indifference of the government, the authorities, and their henchmen, can burn down the houses of the people. We, the people, will raise them up again. Upon the ashes of these criminal fires, we, the people, will build our houses. Ten, twenty, a thousand times, if necessary."

The leader was a persuasive person, a lawyer who was the son of a colonel of the interior. The heir to immense landholdings, he did not, however, own real estate in the capital, and he was out to give the government a drubbing. He had recently graduated from law school; his father had had him elected to congress. As long as it was not a question of agrarian reform, the young leader Ramos da Cunha, of facile and stirring oratory, was even fairly progressive, and this adjective was frequently used by the press to describe him. As a result of the campaign having to do with the invasion of Cat Wood Hill, he was even accused of Communist sympathies. Although these were clearly canards, calumnies of political adversaries, they nevertheless gave him a certain aura as a defender of the people.

But to go back to Dona Filó, perhaps she was the one who benefited most from Jacó Galub's articles. Morally speaking. She was presented as the most devoted of mothers, killing herself to support those seven children. Vague references to a father who had disappeared served as a moral veil, turning her into a deserted wife, victim of the prevailing social order and the husband. Not that we want to detract from Dona Filó's virtures; she was very deserving, and she had few equals when it came to working. But this business of painting her as the victim of a scoundrelly husband was going a little too far. She never had a husband, nor did she want to tie herself to any man permanently. A man, in her opinion, was good for only one purpose: begetting children. After that he caused nothing but work and worry.

Of all those people on the hill, the only one Jacó did not get a picture of was Jesuíno Crazy Cock. He saw Jesuíno going about among them, sensed that it was he who was orienting the others, the counselor to whom they turned at difficult moments, but when Jacó appeared with the photographer, the wary vagabond faded from sight.

Crazy Cock was no less vain or more modest than the others. What he was was a shrewd old man of wide experience who did not want his picture printed in the paper. Once, years before, a photograph of him, taken at the Rampa do Mercado, in the sun with a cigar stub in his mouth and a happy smile, had appeared in an article written with tenderness and poetry by one Odorico Tavares. And the result was that for months the police harassed Jesuíno, detaining him on the slightest pretext and clapping him into jail. All the flatfoots had the newspaper clipping in their pocket with the half-tone of Jesuíno. It availed him nothing that the poet Odorico had called him "the last free man in the city." His freedom was the freedom to be thrown in the clink. So Jesuíno had had his fill of pictures in the papers.

--◦≺{ **6** }≻◦--

As has been repeatedly mentioned, Bullfinch divided himself during those weeks when the events on Cat Wood got under way between the construction of his shack, with all manner of odd details, and his desperate love (all Bullfinch's love affairs were more or less desperate) for Madame Beatriz, fortuneteller and fakir. The building of the shack was slowed down as a consequence of his love. The spieler had little time left for it, busy as he was with the propaganda for the fakir's extraordinary act: she was to be buried alive in homage to the people of Bahia, locked for a month in a coffin—God have mercy!—without food or drink. A marvel, a spectacle *sui generis*, admission only five milreis.

Madame Beatriz had landed in Bahia with her mediumistic powers and her platinum-blond hair "after having visited a number of foreign capitals," as stated in a flyer distributed in the streets of Salvador da Bahia. Capitals such as Aracaju, Maceió, Recife—not exactly foreign, but you can't have everything. Penedo, Estancia, Propriá, Garanhuns, Caruarú, there you have other important cities honored by the visit of the fakir, whose birthplace was a bone of contention between faraway India ("the only woman fakir in the world, the only woman to let herself be buried alive, the clairvoyante Beatriz, born in mysterious India and at present traveling about the world on a

Buddhist mission" according to another manifesto announcing the sensational number) and the pleasant suburban city of Niterói. She had arrived after a swift and melancholy transit through Amargosa, Cruz das Almas, Alagoinhas, cities where the faith in fortunetellers was great but the capacity for adequately recompensing them small, the clients' available funds not being in keeping with the ardor of their faith. She had arrived flat broke, and less than a week later, in the face of the evident economic debacle, she was deserted by her languorous secretary, Dudu Peixoto, also known as Good-Time Dudu, a rogue from Pernambuco who was in the habit of letting rich women support him. When he had met up with Madame Beatriz, she was at her zenith; she had been a great success in Caruarú, and he had accepted from her the title of secretary and her painted lips. On the trip he had been highly demanding: he was accustomed to better food; he had a delicate stomach, and was, moreover, delicate in every way. It nauseated him to see bedbugs, and he turned up his nose at the quality of the rice served at the table. Madame Beatriz, who had gone crazy over his dreamy eyes and black hair, was blind to his shortcomings, begged his forgiveness for making him undergo such humiliations, and promised him the moon when they got to bigger cities, more advanced, better fitted to understand her art and her science.

Unfortunately, the inhabitants of Salvador da Bahia did not show the expected regard for the qualities ("judgment, knowledge, ability, completely confidential," according to the flyer) of the famous fortuneteller.

She had come into contact with Bullfinch through the intervention of the mistress of the cheap boardinghouse where she was staying in Brotas, an old acquaintance of the spieler. She wanted to hire him to distribute the flyer, on which she had spent her last resources. She guaranteed Dudu that she would be swamped by clients as soon as the contents of the announcement became known to the public and their families.

Bullfinch took one look at the platinum-blond hair of Madame Beatriz and was smitten with love. He had never seen anything so pretty, silvery hair like that, except on a movie star. He looked Dudu Peixoto over with contempt and envy. How could a character of that sort, effeminate, a fairy beyond the shadow of a doubt, with his rolling eyes and his waggling bottom, manage to take in a woman of Madame Beatriz's distinction? She must be blind not to see the blatant gestures of her gallant, his suggestive movements. What a pity!

But not even on this account did Bullfinch neglect the distribution of the flyer, which he had accepted with the understanding that he would receive payment for his labors as soon as the clients began to flock in, as could not fail to happen. Beatriz had complete confidence in the effects the reading of the circular would produce. Good-Time Dudu was considerably more skeptical. In order to form an unbiased judgment, the best thing is to read the whole thing, and in that way each can decide for himself. It ran as follows:

MADAME BEATRIZ
OF INTEREST TO EVERYBODY
NOTICE TO THE PEOPLE OF BAHIA

After visiting a number of foreign capitals, she is in this marvelous city, prepared, by means of her science, to satisfy the public and all those who call upon her for scientific, material, and divinatory purposes having to do with life, luck, or some personal problem. One consultation will suffice to convince the person with regard to what he is seeking. Her achievements are marvelous, almost unbelievable, in the fields of business, love, travel, difficulties to be overcome, jeopardized friendships, physical or moral ailments, and everything that has a bearing on your LIFE OR FUTURE.

Secure the marvelous Powder of India to insure luck in love and business. Visit without delay this famous scientist who has her own private office and is in no way to be compared with those charlatans and fakes who make of the noble science of occultism a mere way of earning a living.

Judgment, Knowledge, Ability, completely confi-

dential. Prices within reach of all. No advance appointment necessary. Confidential and private.

EVERY DAY, INCLUDING SUNDAYS AND HOLIDAYS

the famous fortuneteller may be found at 96 Rua Dr.
Giovanni Guimarães, Boa Vista de Brotas.

CONSULT MADAME BEATRIZ

Only a stickler could have asked for clearer, more explicit literature. If there was a shortage of clients, it was
not the fault of the flyer, but of the sad state of the world
today.

A wave of skepticism, of widespread disbelief, a lack of
confidence, is sweeping the great cities at present. A coarse
materialism is keeping men and even women aloof from
the advice of fortunetellers, from their "honest, rapid and
efficient aid," from the remedies they offer for the ills of
life. We live in times of little faith in the occult sciences, but
Madame Beatriz was not to blame for this lack of spiritual-
ism; she was its victim. When Dudu, in need of money for
cigarettes, upbraided her, he was committing a complete
injustice.

When the flyers had been distributed, and well distributed, house by house, with professional pride and the
desire to serve such a beautiful woman, Bullfinch called
two days later, as had been agreed, to receive payment for
his work. He got off the streetcar at the climax of the
tragedy: just as the languorous Dudu—in his left hand his
suitcase with his extra suit and silk shirts, and waving an
ironic good-bye with his right—was coming out of the
door, leaving the uncomfortable boarding-house and the
comfortable and passionate arms of Madame Beatriz. The
fortuneteller, in tears, did not resemble that intrepid, resolute occultist of the "marvelous, almost unbelievable
achievements in the fields of business, love, difficulties to
be overcome." She was torn between rage and pique; her
jealousy overflowed in a stream of words that were hardly
in keeping with a person so confidential and so full of
spirituality. Her mouth was a forge of indecent epithets.
From the door she shouted after the gentleman of the

bedchamber, the delicate and armor-plated Good-Time Dudu: "Swindler! Pimp! Shit of a gigolo! Faggot! A faggot is what you are, Mr. Trash!"

Bullfinch got off the car; Dudu quickly boarded the same vehicle without any concern for the direction in which it was bound, smiled at Bullfinch and made this suggestion: "If you want her, she's all yours. I am fed up."

Bullfinch would gladly have given him a slap or a kick, but the scoundrel was already on the car, swinging his hips, rolling his honeyed eyes at the conductor. A fairy, there could be no doubt about it.

And then Bullfinch garnered the tears and lamentations of Madame Beatriz. The boardinghouse keeper, a fat, easygoing mulatta, left them alone in the parlor. Bullfinch's arrival was providential; she had to get lunch, and she had no time to waste listening to the lamentations of forsaken lovers.

Bullfinch received no payment, naturally. Even if Madame Beatriz had had the money—which was not the case —how could he mention such a coarse, material matter to a poor woman so deeply wounded, her heart bleeding? Not only did he not receive what was due him, but he even left some of his own, not much, true, but only because he did not have more. If he had, he would have, for a woman with hair like that was worthy of any sacrifice. In the clutch of despair, forsaken by lover and clients, Madame Beatriz made up her mind to resort to the "buried-alive" act, the sensational number. She hired Bullfinch as her secretary.

Bullfinch, in view of the fact that the rent was cheap and could be paid later, hired a store on Baixa do Sapateiro, left vacant after a fire. Formerly the shelves and windows had been full of dress materials, colored chintzes, cottons, satins, and silks, all fine quality and cheap for the customers of the New Beirut Store of Abdala Cury. Abdala was unanimously pointed to by investigators, jury, and judge as being solely responsible for the raging fire that burned up the New Beirut Store, having with his own hands poured the gasoline, stretched the electric wire, and provoked a magnificent short circuit. They threw Abdala into jail, and the owner of the property was fighting for the insurance, and the insurance company was fighting against paying, telling him to collect from Abdala. He had been sentenced to a few months, which would pass quickly, and then he would open a new store. Bullfinch had obtained the shop for a month; he himself painted a poster announcing the great event; new flyers were printed (referring to Madame's powers, the fact that she had been born in India, was of the Buddhist religion). Bullfinch outdid himself.

Madame Beatriz, enchanted, never wearied of repeating her gratitude to him. She rolled her eyes at Bullfinch, at times gave him her hand in a gesture of intimacy, she even rested her head—that platinum-blond head—on his shoulder. But it went no farther than that. Bullfinch tried to advance; one day he grabbed hold of her in the back of the store, still all sooty from the fire, and seared her lips thick with lipstick with a long kiss. She did not protest; she let herself be kissed and then closed her eyes for a moment as one deep in thought; when she opened them, she lowered her head and said to Bullfinch in a voice that seemed to come from the other world: "Never do that again. . . . Never."

Never again? To one who wanted to do it over again that very minute, Madame's request was like a dagger thrust. Why not?—he asked without hiding a certain irritation. She felt the umbrage in his voice.

"What I mean is . . . not now . . . because of my concentration."

And she explained to him: she was preparing herself for that tremendous task ahead of her, that sensational number, a month in a coffin with a glass lid, without eating, without drinking. Only by absolute concentration, complete purity of spirit, could she come through such an ordeal alive. Once, when she had undertaken the same number in Buenos Aires, just because she had said a bad word a few days before she entered the coffin, she had not been able to hold out for more than two weeks; she was not as pure as she had to be. She could not even think of "corporeal" things—she pronounced "corporeal" with a kind of disgust —until she emerged from the coffin, until she had passed that month of complete fasting. Afterwards, when she was convalescing, then, who knows? . . .

All this was said with sighs, rolling eyes, and solemn words such as occultism, magnetism, spirituality, and others of the same tenor. Bullfinch listened to her reverently, believing her. But he needed something to sustain him: "Do you like me? Really?"

Madame Beatriz did not answer him with words; she pressed his hand hard, looked into his eyes devouringly, sighed deeply. Nothing she might have said could have been more convincing. Bullfinch grew dizzy with happiness, but—the stupid materialism to which we referred before—he wanted something more explicit: "You mean that after being buried . . . the two of us . . ." He concluded with a gesture that left no room for doubt.

A woman of such spirituality, accustomed to Buddhist morality, that coarse gesture wounded Madame Beatriz, who lowered her eyes and reproached him: "What an ugly thing! . . ."

"But . . . afterwards . . . won't we?"

She pressed his hand once more, sighed again, and through the sigh Bullfinch made out a timid and discreet "yes." Sufficiently audible, however, to leave him happy and utterly devoted to Madame Beatriz, taking full charge of the preparations for the beginning of her sensational number. There was lots to do. The room had to be cleaned up, rearranged in keeping with its new functions as a theater; they had to go to the newspapers to arrange for inteviews—he would talk, Madame just smile—invite a committee of businessmen and important persons to watch over the coffin the day the spectacle opened, get hold of a coffin and a glass lid.

It was not easy to come by either the coffin or the glass lid. But Bullfinch managed: he named as sponsors of the performance, with the privilege of having their name appear on the advertisements, a small funeral parlor in Tabuão and a dealer in glass and china in Pelourinho. The funeral home lent him an old coffin, half broken, without a lid. The dealer gave them on loan a sheet of glass to cover the coffin. It wasn't exactly a lid, but Artur da Guima, at Bullfinch's request, went to work on it, and like the handy person he was, he nailed some strips to the sides of the coffin, and fitted the glass into them. In that way the coffin was hermetically sealed, as the flyers distributed through the streets stated. Holes were bored at the head and the foot of the coffin to let in air.

With so many things to do, Bullfinch had almost completely given up the building of his shack, and he followed the course of events on Cat Wood Hill with scant attention. He showed up there when he had time, chewed the fat for a while, complained about the police, did a little work on his shanty, and left. Madame Beatriz, in deep concentration, was waiting for him for lunch. They lunched as abundantly as was possible, for she needed to nourish herself well for the long fast ahead of her, as she explained to Bullfinch. Taking everything into consideration, he was happy with this latest passion of his; he had to wait only a month, and then the platinum-blond hair and all the rest would be his.

Things were not so rosy for Corporal Martim, either in love or business, if his gambling sessions, his decks of cards, his dice, can be called a business. The chief of police, although his attention was mainly occupied with the lands of Pepe Eight Hundred, was not neglecting his relentless campaign against gambling. A list of cardsharpers had been drawn up by the police, and the name of Corporal Martim—Martim José da Fonseca—stood high on it. Every day new sites were raided—dens or dives, the newspapers that supported the government called them—and some excellent professionals were retired from circulation. Martim had managed to escape; he knew how to look after himself when the occasion arose; he did not show up in his accustomed haunts, at Mercado, Sete Portas, Água dos Meninos. But how was he to earn an honorable living if the police, if the government, interfered?

Poor Carnation-in-his-Buttonhole had been in jail, and charges had been preferred against him. He and eight others had been arrested at Germano's place in connection with a roulette wheel that was said to be fixed. He came out scrawny and dirty after spending eight days in an underground cell without the right to take a bath.

Martim made out, thanks to his wide acquaintance in the field. He knew every place a game might be going on, cards or crap. He picked up some change here and there without trying for too much.

Otália cost him nothing. At most a dish of ice cream, a cool drink. She refused to accept gifts, threatening to break with him if he kept on bringing her dress materials, slippers, trinkets. At the same time, Martim made no more progress than Bullfinch—perhaps less—in the realization of his plans for going to bed. At least Bullfinch had definite promises, could look forward to the moment when Madame Beatriz's spiritual concentration would be over, when the ordeal of being buried alive would have ended, and she would be able to let down the barriers of total abstinence. But Otália had made no promise. Martim accompanied her around the city on interminable walks, long conversations, tender words. But it did not go any farther. He even came to think that she had a lover, carefully kept under wraps. More than one night he kept watch around the brothel, after the girl had gone in, to see if anyone showed up, but he wasted his time on this vigil, just as he did with his questions and inquiries. Nobody knew of any other man except Martim in Otália's life. There were the clients, of course, but they did not count. They went to bed with her, paid their money, left, and that was the end of it.

Martim racked his brains; he could not figure out the girl, her attitude. If she liked him, why didn't she give herself to him? She was no virgin whose object was matrimony. There were times when he felt like leaving her in the street, going away and never seeing her again. But the next day he found himself wanting to see her, hear her voice, look at her little girl's face, touch her soft hair, feel, as they parted, the warmth of her body in their farewell kiss. Nothing like this had ever happened to him before; it was driving him nuts.

Happy he certainly wasn't, the flatfoots threatening him with jail, and that silly, vaporish Otália making a monkey out of him. Martim stretched out in the sun on Cat Wood Hill, trying to figure her out. He was coming to resemble his brother-in-devotion, Bullfinch, always sighing over an impossible love. But he was not prepared to continue in

that state, Martim repeated to himself, determined to put
an end to the situation, to have it out with Otália. Nevertheless, he kept putting if off until the next day.

While he waited for an end to the campaign against
gambling and Otália's nonsense, he helped out his friends
on Cat Wood Hill. He collaborated not only as mason's or
carpenter's assistant but also by keeping morale high with
his guitar or by taking part in the discussions of the more
active residents, who met to decide how best to confront
the threats that had piled up in the last few days. Serious
threats: the chief of police had stated to the press that the
wave of anarchy and subversion of public order that had
begun with the invasion of Cat Wood Hill would be
stamped out by fair means or foul. The flouting of the law
was not going to prevail in Bahia; he would see to that.
Property rights were guaranteed by the Constitution, and
he would uphold respect for the Constitution even at the
cost of blood. He was a guardian of the law; he would not
permit a rabble of vagabonds to overthrow the established
order and set up the rule of communism. That was what he
said, "the rule of communism." Dr. Albuquerque was lit-
erarily inclined; he had written sonnets, and he enjoyed a
gathering where matters pertaining to poetry were discussed. At the moment, however, he was armed for war.
War against Cat Wood Hill and its inhabitants. Against the
eighty-three shacks that had been erected there, housing
some four hundred persons, a small world where a baby
had recently been born, the fruit of the womb of Isabel Big
Toe, the concubine of Jeronimo Ventura, a blacksmith by
trade. Dona Filó had acted as midwife; with all the children she had had, she had learned, so to speak, on her own
flesh. Jesuíno Crazy Cock had helped. When her pains
began, Jeronimo Ventura had set out madly in search of
Jesuíno as though that old rake were a licensed doctor.
Moreover, there on Cat Wood Hill, Jesuíno was a little of
everything: he settled problems, mended walls, gave advice, wrote letters, kept accounts, decided what should be
done at crucial moments.

Now at night Cat Wood Hill was illuminated. At orders
from Jesuíno, a wire from the installation of a beach club
was tapped by Florêncio, an unemployed electrician who

lived on the hill. Makeshift posts were set up, and the shacks were provided with light. In the morning, a truck of the electrical company came around and cut the wire. In the afternoon Florêncio, with the help of the other inhabitants, spliced the wire, and electric light flooded the sands and the shacks of Cat Wood Hill.

7

THE INSTALLATION OF ELECTRICITY on Cat Wood Hill was hailed with enthusiasm by Jacó Galub: "The workers who erected their homes on the idle lands of the millionaire José Perez, better known as Pepe Eight Hundred, harassed by the police and forsaken by the mayor, are continuing to improve the new quarter of the city. They have now supplied it with electricity, even against the wishes of the company. Standard-bearers of progress, the dauntless settlers of Cat Wood are citizens worthy of all esteem."

If the invasion had nothing else to its credit, it would suffice to point out the amount of literature it had given rise to: Jacó's coverage—which won him the journalism award for the year; the speeches of Ramos da Cunha—which were published in pamphlet form at the expense of the state legislature; the moving articles of Marocas, the distinguished columnist of the *Jornal do Estado*; the heroic-social-concrete poem of Pedro Job, which steered a course between Pablo Neruda and the most advanced concretists, entitled "From the Fundamental Heights of Cat Wood the Poet Contemplates the Future of the World."

In the interests of accuracy it should be stated that Pedro Job could not contemplate the future of the world from the heights of Cat Wood because he had never been there. To write his poem, he did not have to leave the bar where he and other local artistic geniuses argued furiously about literature and the movies. Nevertheless, he rose into the Empyrean led by the hand of "Sister Filó, fundamental mother, womb of the newly delivered earth fecundated by heroes," and so on and so forth, with the spotlight on Filó. There he went up hill, the poet Job, "poet of the people bred on struggle and whiskey," to see the future world coming into being at the hands of those people gathered on Cat Wood to build it. Strong the poem was, no doubt about it, at times unintelligible, but stirring, and illustrated by an engraving of Leo Jr.'s, showing a Hercules who more or less resembled Massu, with clenched, raised fist.

On the Hill, the poem did not achieve the success it deserved. Those who read it did not understand it, not even Filó, so enhanced and ennobled: "Oh, Madonna of steel and electronics, your hill is the ship of space and your magnificent children the architects of the collective"—not even she grasped its beauty.

It is, however, worth mentioning that the poem of Pedro Job and the illustration of Leo Jr. were, among all the proofs of solidarity offered to the people of the Hill, the only ones that were really gratis. All the rest, articles, speeches, manifestoes, legal moves, opinions, had their ulterior motives, definite aims looking to benefit their authors in one way or another. Pedro Job aspired to nothing, not even public office or prizes or votes, not even the gratitude of the people he had sung in his poem. The only thing he wanted was to write it and publish it, see it in print. They did not receive, neither he nor the illustrator, one penny from the newspaper. Airton Melo did not pay for literary contributions. He felt that he was doing the poet and engraver a great favor by publishing their poem and illustration, opening the portals of glory to them. Wasn't that enough? He had to pay the reporters; there was no way out of that; and though he paid poorly and slowly, still he paid. But not literature; that would be an insufferable affront.

In spite of the disinterested generosity with which the poem and the illustration were composed and published, even so, with the passing of time, Job benefited by it because his poem became a classic of the new social poetry, quoted in articles, reproduced in anthologies, acclaimed by many, disputed and denied by others, those who look upon social poetry as only that composed in short roundels, in verses of seven syllables, and rhyming in "ão." But the truth is that the poet Job had been devoid of these or any other intention when he had taken up his pen and set down his poem. Moved by one of Galub's articles, his left-wing heart filled with pity for those poor tormented people and with hate for the police, Job had composed his canto. Without any ulterior motive. And in the same spirit Leo Jr. had illustrated it.

The others not only had ulterior but *plus ultra* and at times *plus plus ultra* motives. Even the chief of police, whose campaign against gambling, especially the numbers game, had displeased and annoyed many important people. He hoped by ardently and unflinchingly defending private property to restore his prestige and strengthen his position.

That matter of his campaign against gambling is worth relating. The truth is that it had never been part of Dr. Albuquerque's administrative program to disturb the numbers racket.

On the contrary, when his name began to be considered for the post of chief of police under the new government, of all the allurements the position held out, the most tempting was the control of the numbers game, the connections with the big bankers, and above all, with Otávio Lima, the king of the numbers operations in the state. His chance had finally arrived, thought Dr. Albuquerque, looking around the dinner table at his numerous family, wife, mother-in-law, eight children, and even two of his younger brothers, still in school, all of them dependent on him. Up to then, politics had been more a source of annoyance and vexation than anything else; he had spent all those years in the ranks of the opposition; he was a stubborn individual and, after his own fashion, adamant and consistent with his principles.

His principles had as their goal the profitable relations to be established with the bankers of the numbers game, an immediate raise in the cut paid by those powerful industrialists to the police. In the previous administration the game had been unofficially legalized: a percentage of the daily take was set aside for charitable institutions; the public authorities had no share in the revenue, or at least so it was said and seemed. A police commissioner was named to check on the game and was said to receive a generous gratuity.

As soon as he was appointed, Albuquerque got in touch with Lima and set forth his ideas on the matter. Did they want to continue in that same pleasant immunity, protected by the police, with agencies functioning everywhere? In that event, in addition to the percentage set aside for public charities, another of equal amount would have to be handed over to the police. Lima balked at this; it was too much; no banker would be able to stay in business. Was it possible that Dr. Albuquerque really believed that story of the percentage exclusively for charitable institutions? That was so much hogwash, dust thrown in the eyes of the governor, an honest man who had left the governor's mansion convinced that he had stamped out the vice of the numbers game. But on the side, police deputies and commissioners, congressmen, secretaries of state, policemen, detectives, half of the population, got their cut. Increase the tax? There is no specified tax for the police, doctor. The only recognized tax is that for public institutions, for the work of nuns and friars, homes for the blind, for the deaf and dumb, and so forth. So what was all this talk about a tax, a percentage for the police? If what the doctor had in mind was the tip—and Otávio Lima emphasized the word "tip" as though to rub the nose of this uppity popinjay, with his reputation for incorruptibility, in it—given every month to the chief of police, that, naturally, would be continued, and it added up to a respectable sum.

Albuquerque felt the blood rush to his face. "Tip!" That common creature, who was accustomed to giving orders to his hangers-on, some of them holding high posts in political circles, puffing his cigar, that low Otávio Lima had used the term deliberately and had underscored it with his tone of voice. He would teach him a lesson. He was one of the architects of the new governor's victory, and he would have a free hand in his job as chief of police. For a moment, he looked the "industrialist" Lima over, sprawled there in his armchair, satisfied with himself. Tip! . . . He would teach him a lesson.

Very good, Mr. Lima, if the percentage set aside for the police is not raised to the same amount as that for charitable institutions, then the situation of the numbers game will be reexamined. He, Albuquerque, was not interested in the tips paid out to commissioners, policemen, congressmen, detectives. What he wanted was a tax for the work of the police force, for its most secret services, such as combating subversion, a tax that did not have to be declared publicly, and was, of course, to be paid directly to the chief, with tact and punctuality. As for the tip to which Lima referred, that might have sufficed to buy the conscience of previous heads of the police force, but he, Albuquerque, spurned it, refused to accept it.

Otávio Lima was a good-natured man, he had become rich from gambling, even though he had started at the bottom of the ladder, a cardsharper on the waterfront like Corporal Martim, with whom, incidentally, he had served in the army, though he had never risen above the rank of private. Rather than an accomplished professional gambler —he was not even in Martim's class; he lacked his agility, his ability to size up a situation, and above all, his masterly guile—he was a born organizer. He first opened a small gambling den with a crooked roulette wheel; then he took over the numbers game in Itapagipe after the death of old Bacurau, who for twenty years had been the banker of the district, plodding along, aged and infirm, and satisfied with chicken feed.

From Itapagipe, Otávio Lima set out for the capital and he came, he saw, he conquered. He dominated the other bankers, made himself their leader, giving a bold new form to the organization, linking the various groups in a structure like that of big business, making it economically powerful. He owned factories, houses, apartment buildings, he was a bank director, a shareholder in hotels. But for him, notwithstanding, the most important thing, the cornerstone of all, was the numbers game, a game for everybody, living off the dimes and nickels of the poor. When the gambling houses were closed by government order, he was not affected, whereas other gambling kingpins toppled in swift bankruptcy throughout the rest of the country. The numbers game was invincible; nobody could stop it, root it out. Lima, fortune's darling, liked the good life, women—he kept half a dozen mistresses, had children by all of them, and supported them all, even when he stopped seeing them—drinking and eating well, and sitting down, once in a while, at a real gambling table with players of his own caliber for a game of poker, with scamps like Martim. He did this less and less frequently; his past and the friends of those days were growing more remote. Moreover, the majority of them worked for him. They were sub-bankers, and did all right for themselves. Only the corporal, because of his independence and pride, and Carnation-in-his-Button-hole, because of laziness, did not form part of his organization, were not tied up with him, complete vagabonds.

Throwing money around, heedless of expense, knowing that he was exploited by journalists and politicians, contemptuous of all that gang of hypocrites, political figures, intellectuals, society women willing to let him roll them over in the clover in return for expensive presents, Otávio Lima felt himself much stronger than Dr. Albuquerque. True, he had not supported the present governor in his campaign; as a matter of fact, he had contributed to the fund for his opponent, but that was of small account. There were plenty of people ready to defend him, even at the State House, to defend the *"status quo"* of the numbers game. The gratuities handed out were manifold.

It was with a certain coolness and marked superiority that the industrialist took leave of the new and impetuous chief of police, promising him that he would call a meeting within the next twenty-four hours of the other bankers and transmit to them Dr. Albuquerque's proposition. He personally was against it, and would defend his point of view. Possibly, however, the others would accept it, and if they did, he, Otávio Lima, would abide by the majority decision. He was a democrat.

Dr. Albuquerque was, basically, naïve, but not so much so as to believe in the meeting and the possibility of Otávio Lima's bowing to the ideas of his subordinates or lesser partners in the numbers game. He came away from the interview furious.

Lima telephoned a friend of his who had government connections to find out what the true situation of the chief of police was. Was he really a person of influence? If he was as strong as his friend told him, he had done wrong to treat him as haughtily as he had, to throw that matter of the "tip" in his face, to hold out barely the tips of his fingers to him. Naturally, he was not going to give him the cut he had asked for, but he could raise the amount, split the difference. At the same time he instructed Airton Melo to lambaste the new chief of police in his paper. On what pretext? Any: Lima had no preferences.

There you have the explanation of why, the next day, a deputy of Otávio Lima's went to see police commissioner Ángelo Cuiabá, a close friend of the numbers king and, so he had been told, a friend of Albuquerque's. He was the bearer of a counterproposal which he asked Ángelo to convey to his boss. A fatal mistake. In the first place, there was no friendship between the commissioner and the new chief of police; they barely knew one another, their relations were on a polite, but not intimate, footing. In the second place, Albuquerque was a fanatic about his reputation as an honest man. He felt that this was his capital; he did not want it to be diminished not even in the eyes of a police commissioner. In the third place, during this interval rumors had spread about the secret, hush-hush meeting of the chief of police with the numbers king. The thing had leaked out and was known even at the State House. The governor, who was also interested in this matter of the rake-off, was told about it, and he questioned Albuquerque with a certain severity: "They are saying that you went to see Lima, the numbers racketeer...."

Albuquerque felt the ground giving way under his feet. His face turned red, as though he had been slapped. He answered the governor: "I went to give him notice that as long as I am chief of police the numbers game will not be tolerated in Bahia."

There went the money, but he was keeping his job, his prestige untarnished. What he did not know was that he was signing his resignation at that very moment. The governor swallowed hard without revealing the letdown he had just suffered: there went the numbers cut, so useful and so easy. That was what came of his mania for surrounding himself with customers who prided themselves on their integrity. He'd have to get rid of that dope of an Albuquerque, with his airs, his boasts of incorruptibility, as fast as he could. He couldn't dismiss him out of hand, but he certainly would take advantage of the first opportunity.

"You did exactly right, old fellow. That is my opinion, too. You have carte blanche."

Moreover, advisers whose opinion he respected had assured his Excellency the governor that it was not a bad technique to inaugurate his term in office by lowering the boom on the numbers crowd. It was an attitude which would give a sheen of honesty to the new administration and would make the bankers more amenable when the time came to loosen their purse strings, to negotiate an agreement. Albuquerque was a jackass, no question about it, but he was going to be useful. He was just the man needed for the campaign against gambling: unyielding, stubborn, not even a mule could outdo him in stubbornness. What wouldn't the numbers crowd pay to see him off the force? Besides, Otávio Lima deserved a lesson: he had contributed to the campaign funds of the defeated candidate.

Accordingly, two days later, the governor began to demand action from Albuquerque: "My dear fellow, what about the campaign against gambling? The numbers racket is still going strong."

"It was about that that I came to the State House, Governor. To tell you that I have today ordered the closing of all the gambling dens—the numbers agencies and all those places where the depraved play crap, roulette, cards."

He said nothing about having been approached by commissioner Ángelo Cuiabá with the counteroffer of the numbers bankers. He felt that he was in a vulnerable position, his reputation for decency, so carefully built up, now threatened, and worst of all, in his first important public office, the beginning of his career and his fortune. He had listened to the offer with indignation. Twenty per cent of the amount he had suggested to Otávio Lima at their first meeting. He puffed out his chest, buckled on his mask of incorruptibility, consisting of hard censorious eyes, scowling brow, lower lip protruding in an expression of disdain, and sibilant voice: "I am amazed, Mr. Commissioner. That miscreant who goes by the name of Otávio Lima has made a mistake about me. If I went to see him, it was to inform him that gambling, the numbers game, any form of gambling, had become illegal in this state from the moment I took office. I proposed nothing to him, and I refused to listen to any proposal of his. While I am here, in this chair, the numbers game is out, once and for all."

Ángelo Cuiabá immediately changed his tactics. Otávio Lima had played him a dirty trick, had got him into a jam. Albuquerque wound up: "If I talked with him, it was bearing in mind the previous situation. I did not want to be accused of having made a surprise attack, taking advantage of the immunity which the numbers racket and bankers enjoyed."

All there was left for Ángelo to do was to praise his new chief. As for him, if he had come there on behalf of the numbers crowd, it was only because he had been given certain information, never because . . .

"Let's forget the incident, Commissioner. I know you are an honorable man."

And thus the campaign to "do away with the numbers game once and for all" got under way. It gave rise to serious disturbances both for persons in the highest places, like the governor, on whom friends and party members brought pressure to ease up on such drastic orders, and for the insignificant beat-pounding cops, whose budget suddenly lost the estimable tips from the numbers bankers. Above all, in cleaning out the gambling joints where roulette, baccarat, dice, and poker were played, Commissioner Cuiabá, to whom this part of the campaign was assigned, had invaded the rich homes of some outstanding society figures, where gambling for money went on. The commissioner had laughed at the scandal produced; this would help to bury that fool of an Albuquerque all the faster. The governor, too, was fed up with that carnival and was just waiting for the chance to appoint a new chief of police. He would then make his arrangements with the bankers. But he couldn't dismiss Albuquerue just because he was cleaning up gambling. The chief of police had the backing of the clergy and certain social organizations and was mounted high in the saddle on his reputation for incorruptibility; he was, as everybody said, the person to lend integrity to the government.

Albuquerque, however, felt his prestige waning. Every day the governor transmitted to him complaints, spoke of the flexibility politics called for, went on a rampage when Commissioner Cuiabá invaded the drawing rooms of Senhora Batistini, where distinguished people went to rest from their daily toil, from the hours devoted to care for the progress of the country and its people, and have a fling at the roulette wheel and wink an eye at the pretty women. The governor was not impressed by the fact that Albuquerque—quoting Cuiabá—classified the sumptuous mansion of Senhora Batistini in Graça as a "de luxe brothel" and its mistress as a "sordid procuress." The governor knew, indeed he did, who were the regular visitors at the lively mansion, and who protected the jovial lady who had come from Italy, bringing her civilized customs to Bahia. Her house was a model, of the highest quality, which honored the city. And, above all, she was a useful lady. Who could arrange for a nymphet between fifteen and seventeen at most, and morally degenerate, for our illustrious minister when he visited Bahia and asked for someone with those age and moral qualifications to help him in the study of the grave problems of the country, at night in his apartment? If it were not for the services of the esteemed Senhora Batistini, who would look after the minister, Minister of the Treasury, no less, and the state in such dire need of funds? . . .

It was under these circumstances, with Albuquerque feeling his footing unsteady and menaced on all sides, that the invasion of Cat Wood took place. Here was his chance to rehabilitate himself, to win back lost ground, to launch the other campaign which would give him political solidity, transform him into a real leader of the conservative classes, possibly their candidate for governor in the still distant but already-beginning-to-simmer election. The complaint of the rich landowner, the bastion of the Spanish colony, Commander José Perez, came most opportunely. The subverters of public order, the enemies of the Constitution of the Republic, would be combated without quarter. The journalists on the side of the government had not stinted praise when he, acting firmly but with moderation, as he stated, ordered the shacks burned down.

New shacks, however, were built, and their number increased and the residents multiplied. The *Gazette of Salvador* began running the series of articles by that insolent whelp Galub, a hack with deplorable antecedents, beyond doubt in the pay of the numbers bankers, preaching subversion and demanding his resignation—Albuquerque's—accused by that notoriety-seeking reporter of being the executioner of women and children, an arsonist, the Nero of the suburbs.

The entire press had concerned itself with the case, the opposition papers taking the same demagogic line as the *Gazette of Salvador*, those backing the government supporting the action of Albuquerque but, it seemed to him, somewhat half-heartedly; the paper closest to the governor had insinuated the possibility of a solution that would satisfy everybody. Albuquerque, however, felt himself in a stronger position now. The chamber of commerce, under pressure from Perez, had given him a vote of confidence and had called him "the self-sacrificing defender of order."

They supported him, but demanded action, that he wind up without delay that shameless affair of Cat Wood. If that scandal were not quickly cut short, other lands would be invaded, too, and then what? Who would be able to put an end to the disorder, the anarchy?

At a meeting with his subordinates, Dr. Albuquerque studied the situation. A new onslaught against the shanties on the hill was called for. Destroy them as they had done before; leave not a stone standing and permit no more building. That is to say, defeat the enemy, put him to flight, destroy his property, occupy the site, and prevent his return. When José Perez was consulted, he gave his approval to the plan. Engineers and architects, at his behest, were studying a plan for dividing the land up into building lots. The invasion had frightened Pepe Eight Hundred. The best thing was to divide up and sell off that land, get rid of it. Nobody could feel safe in these times we are living through, with strikes, demonstrations, rallies, left-wing students, even his own grandchildren, who ever heard of such a thing!

Albuquerque summoned his general staff and issued the necessary orders. At the same time, he ordered the campaign against gambling, which had been somewhat neglected because of the pressure of other duties, stepped up. He would attack on two fronts; he felt himself a general, a troop commander, a glorious captain. Only, none of that gave him the desired wealth, the money he needed to feed so many mouths. But he was becoming known, making a name for himself; he was on the right track.

8

THEY DID NOT OCCUPY THE ENEMY POSITIONS; they did not oust anybody; they did not set fire to a single thing; they did not even make it to the top of the hill. They were resoundingly defeated; the tactics and strategy of the chief of police had been of no use. The policemen and detectives fled in disorder, leaving their cars behind. The next morning in his paper, Jacó Galub hailed the bravery of the occupants of Cat Wood, the fearless victors of the battle of the preceding night.

The truth of the matter is that the hill folk were not taken by surprise. The news of the preparation of a new punitive expedition, whose objective was to destroy the shanties and occupy the hill, had leaked out and reached even the newspapers. It had arrived at Cat Wood by diverse channels, one of which was Negro Massu himself. He showed up one afternoon turned into a fury. An acquaintance of his, the relative of a copper, had left him alarmed: within a few days, according to this informant, the police were going to occupy Cat Wood Hill, and this time for good. He gave him details of the preparations. The Negro sat down beside Jesuíno and stated, his big head swinging back and forth, as he scratched the ground with a twig: "Father, let me tell you something. They are not going to set fire to my house. They'll have to kill me first, but I won't go alone. If they come, father, it's going to be a calamity."

Crazy Cock knew that the Negro was prepared to kill and die. He had listened to other dwellers, and felt that they were ready to defend their belongings but did not know how. The majority of them saw only one path open to them: to go to the *Gazette of Salvador,* talk with Galub, call on him for help. Pretty Hair amplified this proposal: why not go to the legislature to see that congressman who had protested against the other attack of the police? They could form a committee. If they got the support of the journalists, the congressmen, the aldermen, the police would give ground. Aside from this, they did not know what to do. Jesuíno, however, had other ideas. Not that he was opposed to the formation of a committee or to looking up the journalists and congressman; they might prevent police action. But he had his doubts. They could not rely on the help of others, on the protection of politicians and journalists. Either they defended themselves or they would wind up losing their houses. What should they do? He would show them, right away. Jesuíno smiled, his rebellious white hair falling over his forehead. He had never had such fun. He was returning to the unforgettable games of his childhood, commanding troops, defending contested positions, defeating enemies. He still bore on his scalp the scar of a cut from a stone thrown by an enemy. He went off to look for Miro, Filó's oldest son, who was one of the leaders of the street Arabs.

The committee of which Dona Filó with her collection of children was the stellar attraction, visited the newspaper offices; the state legislature, where they were received and listened to by Congressman Ramos da Cunha; and the city council, where they were greeted by Licio Santos, elected on a ticket of a minority party with the support of the numbers bookmakers. Accompanied by the congressman and the alderman, the committee made its appearance before the chief of police. Numerically reduced, however, because when the word got around that they were on their way to police headquarters, several of the group, among them Corporal Martim, resigned from the committee; the honor had become too risky. Those who remained were mostly women, including Dona Filó and her children, and Pretty Hair stayed, too. Dr. Albuquerque received them in his office, standing. He shook hands with the congressman and the alderman, nodded curtly to the others. Heading them all, with children straddling her flanks, Dona Filó smiled her toothless smile.

Congressman Ramos da Cunha, his voice emphatic, midway between a conversation and a speech, spoke of the concern of the inhabitants of the hill at the news of measures planned by the police against their houses. He, Congressman Ramos da Cunha, did not want to enter upon the legal aspects of the situation of the occupants of the hill at that moment; he was not interested in knowing who was right, they or Commander Perez. It was not this that had brought him, accompanied by Alderman Licio Santos, to visit the distinguished chief of police. What had brought him was a humanitarian duty, the teaching of Christ: "Help one another." He had come at the head of that committee to appeal to the chief of police to leave the poor in peace, to take to heart the lesson of the Nazarene. As he ended, his voice trembled with oratorical fervor, his index finger raised as though he were on the rostrum of the State House. Dona Filó applauded, as did the other women. An officer growled: "Silence. Either you behave yourselves, or I'll throw you all out."

Dr. Albuquerque took a deep breath, cleared his throat, and replied in no less oratorical fashion. He lacked, however, the resonant voice of the congressman and had a tendency to screech when he got excited: "If I consented to receive a committee representing the riffraff who are illegally occupying land that does not belong to them, it was only, Mr. Congressman, out of consideration for you and your position as leader of the opposition. If it were not for that, these creatures would have come here only under arrest." That was his initial paragraph, and he then went into a long dissertation regarding the crime that had been committed by the invaders of Cat Wood. So the congressman did not want to enter upon that aspect of the question which was the only one that was really important? He, Albuquerque, fully understood why. His colleague, who was an eminent jurist, knew that his argument did not have a leg to stand on. They were dealing with criminals, trespassers on other people's property, nearly all of whom had records of long standing in the police files, social outcasts, dangerous elements. To put them in jail was to benefit the community; to evict them from Cat Wood, a duty incumbent on anyone holding the post of chief of police.

However, inasmuch as the congressman had made an appeal to his sentiments as a believer, a Christian, he was willing to grant the invaders a stay of forty-eight hours. During that time they were to leave the hill of their own free will. In that case, they could take their belongings with them and they would not be arrested or brought to trial. Only those would be arrested and tried who were found on the hill by police agents when at the end of the forty-eight-hour stay they ascended it and set fire to the shacks.

Dramatically he pointed his finger toward the big clock on the wall: exactly 3:43 p.m. They had forty-eight hours from that very moment. This was Wednesday; on Friday at 3:43 on the dot, not one minute before or one minute after, the police would ascend the hill. Anyone found there would be put in jail and tried. He had gone beyond the limits of generosity which duty permitted him, Mr. Congressman, but he had done so as a tribute to the noble leader of the opposition. And to prove his Christian sentiments of tolerance and brotherly love.

With which, as far as he was concerned, the interview was over; the reporters were waiting for a statement from him on the matter. But Alderman Licio Santos, ignored, perhaps deliberately, by the chief of police in his speech, did not resign himself to such an obscure role and took the floor on his own responsibility and at his own risk; the thing was to make himself heard. This Licio Santos was notorious for his lack of scruples; he was mixed up in a number of small shady deals and had been elected to office by Otávio Lima, with numbers money. He was, according to Jacó Galub, "a pleasant and likeable fellow, good company, as long as you did not leave either your wallet or a five-milreis bill within his reach." His extravagant oratory followed no logic and not every phrase made sense. One word trod on the heels of the other, a veritable cascade: "Mr. Chief of Police, I am here because my presence is called for; the people came to seek me out; they found me, and I have come with them. I must be listened to. For better or for worse." He was listened to, but with manifest ill will. Dr. Albuquerque, the incorruptible, did not hide his disgust for that product of the lowest walks of political life. The man was his opposite, they represented different, irreconcilable, schools, totally opposite origins. Behind Dr. Albuquerque were generations of men in public life, even noblemen of the Empire, respectability, that façade of integrity. Behind Licio Santos, there was nothing of all this. Nobody knew anything about his family; he had suddenly emerged from the sewers of the city and had been elected with the money of the numbers racket. But there was one thing in which they resembled one another and were in agreement: in getting rich from politics, in burying their fists deep in the public funds. But whereas the chief of police planned to do so while maintaining and adding to his reputation for austerity, as a model and upright citizen, Licio Santos was in a hurry and did not even try to hide his greed. He rushed headlong into any kind of a deal, big or little, quickly seizing whatever he could get, here, there, anywhere. They represented two different political modes, two really opposed types of public servant, benefactors of the country. The ways in which they tried to make use of power separated them from each other, made Dr. Albuquerque look down his nose at "Licio the Rat" (as he was known to his close friends). But it is not for us, ordinary citizens holding no public office, to take sides with either of these two classes of thieves. It is a proven fact that they all, the noble Albuquerques, the ward-heeler Licios, stole and stole plenty. We are not going to criticize the behavior of one, praise that of the other; we shall remain neutral in this controversy between the saviors of the country.

Licio the Rat squealed out phrases that did not make sense, demanding a longer stay, quoting Ruy Barbosa. The fact was that he was not too conversant with the whole affair. The committee had taken him by surprise and he had accompanied it partly to see if there might not be something in that imbroglio for him, and because, being one of Otávio Lima's henchmen, he was against the chief of police.

The other aldermen had avoided having anything to do

with the occupants of Cat Wood; the mayor, who had connections with the Spanish colony and was a friend of Commander Perez, wholeheartedly supported the action of the chief of police, as did the majority of the city council. The aldermen of the opposition were equally afraid of displeasing the big businessmen, the real-estate owners; they did not want to get involved in that fight. Licio Santos, however, had nothing to lose. On the contrary, his close connections with Otávio Lima automatically put him on the side of the invaders. Therefore he went along with the committee, but he did not know the details of the affair. There in the office of the chief of police, listening to the congressman and Albuquerque, he realized its importance, and with the swiftness and low cunning that characterized him, he grasped the enormous possibilities it offered.

To be sure, he felt the unconcealed contempt of Albuquerque, the lack of enthusiasm on the part of Congressman Ramos da Cunha at having him heading the committee with him—the congressman was of the same stripe of public servant as the chief of police—but Licio the Rat laughed at them, he could put them in his pocket without help from anyone, make them eat out of his hand if he so desired.

His speech mounted in emotion and violence. He demanded a longer stay, at least a week, or better, two weeks, time to find responsible persons, a fair solution that would take into account the legitimate interests of the landowners and the no less legitimate interests of that indigent sector of the city's population. Did the chief of police, perchance, know what hunger was! "Hunger, sir, and of the bitter kind," he proclaimed.

Dr. Albuquerque took advantage of the dramatic pause to interrupt the alderman. He reaffirmed the delay he had granted, forty-eight hours, not a minute more or less. As for the interests of the criminals and the interests of the law, he was obliged to inform the honorable alderman that the two were incompatible.

"There can be no covenant between the law and crime, property and theft, order and anarchy. Mr. Alderman, we either put a stop to subversion or we will be implacably swallowed up in its vortex."

And with this gloomy warning the interview ended. As they were about to leave, Dona Filó, who had no upbringing, came to attention as though she were a soldier, brought her heels together with a click of her old shoes, and saluted the chief of police. Even the policeman laughed. Dr. Albuquerque almost had a stroke: contempt of authority!

Filó was not tossed into jail thanks to the two small children clinging to her flanks. The chief of police was furious. If it had not been for the children, no appeal or intercession would have saved her.

The notice of the delay of forty-eight hours granted the invaders of Cat Wood to leave the hill gave rise to various measures.

When Ramos da Cunha left police headquarters, he went to find Jacó Galub. The affair was conferring a certain prestige on the congressman in the capital, where up to that time he had not had a single voter. He had to arrange with the journalist for an intensification of the campaign against the police and in favor of the squatters. Nothing practical would come of it, naturally; the poor would wind up being thrown out, but he and Jacó would have gained popular prestige while this was happening. It would be useful for him; he could set up committees in the capital, establish bases there which would be important for his political future. As for the journalist, his stories were meeting with growing success; they were arousing an echo outside Bahia, and a magazine in Rio had already asked him for an article on Cat Wood, with photographs. He might even run for alderman in the coming elections.

Licio Santos left police headquarters in a thoughtful mood. He went straight off to talk with Otávio Lima. A bold plan was beginning to shape up in his mind. He smiled gently, recalling Dr. Albuquerque's disgruntled face. That scoundrel with his choirboy, upright-citizen act! Licio knew what his vaunted honesty was worth; he was fully informed of the interview of the chief of police with the numbers king; Otávio had given him all the details. And that rogue had the nerve to cut him short, to look down his nose at him! Licio smiled gently. That business of the invasion of Cat Wood could be very profitable; the question was knowing how to bring it safely to port. And in passing, to kick out of police headquarters that pain in the ass of an Albuquerque, with his lying honesty, his shitty arrogance.

Jesuíno Crazy Cock, too, busy with his tasks on the hill, heard about the time limit and found it sufficient. The defense operations were ahead of schedule; Miro had secured the collaboration of all the street Arabs, and with them Crazy Cock would launch his defensive. He could then depend on the women and finally on the men. His enthusiasm was contagious, he and the kids had a wonderful time, and the others, too, found it entertaining. And when one does a job with pleasure, it is always well done.

Exactly at 3:43 on Friday, under a steady, annoying rain, the police disembarked from their automobiles. This time, to avoid surprises, they left them a good distance away, at the airport near the beach, and came on foot.

In spite of the heavy rain that had been falling all the night before and that morning, turning the whole place into a quagmire, several reporters were on hand, and Jacó Galub, in a show of daring, had climbed the hill and aligned himself with the squatters, so as to be arrested with them. One of the radio networks had set up a portable transmitter there to broadcast developments, and the broadcasters were excitedly announcing every move the police made. Before that, they had transmitted the words of Dona Filó, magnificent in her steadfastness and courage, prepared, so she said, to die there with her seven children defending her shack. And Corporal Martim, led astray by his vanity, took the microphone and made threats, emboldened by his corporal's chevrons. As Jesuíno warned him, he was making a mistake whose consequences we shall duly point out when the moment arrives. We shall take it easy, without rushing; we have plenty of time, and the stills are working, making more and more rum.

Chico Pinóia, too, wearing a waterproof cape, gave an interview over the radio. He, at the head of his men, had come to carry out the orders of the chief of police: raze the shacks that had gone up on the hill, that filthy slum, and occupy the site to prevent future incursions. The police had been overtolerant. They had allowed that trash time to

289

leave. They had not gone because they had not wanted to. Now there were three vans waiting on the beach to carry the prisoners to jail. And at headquarters the charges were already being drawn up. Would they arrest the reporter Galub? They would arrest the devil himself if he were on the hill.

Two trails led to the top of the hill, steep, almost sheer paths. That day, with the rain, they were especially slippery. Both trails were on the side facing the beach in the rear of the hill, bounded by a mangrove swamp full of scrub and pestilential mud. Only the most daring of the youngsters ventured to cross it. Thus the policemen, loaded down with the cans of gasoline, had only these two steep approaches, awash with the rain. They began the ascent, slowly.

They had taken only a few steps, however, when from holes in the hillside, primitive trenches dug by Crazy Cock with the help of the street Arabs, came a hail of stones. The urchins had wonderful aim. One of the policemen, among the first to attempt the ascent, was hit in the middle of the forehead by a stone, lost his footing, rolled down hill through the mud, and when he landed, his own mother would not have recognized him. The rest stopped; one was bleeding from the cheek. Chico Pinóia pulled out his revolver and took command, shouting as he started up: "So this is the way you want it, you outlaws? Now you are going to see, you dogs."

Clutching his revolver, followed by three or four flat-foots, slipping in the mud, he advanced slowly. The broadcasters announced over their microphones: "Commissioner Francisco Lopes in person is going to attempt to scale the hill. Boldly, revolver in hand, prepared for any emergency, Commissioner Pinóia, excuse me, Commissioner Lopes, is in the lead."

And then: "We interrupt our broadcast. The commissioner is no longer in the lead. The commissioner has turned back, threatened by a huge stone, a boulder that is tottering and rolling. . . ."

True enough, with a shove from Massu and Pretty Hair, an enormous rock, in unsteady equilibrium in the middle of the hill, rolled in Chico Pinóia's direction. It was a race.

Not only did the commissioner run, shamefully discarding his revolver, but also flatfoots and spectators, reporters and announcers with their microphones, ran. The boulder crashed at the base of the hill in a welter of mud and confusion.

The announcer of the Second-of-July network was considered the best sports announcer in the city. "Goal," he announced, as though he were broadcasting an important soccer match. "Two to nothing in favor of the outlaws of Cat Wood Hill." Three times the police tried to scale and assault the hill, and three times they failed. The announcers vibrated with enthusiasm: "The detectives fired their revolvers, missing every time. In contrast, the rocks almost invariably hit their mark. Even our teammate Romualdo Matos, who in order to cover events better got close to the spot, was hit on the shoulder by a stone and received bruises and his shirt was torn. But that is the way your Second-of-July network functions, broadcasting directly from the firing line. Build your house on the hill or on the beach, on land bought or invaded, but don't fail to get your furniture at the Supreme Furniture Mart, on Seventh Avenue, number . . ."

At 6:15, more than two hours after the beginning of the attack on the hill, without the police having even reached the shacks, an official car appeared on the scene. Out of it stepped a district chief of police, a member of the governor's cabinet, and a reporter who covered the State House. The district chief of police went over to Chico Pinóia, followed by the cabinet member, while the reporter cracked jokes with the radio crew.

Chico Pinóia, one solid mass of mud, clothes, hands, face—seething with hatred, a hatred that called for blood, beatings, broken heads—demanded reinforcements, military police, orders to shoot to kill: "The only thing those dogs understand is lead!"

But the orders, straight from the governor's desk, were to call off the action that had been initiated. The police were to withdraw.

According to the State House reporter, the governor was meeting in secret session with the party leader, two or three other congressmen, the lawyer of the chamber of com-

SHEPHERDS OF THE NIGHT

merce, and Alderman Licio Santos. They had been locked in for more than two hours. The chief of police had been sent for during the middle of the meeting, and when he left he had not seemed very happy. And it was the governor in person who had issued the order. There was going to be plenty of news breaking. . . .

The police embarked on their return voyage dirty and defeated. When the motors of the vans started up, the whistles of a monumental catcall reached them from the top of the hill, a catcall in which broadcasters, reporters, and spectators all joined. From the top of the hill, Jesuíno had ordered it as marking the end of his command, laughing with contentment, the general of the tattered, the captain of the street Arabs, as though he were one of them, a street waif of Bahia, with a helmet made of tin and cardboard, soggy with rain, playing cops and robbers. He had never had so much fun. Neither he nor Miro, his second in command, his bones showing through his skin, a cigarette stub in his mouth, a knife in his belt.

But the one who descended victorious at the head of the celebrating inhabitants was Jacó Galub, who from that day on was known as the "hero of Cat Wood," as Congressman Ramos da Cunha called him in his memorable speech to the legislature. "The people were not alone, Mr. President; we were there with them in the person of the dauntless journalist Jacó Galub, who from that day on was known as the 'hero of Cat Wood.' " Jacó himself, moreover, let the decisive role he had played in the triumph be glimpsed in his sensational coverage, beginning with the title: "I saw and took part in the battle of Cat Wood." In this report Chico Pinóia was dragged through the street of infamy, described as the most ridiculous and stupid of all the feeble-minded. Whence the threat of bodily injury which highlighted even more the importance of Galub's participation.

That night there was still another moving scene on the hill. The inhabitants celebrated the appearance there of Alderman Licio Santos, who had overcome all obstacles to reach the top of the hill, accompanied by ward heelers and a photographer from O Jornal do Estado. He brought a radio, a gift from the prominent industrialist Otávio Lima for the "good people of Cat Wood," and the unconditional solidarity of Licio Santos, the alderman of the people. He was at their side, with them through thick and through thin, come what might, prepared to stay there, if necessary, and die with them in the defense of their sacred homes, which were under attack.

As for Jesuíno Crazy Cock, he did not attend the presentation of the radio which Dona Filó accepted in the name of all. Jesuíno had not stayed on the hill after victory. He had thought it more prudent to disappear for a few days, to go and have a beer with Jesus at Tibéria's place. A detective, informed of his activities, might appear on the sly and arrest him. He brought with him Corporal Martim, whose harangue at the microphone had seemed to him most imprudent, and young Miro, Dona Filó's oldest son.

He laughed as he told Otália and Tibéria, the other girls and Jesus, how terrified the reporter Jacó had been when the cops began firing shots in the air. He had run into Pretty Hair's house and had found a safe corner to hide in.

And so Jesuíno did not hear the declaration of solidarity of Licio Santos, the testimony of sympathy of Otávio Lima, the backing of all those important people mentioned in the alderman's speech. Pointing to Miro, with his filthy, nappy hair, his restless eyes, his ferret face, Crazy Cock stated: "There's the one who did not let the police up. That customer there, he and the other kids. When the men were ready to give everything up for lost, they bravely fired their rocks down. If the houses are still standing, we can thank them for it."

Jesus wanted to do justice to everybody: "But the reporter, afraid or not afraid, helped. The congressman, too."

Jesuíno shrugged his shoulders, turning his glass of beer around in his hand. The old vagabond was a skeptic who did not believe in the solidarity of anybody. "We are alone in the world, Brother Jesus, Sister Tibéria. But the poor are like weeds; the more you pull them, the deeper roots they send down; the more you yank them out, the thicker they grow."

Miro listened to him and laughed, too. Jesuíno laid a

somewhat unsteady hand—the result of all the rum he had drunk that day, now rounded off with beer—on the shoulder of the street Arab: "This is a good kid. First-class."

But the boy knew that it had all been the work of old Jesuíno Crazy Cock. He knew it, and the people of Cat Wood knew it, even though they did not attach much importance to it. They had all known Jesuíno for a long time; they were aware of his skill, his wisdom, his always managing to find a way, daunted by nothing. A drinker without peer, whom nobody could equal at tasting and judging rum. An indefatigable womanizer, even today with his white hair and wrinkles and years, women preferred him to younger men, as though he had a vintage flavor. It was the distilled wisdom of years, and the people knew all that, and for that very reason they did not attach too much importance to it. Neither did Jesuíno. What he wanted was to amuse himself.

The people of Cat Wood were now gathered around the radio. They had hooked it up, and the music of a samba rolled down the hill, lifting their spirits. Putting her smaller children down, Filó started dancing, and the others followed suit.

9

AFTER THE UNSUCCESSFUL POLICE ACTION, the Cat Wood
affair entered upon two immediate and distinct phases. The
first was one of ebullience.

Articles and reports, editorials and comments, columns
for or against the settlers or the police, depending on the
political affiliations of the newspapers. All of them, however, unanimously praised the prudence of the governor,
his humanitarian attitude in ordering the attack called off,
thus preventing bloodshed and loss of life. In the state
legislature, the impassioned speech of the minority leader,
Congressman Ramos da Cunha, laid the responsibility
squarely at the administration's door. In his reply, the
majority leader, Congressman Reis Sobrinho, accused the
opposition, and particularly its leader, of responsibility for
the disorder and uprising. The opposition had encouraged
the hooligans, the worst elements, the dregs of society, in
order to create difficulties for the administration and put
the government in an embarrassing position. Knowing that
they were the victims of the siren song of the opposition,
and to avoid further suffering, the governor had given
orders to call off the attack and delay the expulsion of the
invaders. But only delay. The government would proceed
to defend the law—let no one mistake generosity for
weakness.

At City Hall, Alderman Licio Santos, now the most

enthusiastic champion of Cat Wood, at least the equal of Jacó Galub, put on a real show. He secured the immediate support of two or three magistrates who were dying for publicity and votes. What the chief of police had done was a shame, he roared from the forum, a crime against the people, that torturer of numbers bankers, that make-believe Robespierre. Why was he hounding the numbers game? Because he had not been given the rake-off he wanted, a limitless cut. This was not idle talk; he could prove it. That Dr. Albuquerque, that deflowered vestal virgin, not satisfied with the tortures inflicted on the lawbreakers he arrested, now wanted to assassinate the workers whose homes had been erected on Cat Wood. And the home of a Brazilian—listen and learn, Mr. Chief of Police!—the home of a Brazilian is sacred, untouchable, guaranteed by the Constitution. Licio Santos raged on. He was trying to make up for lost time, cement his reputation as the most stalwart champion of Cat Wood. He saw in that invasion a gold mine, all that was needed was to know how to work it.

First there was all this agitation; the world seemed turned topsy-turvy. Then came a total lull. If, as gossip had it, there were conferences going on, proposals, conversations, it was all on the q.t.; nothing leaked out. The newspapers said Dr. Albuquerque had submitted his resignation in protest against the conciliatory attitude of the governor, but this report was energetically denied by the chief of police himself. The governor, he stated to the reporters, would act after consulting him and in agreement with him. There was no difference of opinion between them. As for the new measures to be taken to evict the invaders, they were being studied and would soon be put into effect.

The police were furious; they patrolled Cat Wood Hill from a distance, without venturing to go up. At the same time certain of the inhabitants who had played an important part, like Negro Massu, avoided going down; they were safer up there. The police would not forgive the defeat they had suffered, their slipping down steep paths and through mud puddles, the stoning, the final booing.

Once more Jesuíno demonstrated his prudence and good sense by disappearing for a few days, the guest of Tibéria, resting in the sheltering warmth of Laura Sunny-Bottom, whose buttocks were renowned for their size and firmness, and by trying to keep Corporal Martim away from the busy streets.

The trouble with the corporal was that he liked to be in the public eye. On the day of the attack, he had talked into the microphone just to show off. It is hard to resist a radio microphone, there is a special attraction about the apparatus, and a person begins to talk. Like the camera. A reporter shows up with a flash bulb and a guy immediately strikes a pose, his mouth open in a smile showing his back teeth. Jesuíno, however, did not let himself be photographed, nor did he go sounding off into any microphone; he was not a fool. Martim, on the other hand, without thinking of the consequences, with so many reasons not to draw attention to himself, had given free rein to his tongue, had made a mock of the police, telling (and this was the worst thing he did) of the beating that Chico Pinóia had received at the hands of a group of the habitués of the Gafieira do Barão dance hall on the night of the victory dance.

Nor did he pay much attention to Jesuíno's advice about getting lost for a while. As a result, he was almost nabbed near the Church of the Rosary of the Negroes in Pelourinho, where the christening of Massu's son had taken place, as he was coming out of Alonso's store. He had gone to meet Otália, a dramatic and decisive meeting.

Wanted and without funds—there was nowhere to play, his partners having disappeared as a result of the relentless campaign—he had never felt so in need of tangible proof of Otália's love. So he told her, glumly, leaning against the counter of the store, before his empty glass. He had waited with infinite patience up to then. But the hour had come; they could not go in that wishy-washy fashion. After all, she, Otália, was no virgin damsel and he, Corporal Martim, did not intend to play the sucker any longer.

Otália puckered up her eyes and lips, as though on the verge of tears. Martim almost regretted his harsh words. But the tears did not come; all she did was repeat her decision not to go to bed with him. At least, not so soon. The corporal lost his head and took her in his arms by force. There was no other customer in Alonso's store at the moment, and Alonso was somewhere inside. Otália resisted and managed to free herself, asking in a grieved tone: "You don't understand?"

He didn't understand anything. He just wanted her, and she was having fun at his expense.

"If not today, then everything is over between us."

She turned her back and left. Martim got to the door in time to see her round the corner on her way to the brothel. He had another glass of rum before he left, out of sorts over everything—being broke, the police after him, Otália, and himself.

He went out, and had taken only a few steps when the policeman saw him, came toward him, and ordered him to halt. The corporal looked all around, saw no plain-clothes men or other policemen in the immediate vicinity, and with a quick *capoeira* feint knocked the insolent flatfoot off his feet. Then he beat it fast. When the policeman got up and began to call for help, Martim was already disappearing down the hillside.

That night, chewing the bitter cud of careless love, having to hold himself in to keep from going after Otália, Martim, throwing caution to the winds, showed up at the place of Carlos Mule Stink, whose card game was one of the few still going in spite of the police. And if ever there was a joint that needed a lesson it was that booby trap of Mule Stink's, whose nickname came from the strange and overpowering B.O. from his armpits. Mule Stink was a coarse operator, lacking refinement. His decks would not have fooled a blind man and his dice were absolutely crooked. Martim knew all about this, in detail, for Artur da Guima, himself a highly skilled craftsman, had told him about making some dice especially for Mule Stink— crooked ones, naturally. Arthur had even shown him how he had made them; the work was perfect.

Knowing the background of Mule Stink, the corporal was not going into his rat trap to risk the few tarnished nickels Alonso had loaned him. He was going to kill time, chat a little, watch the owner in operation, and perhaps that way he wouldn't think about Otália, would get that obsession out of his mind. After all, a man has to stick to his word. He did not want to see her any more; he was no clown; as far as he was concerned, all was over. And, who knows, there was the off chance of getting up a game of poker—with his deck, naturally.

Carlos Mule Stink's game was hidden in the back of a machinery warehouse. At night the entrance was guarded by a watchman, Carnation-in-his-Buttonhole, who had performed that service for some time. As always, Martim was warmly received; the owner of the establishment had a high regard for him.

There was a small group around a crap table. With Mule Stink covering the bets, who could possibly hope to win with those dice? You can imagine Martim's amazement when he noticed among the players, betting against the banker, Artur da Guima in person, by whose hands those crooked dice had been fashioned. Was he crazy or was he in the pay of the owner of the place, acting as a come-on? Returning Mule Stink's pleasant greeting and refusing his invitation to take a hand in the game, Martim stuck out his lip toward Artur da Guima, as though asking the meaning of his presence there. Mule Stink shrugged his shoulders, and soon afterwards called the game off and sent the players away, saying he had to go out with the corporal. Artur da Guima left glumly, muttering unintelligible phrases.

"He's giving himself hell . . . saying he is a fool and I don't know what all!"

Mule Stink laughed, explaining to Martim that he was not in the least to blame for that crackpot's behavior. Who ever heard of such a thing? The man had made the dice himself, nobody knew what they were like better than he, and still he came to throw his money away on them. How could he prevent it? He once had tried to and Artur had gotten so mad he had wanted to fight him. The old goat was a real crap fiend. As he couldn't find any other place to play, he came barging in there and sat down to bet. If he were the only player, Mule Stink could lose. But there were the others, and after all, Artur came there because he wanted to. Nobody made him; he was of age. Then afterwards he went out into the street, kicking himself, calling himself names.

Martim accepted a swallow of rum, and the two commiserated with each other over the hard times they were going through. Mule Stink asked him to stay a little while. They might be able to get up a poker game. Some suckers from a tobacco-exporting house, and only one of them had the sense he was born with. The other two hardly knew a straight from a flush. Nobody could get rich off them—they must not frighten them away or take them for too much—but it was better than nothing. Martim rubbed his hands. Being flat broke, he was grateful for anything.

Sure enough, half an hour later the three boobs arrived. Martim was introduced as a soldier on leave, and they sat down at the table. They had, however, no more than picked up their cards when the police raided the joint. The watchman at the door to the office was hustled so quickly into the Black Maria that he did not even have time to call out. However, Mule Stink, who never relaxed, heard a suspicious noise, and when the cops appeared, he had time to call to Martim: "Follow me, brother!"

A partly hidden wicket behind a filing cabinet, which opened onto some vacant lots at the back. There they sprinted off while the police loaded the three tobacco-company employees into the van with shoves and slaps.

Martim beat it to the house of Zébedeu, a *compadre* of his, a longshoreman in comfortable circumstances, living in Barbalho. Zébedeu loaned him some money and asked him to go away. The police were looking for him; that very afternoon the image maker Alfredo, in Cabeça, had received a disagreeable visit from the cops. They were looking for the corporal, looking for him everywhere, and a detective by the name of Miguel Charuto, his sworn enemy, was now working with Chico Pinóia and had been specially ordered to nab Martim and clap him into the clink.

Only then did he grasp how serious the situation was. With the help of Zébedeu and Master Manuel, he left for the island of Itaparica. Jesuíno alone was informed as to his whereabouts. In Itaparica he called himself Sergeant Porciúncula, but he did not elaborate on whether he was a member of the army or of the military police. He liked it on the island. Gambling was not banned there, and even though it was not vacation time and there were not many

people around yet, he made out. And then Altiva Conception of the Holy Ghost showed up—what an eyeful of
mulatta!—to help him forget Otália and his absurd infatuation. There were moments when he still remembered and
desired her; he still gnashed his teeth. But he threw himself
on Altiva on the sand by the shore and rode her through
the waves of the sea. He had never seen anyone so like a
siren, and he said to her, as the wind fluttered the coconut
palms and he stroked her belly, the color of copper: "You
are like Yemanjá. . . ."

"And when did you ever sleep with Yemanjá, you low-
down nigger?"

In Bahia the police went on wreaking their wrath. Wing-
Foot had been thrown in the cooler in spite of the fact that
he had left Cat Wood Hill even before the first invasion of
the police. They gave him a working over with the ferule
and only let him go at the request of a client of his, Dr.
Menandro, who, being in urgent need of some frogs he had
ordered from Wing-Foot, went out looking for him and
found the poor devil in the hoosegow, sleeping like a log.

Another who got a going over was Ipicilone. But he, too,
was released, for a certain Dr. Abilafia, a shyster lawyer
under orders from Alderman Licio Santos, solicited a writ
of habeas corpus for all the prisoners against whom no
charges had been preferred. All of them, as soon as they
were released, registered as voters and turned their voting
cards over to the alderman.

With the exception of this feverish police activity, the
only news worth mentioning during those days in connection with the invasion of Cat Wood was the filing of a suit,
by one of the most important lawyers of the city, on behalf
of Commander José Perez, demanding that his property
invaded by squatters be restored to him. The lawyer asked
the court to issue orders for the police to take action, once
and for all, against the violators of the laws and the Constitution.

---❦{ 10 }❦---

THE ONE WHO KEPT APART AND ALOOF from all this vexation was Bullfinch. The developments having to do with the campaign against gambling left him totally indifferent, except as they affected friends of his, such as Martim. We know the store the spieler set by friendship, and Martim was his brother-in-devotion. That was all that worried Bullfinch, whom games of chance had never interested.

"My only vice is women," he would answer when offered a cigarette or asked to take a hand in a poker game. He forgot to mention drink, perhaps because he did not consider it a vice but a necessity, a kind of wonder-working cure for a variety of ills, including those of love.

Without Martim, night in Bahia was not the same. Though in honor of the truth one would have to confess that changes had taken place even before the hasty departure of Martim, who was now for all effects and purposes transformed into Sergeant Porciúncula, honeymooning with Altiva Conception of the Holy Ghost on the beaches of Itaparica. With the invasion of Cat Wood, the friends who had unfailingly met every day at the twilight hour to work out the program for the evening no longer gathered; the calendar of festivities had been totally forgotten; complete anarchy reigned.

Even so, not even the events that came to pass as a result of the invasion managed to disturb Bullfinch. As though he were not an inhabitant of the hill, where he had begun to build his shack, incidentally the oddest of all. There was his chalet, half built, and if not for the vigilance of Jesuíno and Massu, it would long since have been taken over by some opportunist looking for easy pickings. Bullfinch had no thought for anything but Madame Beatriz, the prodigious fakir, at that very moment to be seen fasting, stretched out in a coffin with a glass top, admission five milreis, on Baixa do Sapateiro.

Jesuíno was accustomed to the agitated chronicle of Bullfinch's love affairs (generally frustrated), and his syrupy romanticism no longer impressed him, nor did his illusions and deceptions. But not even Jesuíno, so understanding, could stand to see anyone that naïve. Bullfinch had swallowed that story of the fast hook, line and sinker: he swore by the soul of his mother, he would put his hand in the fire, for Madame Beatriz's honesty. Complete fast, neither food nor drink, for a month. Jesuíno shook his head. Bullfinch would please be patient and forgive him, but he could not believe that. For a person to go a month without eating was difficult, next to impossible. But without drinking, a person could not hold out for even a week. So stop that nonsense and out with the trick, for after all, he, Bullfinch, could have no interest in fooling his friends. They weren't going to tell anybody, spill the beans—were they, Wing-Foot?

Wing-Foot, who was qualified to speak on matters of fasting, agreed. Nobody could fast for a month. A boa constrictor could spend a month without eating, but that was after swallowing a calf, and it took a long time to digest a young bull or heifer. But not people. And much less without drinking. Without food, drink, and a woman, nobody could live. True, there were men who could go for a month without a woman; he had heard tell of them. He, Wing-Foot, however, after four or five days got edgy and sullen, ready to fall upon any woman, no matter who she was. Speaking about such matters, was the lady in question going to spend the month without a man too, or did Bullfinch get into the coffin in the middle of the night for a roll with the corpse?

Without eating, without drinking, and without a man ... She could not have bed relations, not only during her month of fasting—you only had to look at the coffin, hermetically sealed—but not for three weeks beforehand, during which she prepared herself to endure that long penitence, possible only to her, the favorite pupil of the Buddhist bonzes.

"What the devil is that?"

"A religion of the Hindus, people who live all their life long without eating, drinking a swallow of water every six months, wearing a loincloth. . . ."

"That's a lie," Wing-Foot snapped.

Ipicilone spoke up: "I don't know. . . . I have read something about it. It's somewhere in Tibet, the farthest-away place in the world."

"That's a lie," Wing-Foot repeated. "The ones who wear loincloths are the Indians, and they eat like horses."

But Bullfinch was unyielding. How could she eat or drink if he didn't give her food or water and he was the only one who went near her, her private secretary? Didn't he stay in Abdala's old store all day long, collecting the admissions, lifting the curtain so the public (small and unenthusiastic, to be sure) could see how beautiful she looked stretched out in her coffin?

The problem was really curious and interested Jesuíno: "And when you leave, when you come here to have a drink, who takes your place?"

All right, every day, for two hours, at dinnertime, he went out to get something to eat—at noon all he had was a sandwich and a couple of bananas—and to see his friends. His place at the door was taken by the mulatta who ran the boardinghouse, Emilia Green-Sleeves; they knew one another, and she did him the favor of helping out. They had become intimate friends, she and the clairvoyante.

"Emilia Green-Sleeves? One who lives on Giovanni Guimarã Street and had a food stall at the market before she took up with a Turk and started the boardinghouse?"

"That's the one."

"Then there's no need to rack our brains. She's the one who takes food and drink to the so-and-so."

Bullfinch still argued and disputed, but the thorn of doubt had penetrated his breast. Could it be true? Madame Beatriz, for whom he would take an oath, would she be capable of such deceit? Of trusting Emilia because she doubted him? In that case, how could he believe in her promises of happiness after the month of fasting?

With worries of this sort, and head over heels in love, Bullfinch did not become involved in the stormy developments that were taking place. He had only gone up to Cat Wood once, to pay a visit to Massu and old Vevéva and to see the baby.

Nevertheless, there was no lack of exciting news. While the suit brought by Pepe Eight Hundred had been approved by the lower court and was now awaiting action by the court of appeals, Congressman Ramos da Cunha, with the support of his fellow members of the opposition, had presented a draft of a bill which would give the government the right to expropriate the lands of Cat Wood Hill and turn them into state property on which the people could build homes. The repercussions of the bill were considerable, and with it the opposition scored a point. A big meeting was to be held in Sé Square, where various speakers would address the public, among them the sponsor of the bill, the journalist Jacó Galub, the alderman Licio Santos, and the inhabitants of the hill.

It could not be said, quoting the pro-government newspapers, that "the demagogic exploitation by the opposition of the invasion of Cat Wood Hill was a failure, for the much touted meeting consisted of some half dozen loafers with nothing better to do"; nor could one accept the overblown claims of the *Gazette of Salvador*, talking in terms of ten thousand persons "to hear the ardent words of Airton Melo, Ramos da Cunha, Licio Santos, Jacó Galub, and the long-suffering words of the hill dwellers." Neither the one nor the other. A fair crowd, in the neighborhood of fifteen hundred persons, what with listeners and passersby —people waiting for the streetcar and bus—heard and applauded the speakers. Especially Licio Santos, who received an ovation for his tirades, which at times made no sense but were always effective. His words were suited to the baroque setting of the Square, an appropriate frame for that sonorous, astute sermon. Strictly speaking, none of the inhabitants of the hill was present. They were running no risks of this being a fast one the police were pulling. Only

Filó, whom Galub went for in person, appeared on the platform and was pointed out to the crowd, surrounded by her children. She aroused frenzied enthusiasm. The one who spoke in the name of the inhabitants of the hill was Dante Veronezi, a tailor who lived in Itapagipe, a person with political ambitions, always at odds with Licio Santos, his ward boss. His speech was a masterpiece of eloquence, befitting the spot where Father Vieira had unleashed his attack against the Dutch. He described the poverty of the hill dwellers; he was one of them. Homeless, with no place to lay their heads, exposed to the rain and the inclemency of the weather, along with their wives and children. A scene worthy of Dante, of that other Dante, the Italian. But he, a Brazilian citizen, felt acutely, in the flesh of his own small children, the weight of all that misery. As a last resort, they had erected their hovels on the vacant lands of that Spanish millionaire who had made his fortune by taking the bread out of the mouths of the poor. Fortunately, there still existed men like Airton Melo, the noble editor of the *Gazette of Salvador;* like Jacó Galub, "the hero of Cat Wood;" like Congressman Ramos da Cunha, with his bill to liberate the new slaves; like Alderman Licio Santos, that father of the poor, that protector of the hungry, that virtuous citizen comparable only to the great men of the past, Alexander, Hannibal, Napoleon, José Bonifácio . . .

If one of the invaders had spoken, he could not have spoken better or with more conviction. Even Dona Filó, so accustomed to the vicissitudes of life and so little given to tears, felt a lump in her throat and a burning in her eyes when Dante Veronezi pointed to her with his finger, she, his neighbor on the hill, the mother of a dozen children, killing herself day and night over the washtub and the ironing board to support her family. For years and years she had been kicked about from post to pillar with her pitiful orphans; a widow and a decent woman, she did not do as others did. . . . Until finally, with her own hands and the help of the children, the poor things, she had erected her modest little house on Cat Wood Hill. Was it not a crime to evict this loving mother, this veritable saint?

Filó was touched by the applause that greeted her. A real success.

306

Ramos da Cunha's project, which was endorsed at the meeting, aroused repercussions in many quarters. The governor, who was enjoying his day in the sun, did not want to be overshadowed by any demagogue of the opposition. On the other hand, the court of claims, under pressure from Pepe Eight Hundred's lawyer, the renowned jurist of businessmen and property owners, Professor Pinheiro Sales of the law school, had set the date for hearing the Spaniard's suit. One judge had handed down a sentence in his favor, a terse four-line decision ordering the police to evict the squatters. Gossip had it that the sentence had cost fifty contos, in those days a small fortune, not like today when fifty contos wouldn't be enough to buy half a witness, let alone a whole eminent judge. But Attorney Abilafia, who was acting for the Cat Wood Hill dwellers, had carried the case to the court of appeals and had won a stay. The judges of the court received that hot potato; they kicked it around, putting off their decision. They knew that the matter had aroused great political expectations, and they wanted to see from which quarter the wind was blowing. But in the face of Ramos da Cunha's and the meeting's project, Commander Perez's lawyer, with the backing of big business and the conservatives, brought strong pressure to bear on the court, getting it to fix a date to review the decision. He came away from the interview with the presiding judge in great elation, feeling that the matter had been practically decided in their favor. The whole problem consisted in avoiding ruses of the court, which was highly sensitive to the interests of political parties and public figures, and he had circumvented this by getting it to set a date for the hearing.

For this very reason, he was greatly surprised when, on communicating the news to Commander Perez, he did not find in his affluent client the same state of enthusiasm. On the contrary, Pepe Eight Hundred found the court's inclination to delay its decision not only interesting, but even useful. Waiting to see which way the cat jumped, he was no longer in a hurry; the compass needle had come around 180 degrees. Ramos da Cunha's project had alarmed Professor Sales and had made him hasten to present the matter to the presiding judge in an urgent light, insisting that he set the date for the trial. But while this had been going on, the commander had changed his mind about the affair; he did not even rail against the invaders, in his Portuguese with its heavy Spanish accent. The lawyer swallowed a few curses; he did not understand what was going on.

He did not know that a few hours earlier that same day the Spaniard had received, from the hands of the chief engineer of a large firm of realtors and builders, the blueprints of the lands of Cat Wood and the whole strip between the sea and Brotas. A fine job, competently done; the firm was completely trustworthy. Good and well: having drawn up plans, designs, estimates, the technicians stated that they were completely pessimistic with regard to the success of the venture. In their opinion, a long time would have to elapse, decades perhaps, before that parcel of land would increase in value, bring in a worthwhile return. If the commander insisted on dividing it into lots now, he would have to sell them at a very low figure. And possibly not even then would he find buyers.

The blueprints and estimates stayed on Pepe Eight Hundred's desk, alongside the issue of the *Legislative Journal* that carried Ramos da Cunha's project. Wasn't there some way the lawyer could get the court to do an about-face? It wouldn't be a bad idea to wait a few days until they saw what came of all these strange doings. In the last analysis, he, José Perez, was not prepared to play the part of an executioner, an enemy of the people, while all the rest were making ready to profit at his expense. Why, even his grandchildren, so charming and impossible, were calling him a reactionary and accusing him of exploiting the working classes. He, Pepe Perez, who had done nothing his whole life but work, and work hard, like a horse or a draught ox, to give his children and grandchildren a decent livelihood. An enemy of the workers—he, the worker par excellence! Even today, old and tired, he woke up at four in the morning and started work at five, when the so-called workers were still sleeping like logs. He was the worker who was exploited by a gang of good-for-nothings, of stuffed shirts like this lawyer, high-priced and incompetent, all looking for a chance to rob him.

··◦⋄{ 11 }⋄◦··

IT MAY HAVE BEEN FROM THIS CRUCIAL MOMENT in the triumphant career of Professor Pinheiro Sales, when, swallowing his vanity and with his tail between his legs, he had to seek out the presiding judge of the court of appeals and tell him—what excuse could he give?—that he had changed his mind, that his client was no longer in a hurry —it may have been from this humiliating and thankless moment that everything connected with the invasion of Cat Wood took on a farcical air.

Moreover, the presiding judge, a crafty old customer, with plenty of experience with political back-scratching, with the underhanded ways of government ministries, immediately sniffed something in the air. As he put it to his son-in-law, the promising attorney of the Institute for Social Welfare, "the smell of corruption and of vultures around the carrion." Really, Professor Pinheiro Sales, in his black suit, still using a wing collar and stiff-bosomed shirt, did remind one of a vulture, and during that second visit in less than twenty-four hours, of a sad, dejected vulture. But where was the carrion? His Honor did not manage to pinpoint it but he felt that there was in all that mess of the invasion of the hill some very lucrative graft, a juicy mouthful. In a word, it stank. Why in the devil had Professor Sales, so haughty, so self-assured, come back to his office with a hangdog expression to ask him to cancel the hearing, when the evening before he had blustered, demanding a definite date as soon as possible? All of a sudden there was no longer any hurry.

Standing on his dignity, from the loftiness of his post, and also enjoying his small revenge on the lawyer, the presiding judge refused to acquiesce to his demand. The date had been set in agreement with him, even at his request; now it was too late. He couldn't let the court be at the mercy of the whims of lawyers and litigants. Nor could he run the risk of finding himself an accessory to some chicanery. The date of the trial would stand.

A trial that was to take on a sensational quality with all the space the newspapers gave to it. To the trial and the "mass meeting," a popular manifestation without equal, which had been called by Alderman Licio Santos and other "leaders of the people" (as the circular distributed throughout the city described them), among them our already familiar and engaging Dante Veronezi now definitely transformed into the representative of the hill dwellers, their official spokesman. The meeting was to be held in front of the courthouse and would include the hill dwellers and everyone in the city who sympathized with their cause, to "demand from the illustrious court a decision which will give the people the plenitude of their rights."

The one who was never to forget the decision and the meeting, not so much because of the billy blows he received on his shoulders as because of the unforeseen and intimate subsequent developments, was Bullfinch.

He and Madame Beatriz were coming to the end of the duration of the fast, of the irrevocable thirty days—not one less—of the never-before-seen spectacle of being buried alive. The fact of the matter was that it was only the eleventh day, but the signboard on the street door advertising the spectacle stated that the fakir had already been fasting for twenty-six days. On this signboard the number was changed each morning to indicate the number of days that had elapsed since Madame Beatriz's solemn entry into her coffin. But when they reached the fifth day, and only six dispirited visitors had left behind the paltry sum of thirty milreis, Bullfinch, instead of chalking up the number 5, had written 15, and with this they gained ten days: Madame Beatriz, ten days less of fasting; and Bullfinch, too, though his fast was of a different kind—hunger and thirst, true, but not for food. What he hungered for was the buried-alive in person, his thirst was for her lips. Then on the eighth day he picked up three more, for the spectacle's appeal had hit a new low, two measly kids and a soldier who came in for nothing, as the military did not pay.

Bullfinch did not want to get to the bottom of the delicate matter Jesuíno had brought up. The doubts that had assailed him regarding Madame Beatriz's professional honesty he buried in the depths of his unshakeable trust in the misjudged Hindu. Looking at her through the glass to gauge the pallor and emaciation of her face, he observed that she looked plump and satisfied and that her color was good, none of which went with a week of fasting, but she smiled at him and rolled her eyes encouragingly and his doubts evaporated; he desisted from that unworthy spying suggested by his friends.

When he left her alone with Emilia Green-Sleeves, a faint doubt still troubled him. What if he were to come back unexpectedly? Jesuíno asked him, when he came in: "Well, did you unmask the cheat?"

Jesuíno was a skeptic who did not believe in anyone, who doubted everything. Even people as important as Alderman Licio Santos, Congressman Ramos da Cunha and the eminent Dante Veronezi, kindly to the point of paying for drinks for Bullfinch and drinking with him when he invited him to the mass rally: "My dear friend, as a resident of Cat Wood, you cannot be absent."

With help of Filó (to whom a Syrian of Baixa do Sapateiro presented a marked-down dress), Dante took the necessary steps to make sure the rally was a success. Yet Jesuíno Crazy Cock, instead of being filled with enthusiasm, instead of taking charge as he had before, drew back, did not display the least interest.

"Are you going?" he asked Bullfinch. "Not me. Little people should keep out of big shots' affairs. Otherwise they are the ones who pay for the broken dishes. . . . There on the hill, it's one thing; down here below it's another story."

But Bullfinch, flattered by the personal invitation extended to him by the leader Veronezi, turned up. Those who did not show up were the people in general. A few law students who happened to pass that way decided to support the rally, and one of them cut loose with a stirring speech. Only a few came down from the hill. The majority stayed up there, waiting to hear the decision.

Without question the rally would have achieved the expected success according to Licio Santos's statement to the *Gazette of Salvador,* if the presiding judge, having been apprised of the crowd that was gathering before the portals of the august temple of justice and having seen with his own eyes a student haranguing the few early comers from the steps, had not asked for immediate police protection to maintain order and to guarantee the decorum of the court and the independence of its decision.

Policemen in profusion and a squad of mounted police. They started off in brutal fashion, asking no questions, listening to no explanations. The horsemen brought down their night sticks, making everybody run, breaking up the incipient rally in five minutes. Bullfinch received several heavy whacks and narrowly missed being taken off to jail.

Alderman Licio Santos rushed headlong into the courthouse, wound up in the trial room, began to protest against the police. The presiding judge refused to listen to him and even threatened to have him thrown out without taking into account his status of alderman and his official immunity. As for the legitimate spokesman of the hill, our good friend Dante Veronezi, he did land in jail. It did him no good to shout: "I am the secretary of Alderman Dr. Licio Santos. . . ."

One cop advised the other: "That's the so-and-so who's heading the invasion. Load him in."

They loaded him in. They also carried off one of the students, while the others hung around for a while, on the corners, booing the soldiers. But they soon got tired and left. The people of Cat Wood retraced their steps; Jesuíno had been right, as usual.

Bullfinch, his shoulders smarting, set out for Baixa do Sapateiro on his way back to Madame Beatriz. He had asked Emilia Green-Sleeves to take his place that afternoon while he fulfilled his civic duty. At a forced-march step, he made his way to the store transformed into a theater.

Bullfinch's unexpected arrival caused a panic. He found the door closed, the board turned around. With a push he flung the door wide. He was furious and glimpsed the truth. Once more old Jesuíno was right; nobody fooled Crazy Cock.

Sitting comfortably up in her coffin, the glass cover unscrewed, pushed to one side, Madame Beatriz, served by Emilia, was comfortably stuffing herself on a plate of beans, manioc mush, and meat. A bunch of bananas was next on the menu. Emilia brought in plate and pot, bananas and forks, in a kind of leather bag under a layer of knitting wool and some old magazines. She did not even forget a little brush to sweep up the crumbs, proof of perfect organization. Not to mention the bottle of beer and the two glasses. Bullfinch bellowed with rage.

Emilia slid through the door with an agility that would have seemed impossible in a person of her size. Madame Beatriz dropped the plate, covered her face with her hands, and burst into sobs and vows: "I swear it is the first time . . ." She went on: it had never been her intention to fool the public, much less Bullfinch; her intention had really been to fast the whole month. But because of Bullfinch . . .

Bullfinch was furious; his ribs burned—he had really received a drubbing—and now to see the rosy cheeks of Madame Beatriz, her fat jowls—she had put on at least five pounds during her fast! Bullfinch was in no mood to listen to excuses, but he paused when she, laboring for breath, said it was his fault. He wanted to see how far her impudence would go.

Yes, because of Bullfinch. . . . Weak, without strength, shut up in that coffin like a corpse, she saw, through the glass, Bullfinch moving about the room smiling at her, and against all her will, she had evil thoughts, saw herself lying beside him, and those vile, sinful desires had exhausted her spiritual concentration, and he had lost her ability to withstand the fast. . . .

On any other occasion this balderdash would have mollified Bullfinch, filled his eyes with pity and tenderness, made his heart throb. But he was furious; he had been beaten by the police; he had stuck his nose into other folks' business in spite of Jesuíno's advice; and now this broad feeding him that stuff about the indecent thoughts which gave her an appetite! That was a little too much! He was the one who had gone hungry or practically so, cutting down on his meals in order to hand over almost intact the meager daily intake to Emilia, entrusted by Madame Beatriz with administering her finances and filling her crop. Even beer. She deprived herself of nothing. And now all that rigmarole to pull the wool over his eyes. Bullfinch, in the course of his many and tormenting passions, had come across a good many impudent hussies, but never one like this.

With a kick, he closed the street door once more. His sides hurt; the skin was scraped off his arm; his shoulder was almost out of place. He raised his hand and it exploded against Madame's face. The slap fell pleasantly on his ears, and he dealt her another. The spiritual Hindu gave a scream, grabbing his arm, begging his forgiveness. But now as he grabbed her by the hair, holding her off the ground by the head, she threw her arms around his chest, and as he applied the third slap, she put her mouth to his and kissed him wildly. When Bullfinch finally stopped beating her, he felt himself her captive in a kiss that had no end. At long last a woman—and what a woman!—had fallen madly in love with him, was giving herself to him, overcome, melting with love. Letting go of her hair, he quickly and brutally ripped her dress of red tulle imitating foreign clothing, Hindu saris, and right there, in the coffin, Bullfinch made up for his prolonged fast, satisfied himself completely. With desire and desperation, hunger of long standing and pain in his ribs. He settled all his old scores. The coffin, which was made for the dead, could not stand the weight of all that seething life and collapsed into old boards. The two lovers rolled on the floor of the store to which Abdala had set fire; the glass cover was shattered into a thousand pieces, but they neither saw nor heard. Upon the ashes, the wood, the glass, they satisfied their hunger, slaked their thirst, laughed at all that silly sham, and once more consumed themselves in one another's fire.

They decided, after a careful casting up of accounts of the moving spectacle of "buried alive," to close the show that very afternoon, handing over the key to the clerk of the store next door. There wasn't even a coffin left in which to fast. Bullfinch was going to finish his shack on the hill; there Madame Beatriz would rest, recuperating from her wearisome act. Bullfinch never lacked for work; she could tell fortunes, either by palm reading or by the cards, and she would surely have customers on the hill, where a tavern and a store of sorts had already been opened.

While Bullfinch was finding love by such arduous and complicated routes, the court of appeals, free of pressure, met to decide the suit of Commander José Perez against the invaders of Cat Wood. The relator, even though he lamented the brevity of the judge's sentence, the extreme economy of his arguments, upheld it. Two of the judges voted in favor. The third, however, asked to see the documents, and the decision was postponed for a week. Professor Pinheiro Sales gave a sigh of relief; he had arranged that request for the documents at the last minute, when he thought that all was lost, that is to say, ridiculous though it sounds, when his case was practically won. This is an example of how entangled the plot of the story of the invasion of Cat Wood Hill became. So entangled that afterwards nobody could prove anything, pro or con, say what was good or what was bad, what was right, what was crazy.

Jacó Galub and Licio Santos left the courtroom in a state of high excitement, talking about the need to take drastic measures, as the bias of the court was manifest. Within a week the inhabitants of the hill would be condemned to lose their shacks. Licio, particularly, was in a hurry; it was time to begin to reap the harvest he had sown days before. At that very moment in the state legislature, one of the congressmen was attacking Ramos da Cunha's proposed bill, calling it demagogic and unconstitutional. He informed the House of the decision of the majority of the government members to vote against it if it came before the plenary session.

As for Professor Pinheiro Sales, he could not decide whether he had won or lost. A twofold victory, perhaps. But his client, a Spaniard of limited intelligence and boundless ill breeding, said to him when he made his report: "It's a good thing the decision was put off. Perhaps a week will be enough. And you can forget about this case, Doctor. Leave it to me. I'll handle and decide about it myself."

On Commander José Perez's desk there was a card from Licio Santos, asking for an appointment. The alderman was a tenant of his, living in one of his houses, at times five or six months in arrears with his rent. He was a foxy article, always getting himself into tight corners, but, as a rule, getting out of them well. He was mixed up in this monkey business of the lands, and he might be as useful as anyone else, as Ramos da Cunha or Airton Melo. Certainly cheaper. He called in one of his employees and sent him off with a message to Licio Santos.

·--◦◦❧{ 12 }❧◦◦--·

THAT WEEK BETWEEN THE TWO SESSIONS of the court of appeals at which the suit of Commander Eight Hundred Grams vs. The Squatters of Cat Wood Hill was heard was characterized by the exacerbation of positions toward the invasion, pro and con, to the accompaniment of a welter of words, spoken and written, in newspapers and on platforms. One had the impression that war was imminent, with both sides menacingly mobilizing and with Dr. Albuquerque suddenly back in the limelight like a movie star and the lieutenant governor taking a definite stand.

All of this impressed the public greatly and there were those who predicted grave and possibly tragic consequences, fearing even for the fate of the state and the security of the regime. Not to become engulfed in pessimism, however, it was enough for the man in the street to be able to read between the lines in the newspapers and to listen to the conversation in the lobbies of the legislature rather than to the speeches on the rostrum. At no time was the storm over the invasion of Cat Wood as great as it seemed. The accusations against the invaders; the brilliant campaign of solidarity with the inhabitants carried on by journalists, congressmen, popular leaders, at times whole parties; the threats of conflict with blood flowing—might they not have as their objective covering up the trail of the negotiators, muffling their voices? It is not incumbent on us, removed from discussions and agreements through lack of political standing or social importance, to bring to light this scheme to achieve peace and quiet, which turned out to everyone's taste, without exception. The sole exception being, perhaps, the poet Pedro Job, who protested in his cups against this "wholesale graft" at the expense of the people of Cat Wood. But we all know what store to set by these bitter accusations of poets, especially drunken poets. Might not the fact that he was on bad terms with the journalist Galub because of a girl from Dorinha's brothel on Ladeira da Montanha have had something to do with the poet's accusation? To that apple of discord, by name Maricena, Job had indited that inspired lyrical composition, a work of genius in the opinion of his bosom and bar friends, "Maricena, Virgin of the Bawdyhouse, Gravid by Poet and by Prayer." While Job was working on his poem "of truly revolutionary lyric reverberations," as the critic Nero Milton wrote, the journalist had taken over the girl, leaving to the poet only glory and cuckoldry.

To gauge the violence of the debate that sprang up around the invasion of Cat Wood during that week preceding the final events, it is worth examining three or four incidents which had wide repercussions on public opinion. The first had to do with the stand taken by the lieutenant governor of the state, an old and powerful industrialist, an authentic representative of the conservative classes. We begin with him out of deference to his position. There are those who do not attach much importance to the office of lieutenant governor, looking on it as more or less honorary and nothing more. But just let the governor suddenly kick the bucket, turn into pure spirit arisen to the glory of God, and who takes his place, who will bind and unbind, distribute as he sees fit jobs and public funds?

Elected by the opposition, the lieutenant governor had taken a discreet attitude with regard to public affairs and grave problems in order to avoid friction with the governor. On the other hand, his close connection with the moneyed class by reason of his being one of its outstanding leaders gave rise to the opinion that he would be in agreement with the official position of the government in combating the squatters of Cat Wood, "refusing them bread and water," as Dr. Albuquerque, the chief of police, put it

in an interview of his to which we shall refer farther on. So
you can imagine the general surprise when the office of his
Excellency the lieutenant governor issued a note affirming
his solidarity with the people of Cat Wood. The note,
naturally, did not praise or support the invasion. On the
contrary, it criticized the mistaken method employed by
the people to settle the painful and crucial problem of the
lack of housing. But the problem existed; it was impossible
to deny it; and the invasion of the lands of Commander
Perez was a consequence of this and should be viewed and
handled as such. After analyzing the problem, the lieutenant governor suggested concrete measures. To the people
of Cat Wood, his solidarity and understanding. They
should not be treated as though they were criminals, for
they were not. They deserved the consideration due insur-
gents, whose acts do not obey logic or good sense. However, the real problem was not the invasion (and perhaps
for that reason the lieutenant governor offered no solution
to the invasion, strictly speaking, of Cat Wood), but the
lack of housing. To that very serious social problem, which
threatened the life of the city, he pointed out a fair solution. It was up to the government to consider the immediate construction of homes for workers on the outskirts of
the city—cheap, comfortable buildings. There was no lack
of vacant land and capable planners. The work could be
done by the future occupants. The document decribed the
project in detail; it aroused general praise; one sensed in it
the hand of the statesman, the administrator. There were
plenty who said and believed it: "If he were the governor
and not the lieutenant governor, everything would have
been settled long ago." And the eternal malcontents appeared, too, the professional character assassins, insinuating
the biggest kind of a hidden deal in the solution proposed
by the lieutenant governor. Who owned the mammoth
construction company that specialized in factories and
workers' housing? Beyond doubt, the lieutenant governor
had a controlling share in the enterprise, but it is political
pettiness to attribute such sordid intentions to one who is
seeking the public good. His proposal ended by affirming
anew his solidarity with the invaders of the hill: his heart
beat in keeping with the suffering of those good people.

Meanwhile, in the state legislature, the members of the party in power really trounced Ramos da Cunha and his expropriation project. They dragged him through the mire: never had such a demagogic proposal been presented; how could the state take it upon itself to expropriate lands invaded by squatters? Imagine! Let the congressmen establish this precedent just once, and they would do nothing else during the entire session except approve bills of expropriation, for the idlers and swindlers asked nothing better than to build houses on land that was not yet subdivided. Before long, shacks would be erected alongside the Lighthouse of Barra and the Christ on Barra Avenue. Ridiculous! Playing the role of a devoted friend of the people, the leader of the opposition had lost his head. He was sponsoring the bill for publicity purposes, to make his name known. Possibly it was known in Buriti da Serra, to the voters of the distant boondocks, but as yet it aroused no echo in the capital. And this echo, nothing else, was the ultimate objective of his project.

Ramos da Cunha took the floor again and defended his project. Demagogic? Then why didn't the government present a non-demagogic project to solve the problem? He would support it. They could heap insults on him; the government bloc could hold him up to ridicule, attempt to give him a bad name with the people of Bahia, but they would accomplish nothing. The workers, the honest citizens who had been forced by grievous poverty to put up their houses on Cat Wood Hill, knew whom they could count on, who were their friends and who their enemies. He, Ramos da Cunha, was a friend of the people. How many of his political adversaries could say the same? Certainly not those uncompromising critics of his project. Might it not be that they were seeking the electoral support of the great landowners, trying to get on the good side of certain foreign colonies? If he, Ramos da Cunha, was, as his adversaries accused him of doing, trying to ingratiate himself with the people, they, the majority members, were trying to curry favor with the national and foreign magnates.

Workers, that pack of loafers established on the hill? Another congressman had taken the floor and was mauling

Ramos da Cunha and the inhabitants of Cat Wood, whom he converted into a conglomeration of thieves, card-sharpers, beggars, prostitutes, vagabonds of every description, the scum of the city.

Without question, there were among the invaders people who were not too fond of work, but to flatly deny the existence of workers on Cat Wood Hill was an exaggeration.

Bricklayers, blacksmiths, carpenters, streetcar conductors, teamsters, electricians, practitioners of diverse trades, had built their shacks there. And what right had a congressman to call these people the scum of the city? Whoever he may be, whatever profession he follows, a man is always worthy of respect, a woman of consideration. Perchance a prostitute does not work hard? Her calling may not be edifying, but does she follow it because she chose it of her own free will or because she was dragged into it by the undertow of life? As for the work of a virtuoso like Martim, it is not only wearing and difficult but beautiful, a sight to be seen and admired. How many among those congressmen would be capable of handling a deck of cards or a shaker and dice with the expertise, delicacy, style, of Martim? As we said in the beginning, we are not going to take sides; we are not here to arraign anyone, but only to tell the story of the invasion, the setting of the loves (which is really our theme) of Martim and Otália, of Bullfinch and Madame Beatriz, the renowed occultist. But we must admit that it is not easy to hold our peace when some congressman who is undoubtedly salting away a fortune made on shady deals, lining his pockets with the taxpayers' funds, living at our expense, classifies upright citizens and agreeable citizenesses worthy of esteem and consideration on every count as "scum of the city." People of that sort gratuitously think themselves superior.

This, then, was the tenor of the legislature, with a spate of speeches bearing on the case of Cat Wood Hill. Ramos da Cunha's project seemed definitely doomed. The tension among the congressmen grew to the point where they were actually threatening one another with bodily assault.

And speaking of threats of aggression, the journalist

Jacó Galub brought to public attention in the pages of the *Gazette of Salvador* the fact that he had been threatened by the police, that his life was in danger. The flatfoots and Chico Pinóia were boasting to the four winds about their decision to "teach that reporter a lesson." Jacó, supported by the Newspaper Guild, laid the blame for whatever happened to him at the door of the chief of police, Dr. Albuquerque. "I have a wife and three children," he wrote. "If I should be attacked by Chico Pinóia or any stool pigeon of the police, I shall react like a man. And if I should fall on the field of battle, sacrificed by the enemies of the people, Dr. Albuquerque, state chief of police, will be responsible for my children becoming orphans, my wife a widow."

The chief of police called in the journalists. Jacó Galub could move freely about the city; he need have no fear. He would not be attacked by the police. There was never any intention in any division of the force to threaten the journalist. But he should be on guard against that herd of shady characters he was associating with, the invaders of Cat Wood, who were capable of attacking him and putting the blame on the police. To these he, Dr. Albuquerque, and his subordinates on the force refused "bread and water," and they were only awaiting the decision of the court of appeals to evict them once and for all from Cat Wood. Thus no one could speak of violence, of taking the law into one's own hands. That shindy, that subversion of law and moral values, was approaching its end. He, Dr. Albuquerque, whose occupancy of the post of chief of police had already distinguished itself by putting an end to gambling in the city, by eradicating the numbers game, would render the city another outstanding service by bringing to an end this dangerous attempt to subvert order, whose origins were unknown but suspect and whose objectives were the disintegration of society. To tolerate this invasion was to create the climate for chaos, uprising, revolution. . . . Revolution (pronouncing the word in a dramatic shuddering tone and with ominous glances)—there you have the real objective of those who are pulling the strings, inventing invasions, meetings, rallies.

For the congressmen of the governing party, the people

of Cat Wood were the dregs of the city. For Dr. Albuquerque, the dismayed functionary who had not yet managed to enjoy the famed benefits of his post, who had made a mess of things from the start, putting his foot in it when he tried to do business with the numbers bankers, and who was now trying to get out of a tight spot with this story of the invasion and to curry favor with the city real-estate owners, for Dr. Albuquerque, somewhat naïve and dim-witted, the inhabitants of the hill were terrifying revolutionaries. True, they did not cease to be bandits on this account. Bandits, misfits, pack of scoundrels. Nevertheless, revolutionaries, covering with this romantic and political mantle their real condition. Dr. Albuquerque had said this so many times that he had come to believe it. He wound up seeing the social revolution on every street corner, and in every narrow alley a Bolshevik with dagger between his teeth, ready to slit his belly open. Even today, after such a lapse of time, when so many other invasions have taken place, when above the waters of the mangrove swamps the city of the palafittes arose, the great invasion of the marshes, when the events of Cat Wood have been completely forgotten and we here barely recall them as we sit sipping our rum, even today Dr. Albuquerque is still terrified by the revolution, and more and more, predicting its imminence if the administrators lack the good sense to reappoint him to the post of chief of police. Ah, if he got back there again, this time he would not make the mistake of a run-in with the numbers crowd!

We shall make no mention of Alderman Licio Santos or of the editor of the *Gazette of Salvador*, Dr. Airton Melo, or of others less known and mentioned, as they were all in such a state of activity, running from one side to another, from the office of José Perez to the State House, from the State House to the legislature, from the legislature to the home of the lieutenant governor—excellent whiskey!— from the home of the lieutenant governor to that of Otávio Lima—not only excellent whiskey, but also French cognac and Italian Fernet. (The king of the numbers game knew how to look after himself and his visitors.) We shall leave them to their discreet negotiations, and not because at the moment they are not speaking out in the columns of their newspaper or from the rostrum of City Hall shall we doubt their stalwart support of the inhabitants of Cat Wood or that they are true friends of the people.

Including Commander José Perez? And why not? If we go more deeply into the biography of this outstanding bastion of private property, we will find various good turns rendered to the community, duly noted by the press at the time, some of which were outstanding services. Was it not he who contributed a generous sum to the construction of the Church of St. Gabriel in the workingmen's quarter of Liberdade—a new housing development, recently laid out streets thickly settled by workmen, artisans, clerks, poor people for the most part, who did not yet have their indispensable church? As far as religion was concerned, before the generous contribution of the commander, there existed in the populous area only two spiritualist tents and three voodoo centers. It was Pepe Eight Hundred—who now has five flourishing bakeries in Liberdade and its environs—who dug down in his pocket, and brought out the money that made possible the faith for those neglected people. Other outstanding services? Isn't the building of a church enough? All right then: didn't he contribute on more than one occasion to the labors of the Spanish missionaries in China, to the conversion of Negroes of lost tribes in the heart of Africa? Or do we lack feelings of human solidarity and regard as people only our own, indifferent to the suffering of pagans of other continents?

⋯⊰{ 13 }⊱⋯

AND THE PEOPLE OF CAT WOOD HILL, the celebrated invaders, what were they doing, how were they acting and reacting to all this controversial movement of which they were the center? Are we not, perhaps, forgetting them, and giving too much importance to commanders, congressmen, reporters, politicians, and economists? Dragged along unconsciously by the vanity of rubbing elbows with these prominent people whose names appear in the society columns? After all, whose adventures should be related? Are not, perchance, the invaders of the lands of the commander—Negro Massu and Pretty Hair, Dona Filó and Dagmar, Miro and old Jesuíno Crazy Cock, and all the rest—the real heroes of this story? Why relegate them to oblivion, wasting so many words on Congressman Ramos da Cunha, Alderman Licio Santos, and other scoundrels of politics and yellow journalism, by this prolonged silence about the people of the hill? Do you want to know the truth?

We are not talking about them because there is very little to tell, no incidents or episodes of special interest. Throughout this story of the invasion, the people of the hill were the ones who did the least talking and explaining. There they were in their shacks, living. Living: there you have the whole thing in a nutshell. Without vaulting ambitions, without turmoil, without acts of derring-do, just living. Amid all that uproar and hubbub—evicted, not evicted, torn down, not torn down—with so many people milling around them, attacking them or praising them—bandits of the worst kind, subversives, people worthy of every consideration, good people, humble and exploited, depending on the newspaper and the commentator—they managed to achieve the greatest thing: they managed to live when everything conspired to make such an endeavor impossible. As Jesuíno said, a poor person does more than should be expected of him by just living, living in the face of such wretchedness, difficulties of every sort, dire poverty, sickness, the lack of all help, living when there would seem to be reason only to die. Nevertheless, they lived; they were stubborn people; they did not let themselves be liquidated easily. Their capacity for resisting poverty, hunger, sickness came from a long way back; it was born on the slave ships and nourished in servitude. They had become invulnerable, hard to beat down.

And not satisfied just with living, they even lived happily. The harder things became, the more they laughed, and to the sound of guitars and mouth organs, the music and words of songs were born and rose upward on Cat Wood Hill, on the highway of Liberdade, in Retiro, in all the poor quarters of Bahia. They confronted misery with gaiety; they guffawed in the face of poverty; they kept going. The children, when they did not quickly become cherubs in heaven, chosen by God and by worms, hunger, lack of care, were educated in that harsh and happy school of life; they inherited from their parents the resistance and the capacity for laughter and living. They did not give up; they refused to submit to fate, humiliated and conquered. Not at all. They resisted everything; they stood up to life, and they did not live it naked and cold. They dressed it in laughter and music, in human warmth, in courtesy, in that civilization of the Bahian people.

That is what these common folk are like, hard nuts to crack; that is what we are like, the people, gay and stubborn. The upper crust are the ones who are soft, dependent on the drugstore, on barbiturates, ravaged by anxiety and psychoanalysis, full of complexes, from Oedipus to Electra, wanting to sleep with their mother, fornicate with their father, finding it chic to be a fairy, and other similar revolting things.

For the people of the hill, however, all that huggermugger did not make them lose a minute's sleep, did not interfere with their life. When the police appeared the first time and burned the shacks they had put up, some of them thought of leaving, of looking for another place to live. But Jesuíno Crazy Cock, respected for his wisdom and his gray hair, an *obá*, had said: "We will build our houses again," and so they had done. This was included in their formula for enduring and living. They followed Jesuíno's advice and left the important decisions to him. The old man was an ace, worthy of their confidence.

Others came, and new shacks went up. The police had returned; Jesuíno and the street Arabs had dug play trenches, piling up the earth around the rocks, collecting stones, rolling down boulders. The police had run away; it had been a great lark; they had all laughed and celebrated it.

Finally everybody was in the act: terrible arguments, the cops chasing people, throwing the innocent in jail, beating them, the newspapers vociferating, a bill before the House, court action, the very devil. And they living. If the police attempted to return, they would resist. Jesuíno was once more in command of the urchins; they had opened a hidden path through the swamp; they were preparing once more to confront the police. The police and the judges of the court of appeals.

They had built their shacks; they were stubborn; they were staying there in spite of all the threats. They were living. As for killing themselves, nobody did that except the Negress Genoveva, who soaked her clothes in kerosene and set fire to them, but that is understandable: it was love, the mulatto Ciriaco, a ukulele player, had left her for another. The important thing was to go on living, not to let themselves be crushed or yield to sadness. They laughed and sang; in one of the shacks a dance hall was functioning, with gay dances on Saturdays and Sundays, *capoeira* matches in the afternoons. They greeted their divinities on festival nights, fulfilling their religious obligations. They lived and loved. Pretty Hair threatened to slit the gullet of

Lidio, who had the airs of a movie star, if he ever again ventured to wink his eye at the beautiful Dagmar.

And that Jacinto, a highfalutin young stud whom we spoke about—do you remember?—built his shack on Cat Wood, and set up housekeeping there with Maria José, a light mulatta who was plenty tough. She gave rise to trouble, for on the excuse of helping old Vevéva to look after the child, she wound up serving Massu as a mattress. The Negro's movements were restricted to the top of the hill, as the flatfoots were waiting anxiously for him down below. Without freedom of locomotion, unable to visit his friends in saloons and grogshops or to go to the docks to talk, Massu was like a caged animal. For that reason, Maria José was a great comfort to him. A sour note in the *entente cordiale* was that disagreeable Jacinto. Instead of feeling proud of the success of his girl friend, capable of pouring the balm of happiness on the troubled heart of Massu, a man as important as he, the *compadre* of Ogun, Jacinto took it very much amiss, downed several glasses of rum, armed himself with a knife, and came seeking satisfaction. Negro Massu, in spite of the comfort Maria José afforded him, was in no mood for jokes; shouts did not set well on his stomach. In the end, that Jacinto showed himself to be a person without any upbringing; he had been mistreating Maria José, and now he had come to stand in front of Massu's shack, calling him names and scandalizing the neighborhood. Massu dragged him to the broadest trail, the best pathway down the hill, and gave him a shove with his foot. And he advised him not to come back and to leave the shack to his ex-consort as her dower right in their joint property. He could keep the out-size horns as his share.

Jacinto returned, however, some days later, looking for Otália. He had cherished a passion of long standing for her, ever since the girl had come to Bahia. He had met her that first night, when Carnation-in-his-Buttonhole had played that joke of hiding her luggage. He had never been able to go to bed with her; there had never been an opportunity, he thought to himself. He followed from a distance the itinerary traveled by her and Martim in that love affair which was the talk of the dance halls and docks.

For Jacinto, a person little given to imagination and poetry, that story about a romantic idyll, a platonic love, gave him a big laugh. A fat chance of his being taken in by such crap. He new Corporal Martim, and his secret desire was to imitate him, resemble him, behave the way he did with women: superior, condescending, letting himself be loved, taking little cheek from them. He did not take the least stock in that story that was going the rounds about the corporal dying of love, walking with his little finger linked to Otália's without getting to first base. He considered Otália lost to him forever unless Martim should get tired of her and beat it.

And this was what happened unexpectedly. Not that he got tired of her, but to escape the persecution of the police, the corporal changed abode, disappeared without leaving any forwarding address. At any rate, Jacinto did not manage to learn the whereabouts of the traveler, in spite of inquiring among all his acquaintances. He did not want to make a play for Otália if the corporal was anywhere around. Martim was not one to accept with good grace a volunteer partner. But when Otália, at Tibéria's decision, moved into the shack on Cat Wood to recuperate, Jacinto began to show up there once more, all airs and wearing a necktie.

The house Tibéria and Jesús had built on top of Cat Wood was for them to retire to when they grew too old to work. In the meantime they used it as a vacation spot and as a retreat for girls of the brothel in need of rest or of hiding from some importunate character, a tiresome sweetheart or unbearable suitor. At any rate, that was what Tibéria reserved it for, though after what happened to Otália, she took such an aversion to the place that she was ready to sell it at any price.

Martim had no sooner put on his disappearing act—it devolved upon Jesuíno to notify friends and acquaintances, Tibéria and Otália, of the enforced disappearance of the corporal, adding that he did not know where Martim had gone—that Otália went into a decline. For no good reason that anyone could account for. She developed a weakness in her legs, her body, a dullness of eye; all she wanted to do was to stay in bed; she had no desire for anything; she

refused each and every client, even the most openhanded
and steady, like Mr. Agnaldo of the Miraculous Pharmacy
from Terreiro de Jesus, who never missed a Wednesday
late in the afternoon. He not only paid well but he always
brought a present: a box of cough drops, a bottle of cough
syrup, a cake of soap. She turned away Mr. Agnaldo, old
Militão of the notary's office on Sé Square, and all the
chance customers. She did not want to leave her room,
would come to the dining room only after much coaxing,
and would hardly touch her food. She never set foot out of
the house again. In bed, with her doll beside her, her eyes
lost in space, thin and pale-cheeked.

Tibéria was deeply disturbed. Her girls called her
Mother, and her friends, too. She deserved the name, for
she looked after the girls as though they were her daughters. She had never taken such a fancy or become so attached to any of them as to this little Otália, such a child
in years and ways and so early cast into prostitution.

Because old Batista, her father, who had a farm near
Bonfim, was not a person to joke with, and when he
learned what had happened, that the son of Colonel Barbosa had deflowered the poor little thing, still greener than
an unripe guava, he turned into a mad dog, grabbed a
stick, and beat her until she was black and blue. Then he
threw her out, he would not have a whore in his house.
The place for a whore was on the street corner, the place
for a fallen woman was in the red-light district. Let her go
with her sister, who had been a whore for two years now,
but that one had not gone straight from her father's house
to the brothel. She had got married first; her husband had
run off to the south, and she had had to find some way to
support herself. Whereas Otália had left straight from
home, thrown out by the old man, furious at seeing his
fifteen-year-old daughter, as pretty as a saint, already dishonored, good for nothing but a whore.

Martim only learned many of these details when everything was over, from Tibéria, who was a person of the
greatest discretion, the best madam Bahia had ever known.
We do not say this out of friendship; we are not praising
her because we are linked by ties of long association. Who
doesn't know Tibéria and doesn't admire her talents? There

is nobody better known or more highly regarded; at her brothel they are all one family, not each for himself and devil take the hindmost. One big family, and Otália was the baby of the household, petted, indulged.

Martim came to know how the thing had happened. When Colonel Barbosa's son, a young, good-looking student, had stolen Otália's cherry, she was not yet fifteen but she had the body and breasts of a woman. But only outwardly a woman. Inwardly she was a child; even in the brothel what she wanted was to play with her doll and be courted like an innocent damsel, be courted by Martim and then become engaged to him, with ring and everything. That was the way she was. She made dresses for the doll and put it to bed.

There on the side street where she lived with her father, old Batista, the student spied her and showed up several times. He gave her some candy, and one day he said to her: "You are big enough to get married, my lass. How would you like to marry me?" She would have preferred to be engaged for a while; that seemed so nice. But even so, she accepted with the greatest pleasure, and all she asked for was veil and bridal wreath. She did not know, poor thing, that the young man was talking double talk and that in his high-flown language getting married meant deflowering her on the riverbank. Otália was still waiting for the veil and the bridal wreath, and what she got was a beating from old Batista and being thrown into the street. What could she do except go where her sister was, Teresa by name and a real vixen?

In the brothel, where she conscientiously attended to the clients, in her free hours she was like a child, utterly devoid of malice, wanting only to be courted by the corporal, go walking with him, hand in hand, until the day of their engagement came.

The corporal disappeared, wanted by the police. Besides, he was fed up with that senseless infatuation that led nowhere. He knew nothing of Otália's past; all he could think was that Otália must have a screw loose. Who ever heard of a whore wanting to be engaged, waiting for a wedding ring, the priest's blessing, to go to bed with her man and make love with him? So, hounded and disgusted, Martim

struck camp, and to make even surer, changed his name
and promoted himself to sergeant. Otália was never again
the same. She took to her bed, growing weaker every day.
Tibéria thought the best thing to do was to get her away
from the brothel, and she suggested to her that she spend a
while in the house on the hill where her friends lived,
Negro Massu, Bullfinch, who was now shacked up with a
bleached-blonde fortuneteller, not to mention Jesuíno,
without a house there or anywhere, but commander-in-
chief of the hill, in charge of attack and defense, having
more fun all the time.

That Jacinto, as soon as he knew that Otália was on the
hill, showed up in the hope of knocking her eye out with
his fancied good looks. But the girl, if she noticed him, did
not pay the least attention to the uppity creature. She paid
no attention to anything except her doll and the memory of
Corporal Martim, her suitor to whom she would become
engaged, and, one day, marry. She stayed in the house,
stretched out on the cot, far from everything, and only
when Massu's little boy came to play beside her bed did
she caress him and smile. It would be enough for her to get
married, but if in the bargain she should have a child, then
her cup of happiness would be full to overflowing.

What more is there to be told about the people of the
hill? Well, they went on living, and it is no small thing to
live when one is poor and the police are threatening to set
fire to one's house. Living as best they could, without setting much store by all the toil and moil of politicians and
newspapermen, big shots, all birds of a feather.

Of news worth mentioning on the hill, there was perhaps
one single item. What had happened was that for some
time, perhaps because of all these complications, the population of the hill had reached a standstill and new houses
had not been built. Or because the well dug by the inhabitants was inadequate for the needs of those residing there,
or because of the electric connection, which provided a
measly light that was good only for lovers. However, in
recent days, during that tense week between the two sessions of the court of appeals, there had appeared on Cat
Wood masons and carpenters with their trowels, their
plumb lines, their saws, who had begun to build houses.

Public-utilities trucks dumped sacks of cement, bricks, and tiles at the foot of the hill. Two whole streets of spruce bungalows, each like the other, were quickly put up. White-washed inside and out, with blue doors and windows, really nice. Nobody knew to whom they belonged; the construction foreman was closemouthed, and if he had the solution to the riddle, he was not telling it. They had to belong to someone. Looking at the trucks, Wing-Foot suggested that they might belong to the state, perhaps for the families of employees. Or to set up a nursery for mulattas. Wing-Foot was still waiting for the mulattas he had ordered from France a long while back. He was worried for fear the ship might have foundered or someone had robbed him of the girls on the way. More than four hundred in all.

Wing-Foot suggested the theory of the state to see if he could in that way satisfy the curiosity of Jesuíno, who was crazy to know to whom those new buildings belonged. The old rascal, with Miro and the other kids, had taken measures to be ready for the police when the court issued its decision. He distrustfully eyed the walls of those buildings that looked like real houses, shook his head, but just in case of doubt and for the sake of amusement, he went on with his preparations to meet any aggression. "Cat Wood Hill will defend itself to the last man," Jacó Galub wrote, and laid the responsibility at the door of the government. "There is still time for the governor to remove the chief of police and heed the just complaints of the people." Jesuíno shook his head, which was covered with an extraordinary hat. The whites there below—white by reason of wealth, not color—were capable of finally coming to an understanding, and that would be the end of his fun. They were big shots, and big shots always reach an understanding; quarrels among them do not thrive.

Wing-Foot agreed. He had been beaten up at the police station, and he would enjoy giving Jesuíno a helping hand to make the flatfoots run. Crazy Cock had gotten hold of—God only knows how—one of those metal hats, like an enineer's helmet, which completely covered his head, but his rebellious gray hair escaped on every side. This detracted from the martial air he longed for; he looked more like a poet. The breeze blew over the hill, stirring the coconut fronds, the inhabitants went on living, laughing, singing, working, eating, having children. With the new houses, Cat Wood had taken on the air of a development.

"Such clever people," Wing-Foot commented. "A couple of days ago this was a swamp, a briar patch, and now it's just like a city. These humdingers of smart folks! . . ."

Jesuíno gave his catarrh-and-tobacco-hoarsened laugh. He enjoyed that business of the invasion. He knew where there was some vacant land beyond Liberdade, and he was thinking about taking some friends to put up shacks there. Why didn't Wing-Foot come with them?

"Do they have mulattas there? The real kind?"

If they did, he would come and help. But not live there. Wing-Foot preferred living alone, at peace off in his own corner.

⋯⊷❮ **14** ❯⊶⋯

THE SHACKING UP OF BULLFINCH and Madame Beatriz, the
fortuneteller for whom the future was an open book, coincided with the first session of the court of appeals at which
the suit of Commander José Perez—Pepe Eight Hundred,
the onetime thief who used to give short weight on trum-
pery scales and who now, a pillar of society and righteous-
ness, cheats with electronic scales—against the invaders of
his lands on Cat Wood Hill was scheduled to be heard. The
second session, at which the invaders were found guilty,
coincided with the marriage of Otália and Corporal
Martim.

Otália died at nightfall, when sentence already had been
passed and was waiting only to be copied and transmitted
to the chief of police, who was eager to carry it out, his
preparations carefully made and his men selected. Tibéria
had gone to her house on Cat Wood early the evening
before, and Jesus, too, came and stayed the night. The girls
appeared later, when the doctor pronounced the case hopeless. Taking advantage of Jesus's presence and Otália's fit-
ful sleep, Tibéria went out looking for Jesuíno. The old
rake had gone down to the city to join his drinking cronies.
The next day, with that business of the sentence, he would
not be able to leave the hill. Tibéria found him without too
much trouble, knowing, as she did, his itinerary. She
wanted Martim's address so that she could send him a
message.

At first, Jesuíno denied all knowledge of it, clammed up, but when Tibéria explained the reason to him, he came through: Corporal Martim's theater of activity was now Itaparica, but he was known there neither as corporal nor Martim. He had become Sergeant Porciúncula, making time, so it was said, with that superb Altiva Conception of the Holy Ghost, who was really an eyeful. He offered to get a message to him with all possible haste, and before daybreak he sent off the master of a fishing smack with orders to bring Martim back with him. And after he had sent him, he took the path to the hill without even recalling the session of the court set for the afternoon, so distressed he was, so heavyhearted. Otália was his favorite; the night of her arrival in Bonfim she had asked for his blessing and had knelt at his feet. Why did it have to be she, with so many old, mean people around, whom nobody would miss if they died, nor would a tear be shed? Why did it have to be she, so gay and sweet, with her comeliness, her doll, her smile, her dancing, her pretty ways, her love? Why did it have to be she, who had just begun to live? With all the dirty dogs who deserved to die. It was an injustice, and old Jesuíno Crazy Cock had a horror of injustice.

The message reached Sergeant Porciúncula in the middle of the afternoon, because that very day he had gone to Mar Grande, where a kind of club had been founded by dockworkers and fishermen. It had no fixed address or funds, but it had got hold of some decks of cards. When he learned about it, the sergeant was eager to give his support to those brave sportsmen, his expert aid.

In the smack, standing beside the tiller, motionless, his lips compressed, his face all anxiety, he looked like a stone statue, and he wanted only one thing: to arrive, to run to the hill, to take her hands in his and beg her to live. Once she had said to him: "Don't you understand?"

No, at that time he had not understood. When she looked into his eyes and asked him that question, he was in a hurry and a fury. He had left to escape the police and also to get away from Otália, not to see her any more, to forget her. In the glowing body of Altiva Conception of the Holy Ghost, in the leaping flames of her breasts, in the ember of her belly, he had burned the memory of Otália, the ingenuous taste of her lips, her air of a girl and sweetheart. He had quickly filled the emptiness she had left with days of reckless gambling, with nights of love along the seashore under the canopy of stars. But now he understood; his eyes had been opened, and he felt his heart shrinking in the depths of his breast, all fear, nothing but fear, the fear of losing her. Where were the sea breezes that were taking so long to carry that boat to the wharf of Bahia?

When he finally reached Cat Wood Hill at nightfall, Otália no longer had the strength to speak and could only seek him out with her eyes. Tibéria explained to the corporal the request she had made when her agony set in, on the threshold of death. Otália wanted to be buried in a wedding dress, with veil and wreath. Tibéria knew who the groom was: Corporal Martim; they were engaged to be married, very soon, during the festivities of June.

It was a crazy request—who ever heard of a whore being buried in a wedding dress?—but it was a request made at the hour of death, and it had to be granted.

At sight of Martim, Otália recovered her speech. In a thread of a voice, a faint whisper, she called for her dress. There was as yet no dress of any sort, let alone a wedding dress. Martim did not know what to do. That was an expensive item and, to make matters worse, it was night and the stores were closed. But would you believe that they managed it? There in her bed, dying, Otália waited. All the womenfolk, those of Tibéria's brothel, the neighbors on the hill, acquaintances in other whorehouses, a swarm of harlots, a gaggle of strumpets, had all turned into seamstresses, sewing the dress and the veil and the wreath. In a second they had collected money for a bouquet, had got hold of cloth, lace, medallions, slippers, silk stockings, gloves—imagine, white gloves! One sewed this, one sewed that, another stitched on a ribbon . . .

Not even Madame Beatriz had ever seen a wedding gown like that, so sumptuous and elegant, nor a more charming veil and wreath. And mind you, the fortuneteller had not only traveled widely but was very knowledgeable in the matter of trousseaux. Before she had gone out into the world, consoling the afflicted, she had had a dressmaker's establishment in Niterói.

Then they dressed the bride, the train of her dress hanging over the side of the bed and cascading onto the floor. The room was full of the girls and friends. Tibéria came with the bouquet and put it in Otália's hands. They raised the pillow and lifted up the girl's head. There had never been such a beautiful bride, so serene, so sweet, so happy at the hour of her marriage.

Corporal Martim, the groom, sat down on the side of the bed and took the hand of his bride. Clarice, one of the girls who had been married, tearfully pulled off her wedding ring and handed it to Martim. He slipped it slowly on Otália's finger and watched her face. She was smiling; one could not believe that she was dying, she was so satisfied and happy. When Martim raised his eyes, it was to see Tibéria in front of him, facing him and Otália. It was as though Tibéria had become a priest, attired in the vestments to consecrate a marriage, with rosary and everything, a fat priest with the air of a saint. She lifted her hand and blessed the couple. Martim lowered his head and kissed Otália's lips, feeling on his her last breath come from far, far away.

Then Otália asked them all to go out, smiled with her mouth and her eyes, her face radiant. Such a happy bride had never been seen before. They all left on tiptoe except Martim, whose hand she was holding. With a great effort she moved over in the bed, making room for him. The corporal stretched out, unable to speak. What would life be like without Otália, such a meaningless life, such a meaningless death? Otália raised her head, and let it sink gently on the corporal's broad breast, closed her eyes, smiling.

In the doorway Tibéria stifled a sob. Otália smiled on.

15

AT THE END OF THE AFTERNOON following the decision of
the court of appeals, when the police cars—in a display of
strength, as though preparing to engage an army and storm
nearly impregnable outposts—were approaching Cat Wood
Hill, Otália's funeral procession was descending the steep
slope. The policemen and detectives, under the command
of Chico Pinóia and Miguel Charuto, were armed with
machine guns, rifles, tear-gas bombs, and a thirst for revenge. This time they would not come back in flight; they
did not intend to leave a stone standing, the empty paddy
wagons would return full.

From the top of the hill, Jesuíno Crazy Cock watched
the funeral disappearing in the distance, the police squad
arriving. He was carrying in his hand that astounding engineer's hat transformed into a soldier's helmet, and he put
it on his head. Beside him, Miro, his second-in-command,
was awaiting orders. Mounds of stones had been piled up
during the night while they stood sentry duty, and the boys
slipped in and out among them. Some of them lived on the
hill in the houses that had been built by the invaders. But
the majority had come there in a gesture of solidarity to
defy the police. The whole vast and invincible organization
of the street Arabs, without written rules, without chosen
leaders, but powerful and feared, had gone into action.
Those boys with ferret faces, clothed in rags, come from

the corners of the most remote streets. The waifs of Bahia, students in life's harsh school, learning to live and laugh in the face of poverty and despair. There they were, those enemies of the city, as they had so often been called by reporters, judges, and sociologists.

The funeral procession, accompanied by Tibéria and the girls, moved along at a fairly brisk pace. Those weary women had lost the previous night sitting up with Otália; they could not miss work two nights running. Twilight was falling over the sea as Otália, all in white, with veil and wreath, took her last walk in her coffin. The pallbearers were Corporal Martim and Jesus, Wing-Foot and Bullfinch, Ipicilone and Carnation-in-his-Buttonhole.

It was the first funeral to come down from Cat Wood, but four children had already been born there, three girls and a boy. As for developments and the court's decision, the journalist Jacó Galub had come up the night before in the company of that pleasant Dante Veronezi and had told them not to be frightened by the "snarling of the chief of police," for the matter would be settled to everybody's satisfaction; no one would be evicted from the hill; nobody's shack would be torn down. Why, then, on the afternoon of Otália's funeral, that display of police strength? Crazy Cock and the boys, just in case, assumed their battle posts. One of them was sent to notify Jacó.

Once the court reached its decision, everything moved very swiftly. What had happened to those opposed, truculent, irreconcilable points of view? Through love of the people, in the unyielding defense of their interests and claims, all the difficulties had been overcome; the differences of opinion had been ironed out; the antagonistic forces had met and become reconciled. We shall speak of this, of this feast of true patriotism which brought together men of the opposition and the government, leaders of the conservative and popular classes, their hearts beating as one to the rhythm of the love of the people. Forgive us for repeating the words "love of the people" so many times, but if it was really so great, if all was fraught with this love and nourished by it, we see no reason for not repeating the expression, even at the sacrifice of style. After all, we are not a classic, nor have we any special responsibility as regards the purity and elegance of the language. All we want to do is to tell the story and give praise where praise is due. Besides, in order not to overlook anybody, the best thing is to praise them all, the whole lot of them, without exception.

The reconciliation of so many illustrious men separated by political differences was the grandiose and basic theme of the many speeches, articles, editorials, written during the final phase of the problem of Cat Wood Hill.

"Our campaign victorious! Triumph of the people and the *Gazette of Salvador*," ran the proud headlines of the paper, borne out by the scream of its siren summoning the crowds. The siren of the *Gazette of Salvador* was sounded only on the gravest occasions, in the case of stop-press news.

The turbulent problem of Cat Wood was settled to the satisfaction of all, stated the newspaper, less than forty-eight hours after the court had handed down its decision, an interval that broke a number of bureaucratic and legislative records. Love of the people works miracles. An outstanding example of patriotism to be emulated by the rising generations so imbued with radical ideas. A triumph for honest journalism at the service of the people.

The presiding judge of the court of appeals was a crafty, shrewd old fellow, who was aware of the negotiations in progress involving the divers interested parties: the distinguished Commander José Perez; the spirited lawmaker and leader of the opposition, Ramos da Cunha; the governor; the lieutenant governor; the mayor; the aldermen; the indefatigable Licio Santos; and Dr. Airton Melo, an outstanding member of the press; as well as Jacó Galub, the bold journalist, whose fearless procedure deserved, in addition to praise, a fair compensation. Not to mention that popular businessman—perhaps the only person who enjoyed general popularity—Otávio Lima, whose presence at the talks may perhaps call for an explanation. The truth, however, is that nobody asked for such an explanation, so why should we go looking for it and setting it down? Why should we be more exacting than the many distinguished men concerned with this matter? The presence of Otávio Lima was accepted as a matter of course; in fact, it may be stated that he played a decisive role in the success of the negotiations. In solving that intricate problem, the governor wanted to hear the most varied opinions, thus revealing his democratic spirit and his statesman's vision.

The only ones who were not heard were the inhabitants of the hill, nor was this necessary. Were not all those meetings and gatherings being held for the purpose of safeguarding their interests? Were there not present and active all those sincere patriots, devoted friends of the people? Not to mention the modest but agreeable presence of Dante Veronezi, whose status as a man of the hill, as undisputed and respected leader of the invasion, nobody could any longer gainsay: two rows of houses, put up in the twinkling of an eye, belonged to him and were already being rented at a good price. In the gatherings on the hill, Dante came and went, and convinced Jesuíno and the inhabitants that their preparations for combat were unnecessary. "The men are settling everything." Instead of barricades, trenches, stones and cans of boiling water, they should be preparing paper flags, posters of welcome, Roman candles, fireworks, to celebrate, to honor the occasion in the public square. The police had surrounded the hill, but Dante Veronezi crossed intrepidly among the cars and machine guns. A poster was being printed at the expense and under the direction of the young leader which read:

HURRAH FOR DANTE VERONEZI, OUR CANDIDATE!

Left a little vague on purpose, without specifying the job for which he was being nominated and supported. In view of the triumphal course of events, Dante began to think seriously about the possibilities of his being elected to the state legislature. The post of alderman was in the bag. But, who knows, he might be in line for the legislature. . . . In any case, a candidate. Dona Filó, for whose youngest child Dante was going to act as godfather, was directing his propaganda on the hill.

The presiding judge of the court of appeals was cognizant of all this. "All this" naturally did not include the affectionate and moral relationship between Dante and

Filó. We are referring to the talks, the negotiations in progress. The presiding judge was no fool; he was not like that dolt of an Albuquerque who held the post of chief of police. Moreover, he knew the obligation of the court, its responsibility, the duty it had to perform: to see that the laws were respected, especially that article of the Constitution which guaranteed the inviolability of private property. Let the politicians work out the best arrangement, the shrewdest fix, that was what they were in politics for. It was incumbent on the court to reaffirm the constitutional right to the ownership of the land and condemn the crime implicit in the lack of respect for this sacred right, the crime committed by the invaders of Cat Wood. The sentence of the court was a masterpiece of jurisprudence and slyness. "Justice is blind," it repeated, adding, nevertheless, to the old cliché a few words of regret that it was not in the power of the court to turn its gaze on the moving image of Dona Filó, the long-suffering and devoted mother of so many children clamoring for a roof over their heads. Justice is blind, and judges are obliged to turn a deaf ear to such clamors. It was incumbent on the legislative and executive branches of the government to seek a political solution to the problem, respecting the rights of property guaranteed by the Constitution while looking after the interests of the underprivileged masses. The court trusted that God, the fountainhead of wisdom, would illumine the leaders and the legislators, and entrusted, inasmuch as it could not do otherwise, to the power and the prudence of the police the execution of the sentence against the invaders of the hill, who were to be evicted and the land returned to its legal owner.

A brilliant decision whereby the court reaffirmed its position as guardian of private property, but at the same time seemed to insinuate, to suggest, a political solution. Thus, any decision which rendered the adverse sentence null and void would seem to proceed from the sentence itself, from the wisdom of the court. Weren't the governor and the legislators cooking up some kind of a deal behind the court's and the police's back? The chief of police was a bumptious fool, but he, the presiding judge of the court, was not going to let himself be taken in. No scoundrel was going to pass himself off as a good fellow at his expense. Thanks to the sentence bristling with sound judgment and shrewdness, the judge appeared as the real mastermind behind any compromise solution. He gave orders to the court clerk not to transmit the decision to the police until he expressly instructed him to do so.

Only Dr. Albuquerque, astride his genealogy and ambition, his self-importance, was unaware of the intense activity mushrooming in the shadow of the controversy over Cat Wood Hill. His position had never seemed to him more brilliant or assured. The evening before, while trying to get to the bottom of certain rumors being spread by the press, he had heard from the lips of the governor himself the reiteration of his complete confidence. His Excellency had added that the problem of Cat Wood lay completely outside his powers as governor. It was up to the law to decide and for the police to carry out the mandate of the court. Dr. Albuquerque had left the governor's mansion walking on air. At the door, he passed Licio Santos, who was coming in, and whose ceremonious greeting he answered curtly. Had it not been for the fact that the rascal was protected by the immunity of his office, he would throw him in the calaboose.

The newspapers of the opposition, presenting the chief of police as a die-hard, painting him in sinister colors, were doing him a big favor without realizing it. They accredited him in the eyes of the conservative classes as a firm, resolute leader. Whereas others wavered, toadying to the populace for the sake of its votes, he appeared as the dauntless champion of the property owners. When the time came, who would be the natural leader of all those who feared the wave of subversion, the alarming rumors of socialism whose herald trumpets had sounded—in his considered judgment—on the heights of Cat Wood Hill? When the time came for the casting up of accounts, who would be best fitted to govern the state with an iron hand? In his office, waiting for the decision of the court to be officially delivered to him, Dr. Albuquerque saw himself in the State House by acclamation, and across from him, humiliated and broken, the king of the numbers racket, that s.o.b. of an Otávio Lima.

It would be an exaggeration to say that Dr. Albuquerque was the only one whom events took by surprise. There were also several second-string congressmen, one or two cabinet officials, who knew nothing, had their head in the clouds, and barely had time to run and applaud. Moreover, things happened so fast that Congressman Polidoro Castro —Castrinho, as the French whores used to call him, an ex-pimp of Carlos Gomes Street when it was a red-light district—was left in a ridiculous position. This Castro, whose name while he was a student had appeared frequently on the police blotter, had shaken the dust of Bahia from his feet and had left for the interior, where he married the daughter of a rancher and became a lawyer of egregious moral qualities. Now balding, he had returned to the capital, appointed to replace the congressman of his district while the latter was taking a trip to Europe at the government's expense, thus making everybody happy. Wild to make a name for himself in the legislature, he saw his chance in Ramos da Cunha's project. He became its most relentless and insatiable foe; he took it apart paragraph by paragraph, and with the pettifogging erudition of a provincial lawyer and the Cartesian logic of a lover of old French whores, he more or less reduced to tatters that "pile of demogogic poppycock of our fiery backland Mirabeau." All this was being threshed out in three long and irrefutable speeches.

With manifest pleasure he was on the point of launching into the third, carried away with admiration for the force of his arguments, his references, some of them in Latin, and the tone of his voice, on the afternoon following the decision. He was referring to it time and again, to the coincidence between the juridical reasoning of his speeches and that of the "luminous lesson of the court," when the majority leader came quickly into the legislature from the State House. He glanced at the speaker out of the tail of his eye, whispered a few words to several of the government congressmen, turned toward Ramos da Cunha, who was heckling Polidoro, and took him over to a corner, where they sat whispering together. Polidoro Castro, intoxicated with his own voice, did not pay much attention to the leader. Not even when he saw him come over to the rostrum and whisper something into the ear of the Speaker of the House. He emerged from his enthrallment, from his admiration of his own intelligence, only when the bell rang and the Speaker said to him: "The distinguished member of the House has used up his time."

It was not possible; he had the right to two hours, he had not even used up the first, the Speaker was mistaken. No, the Speaker was not mistaken, but the distinguished legislator was. His time was really up. As he turned toward the Speaker, prepared to argue the point, Polidoro caught sight of the party leader and understood. Beyond doubt some important political communication to be made to the House. The leader wanted the floor. It did not matter, Polidoro would make a fourth speech. "I am just about finished, Mr. Speaker."

He concluded his comments, promising to go on with them in a final oration which would be devastating. Why in the devil was Ramos da Cunha smiling in the face of such a serious threat? Not only smiling, but he sat down beside him in the front row to listen to the party leader, who was standing on the rostrum, clearing his throat, before the attentive full assembly. Ramos da Cunha, his project demolished, was looking at the ceiling, his moral sensibility blunted, thought Polidoro.

The party leader asked for the attention of his fellow members. He had just come from the State House, and he was speaking in the name of the governor. The silence typical of momentous occasions gave greater weight to the leader's words. He had come from the State House, he repeated, and he was gratified by his intimacy with the rooms and corridors of the mansion, where he, the party leader, came and went without having to make a previous appointment. There in the company of His Excellency the governor, the lieutenant governor, the mayor of the capital, the Secretary of Transport and Public Works, and other authorities, he had taken part in the lengthy meeting in which the thorny problem of the invasion of Cat Wood Hill was considered from its many and complex angles.

He paused, raising his right arm to reinforce his words. The illustrious governor of the state—he said—whose previous humane intervention they could thank for having spared the populace, driven by necessity to the invasion and occupation of Cat Wood, bloodshed; His Excellency, ever alert and zealous for the cause of the people, now with his hands tied, unable to prevent the police action ordered by the court of appeals to implement its decision; His Excellency, the praiseworthy governor—he repeated fulsomely, his spittle exploding in a shower of saliva—backed by the very words of the decree advising the executive and the legislature to seek a political solution that would avoid police intervention; His Excellency, that outstanding example of a statesman concerned with the needs of the people, that humanitarian, had made up his mind to give further proof of his loftiness of sentiments, of his political impartiality, and of his love for the people. In the state legislature, there in that house of the Law and the People, a bill was under discussion proposing that the lands of Cat Wood Hill be expropriated, a bill sponsored by the noble leader of the opposition, Dr. Ramos da Cunha, whose talent and culture did not belong exclusively to the minority, but to the legislature *in toto*, to the State of Bahia, to Brazil (Applause, Hear, Hear, and the voice of Ramos da Cunha murmuring: "Your Excellency is too generous my noble colleague"). Well, then, in the name and by the decision of His Excellency the governor, he had come to inform the assembly of the unanimous support of the government bloc, that is to say, the majority of the members, for the patriotic project of the leader of the opposition. When it was a question of the people, there was neither government nor opposition, but only legislators at the service of the people's interests. These had been the words of the governor, and the leader was only repeating his admirable sentiments. Therefore he, the leader, would now transfer to the hands of the Speaker the petition signed by himself and the minority leader, asking for a vote as quickly as possible. In conclusion, he wished to say how proud it made him to serve such an exponential figure as the present head of the government. In the history of Brazil, the counterpart to his magnificent and magnanimous gesture was to be found only in that of Princess Isabel the Redeemer when she signed the bill decreeing the abolition of slavery. His Excellency the governor was the new

Princess Isabel, the new Redeemer. He returned to his seat amid a thunderous ovation.

No sooner had the applause died down (the orator was still receiving embraces) than the resourceful Polidoro Castro was back on the rostrum, giving rise to a certain speculation and excitement, for there were those who thought the principal critic of the project might do something rash, like breaking with the government, standing alone, equidistant from both majority and minority.

"Get ready for a blast of hot air," wisecracked reporter Mauro Junior in the press section.

On the platform, his arms spread wide, Polidoro Castro thundered: "Mr. President, I want to be the first to congratulate His Excellency the illustrious governor of the state for this historic, I would. say immortal, decision which the noble leader of the majority has just communicated to us in his eloquent words. I have had occasion to analyze the project of our illustrious colleague Ramos da Cunha, whose talent glitters like a diamantine star in the heaven of the Fatherland, and if I debated it as I did, it was never with the idea of detracting from its indisputable merits. Mr. Speaker, what I want to say is that I am squarely behind the project, that it has my complete support. And I take advantage of the occasion to transmit to the governor my unconditional solidarity. . . ."

Mauro Junior, the journalist, resumed his seat: "Nobody can get the better of that Polidoro. . . . He's too smart. It was not by accident that he got money from those French tarts. Has he got brass!"

The project received its first hearing posthaste. The newspaper offices were boiling over; the journalists had a ball with that quotation of the majority leader in which he presented the governor in travesty as Princess Isabel. Polidoro Castro's impassioned support took some by surprise. But what right had they to set bounds to his patriotic fervor?

The latest news was to the effect that technicians and experts from the office of the Secretary of Transport and Public Works were in conference with Commander José Perez, his lawyers, and his engineers. They could not arrive at an agreement with regard to the evaluation of the land, calculated by the square meter. The experts pointed out the distance from the city, the absence of communications and improvements, the lack of demand for property in that area. Commander José Perez, with the backing of plans, blueprints, estimates, considered the price offered by the arbitrators ridiculous. They wanted to play the good guys? They wanted applause and votes? He had no objection to this as long as it was not at his expense, if he was not the only one to pay the piper. How did they have the nerve to offer him that absurd price, when all the studies, estimates, and plans were ready and the date for the sale of lots had been set? And him with a court decision in his favor. Did they know the price the lots would bring by the square meter? And the value of the decision?

Licio Santos went from one side to the other, from the commander to the experts. Wherever there was money, there was he, and on every fee he got his cut, from every nickel that changed hands in this whole business of the invasion of Cat Wood Hill he got his percentage. He went from the governor to the lieutenant governor, from the mayor to the Speaker of the House, from Airton Melo to Jacó Galub. He carried the messages of Otávio Lima, for together with the lands of Cat Wood the problem of the numbers game was being settled. At the same time, a single political front, rallying all the different parties behind the government, was being formed. There was talk of Ramos da Cunha for one cabinet post, Airton Melo for another. Substitutes were suggested to replace Dr. Albuquerque as chief of police.

By the end of the afternoon, the first vote on the bill had been taken. The majority and minority leaders both requested a special session of the committees of Justice and Appropriations that very night, so the project could be submitted to final vote the following day and put into effect immediately.

At police headquarters, nervous and importunate, Dr. Albuquerque was awaiting the court's decision. He could not understand that delay. The decision had been issued by the court twenty-four hours before; how was it that it had not yet reached him? Bureaucratic negligence, assuming nothing worse. The news from the legislature and the State

House worried him. He had tried to get in touch with the governor; his Excellency was not in, nobody knew his whereabouts. Dr. Albuquerque decided to act on his own initiative.

He ordered the hill surrounded. The police, well armed and employing a number of cars, were to occupy the entire base of the hill. Camp there. Let no one come down. Whoever descended was to be arrested and thrown into one of the Black Marias there to bring in the prisoners. As soon as the official court decision reached him, orders for the occupation of the hill and the destruction of the shacks would be issued. At latest, by morning of the next day, Chico Pinóia, who was entrusted with carrying out this important task, asked if he was really authorized to employ firm measures.

"With all firmness. If they attempt to resist, use force. Take stern reprisals for any attempt to attack or demoralize the police. I do not want to see the police made to look ridiculous again at the hands of hooligans."

"It won't happen this time, you can rest assured, sir."

Just as they were coming to the hill, the police met a funeral procession going by. Chico Pinóia's lips parted in a smile of decaying teeth. He remarked to Miguel Charuto who was sitting beside him in the car: "If they try any funny business, there are going to be a lot of funerals."

What Miguel Charuto wanted to do was to throw Corporal Martim into the clink. And if, to boot, he could smash his face in, so much the better.

What he did not know was that at the gate of the cemetery Corporal Martim had ceased to exist. He had shaken hands with his friends, kissed the fat and suddenly aged face of Tibéria. Militão's big coastwise vessel, the three-masted *Flower of the Waves*, was waiting for him, ready to set sail. It was bound for Penedo in Alagoas and was taking Martim as a passenger at the request of Master Manuel. But Martim was no longer Martim. His face, as though carved out of stone, bore no resemblance to the roguish, gay, smiling countenance of the former corporal of the army. His parched, tearless eyes were not the warm, merry eyes of Martim. He was taking leave for good of his rank and name. Corporal Martim no longer existed; how could he live without Otália? On that nocturnal sea he was empty, drained, he was nobody; he felt the weight of that dead head on his breast, the silky hair, the bridal veil.

Later, when he reached the unknown city, he would be another person; he would start over again. With the same deftness at shuffling a deck of cards, the same adroitness at tossing the dice, but that roguery, that capacity for living life to the full every minute, that wit, that charm, were no more. Sergeant Porciúncula, his shoulders a little bent, as though bowed under a weight. He was carrying his corpse, which he never wanted to lay down, to rest from its heavy weight. He never opened his lips to tell his story; he never shared it with anyone. On his back, Otália in her wedding dress, bowing down his shoulders.

⸺⸳❧{ 16 }❧⸳⸺

DANTE VERONEZI ASCENDED THE HILL without difficulty, crossed through the armed police, past the loaded and aimed machine guns. They did not try to stop him, they said nothing to him. Their orders were not to let anyone leave the encircled hill. And so when Veronezi, accompanied by the construction foreman who had been in charge of the building of the two streets of houses, wanted to go back to the city, he was prevented from doing so, arrested, and thrown into a paddy wagon together with the foreman. There they would have spent the night if Miguel Charuto had not happened to be acquainted with him and had he not put in a word for him with Chico Pinóia. Dante had kicked up a real hullabaloo in the paddy wagon. Chico Pinóia decided to send them to police headquarters in a car. There the chief could decide what to do.

The arrest of the leader Veronezi was observed from the hilltop by the residents. Jesuíno resumed his bellicose preparations, sent a boy to the city to advise Jacó Galub of what had happened. The urchin took the recently cut trail on the side of the hill facing the swamp, which ran hidden by the bushes. No policeman could have caught him in the stinking mud of the swamp. In a little while he was on his way to the city, bumming a ride on a truck, to carry Jesuíno's message.

Even before the boy returned—he had been delayed in

the office of the *Gazette of Salvador* while his picture was being taken and he was telling his story to the reporters— Alderman Licio Santos was coming up the hill bringing the news of the release of Dante and the foreman, which he had arranged for under direct orders from the governor. He also informed them of the unanimous vote in the legislature on the first ballot in favor of the project being converted into law. It was in the hands of the committees meeting that night. The next day the second and final vote would be cast, the governor would sign the law, and they would be the owners of their homes. Licio Santos was proud and happy to have contributed with his words and deed to this victory of the people. A friend of the people, he, and in the Board of Aldermen, their true representative.

All this he conveyed in a resounding speech from the door of one of the bungalows built by Dante, with a plaque over the door reading:

ELECTION POST

OF

ALDERMAN LICIO SANTOS

AND

DANTE VERONEZI

The inhabitants had assembled to hear him. Among his high-flown figures of speech—"the poet of the slaves once said that the public square belongs to the people as the sky belongs to the condor"—Licio introduced amusing quips— "and I say that the hill belongs to the people as the bone belongs to the dog"—which made his audience laugh. He gave the chief of police hell, prophesying his immediate dismissal. Possibly that Albuquerque was no longer in office, had already been kicked out.

He still was. The order of the governor for the release of Dante Veronezi arrived with a recommendation: great prudence in any action against the inhabitants of Cat Wood. For the first time Dr. Albuquerque felt his position insecure. He ordered the charges against Veronezi dropped (Licio Santos was waiting in the other room; the chief of police had refused to receive him) and set out for the

Executive Mansion. He needed to see the governor, come to an understanding with him. But hardly a light showed in the building. After a fatiguing day his Excellency had gone out alone for an informal stroll and had not said where he was going or when he would be back. The chief of police waited a little while. Finally he decided to return to headquarters, leaving this message: he would spend the night in his office, in civic vigil, awaiting the governor's orders there. But as at two in the morning he had not yet received any word, and he was dead for sleep, he went home with downcast face and heavy heart. As he left, he saw Commissioner Angelo Cuiabá on the corner, laughing and talking with a group of policemen. He even caught a scrap of a phrase, cut short by the enthusiasm with which it was hailed: "They are talking about Congressman Morais Neto for the job; anybody would be better than that jackass. . . ."

He got into his car with the air of a person who has just heard his own funeral eulogy. Neither numbers money nor the leadership of the conservatives. But he would fall with dignity. "I fell with head high," he said to his wife, who was waiting up for him, she, too, nervous with the gossip she had heard from the neighbors. His reputation for honesty, incorruptibility, was still intact. His wife, a little tired of this pompous folderol, of this profitless self-esteem, reminded him that it was hard to fall with head high. As for incorruptibility, it was a nice word but buttered no parsnips. Dr. Albuquerque then sat down on the edge of the bed, and covered his face with his hands: "What do you want me to do?"

"At least have the satisfaction of handing in your resignation."

"Do you think I should? And what if things change and the governor, in spite of everything, keeps me on in the job? Why rush?"

His wife shrugged her shoulders. She was tired and wanted to sleep. "If you don't hand in your resignation, even your dignity will be gone. You'll have nothing left."

"I'll think it over. . . . Tomorrow I'll decide. . . ."

The next morning he was awakened by a message from the State House: the governor wanted to see him at once. His wife had gotten up to let the messenger in, and he stood in the doorway looking at her with an expression that filled her with pity. That poor husband, so self-satisfied and so good for nothing! She and she alone could gauge the full extent of his incapacity, his fatuity. But he stood there with such a Godforsaken air that she came over to his side. Dr. Albuquerque's head drooped; this was the end.

"The governor wants to see you."

"At this time of day that can only mean . . ."

"Never mind. . . . We'll get along somehow. You did your duty."

But he knew what his wife really thought of him, the regard in which she held him. It got him nowhere to boast of his honesty, strike noble poses; he neither fooled nor convinced her.

"Defeated by that pack of lowlifes."

She never knew if he was referring to the governor and the legislators or had the people of Cat Wood Hill in mind. She helped him get dressed: Dr. Albuquerque still used a starched collar.

At the State House, the governor reiterated his respect, his esteem, his gratitude, and his desire to have him in his government; he conferred luster and respectability on it. But in another post. They would give this careful consideration later on. That of chief of police in this moment of political reorganization, of mutual concessions, called for a head of department more ductile than Dr. Albuquerque, less inflexible. That inflexibility was a valuable asset not only for the present government but for the whole public life of Bahia. Dr. Albuquerque was a model for future generations. Politics, however, had its own rules, its darker side, called for give and take, concessions, agreements, even certain deals. And his distinguished friend was not a man for deals.

Dr. Albuquerque lowered his head. What did he care about all that praise? He was leaving the post of chief of police empty-handed, the way he had come into it. And with what high and well-laid hopes he had entered! Honest, uncompromising, incorruptible—a jackass, a dope. He looked at the governor smiling across from him, pronouncing all those flattering phrases, outdoing himself in politeness. Clean hands, a model of uprightness, leaving a sensitive post of that sort as poor as when he accepted it. What he felt like doing was getting up and sending the governor, along with honesty, inflexibility, and incorruptibility, to hell.

He arose, buttoned his coat, and bowed to the governor: "In half an hour Your Excellency will have my request to be relieved of my duties."

The governor, in turn, arose, embraced him warmly, and reiterated, almost sincerely, his regard for him: "Thank you very much, my friend."

The resignation made no reference either to the numbers game—Commissioner Angelo Cuiabá had made a point of informing the chief of police the minute he saw him show up so early that morning that the restrictions on gambling were about to be lifted, thanks to an agreement reached the night before, when the governor had visited the home of Otávio Lima, the house where he lived with his lawfully wedded wife—nor to the events of Cat Wood Hill. Poor health, doctor's orders, need for rest—these were the reasons given in the carefully worded resignation: "Although I had on more than one occasion asked to be relieved of the difficult task I had been assigned, my request was not granted and, at the sacrifice of my health, I heeded the pleas of Your Excellency that I continue. This time, however . . ."

The governor accepted his resignation, answering it at once with a letter in which he praised the ex-chief of police, a master of jurisprudence and an example of integrity. A newspaperman whom Albuquerque had given a sinecure in the police department, prepared a radio broadcast. He paid his debt of gratitude by giving out a version favorable to the ex-chief of police: Albuquerque had resigned because he refused to be a party to the new scandal of the numbers game. With his departure, the government was definitively wallowing in the gambling mire.

The news of the resignation of the chief of police reached Cat Wood around noon and was hailed by the inhabitants. One of the boys, who was a kind of liaison officer between the besieged dwellers and the city, brought a message from Licio Santos. The chief of police had resigned; the expropriation project had been approved by the committee in a further and swift discussion, was going to be voted on at an extraordinary session of both houses, and would surely be passed that very day. The inhabitants were to get ready for the great rally to celebrate this triumph, to which everyone was being invited by newspaper and radio, a rally of support for the government, a monster meeting in front of the Congressional Building.

The morning newspapers had invited the people to lend prestige, by their presence in the Municipal Square, to the meritorious act of the governor. In the *Gazette of Salvador*, in addition to the enthusiastic coverage by Jacó Galub of "the horrors of the last siege of Cat Wood by the murdering minions of Albuquerque, buzzards doing a vulture's work," narrating and dramatizing the arrest of Dante Veronezi, reproducing the picturesque statements of Woodpecker, the street Arab who had brought the message, and reproducing, too, his aggressive and sympathetic mug, with his hair falling over his forehead, a cigarette butt dangling from the corner of his mouth—in addition to this story announcing the end of all that unjust persecution, there was an editorial signed by Airton Melo, the editor. Only on rare occasions did he sign an article. He did so that morning to applaud the act of the governor. Even though he was in the opposite political camp, he knew how to recognize grandeur wherever it appeared. His Excellency had won the admiration of the entire state. And that was why he, Airton Melo, had agreed to be one of the speakers at the rally scheduled for the afternoon.

The occupants of the hill were getting ready. Posters, flags, a banner cheering the governor. The street Arabs went out through the swamp to see what news they could pick up. The police had surrounded that side of the hill, too, had set up their machine guns there. But the boys slipped through the bushes on their cat feet, and by the time the cops caught on to what had happened, they were already a long way off, thumbing a ride from a truck.

The one snag the negotiators had trouble getting around was the price of the land. Commander José Perez had set his figure, and he would not shade it, standing firm on the plans, the blueprints, the estimates of the division into lots. Friends had intervened, and a meeting between the governor and the bastion of the meritorious Spanish colony was arranged. They finally reached an agreement. Commander José Perez, to facilitate a solution and do his share toward bettering the lot of the people, the poor people of the hill, made a slight reduction—or a great sacrifice—depending on how you want to look at it. The experts modified their initial expertise. Incidentally, one of them refused to sign the new document, considering the deal too outrageous. A number of people had their feet in that trough, a number of names were mentioned, but the only one we can go bail for was Licio Santos, indefatigable and in high spirits.

At the foot of Cat Wood Hill, the police, completely overlooked in the confusion of the chief of police's resignation, and his successor still to be appointed, kept up their siege of the hill and arrested and threw in the Black Marias anyone who ventured down. Three of the dwellers were under arrest, but Jacó and Licio promised to have them sprung as soon as they had a minute's time. They were terribly busy with the rally. They would advise them when it was to be held, as soon as they knew. It would certainly be toward the end of the afternoon.

Jesuíno, whose war games were over, took charge of the preparation for Cat Wood's share in the celebration. That, too, was fun and brought in a few cents. Not to mention Licio Santos's promise: unlimited quantities of rum and beer to celebrate the victory. Crazy Cock, who had never been known to have any occupation, who was regarded as the irreconcilable enemy of any and all work, was ready to become a professional invader of lands, he informed Miro laughingly, as he pasted cardboard posters on long laths of wood. He knew of nothing more entertaining. He was already planning a new invasion: a stretch of land beyond Liberdade, at a spot known as Turk's Furrow.

At two o'clock that afternoon, amid great civic enthusiasm of the legislators, the project of Ramos da Cunha was passed in final form. The Speaker was going to appoint a committee to take it to the governor for his signature. But at the suggestion of Polidoro Castro, it was decided that they should all go to the State House in a group. The signing was set for six that afternoon, leaving time to get ready for the great rally.

All the radio stations were issuing bulletins every five minutes inviting officials and the people to appear in the Municipal Square in front of the State House at six o'clock to witness the historic act of the signing by the governor of the law passed by the legislature expropriating the lands of Cat Wood Hill. They mentioned, among others, the party whip and the opposition leader, the newspaper publisher Airton Melo, the alderman Licio Santos, the governor himself. State and municipal trucks were standing by to carry people to the meeting; all resources had been mobilized to insure the resounding success of this spontaneous manifestation of the people.

--➤{ 17 }❖--

So MUCH TO DO. SO MANY ARRANGEMENTS to be made, with
things happening one on top of the other—meetings at the
State House, talks, conferences, discussions about the new
chief of police and the revamping of the cabinet—that they
forgot all about the police besieging the hill on that war
footing, with machine guns and everything, and they forgot
about the inhabitants of the hill. The Square was brimful
of people, buses and trucks unloading demonstrators with
posters and placards; the members of the legislature arrived
in a group, the government and opposition leader in the
same car; politicians got out of their automobiles in front
of the State House; the mayor was coming down the steps
of the City Hall to cross the square and join the governor
when Jacó Galub, in one of the rooms of the State House,
happened to remember the people of the hill. Licio Santos
was standing beside him.

"What about the people from the hill?"

"Good Lord! We'll have to send for them."

Jacó remembered the boy who was waiting at the newspaper office in case of any important message. "Please God
the telephone is working!" He got the connection, and a
few minutes later the street Arab had set out in a taxi,
carrying Jacó's belated summons. A truck was being sent
to bring in the hill's inhabitants. They were to come down
to the foot and wait for it.

At this point they also recalled the police siege. They set out to find the new chief of police, who had been appointed and installed in office half an hour before, a congressman who happened to be a cousin of the governor's wife and a friend of Otávio Lima; in this way the numbers affair stayed in the family. The man was startled: the hill besieged? Yes, he had read about it in the paper. To tell the truth, he was not too well posted on that whole business; he had not been in the capital but vacationing on his ranch in Cruz das Almas when the governor had hastily summoned him. He would take the necessary measures; they could rest assured. Incidentally, what measures? He did not know. Very simple, his two callers informed him. It was just a question of sending a captain or a commissioner with orders for the police to return to headquarters. They had been besieging the hill for over twenty-four hours, eating sandwiches and drinking tepid water, the orders of that jackass of an Albuquerque, and they were ready to mutiny.

Mutiny is not the right word. They were not mutinous but bored to death, furious, hungry, having spent a sleepless night, eaten alive by mosquitoes—there were millions of mosquitoes in the swamp. The police were the only ones who had no knowledge of the magnificent celebration, the spectacular rally. Stuck off there, besieging that obscenity of a hill. If only one of those devils would come down to be arrested, get a going over. The night before they had arrested three, who were in the paddy wagon, hungry, thirsty, and roasting with the heat. Chico Pinóia paced back and forth, snorting with hate. Miguel Charuto asked only to lay hands on Corporal Martim to teach him a lesson.

Just then on the top of the hill the crowd loomed up. To Chico Pinóia, they looked dangerous, armed with sticks and stones. In the van, flourishing a marshal's baton, went Jesuíno Crazy Cock. The fact of the matter was that they were coming down, as instructed, to wait for the truck that was to transport them to the Municipal Square. What Jesuíno was carrying was a banner rolled on two thin strips of wood.

The young liaison officer had left the taxi a good distance from the hill, had crossed the swamp, and had slipped up the hill unnoticed bearing Jacó's and Licio's message. Jesuíno assembled the inhabitants, who were more or less ready; they picked up the banners and posters and followed Crazy Cock, who was proudly wearing that ludicrous steel helmet.

Below, Miguel Charuto fell back and took aim: "They're coming to attack us! . . ."

Chico Pinóia pulled out his revolver and shouted Albuquerque's orders to the police. He smiled. He was going to avenge himself for his previous defeat and for the night of mosquitoes, the long wait in the broiling sun, the lack of food worthy of the name, the dirty, warm water. He felt repaid for everything.

The inhabitants disappeared around a turn in the road. Later on they would be clearly visible. Chico Pinóia laughed, satisfied. Miguel Charuto chose his position. What he wanted was to lay hands on that son-of-a-bitch of a Martim.

The figure of Jesuíno Crazy Cock stood out against the red twilight horizon. "Fire!" ordered Chico Pinóia, and the machine gun mowed down the bushes, threw up the earth, and devoured Jesuíno's breast. He was atop a big rock; he staggered, tried to hold on to his hat; his body sagged, then went rolling head over heels into the swamp, where the mud swallowed him. The other inhabitants withdrew to the top of the hill. The banner Jesuíno was carrying had fallen a little below the rock; the device on it read:

HAIL, FRIENDS OF THE PEOPLE

Immediately afterwards, the automobile carrying Commissioner Angelo Cuiabá and the truck coming for the inhabitants of Cat Wood arrived almost simultaneously. The commissioner was bringing orders to call off the siege, to release the prisoners, if there were any, and for the police and police cars to return to Headquarters. If any of them wanted to go to the rally, he could.

He asked if everything was going well. Chico Pinóia reported that everything was fine; they had arrested three characters as they tried to leave the hill, and he was going to release them. Aside from that there had been, moments before, an attempted attack by the inhabitants. He had ordered a burst of machine gun fire, just to put the fear of God into them, and they had given up the idea.

"Nobody was wounded? Or killed?"

"Nobody."

The police withdrew, a few of the hill dwellers picked up banners and posters, Dona Filó in the lead with her children. But not all the children: the two oldest did not go. Miro went down to the swamp.

In the Square, the rally reached its apex. The speech of the party leader produced a sensation as he repeated that highly effective simile: His Excellency the governor was the Princess Isabel of today, redeeming the slaves of the social order. Airton Melo and Ramos da Cunha did not fall behind. And the governor, on the State House balcony as he signed into law the bill expropriating the lands of Cat Wood Hill to the applause of the crowd, could not hide the tears that welled up in his eyes. With these tears running down his cheeks, he began his memorable speech. In the window at his side, the industrialist Otávio Lima, puffing a fragrant cigar, smiled contentedly at the enthusiastic crowd, many of whom were acquaintances of his, members of his organization, runners at liberty once more. Nice people, not one of them had failed to show up.

It was a scene of indescribable emotion, calling for a Camões to put it into verse and thereby immortalize it: the governor embracing Dona Filó when she, all set about with children, reached the balcony of the State House and he, the head of the state, the Father of the People, enfolded her in his arms.

The celebration lasted far into the night. Otávio Lima ordered beer and rum served, and a platform was set up in the Square for dancing.

It was a moonless night, thick with clouds, almost starless, the sultry atmosphere foretelling a storm. In the rotting swamp, Miro and the street Arabs, using long wooden poles, were trying to find Jesuíno Crazy Cock's body. Wing-Foot and Bullfinch had joined the search, as had Ipicilone and Carnation-in-his-Buttonhole and several others. They spent the whole night, but to no avail. The reddish light of the fireflies flickered above the mire of the swamp. Jesuíno had disappeared in the mud and there was no way of finding him. What they did find was that extraordinary hat, one of those used by engineers, the helmet of a soldier or a commanding officer. But Crazy Cock had never managed to look like a soldier; with his gray hair fluttering in the wind, what he had looked like was a poet.

-•⚜{ 18 }⚜•-

WITH THE RALLY turning into a joyful celebration, with dancing and drink, the story of the invasion of Cat Wood Hill ended. It had what is known as a happy ending. Everyone came away satisfied; each got his just deserts.

The governor had won that completely spontaneous and sincere (just ask Otávio Lima) demonstration of the affection of the people. Not to mention the political advantage, with the opposition eating out of his hand. Ramos da Cunha was made Secretary of Agriculture, Airton Melo of Justice, in return for their services. The government was strengthened; a political truce was established.

Commander José Perez sold his lands for their weight in gold. He gave his grandson and granddaughter each a new automobile. Both of them were great revolutionaries imbued with all the latest theories. We already know about the change Licio Santos managed to pick up here and there wherever there happened to be money in this affair. His election as state congressman seems assured; he is today a very popular man. And also the election of Dante Veronezi as alderman. He is the candidate of the invasions, for the invasions, even though Jesuíno Crazy Cock is no longer on hand to command them, have continued and multiplied. In each of them Dante has rows of houses. Jacó Galub, the hero of Cat Wood Hill, was named press secretary of the legislature and received the award for journalism, as already stated, for his coverage of the invasion.

365

As for the people of the hill, there they are on the hill. They stayed on in their shacks, stubbornly living. Dona Filó devotes herself to politics; she is Dante's ward boss. If it were not for the fact that she cannot read or write, she might be elected to the city council herself.

And what about Dr. Albuquerque? Would that master of law, that incorruptible legal luminary, be the only loser? We can divulge the good news: he, too, received his reward. There was a vacancy in the State Auditing Board, and in spite of the many candidates, the governor remembered his ex-chief of police and appointed him. If in the history of the invasion of the hill, among all those friends of the people, he had played the role of enemy, of villain, not on that account should he be forgotten when the spoils were being divided up. From his responsible post as counselor of the Auditing Board he hopes to be called one day to become the candidate of the conservative classes for governor of the state or merely Secretary of State or even to return to the post of chief of police. He would like that job back, that business of the numbers racket still stuck in his craw. It was rumored that the governor (and all his family) were getting filthy rich on their cut. Dirty dogs, thought Dr. Albuquerque, still stiff-necked.

And who else? The body of Jesuíno was never found. There were even those who doubted that he had died: they said he had gone away and changed his name like Corporal Martim, who became Sergeant Porciúncula. Rumors of this sort circulated for several months until once, at a great voodoo celebration in Aldeia de Angola—where the priest Jeremoabo is possessed by the Caboclo deity Maré Alta and lays on hands and gives health—there descended into the girl Antonia of the Annunciation—a votary who as yet had no special divinity, an eyeful of a mulatta—a new Caboclo deity unknown up to that time.

He came down for the first time at the ceremonial grounds and said his name was Caboclo Crazy Cock. His dance was spectacular; he invented new steps; he did not get tired; he could spend the whole night without resting, calling for songs. He cured sicknesses; he found a solution to problems, all problems, and was infallible in matters of love. He liked a drink and he had a nice way of talking.

It could be none other than Jesuíno, for he was never known to descend into an old votary, a damaged instrument, a skinny horse. He descended only into the most beautiful, and he did not care if they were devotees of another deity. As long as they were pretty, that was all he asked; he spent the night in them, dancing, Jesuíno Crazy Cock, now a god, a divinity of the Caboclo *candomblé*, a minor god of the people of Bahia.

Glossary

Afoxé. Carnival group with African influence, typical of Bahia.

Aldeia de Angola. A Caboclo voodoo center, that is to say, one in which there is a mixture of African and Indian rites.

Andrada e Silva, José Bonifacio de (1827–86). Tutor of Emperor Pedro II. Statesman, jurist, poet, who brought his great moral authority and eloquence to bear on the campaign for the total abolition of slavery in 1886. "My heart did what it could," he said on his deathbed a few days after the triumph of the cause.

Âtoto. Form of addressing Omolu.

Axê. Temple at voodoo ceremonial center. The "Caille" of Haitian rites.

Babalaô. Witch doctor.

Babalorixá. Head of voodoo center (male).

Barbosa, Ruy (1849–1923). One of the Brazilians best known beyond the national frontiers. Statesman, jurist, writer. During dictatorship of Marshal Peixoto he went into voluntary exile in England, where he wrote his most important literary work *Cartas da Inglaterra.* On his return to Brazil in 1907 he was appointed to the Permanent Court of International Justice (The Hague).

Berimbau. Word of unknown origin (also spelled *berimbao, birimbao*) used in Brazil for two musical instruments: a musical bow of which the string passes through a gourd resonator held against the player's chest or stomach and is tapped with a small stick; and a form of Jew's harp.

Bonifacio, José: See *Andrada e Silva, José Bonifacio de.*

Bori. Purification rites for those already initiated in the *candomblé.*

Candomblé. Strictly speaking, each of the great annual celebrations of the Afro-Brazilian cult. Also used to describe voodoo ceremonies in general.

Candomblé de Caboclo. Cult in which African and Indian rites are intermingled.

Capoeira. Style of fighting brought from Africa by Negroes of Angola in the sixteenth century. In its purest form it involves the use of hands, feet, and especially head butting, although at times razor and dagger were employed.

Comadre, Compadre. Literally, godfather, godmother, in relation to godchild's parents. By extension, intimate friend, crony.

Carybé. Hector Júlio Páride Bernabó, born in Buenos Aires in 1911 of Italian father and Brazilian mother. Today one of outstanding artists of Bahia and Brazil. He has two huge murals in the American Airlines Building at Kennedy Airport.

Dendê. The African oil palm grown in Brazil from whose fruit *dendê* oil, which is much used in cooking, is extracted.

Egun. Spirits of the dead who participate in voodoo rites.

Euá. Goddess of the waters, tutelary spirit of fountains and springs.

Exê ê ê Babá. Ritual greeting to the spirits (*eguns*) which are also called *babá* ("Father").

Exu. Messenger of the other deities, malicious and easily irritable. Given his bad disposition and his role of

messenger of the other *orixás*, he receives his sacrifice
before any of the other divinities to keep him in a
good humor. Often syncretized with the devil. "Legba"
in Haitian voodoo.

Feijoada. Typical Brazilian dish made of black beans
cooked with pork sausage, dried beef, and peppers
and served with rice and manioc meal.

Gallego. Literally, a native of Galicia in northern Spain.
As many immigrants to America were from this
region, the term has become synonymous with "Spaniard" in Argentina and Brazil.

Gafieira do Barão. Famous dance hall in Bahia frequented by servants, soldiers, sailors, and idlers.

Iawôs. Handmaidens through whom the *orixás* or deities
manifest themselves. Spiritual daughters and mystic
spouses of the divinity who chooses them.

Iansã or *Yansã.* Wife of Xangô, goddess of the winds,
domineering of temperament. Syncretized with St.
Barbara.

Iyalorixá. Priestess of voodoo ceremonies.

Modinha. A sentimental ballad or folk song of the nine-
teenth century.

Nãnãn Buroko. Mother of Omolu. The oldest of the
divinities of the waters. Syncretized with St. Anne.

Neruda, Pablo (1904–). Chilean poet of advanced
poetic technique and social ideas.

Obã. Male dignitary in the *candomblé.*

Ogan. Dignitary of the *candomblé.* It is the duty of the
ogans to look after the ceremonial site.

Ogun. God of iron. Patron of blacksmiths, warriors,
farmers, and all who use iron. Brother of Exu and
Oxóssi. Syncretized with St. Anthony.

Omolu. God of smallpox and sickness. Syncretized with
St. Lazarus or St. Roque. His dance mimics suffering,
ailments, convulsions, lameness.

Opa Afonja.   One of the great voodoo centers of Bahia.

Orixá.   General term for Negro god or divinity. Cf. *loa* of Haiti.

Orobo.   One of the names of the cola nut.

Ossani.   Divinity of medicinal and liturgical plants. No ceremony can be carried out without his being present. He is greeted by cry: *Eue o!*

Oxalá.   God of creation. This great spirit is symbolized by pieces of marble in a ring of lead. Syncretized with Our Lord of Bonfim.

Oxóssi.   God of hunters, whose emblems are a bow and arrow. Syncretized with St. George.

Oxum.   Second wife of Xangô. Divinity of Oxun River, coquettish and vain. Syncretized with Our Lady of Candlemass.

Oxumarê.   The rainbow. Symbolized by copper snakes. Syncretized with St. Bartholomew.

Pataco.   Old silver Brazilian coin worth two milreis.

Peji.   Altar or shrine in *candomblé* center.

Sampaio, Mirabeau.   Sculptor and designer, one of the outstanding figures in modern art in Bahia. Holds Chair of Sculpture in the School of Fine Arts of the University of Bahia.

Terreiro de Jesus.   Colonial Square in Bahia, the site of some of the most beautiful churches in the city.

Yemanjá.   Goddess of the waters, mother of the other divinities. Syncretized with Our Lady of Conception.

Xangô.   God of thunder and lightning. Syncretized with St. Jerome. His dance has the virile grace of a warrior for he was a king of the Yoruba nation.